I0609774

THE
DEAD
FED
SAID

CONETTA
TAYLOR

WHAT'S BEING SAID ABOUT THIS DEBUT NOVEL

Christmas time is full of surprises, and so is Taylor's first book. If you like charm, suspense and intrigue neatly wrapped in a bundle and tied with holly, you will like The Dead Fed Said.

Keep an eye on this author!

- Lori Copeland, best-selling USA Today and Publishers Weekly author.

Wow! This was such a fantastic read! I truly enjoyed getting to follow this journey and see the progression of the characters and plot, and all the twists. Great work!

- Addison Williams, Editor

In this delightful tale, Mrs. Taylor guides us through the story of a woman's struggle to live up to the standards set forth in the will of her beloved grandfather. There is mystery, supernatural occurrences and a budding romance sprinkled throughout this novel. Will Letsea live up to the strident demands made of her by the grandfather? Or will she succumb to her growing feelings for a man who may not be who she thinks he is.

This novel is a page turner. Do not start it late at night or you won't get any sleep.

- Award Winning Author, J.C. Fields

"Taylor's debut novel weaves a perfect combination of murder, romance and intrigue.

- Shirley McCann, Author

"Taylor writes a passionate love story filled with page turning twists and turns thwarted by an insistent ghost seeking justice for its murder."

- Michael Lee, Author

Copyright © 2024 Conetta Taylor
All cover art copyright © 2024 Conetta Taylor
All Rights Reserved

This is a work of fiction. Although, Paul E. Reynolds was a real person, to date his is still the only unsolved murder of an FBI agent. With the exception of historical facts, as found in newspapers, articles on the internet, and historical locations all further characters are a figment of the author's imagination. All other characters, names, places, all conversations and incidents are either the product of the author's imagination or are used fictitiously, and any resemblance to any actual persons, living or dead, businesses, organizations, events or locales is entirely coincidental.

No part of this book may be reproduced or transmitted in any form or by any means, electronic or mechanical, including photocopying, recording, or by any information storage and retrieval system, without permission in writing from the author.

Publishing Coordinator – Sharon Kizziah-Holmes
Cover Design – Jaycee DeLorenzo

Paperback-Press
an imprint of A & S Publishing
Paperback Press, LLC
Springfield, Missouri

ISBN - 978-1-964559-14-8

LETTER OF DEDICATION

Dearest Thom,

I dedicate this debut novel to you, my loving husband. We met through the grace of God. With each memory of our friend, Roseanne, I still recall her words, "You *have to* meet this Thom Taylor. You two are perfect for each other."

During our first conversation we discussed our hobbies, childhood experiences, dreams, and belief in God. That's when I knew what she meant.

Thom, I fell in love with the young man you were and have been blessed since our beginning. My heart is filled with gratitude for the love and compassion which radiates from yours. You are a man of inspiring faith, loyalty, understanding, strength, and wisdom. In our time together I continue to adore the authentic core of who you are. I treasure our ventures and journeys, a little hair-raising at times, and calm, sacred, and downright hilarious at others. You have watched over me, protected me, supported and honored me.

Dearest, in your own magical way you keep life interesting, that's for sure! What a joy! A blessed reminder to look above, deeper into, or beyond the appearance of a situation. To trust The Divine for a higher meaning, whether we ever understand it or not, and find peace. What a genuine inspirational and supportive man I married, all those years ago. I love that we have humor and laughter in our lives.

You are my light, my knight, my life's partner. It thrills my heart to still have and to hold, to love, cherish, and honor the devoted man you are today. You continue to enrich my life, heart and soul. I wish everyone could experience such love in their lives.

Thank you, Dear for being in mine.

Your wife, Conetta

CHAPTER 1

"A killer thriller, hm?"

"It has been called that," author, Gunner Hardyn Chase said with a wide grin.

Letsea Brechenworth acknowledged the author when he stood in greeting as she approached his table at the local holiday arts and craft show. A courteous man, who wrote high-impact action thrillers. Ironic, to sell powerful deadly force stories while the intercom played the tune to "You're a Mean One, Mr. Grinch."

"I've read this. If I remember, a good read. Isn't it about an FBI agent?" Chase's pleasantness charmed her senses.

"That's my first book, and yes, in the entire first series, the main character is FBI."

He gestured to the assemblage of books on his display table. His mannerisms and friendliness spoke of his enthusiasm for his craft.

"You have been busy." She perused his exhibit, a full array of book cover designs.

"Writing is my pleasure."

Letsea noticed the gleam in his eyes. "Are you retired FBI?"

"No, I do know some who are. Are you FBI?" he asked.

She parted her lips slightly then simpered. "You mean a man, or woman in black? No thank you. Yellow and greens are more my fashion colors. Although, somewhere in my family history there *was* a murdered FBI agent. They never solved his case."

Gunner Chase tilted his head. "Sounds intriguing."

"It does, doesn't it?" She shuffled back a couple steps.

"What do you know about it?" he asked.

"Not much. On assignment and someone shot him—graveyard

dead."

"What was his name?"

"Offhand, I don't remember." She closed her eyes and tried to recall.

"I'd be interested in learning the story of your FBI relative."

Her cell phone interrupted with little sister's ringtone, "Knock Three Times." She offered an apologetic glance. "Excuse me. I need to answer this. I'll take one of each of your books. Will you autograph them please?" She stepped away for privacy. "Gwendolene. What's up?"

"The music director called. I need for you to take the kids to a last-minute rehearsal tomorrow. I already have plans. They love spending time with their favorite aunt. Please?"

Letsea sighed at her sister's plea, although as guilty as their parents for spoiling baby girl. Besides, she welcomed time with the kids. "Yes, Sis, they're all mine. I'll take them."

"By the way, will you bring some of Pauline's omelets? I mean, since you're coming here anyway."

When Gwen finally hung up, Letsea turned her full attention to the author. She paid him with cash. "Do you live here in St. Charles or St. Louis?"

"In the Ozarks."

"I'm glad you're here. I'm ready to begin a new series for winter reading."

The novelist extended a hand to her. "My business card, should you decide to share your relative's information. My private phone number. I'm interested in hearing his story. I appreciate your purchase. Hold on tight during your reading adventures." He handed her a fancy black-and-white shopping bag adorned with illustrations of his name and book titles.

They shook hands. "I look forward to the read, Mr. Chase. Happy Thanksgiving to you."

Letsea walked away grateful she'd only told him of an obscure great uncle. *Mr. Thriller Writer was easy to talk with.* Although, generational uncles were safe topics, *weren't they?* She was relieved, after all it wasn't like she shared information of her parents' demise. She remembered the dreadful ordeal with the American Embassy in the DRC, FBI, and all those other agencies involved with international kidnapping and hostage recovery.

CHAPTER 2

The next day

Inside the community center, Letsea and the children removed their coats. The children dashed down the hall. "Walk," she urged while holding their coats. "I'll be right there."

Four-year-old Chip stopped. "Aunt Letsea, will you wait out here?"

"Why? I've watched you rehearse before."

"We're getting it polished."

Other children brushed past her, running down the hallway. "Where are the others' parents?"

"Mostly, they drop them off."

"Okay, I'll be right out here."

"Thanks!" As they turned a corner, three-year-old Lauren waved, her long blonde curls swung as she rushed on.

She considered which parent they took after. Doyle, a perfectionist, with goals aimed to succeed in family and career. Gwendolene needed other's approval. And they did. Gwen won beauty contests one after another and still modeled for local fashion shows.

Across the wide entrance hall from the coatrack were several comfortable chairs.

A couple of older women, a high school English teacher and her favorite waitress of all time, were in a deep *tête-à-tête*. She crossed by unnoticed. Letsea sat and reached into a tote bag for the first in the series of the new books. *Ah, reading time.*

Alice and Mrs. Ormsby were not whispering by any means.

"So, have you located a house?" asked her old high school English teacher.

"We're still looking. I don't know how we're supposed to find something with the measly amount the highway department's paying for our house. It's long paid off, and real estate has skyrocketed. It's wreaking havoc with our retirement funds."

Letsea's heart softened for Alice. Eminent domain. Necessity was understandable, though, it should never put a hardship on people forced out of a place they own and often love.

"When do you have to be out?"

"By the end of the year. Our boy is taking off the entire month of December to help us move."

A whole month? Nice son.

"Where to?" Mrs. Ormsby asked.

"His house. He invited us to stay with him," said Alice.

Even nicer. Letsea touched fingertips to her heart.

"He is a blessing to you, Alice," said Mrs. Ormsby.

No joke.

"He always has been. His sisters have tested our patience a few times though."

The ladies snickered.

"I can't believe he never found a wife."

That caught Letsea's attention. Sweet Alice had a son who never married?

"I remember in high school the girls would trip over their own feet to have a chance to talk to him, then blush. But he was always polite," said Mrs. Ormsby.

Letsea glanced at the ladies.

"He travels. It's difficult to maintain a relationship when you're not home. He finally settled into his new house. Now he'll have us underfoot. I never know what to expect. Out-of-the-blue, he announces he's flying out and can't reveal where, for an undetermined length of time."

"It's job related though?"

"Sure it is, but it keeps me in a state of worry."

"Alice, you'll be house sitters. Can't expect him to have a normal job. He's an out-of-the-box thinker. Such a dapper young man, smart, flexible, sense of humor, plus he sings and dances, to boot."

The ideal man. Letsea briefly closed her eyes.

Alice softened her voice. "I had an embarrassing crush on his father. When Rick finally asked me out, I thought I might faint."

They chortled like teenagers.

Letsea considered her unfulfilled aspirations for a husband. She'd like an Apollo. A Greek god of music and manly beauty. The personification of charm. *Yes please!*

"He's so analytical. Lives by numbers."

"Won't he retire soon?"

"Soon. I hope with a nice pension. He never speaks of it, but it'll be years before he can apply for Social Security." She cleared her throat. "He's not old yet."

They stood and began searching through the coats on the coatrack.

"I'll swan, Alice, if he'd retire, he wouldn't have to travel. He could collect his pension. Maybe do people's taxes. Even find a nice wife and give you grandchildren."

Me, me, me! Letsea wanted to wave her hand like a student who knew the answer. She understood numbers, and sighed at thoughts of having children of her own. Fat chance of an epitome of a gentleman agreeing to her grandfather's trust stipulations. No luck so far.

Alice looked downward. "Aw, yes. I do want more grandchildren. The ones I have adore their uncle. He'd make an ideal father."

"A regular paragon," Letsea said aloud. Then looked up, startled to have voiced her last thought. "Sorry. I didn't mean to eavesdrop."

"About right," said Mrs. Ormsby, looking up, then added. "Well, if it isn't Miss Brechenworth."

Letsea froze. Was she being admonished for listening in, or did the retired teacher agree the man was a paragon?

"Alice. That's not your coat you're putting on," apprised Mrs. Ormsby.

"Silly me." Alice began chasing a sleeve to pull it off. Mrs. Ormsby grabbed for it.

Letsea noticed Alice stood on the tip of the belt and she arose to assist. "Here, let me help. Lift your left foot for a moment."

"Oh!" Alice laughed. "Miss Brechenworth, thank you."

Letsea was used to being addressed by her surname. It came with her role in the family. She would *always* be a Brechenworth. By and large, to know the other person's first name and not their last was awkward. "Hello, Alice. It's nice to see you. I miss you at the Settlement Tea Room."

"I retired."

"Congratulations. Please, call me Letsea. I'm sure I've mentioned it before."

"Letsea," Alice said, as if testing the use of her first name and squeezed her hand.

"Alice, I didn't mean to intrude. I happened to overhear."

Alice shook her head. "Not at all."

"Posh," Mrs. Ormsby said boldly. "You *should* meet her son. Really," she inserted pointedly with direct eye-to-eye contact. "I've yet to see you in the society announcement page in regard to a wedding."

The two ladies chuckled with a nervous twitter. The comment stung, however. Mrs. Ormsby always did have a way of creating excruciating embarrassment. Letsea avoided comment and hung the mistaken coat while Alice searched for hers.

"Letsea, you can meet my 'paragon' to the world shortly. He should be right here."

Letsea shyly admitted, "At this point I'd probably stammer and blush." Her mouth went dry. She did want a glimpse of this winsome gentleman. *Surely, he's mortal! Right?* She patted Alice's arm. "Happy retirement. And, Mrs. Ormsby, nice to see you again."

She casually moved down the hall where several young ballerinas in white tutus hopped and giggled. She remembered those times. The excitement preparing for the big day. *The Nutcracker Suite*. The honor of having been Clara, such a highlight in her young life.

When she glanced back, the ladies were gone. She didn't want to be conspicuous, although a glimpse of this mystery son of Alice could be pleasant. She hurried to look out a window.

The paragon opened a car door for his mother. From behind, he looked fit. Firm. Fine.

He wore jeans and a blue cable-knit sweater, the Aran Islands of

Ireland style. Heat rose to her cheeks. Her eyes focused on his dark hair beneath the Irish flat cap. Yes, decidedly a gentleman, as he closed the passenger door to a sporty car and walked around.

Oh, snap! Missed his face. What *was* visible looked mighty fine, indeed. She watched them drive away. Hm. Alice's son, not married either. What were the odds?

She sat, closed her eyes, and sighed. *Good heavens!* Seth! She forgot about Seth and drummed her fingers on the chair arm. He'd been too busy for months. Probably time to let him go.

When she opened her eyes, Lauren stood in front of her. "Ready, honey?" She patted her lap.

"I am. Chip's not."

She held her niece, and daydreamed. Mighty fine, indeed.

CHAPTER 3

Later, same day

Two men stood across the street from one of the oldest homes in St. Charles, Missouri. One leggy, lanky, and adust. The other short, podgy, and pale.

Neither man had a razor cross his face for several days.

"What do you think, Charlie?" Otis struck a match against the concrete and lit a cigarette butt he found on the ground.

"I think that might kill you. You have no idea who else's lips were on it."

"That's not what I meant. 'Sides, the sooner they kill me, the less time I'll suffer. So, Charlie, tell me what you think. Did I find a good job for us or what?"

"Have you looked for security cameras?"

"Appears next to nonexistent."

"Good. That's how we want it. The broad is worth a fortune. Some people with big old houses are next to bankrupt from trying to maintain them."

"Not this one. Has so much she doesn't know what to do with it."

"I like 'em stupid. I've got plenty of things I can do with her money."

"You mean, *we* do."

"Yeah, little buddy, *we* do. Come on, let's head over to the riverbank."

The two walked a few blocks, peeked in people's mailboxes

when they thought no one would see, then crossed an empty lot eastbound toward the famed Missouri River.

"By the way, I'll hold on to that paper you've been carryin', listing the broad's income."

"Sure, Charlie, whatever you say."

"Otis, I'll say this." Charlie surveyed the space around them. Once assured, no chance of being overheard, he said, "It seems to have potential. Let's keep watch and see what we might have to deal with. You're sure it was really quiet there last Christmas?"

Otis gave a rapid nod. "As a cemetery."

"Good job, little buddy."

"Charlie, do you still have access to a car?"

"Yeah, sure. I know enough secrets. Borrowin' a vehicle should be no problem."

"Good."

Like a stray dog with a pack of fleas, Otis scratched his bewhiskered cheeks with vigor and intensiveness. "Well now, *that* can't be good." He examined his fingernails.

Charlie crossed his arms. "We need to clean up. Not good to be noticed when plottin'."

CHAPTER 4

Thanksgiving Day at the Brechenworth estate

"Aunt Mae, what do you remember about a great-uncle, an FBI agent, who was murdered?"

"Letsea! Why on earth bring that up? Especially over Thanksgiving dinner with the children present," her aunt chided and pursed her lips.

"Aunt Mae," interrupted Gwendolene. "I love your new short hairstyle. When did you decide to change from the braided bun?"

Her one and only aunt gave a shy bat of her eyelashes.

"Last month, child. I felt a spark and decided to update. Come around more often and avoid surprises. Speaking of, Letsea, it wouldn't hurt you to update, too. Your Gibson-girl style is so Edwardian."

Letsea, her family, and guests all looked to the new Uncle Robert, the "spark."

Letsea's jaw tightened. Hm. What was wrong with her look? Just because Auntie cut her hair didn't mean she had to follow suit. There were differences between her and her aunt. Responsibilities compelled her to give up choir when rehearsals became too demanding. It behooved her to invest time wisely. It took organization to manage the estate, her inheritance, her own finances, Auntie's accounts, and use care with involvement in charities.

Fond of her own hairstyle, not even a sign of gray, she poked a finger to her caramel-blonde updo then quickly dropped her hand to her lap.

Decades ago, Aunt Mae married her way into an elegant society, in much the same way her mother had. As a widow, Auntie became socially independent. Stubborn to accept Letsea's advice, Aunt Mae hesitated on the prenuptial agreement with her new husband, although the man, devoted to her aunt, had little choice in her financial decisions. The arrangement also left Auntie out of Robert's legal and financial affairs. Common sense came into play, and it didn't appear to interfere with their romance. They made an adorable senior couple. Still, one needed to be sensible, even in matters of the heart.

Letsea tried again. "Our great-great uncle with the FBI. He's been on my mind. What was his situation? And do you remember his name."

"Honey, there's a lot of things I don't care to remember. It wouldn't hurt you to forget a few of them too."

"I already have. Mother received a little family history booklet in the mail years ago. I read it, now I can't remember where he fit in the family. I can't even find the booklet. I know where it should be, but it's not there. Did you get one?"

"Letsea Nadene Brechenworth, I'm glad you can't find it. Now I appeal to you to use your better judgment. Drop the subject."

Gwendolene got up from her side of the expansive table, spaciously seating only twelve, and walked around to whisper in Letsea's ear. "Why upset Aunt Mae? Obviously, she doesn't want to discuss him."

Letsea whispered, "Why not?"

"You know why. Because of Mommy and Daddy being killed by those kidnappers."

Gwen's husband attempted to change topics. "Has anyone read a good book lately?"

CHAPTER 5

Following a daunting dinner discourse, family and friends relocated into the front parlor.

Doyle held Letsea back. "Sorry I asked. I didn't mean to dig the hole deeper. Aunt Mae's rather antagonistic toward your reading choices. Disgruntled, yes. First time I've seen her ablaze."

Doyle's humor was a welcome relief. "Being domineering is her nature. This was a 'healthy debate.'"

"You don't say?" He rolled his eyes. "I'm glad Gwen didn't take after her demeanor."

She tilted her head. "Really?" Guess it's true. Love *is* blind.

"Hey, change of topic. How's your boyfriend? I expected Seth to be here today."

"So did I. He's stressed over a case he's working on." She gripped a chairback and edged the toe of her shoe along a floral pattern in the thick wool area rug. "It's been months." She knew what she needed to do. Set Seth free and run like the dickens.

"You mean where he's helping his client sue the most formidable law firm in the city?"

"You know?"

"Who doesn't? His client clamored all over the city for an attorney audacious enough to tackle the legal magnate." Doyle quipped, "Sure, no call for tension there."

"If he loses, he's done for," she said.

"Don't kid yourself, Lets. Even if he wins, he's going to have to leave the area. An independent attorney suing a major law firm over professional misconduct is a suicide mission. I'll be sorry to see him go. The man has guts. No other counsel dared touch it."

Letsea knew. *When we fail to make a decision, the universe does it for us. Goodbye Seth.*

Doyle cleared his throat. "So, what's the story on this murdered ancestral uncle? Fess up, Lets, you know your forefathers are that of my children as well."

"I can't remember, and you heard Aunt Mae. There's no discussing him. I get it. I do."

The servers and catering staff hired for the day came in to clear the table. She gave her employees the long weekend off. Letsea and Doyle strolled into the large hallway.

"What's with this book you're reading now?"

"It's a series and I'm hooked on it. There's something regarding the main character. It keeps me thinking about that great uncle in our family."

"Out of curiosity, what's this obsession you have with thriller books?"

"I get satisfaction in seeing the villains get the retribution due to them. Victims deserve some attempt at justice. Considering they never solved our parents' case, it's an issue for me."

"I can understand that. Gwennie still has nightmares and she was little at the time."

To avoid further discussion of the kidnapping and murders, she changed the subject. "Doyle, I understand your whole family is coming for Christmas."

"They want to see the kids sing."

"Who doesn't?" They paused in the hall. "Where do their angelic voices come from?"

Doyle rubbed his face. "Gwen says it's from her. They certainly don't get it from me."

Letsea said, "She's probably right. Our ancestors were known to sing. Just not the caliber of those two. Come, it's time to switch gears and join the others for hot chocolate or a *copita* of sherry." Always a joy to have family over. The big old house wasn't as lonely when they were present. "Your family is welcome to stay here, you know."

"Thanks anyway, Gwen made arrangements at a hotel." Doyle said, "Hey, what does the family history book look like?"

"I remember photocopied sheets folded and stapled. There's a picture of Mom's great grandmother on front...or two greats."

Doyle asked, "So you aren't exactly the family historian?"

Before they stepped into the parlor, she poked his arm and said, "I think I'm the best shot you've got at it. A lot of good it'll do if I can't find answers."

Doyle laughed out loud.

"Fortunately, Father's side of the family is well documented. Did you know there's a room in this place filled with trunks of memorabilia?"

Doyle leaned toward her right ear. "I'm not surprised. Do you even know where it is? We should plan an expedition party to find it. That'll be fun."

Gwendolene never showed enough interest to explore all the rooms in the old house, much less their family's history. Her penchant leaned toward things new and modern.

"What's funny?" came Aunt Mae's brusque tone. "Letsea, come be our hostess."

As they entered the main parlor, Uncle Robert cocked his head toward the large bay window. "Do you know that man standing on your lawn?"

Letsea stared out the front window. "Not that I know of." She forgot to close the gate.

Doyle headed outside.

Gwendolene's voice, was a mere whisper, "What do you suppose he wants?"

Letsea put an arm around her sister and pulled her in for a hug. "I haven't a clue. But look at your fearless husband. He's all in charge. Doyle will see what the stranger wants."

With all the staff off for the long weekend, why hadn't she replaced security coverage? At night, after everyone went home, she would be left alone in the big house.

Having left Gwendolene in the parlor, Letsea headed outdoors. She refused to bury her head in the sand. Why didn't the unknown man come to the door? What did he want?

CHAPTER 6

Early morning of the first Monday of December

Letsea closed down her phone after another unsuccessful monthly contact with the Embassy authorities in the Democratic Republic of the Congo. No news on her parents' cold case.

She concentrated on a bank of large monitors in her home office, searching for signs of *cup and handle patterns* in the stock market charts. Book three of the thriller series awaited her attention on the long, black granite desktop. The crystal specks gave it the deep galaxy appearance, exactly where her thoughts were adrift. Stargazing in the bright white room.

Cavernous dives in Friday's market close of Dow Jones, as anticipation of poor November company reports spread across media. Holiday sales weren't rescuing bad decisions.

Pedicured bare toes flexed the Icelandic sheep's wool rug beneath the desk. Rex-Kitty draped over her lap as she rested back and absent-mindedly stroked the cat's chest. He batted at her bracelet.

Burdensome thoughts of the stranger in the yard on Thanksgiving weighed and stayed. He claimed to be a neighbor. When she couldn't place him, he corrected himself, saying he was visiting family and looking for their little dog who took off on adventure. Around the age her parents would have been, something familiar concerning him worried her.

Question everything! her grandfather insisted.

"Knock three times…" At the ringtone, she rolled her eyes. What does Gwen need at this hour? She answered, "Hey, early bird, what's going on?"

"Letsea, will you take the kids to the zoo tomorrow? Their choir is singing there."

"Sorry, kiddo, I can't. I'm meeting Seth for lunch."

"Oh please. You can see him anytime."

"As it turns out, I can't. He's been too busy. I think he has good news, he sounded—"

"Please, Lets, please."

"What's going on with your schedule, honey?"

"You know I have allergies," she whined.

Letsea's senses danced with humor, glad they weren't on video chat. Gwendolene Brechenworth Davis feigned allergies because her kids begged for a dog. With a very active family, she didn't want pet responsibilities for anything more energetic than a Betta fish.

Gwen even showed signs of sensitivity to Rex-Kitty, when she happened to see the cat. Letsea understood the Cornish Rex to be the last pet to cause allergies. With the one layer of hair, instead of three, Kitty didn't shed or have much dander. One of the upsides to a cat having free rein in a house with over forty-thousand square feet.

"Please!"

"What time do the children need to be there?" Letsea asked.

"Noon. Performance starts at one o'clock."

"Gwen, you take them. After my date, I'll strive to catch the performance. If your allergies are inflamed, you can leave and I'll take over. I'll see you tomorrow at the zoo."

Marcia, her confidential secretary, said, "Morning. Would you like breakfast in here?"

"You're an early bird, too. Excellent plan. Thank you."

Methodical Marcia, gone without another word.

Letsea turned to look across the room and out the windows. Still dark outside. She hoped for Tuesday to be sunny and warmer.

She tried to refocus on the charts. Still, diverted by the stray thought of whether or not Alice's son, the seafaring paragon, also kept an eye on the stock market. *Isn't he an accountant?* Mrs. Ormsby and Alice spoke of him quite favorably.

Why thoughts of him? All she saw was his backside. The ladies said they wanted to introduce him to her. Had she not taken the stroll toward the ballerinas, there would be a face to put in her reverie. She smoothed her feet across the luxurious rug that her father purchased for her as a teenager, in Iceland. Her pleasures were simple. Weren't they?

Pleasures? After months apart, Seth finally set a date with her. *Where's the elation?*

Perhaps, she drew the line at being stood up for the holiday dinner with her family.

CHAPTER 7

Tuesday, 10:45 a.m.

One of Letsea's favorite eating establishments, at the old train station, was dually located near Seth's office and his apartment. They met in the Grand Hall of Union Station, shared a brief kiss, then walked hand in hand to the restaurant.

"I almost forgot what you look like," teased Letsea, in an effort to be lighthearted over an annoying topic. Why did he practically ignore her for a whole season?

"Baby, I haven't forgotten you. You're as gorgeous as ever."

His fixed grin gave him the air of youthfulness. Seth, four years younger, in a caretaking fashion, she reached over to tug his shaggy blond hair. "You need a trim."

"Yeah," he agreed. "I've been busy."

"I know you have."

The waitress arrived.

Letsea fingered the white tablecloth. "I know what I'll have. A cup of vegetable soup, Bibb salad with salmon, with half a glass of white Pinot Noir please."

"Half a glass?" Seth said, and ordered his favorite, "Heirloom salad with shrimp and bring the wine in a bottle please."

"A whole bottle?" Letsea asked with reserved enthusiasm. "Are we celebrating?"

Seth beamed. "We've settled. No trial. They delivered the check this morning."

Letsea clapped her hands in excitement. "Congratulations! Lump sum or structured?"

Seth leaned toward her and spoke in a soft voice, "Lump. Oh,

Letsea, I feel exhilarated. I've never been happier to close a case in my life."

"Doyle said you really took a risk on this one."

His chin raised. "I did, providentially I won."

The wine delivered, after a brief tasting, the waitress poured half a glass for each. After she left, Seth took the wine bottle, and with a flourish he filled both glasses.

Letsea raised her stemware toward him. "A toast to your due diligence."

"My client is thrilled. He reaped several times what his initial investment might have brought him from the company who cheated him." He sat back and excessively swirled the smidgen of wine left in his glass. After sipping, she set hers down. And he reached to top it off.

"Oh, no more, Seth." She placed her fingers over the rim. "I'm very happy for you."

Her soup arrived.

"Although the payout is exciting, I'm afraid I have bad news." He hesitated and leaned forward, his face solemn. Instead of looking her in the eyes, he looked over her shoulder.

"You're moving," she said, silently thanking Doyle for the warning. Since Thanksgiving Day, she prepared herself for the official split and was fine with it.

He looked downward. "If I stay, every law firm in the area will chew me up and spit me out. I'm not so sure, I may deserve it."

"Someone needed to put them in their place. A law firm can't ignore filing deadlines and expect their clients to be understanding of it. Nondisclosure agreement, I presume?"

"Definitely. I wouldn't have gotten such a large pre-trial settlement offer without one."

"What are your plans?" she asked. They paused while the waitress served. She thought this most likely their last meal together.

"My father has been wanting me to join his firm since my first day of law school. Any chance you want to move to Philadelphia?"

She accepted his leaving. Seth wasn't thrilled with conforming to the stipulations in the trust fund. A subject she feebly broached with him after they dated for a year. Since he continued to see her, she thought eventually he'd propose. Years later, boyfriend number three bites the dust! After a shrug, a twinge of pain in her neck.

"Saint Charles is my home. You know I love it here and I have family obligations."

He leaned closer. "Aw, baby, don't blame me for trying."

"Is your father prepared to take on any backlash that may follow you from this case?"

Seth scoffed, "You've not met Father—"

No, and why not, Seth?

"He's hard as nails and much sharper. Wherever he's known, others may well quake in his presence."

Letsea relaxed seeing Seth at ease. She knew he made the right decision for his career. Besides, Grandmama always said, "As soon as you know they aren't the forever one, run."

He reached across the table for her hand. "I've enjoyed our time together."

For everything there is a season. And she knew his words were the sound of closure.

"You're the classiest lady I've ever known, probably will ever meet." He gently squeezed his fingers to her palm.

"Heads-up. Don't ever tell your future wife you said that to another woman."

He patted her hand. "See? That's what I'm referring to. Classy all the way, baby."

Letsea looked down and studied the food on the plate and pondered. *Yet, not important enough to slip in some time to see me for three full months while you focused on your career.*

They ate their meal in uncomfortable silence. She wanted to get out of there.

"I'll miss you, Seth." Not as much as she may have. She already got a head start in expecting and accepting the inevitable, relieved it came from him and not her. Seth didn't need to know that. *Depart in good graces,* her mother taught her.

They were leaving when a fellow attorney pulled Seth aside for private conversation. Letsea waited patiently under the famed Whispering Arch in the Grand Hall.

Her thoughts of relief of Seth's leaving were interrupted by a deep masculine voice of stifling conviction.

I was murdered!

CHAPTER 8

Letsea swayed. Seth was still in deep discussion upstairs in the huge lobby. She gasped and backed against the arched wall. Surely her imagination duped her. Perhaps her father's spirit after all these years? "What?" she whispered.

I...was...murdered! A voice with grit.

She visualized a muscle clenched in a man's jaw. Except no one, nada at the other end of the arch. Her brain scrambled for an explanation.

"Who?" she breathed. She looked up the staircase to see if anyone, anywhere, might be watching her. No doubt someone's idea of a practical joke. *Not funny, fool!* Did some random bamboozler know her parents were murdered? *No, they did not. Idiot!*

A group of baseball players entered through the front doors. Out of season, still wearing jeans and team sweatshirts, she recognized several faces. They goofed around at the mysterious archway, lingered and played with whispers. She stepped aside and wondered if any of the athletes might have heard the deadly declaration.

One of the cheery young ballplayers headed her direction. The closer he got, the larger his smile.

"Sorry, baby."

She jumped as Seth put his fingers on her elbow and tugged toward the door. She glanced over her shoulder at the man wearing the big red bird. He made a sad face and raised a hand to his heart to indicate his loss.

Seth dumped her. Why should he feel a need to keep her from meeting someone new? *Go Cardinals!*

"I'll walk you to your car. Or did you use the valet?"

"Valet," she whispered. She felt someone's eyes on her, and the tendons on the back of her neck stood out.

After handing over her claim ticket, they waited curbside.

"I have a favor to ask of you." Seth cleared his throat and rubbed the back of his neck. "I'm flying out to Philadelphia tomorrow. In a couple of days, I have a moving company who's going to pack up my belongings and truck them out for me. Would you mind so much to be there when they do? And to make sure the cleaning crew does a good job on the apartment. I'd like to know I'll get my deposit back."

Of all the gall!

"What? You mean you've already made your moving plans?" Still dazed by the unattached voice in the archway, to learn Seth already planned his move without mentioning a word of it to her, until the day before he left, stung. "You're flying? Are you leaving your car at the office? Isn't Roslyn, your secretary, more equipped to handle those details?"

"She'll be swamped closing down the office and packing files. The girl's been running wild these last weeks while I wrapped up my other cases. I can leave my car in the parking garage until the end of the month, but I need to meet with Father and Grandfather this week."

"You've known for some time you were planning to leave."

"I told you I haven't had a spare minute lately." Seth handed her a typed page of instructions and placed a key in her palm.

She stared at it and mulled over his insolence. Three years of dating and he never offered her a key to his apartment. Such effrontery to hand over one to an unoccupied space. Letsea wanted to slap him. Instead, she opened and closed her mouth without speaking then clenched her lips. Mother's words were gold, *Depart in good graces.*

Relieved to see her car approach, not saying what she really wanted to say, she politely asked, "Seth, did you walk here? Do you need a ride back to your building?"

"The walk will do me good."

"Yes, it will," she said, relieved.

"Unless you want to come up to celebrate my victory." He wiggled his eyebrows and gave a broad smile.

"Thanks anyway, I think we've already reached the point of separation. Besides, I promised my sister I'd meet her and the kids at the zoo."

"Letsea, you should beware of Gwen. She walks all over you."

Apparently, little sis wasn't the only one.

She glanced back to the front doors of the hotel lobby of Union Station. She chose to be more concerned with the unattached voice of he who was murdered.

CHAPTER 9

Tuesday, 12:35 p.m.

Letsea drove to the downtown area and parked with a clear view of the historic Gateway Arch next to the mighty Mississippi River. The sky overcast and water choppy, a pinhole ray of light shone on the gigantic stainless steel monument. Did the huge arch also have some way of relaying whispers? As a distraction, she picked up the thriller novel and read a couple of paragraphs.

Concentration eluded her, so she slammed the novel closed. "Was it my imagination back there or what?" She took a couple of slow deep breaths to clear her thoughts, but it didn't work. "It's your fault, FBI agent," she accused the fictional character in the book. Because of this made-up character, thoughts were of her parents and that great uncle FBI agent—from when? Early twentieth century? She wished she could remember more of what she read regarding him. A glance at the clock sent her hurriedly in the direction of the zoo.

In time to watch the children sing, but after the performance, Gwen stood amidst the choir's reception line meeting zoo guests who were oohing and awing in astonishment of her young children's beautiful and mature voices.

Not surprising, Gwen showed no signs of allergies to zoo animals.

Letsea arrived home feeling a bit overwhelmed at the thought of killer thrillers. Parked in the oversized garage behind the mansion, she pulled up a search engine on her smart phone. She spoke into the microphone, "Unsolved murder of FBI agents."

"The FBI Wall of Honor remembers Special Agent Paul E. Reynolds, who died of a gunshot wound to the heart under mysterious circumstances, August 1929."

Other articles read:

"Reynolds is memorialized in the Bureau's Wall of Honor."

"A thorough and intensive investigation failed to shed any light on his murder."

"His loss remains the sole unsolved line-of-duty death of an FBI agent in U.S. history."

The only killing unsolved? Her heart beat quicker as her mind raced. It must be him. Where did the name Reynolds come into her family tree?

Why on earth, or... She amended her thought. *Not of this earth.* Why did the voice speak to her? The internet clearly read "unsolved killing." She touched a link and began reading an excerpt of an old newspaper clipping.

"His waterlogged body was found in an irrigation canal. He had been shot in the heart at close range." It took place in Phoenix, August 9, 1929. "That's him," she exclaimed, beginning to remember a little of what she originally read years ago, although not this extensive. Her ancestor, murdered in Arizona, in the 1920s. *This is him.* The authorities suspected members of a drug ring responsible for his death. A drug ring, way back then? Wasn't alcohol the issue in those days?

Her phone rang and she jumped, fumbling it. "Hello?"

"Letsea, it's Marcia. There's someone on the house phone for you. I wouldn't have disturbed you, but I noticed you drove in a little while ago. Are you all right?"

"Fine. Thanks, Marcia. Who's on the phone?"

"This is the second time this man has called today. He wants to talk with you regarding a company's annual meeting. Mr. White says you own stock in the company he's with. He makes it sound important. I mean to tell you he comes across like a scam artist. His voice sounds just like a guy who called yesterday and refused to tell me what he wanted. He won't let me relay a message. Shall I tell him to hold? Or I can tell him to never call again."

"Marcia. You're too efficient for even me. No, tell him you are the one he needs to talk with. I'd like to get in on the tail end of the market before closing bell. I'll be right in."

"Yes, ma'am."

Letsea looked at her phone. She accidently closed down the articles from the web. Oh well. She grabbed her purse and the novel.

1920s. His waterlogged body found in a canal. Shot in the heart. *Could the whisper have been from my great-uncle Agent Reynolds?* It didn't make sense. If his point was to clarify he had been murdered, wasn't that already established? What would he want with her a century later? *If* it *was* Reynolds' voice.

CHAPTER 10

Dark, early hours of Wednesday morning

Red-eyed from a late night of re-reading an online article from a 1929 Phoenix newspaper, Letsea tried to glean a sense of the personality of Agent Paul Reynolds. Definitely the same relative she remembered from the family history booklet.

Had Reynolds' spirit found a way to communicate through the Whispering Arch? How many people had heard the declaration, "I was murdered"?

Or did he single her out? If so, why? At 3:00 a.m., she tossed her covers off.

The newspaper article said Reynolds spent the day studying a mass of papers in the hotel lobby where he stayed. On Friday, he intently worked until nine in the evening then got up and packed his briefcase. He told the desk clerk he'd be back in a couple of hours.

Reynolds rented a Chevrolet coupe from the car rental service across the street from the hotel. He jovially told the attendant he was going for a swim and would be back later that evening.

He never returned.

Foiled by the lack of sleep, Letsea sat up and rubbed her eyes. Empathetic with her uncle, she knew paperwork could be overbearing. Worse, were her ancestors in danger due to his occupation?

An August evening. When did air-conditioning come into the picture? A summer's night in the Southwest City of Phoenix. No doubt the man wanted to cool down. In a canal? Surely not. One journalist interviewed a friend of his who said he expected Paul to arrive for a late evening swim in his pool. He never showed.

Uncle Paul appeared to have some wealthy and maybe influential friends. Why not? Mom's great-grandfather wasn't without status in the field of communications and electrical engineering. Letsea remembered her grandmother kept letters and a series of textbooks he had written.

Paul Reynolds' friends may have been powerful, how? Politically? Financially? Did he work undercover? What did his friends think he did for a living if he kept his true identity a secret?

The memory of the disembodied voice at the station became a driving force. What if it were voice-throwing trickery? Perhaps it arose from being upset with Seth more than she realized. Her imagination might have gone haywire.

If a spirit from beyond, it could be anybody's. It didn't sound like Father. "I was murdered." If Reynolds, surely he didn't expect her to solve his murder nearly a century after the fact.

What could she do about it?

For the time being, she needed sleep.

During the night of restless tossing, Letsea got up and strolled to the tower. Once little Gwennie's favorite room. Fondly, she thought of *the little snippet*, as Grandad called Gwendolene. A snippet of trouble, a snippet of sweetness. To be so young, she had a mighty big presence, still did. Bright, willful, demanding, and yet so very cute and lovable. Letsea entered the round room and sat on the curved cushioned window seat. She pulled a plush toy polar bear onto her lap, hugged it, and remembered the warmth that used to fill the nursery.

A day from law school came to mind. Grandfather flew in to Cambridge to break the news to her that her parents were reported missing. He brought her home and said not to tell Gwendolene. "Sis is just a child and shouldn't be burdened with such news."

Until college, she and little Gwen stayed in the "big house" every time their parents traveled without them. She loved her grandparents deeply, but she loved to travel and see the world with Mommy and Daddy, as they liked to be called.

Distracted by memories, she squeezed the bear close as grief overwhelmed her. An attempt to blink back the tears which welled in her eyes. "Daddy? Did I hear you at the train station?"

Silence was her answer.

She untangled the polar bear from a scrunched tight ball.

She thought of how fun her parents were. They loved adventure, taking risks, and parties. Although they managed some good investments over the years, they were not known to be overachievers in the world of business. However, they could do cross-country dogsled races with the best of them. Swim with sharks and climb mountains. They liked to explore ancient villages, rainforests, and other countries....

A glance beyond the curved glass revealed a snowfall of huge flakes. All to be gone by morning, others may never know of the lovely night scene. The yard lights below were old-fashioned gas lanterns. Sentimental toward living in the old house, just not alone, Letsea wondered, where was her perfect life? A husband and children to love and raise. Sons and daughters to carry the heritage into the future would be a dream come true.

She wished for Gwen's family to live here with her. She couldn't spend enough time with Chip and Lauren. These halls longed for the sound of children's play. So did she.

Doyle's position was understandable. Gwen explained, he wanted to be the head of his own household. Important for him to thrive in his responsibilities as husband and father, as provider and protector.

He privately made his point to her. How would Gwen ever learn to take responsibility for her actions if her big sister kept pulling "little Gwen" out of difficulties? She missed her family. All four grandparents died of broken hearts in their loss of her parents. If it hadn't been for Gwen, she may have too.

Her adult life had been a long, hard trek. She wished for a man, unlike Seth, who really cared for her. One who wanted fatherhood. She sniffled. At over forty, not only did her biological clock tick, an entire symphony of warnings blared notifications in her mind.

She heard, "Meow." Rex Kitty stood in the open doorway. Large blue eyes and a tilt of his head, he called to her. As of now, she'd have to accept he was the sole male in her life and she loved him. She patted her lap.

"Meow."

"Come here." The cat refused to cross the threshold. Why

wouldn't he enter?

"Meow, meow, meow."

"What's wrong?" As if beckoning her to come out. "Okay, okay. I'm coming."

A shiver ran up her spine. From the chill of air through curved windows, or something else?

She shook the feeling, kissed the polar bear on the snout, left it on the window seat with a dozen other plush toys. She picked up the cat and went to her bedroom. By good luck, she witnessed the first snowfall of the season. Mother always called it a sign of purity and awareness of God's blessings.

A call to FBI Headquarters for the latest information on Agent Paul Reynolds was in order. She needed him out of her head once and for all.

CHAPTER 11

Wednesday, 1:18 p.m.

"OH, snap!"
Letsea slapped her fingertips to her desk and stared at her cell phone. The calls to FBI Headquarters provided no new insights and they shut down her search engine!

Never had she experienced anything like that before! She pushed her chair away from the desk and got up to pace. *What's wrong with trying to learn the history of an agent killed nearly a hundred years before?* She stopped to stare out the north windows, to overlook the acreage behind the house. What did she do in error?

When she assertedly set out to find information, it was deemed *restricted*. A large blue circle spun in rapid succession. Her endeavor thwarted. It requested a passcode. All attempts to log on were refused, and it ended with her search engine being officially locked down. *Access Denied.* She needed to uninstall and reinstall a new app.

With her computer, she explored pedigree charts and family group archives. She got lost somewhere in compiled records before realization hit. She knew little of her mom's side of family history. When her maternal grandparents came for visits, her parents usually whisked the whole family off to adventures like canoe trips, museums, and gardens. They were together, albeit they didn't sit and reminisce. Their visits to them in Vale were mostly spent skiing. To seek birth and death records led nowhere. She needed to know full names, birth locations, and dates.

Ultimately, she decided to visit the one person who knew answers. Aunt Mae.

She pulled into her aunt's driveway beside the historic red-brick Italianate-style house. Uncle Robert approached and opened her car door. "Letsea, nice to see you."

He became her aunt's everything imaginable, from gardener to cook to home renovator. "Why does she have you outside?"

"You know why. She's old and just plain mean." He winked and smiled.

Letsea cracked a grin and tapped the toe of a shoe to a box of Christmas lights. "Putting up decorations in the cold?"

"That's what I told her. They should've been up before Halloween. The old curmudgeon wouldn't allow it. She said the trick or treaters might pop the light bulbs."

"They wouldn't if she were nice and gave them lots of candy."

Robert shook his finger at Letsea. "You tell her, will you? I like to see their cute costumes. My Missus didn't even want to turn on the porch light."

She chuckled, as per her habit, rang the doorbell three times to announce her presence, then walked on in. Aunt Mae stood peering out the parlor window. "Auntie, what's going on?"

"Old fool. Christmas lights, of all things. I bet he'll climb a ladder. What if he were to fall?"

After a hug and a kiss to her aunt's cheek she said, "You'd call an ambulance, have him recover in bed, and hire ten people to do all the work he does around here."

Auntie's eyes narrowed and her lips pursed. "Don't you sass me, girl!"

"Okay. That's not why I'm here."

"To pay my bills?"

She drew a deep breath and plunged forward. "Yes. I also want to know where Uncle Paul Reynolds fit into our family history?"

"Girl, it's never-ending persistence with you, isn't it?"

"I have questions. He's part of my family too."

Aunt Mae huffed and sat in her favorite overstuffed chair. "Not our uncle, child. No blood relation. He was Mildred's first husband, and that's all I care to say on the matter."

"It's not like he left willingly. He...died."

Aunt Mae stared and raised her chin. Letsea knew Aunt Mae's inclination to button up in a code of silence if she even uttered the word murder.

"True."

"And an FBI agent. So, who in our family did Mildred marry next?"

"Your second-great-grandfather's brother Raymond. He adopted and loved Mildred's little boy, their only child. I understand they were quite happy."

Letsea's voice squeaked in surprise, "Paul Reynolds had a son?"

"Yes, but he died as a young man."

"How young? Did he have any—"

Mae put up her hand. "Stop, child. That whole side of the family lived in the Northwest. There's plenty of family I've never met."

"I suppose Uncle Raymond and Aunt Mildred have passed away by now, hm?"

Auntie squinted. "They were born in the eighteen hundreds. What do you think, girl?"

"Where are they buried?"

"I'm not sure. Probably in the Northwest somewhere. Can we change the subject now? I don't feel like discussing family that's gone before me. I'm on the precipice as it is. Did you hear we have a warm front coming? Cold be gone for all I care. You wouldn't believe the heating bills every winter."

She sighed. "I'm well aware of your utility expenses, Auntie. I've been tending to your bills and bank accounts for years, remember? Maybe Robert can talk you into updating the insulation and H/VAC. Try solar panels. They've saved me a fortune."

She pressed for more information. "One more question and I'll leave it alone for now. Where is Paul Reynolds buried?"

Aunt Mae tilted her head, closed one eye, and stared way too long. "Fine. Idaho, I think. That's it, I'm done. Now, girlie, tell me, are you still planning to have the Christmas tea for the community volunteers at the manor this month?"

"Yes. Check your mail for the invitation. You aren't so mad at me you won't attend, are you?"

"Honey, you remind me of your mother." Aunt Mae touched

her cheek. "You have her fair porcelain-like complexion, and like her; you're a regular social butterfly. I will not miss your Christmas teas until I'm dead and cold in the ground. I want to bring Robert, you know."

Gwendolene was the true family socialite, she thought. "Space is tight this year, but no matter, Uncle Robert's always welcome. Besides, he's volunteering with you at the park gardens and at the senior center. While I'm here, I'll write checks for your bills and I have cash on hand from your account."

"Good." Mae stood. "Now come to the dining room and take tea with me. I need to explain Robert's offer to take over paying our bills so you won't have to. It'll give you some free time. That reminds me, will you pull a receipt out for me? This newest shredder has already jammed. Irritating gizmo. I can't stand those things."

"You should have bought the deluxe model. Those cheap ones don't last long."

"The one like yours is so expensive," Aunt Mae grumbled.

"You can afford it, besides a good one will last years longer, without jams."

Mae groaned, "It's so frustrating when it clogs."

CHAPTER 12

Robert rested on an outdoor sofa in the portico facing the driveway. Letsea sat near him. "Auntie frets over you. I don't think she could handle it if you hurt yourself. It took too many years for you two to meet up again. I'm still amazed. High-school sweethearts. Both of you in successful marriages with silver anniversaries. Both widowed, then running into each other on a garden tour. It's so romantic." She nudged her shoulder against his. "No ladders, all right? Stay safe."

"Aah yes, Mae likes to worry. It makes her feel useful. The Christmas light hangers will be here any minute to string out and hang the little pretties. My climbing days are officially over. Now I direct."

"Good." She patted his arm. "They hung my lights a few days ago."

"Did you come to drill her concerning that murdered agent?"

"She shared a little. Did she tell you?"

"Some scandal her grandparents kept hushed. You do know it's *before* her time. Right, Lets?"

"I don't get it. A federal agent. What happened to make the family want to ignore his murder?"

"As a G-man, maybe it's classified."

Her jaw dropped. "It's possible. I called FBI Headquarters for an update. They didn't share anything other than the epitaph on the Wall of Honor. It happened during the Prohibition Era. Robert, what do you know about the 1920s?"

He paused, before he said. "That was before my time, too. I'm old, but not *that* old."

Letsea cringed. "I know, sorry."

Robert explained, "I do know my grandparents lived through it and I can assure you they recalled it as a time of unrest. The entire decade was a notorious time in history. A challenge for anyone in the field of law enforcement. What do you know of the era?"

"The Eighteenth Amendment declared it illegal to produce, import, export, or sell intoxicating liquors. Soon after a ratification added to make it illegal to *drink* it as well. Oops."

"Exactly right. I bet you'd never make such an error."

"Never bet," she said. "Law school was methodical at drilling procedure into us. 'When you write a bill, contract, or an agreement of any kind—cover all your bases!' Then what?" she asked.

"No one could legally have anything to do with alcohol, except as a prescribed medication. They weren't even allowed to crash a bottle of wine over the bow of a boat."

"Must have been difficult for those who enjoyed a drink. Even I like a glass of wine now and then." Letsea remembered the sips of wine with Seth. Could that have been the cause of her hearing the voice? *No, don't be silly.* Still, she'd not like being refused the choice to partake or not.

"A lot of people challenged it in the courts, dear. Both state and federal, everyone saw the law from their own perspective."

"I don't get it, why did they make it law in the first place?"

"Citizens pushed for it, for years. A lot of people got tired of seeing drunks gambling their pay away, leaving wives and children without necessities. They saw liquor as the core problem instead of the reason people were indulging in the first place."

Letsea asked, "What do you mean?"

"They thought by creating a prohibition, they'd save lives. After all, when people aren't accountable for their actions, there are figureheads who want to force them into compliance. To own up and take responsibility, even if it meant putting them in jail. Understand?"

"I do. It didn't work, though, people still managed to buy liquor, right?"

"Speakeasies and direct sales. They were illegal and it was a different dimension of control."

"Those who made the law probably thought it wouldn't apply to them."

"Right. They didn't see they had a problem with alcohol. The law, meant to protect the families of, and abusers from themselves."

"In essence, they were breaking the very law they put into place, every time they partook in an occasional drink. Oh man, they were doomed by their own actions."

"There's an acceptable way to put it," Robert agreed. "America coming out of World War I. They grieved and needed to forget the horrors of death and injury."

Letsea stood to leave. "Thanks for the history lesson."

Robert walked with her and opened the car door. "Letsea, remember severe consequences can develop from people with good intentions. The government created a void and swinging doors with prohibition. It turned against them and became a radical deadly force of crime activity. We still deal with it today. Fortunately, America seemed to dance their way through the Roaring Twenties. Dance halls were popular. Then again, many of them were fronts for speakeasies. Owned by crime bosses."

"Point taken, Uncle Robert. Oh hey, do you think they also had a problem with illegal drugs?"

"When was there *not* a problem is more the question. Where there is a need, there is someone willing to meet it, to supply it, for a cost. The law opened a door wide for the Mafia to come through. They deepened liquor and the drug trade while they were at it."

"Where there is need, keep a watchful eye for greed. It sounds like they suspected Agent Reynolds died from a drug ring at work," she said as she started her car.

"All because of well-intentioned laws, designed to rule the masses," said Robert.

Letsea agreed. "Their game plan is to create discord. The more we disagree, the weaker we'll all be. The key is to see higher, be kind, and always look for good. United we stand, right?"

CHAPTER 13

Thursday morning

A vibration in the man's shirt pocket was followed by a sigh.

Special Agent Godrick Lockhart, the Third, FBI, known to work colleagues as Lock. Family and friends were a different story, they still called him Trey. Therein lay the duality of his life. He set barbells on his bedroom floor to answer his cell phone. "Hello."

"Lock, I've got an assignment for you."

"Whoa, Chief. Don't you want someone else? It's December. I have the whole month off, remember?"

"I happen to know you're the best man for this job. You can handle it in a jiff. No flights. It's pretty simple and in your own backyard. Right there in St. Charles, Missouri."

Lock didn't say anything. He earned his free time. Still, Chief was both boss and friend.

"Come on. It's no big deal and it's something I need to have checked out now."

"What?"

"I'm glad you asked."

Lock rolled his eyes. He should have remained quiet.

"I've been sent notice a woman in your town has been searching government websites and making phone calls, digging for information on a former FBI agent."

Lock said, "Maybe she wants a background check before she

dates him."

"I doubt it. The agent died in 1929."

Lock sat on the edge of his bed. "What are we talking here?"

"Agent Paul E. Reynolds from the Wall of Honors."

"Oh, black-eyed peas! Are you kidding me? Do you mean the murdered prohibition agent, with the case never solved?"

"You got it."

"I thought the door to that closed decades ago."

"It swings like the hinges of the door to hell. It's Hoover's doing. He said it reflects the integrity of our bureau and tried to force the case closed. Like all cold cases, it'll remain open until it's finally solved."

"Do they even have evidence to extract DNA?"

His boss cleared his throat. "Probably not. Lock, I need for you to nip it in the bud. Check your email. I sent you our 'authorized version' of the case file on Reynolds. I also forwarded what we have on Miss Inquiring Mind. NSA info., driver's license, etcetera. Read between the lines, Lock. Find the connection. I hope she's not another journalist. Her name is Letsea Brechenworth, of St. Charles. Research her, call me back ASAP, and you can still enjoy your vacation." *Click.*

Lock recognized her name. *That's a no-brainer.* No doubt everyone in St. Charles knew of Letsea Brechenworth. For more than one reason. His mom mentioned she recently ran into her.

He walked upstairs to his home office, read his email, leaned forward, and dropped his forehead to his palm.

An hour later, Lock called his boss.

"Right off the bat, here's what we have on Brechenworth. Single, never married. No children. Forty-one. Income is only seventy-eight thou per annum and comes from a trust. Her earned income is in real estate and it's reinvested. She has one younger sister."

"Lock, why did you say 'only' seventy-eight K? That's not bad for an average income in Missouri, is it?"

"Not at all. Chief, she doesn't work, remember? She's a trust fund baby and happens to live in one of the more impressive houses in our region. Plus, she has the potential to earn a lot more."

"How's that?" the chief asked.

"The woman's an elite law school grad. Has her license in

Illinois, Massachusetts, Missouri, and Washington D.C."

"Frack! A D.C. attorney doing research on this guy."

"You'll be interested in these next notations. Her great-great-grandfather was Lemuel Brechenworth, as in the well-to-doer in the nineteenth and twentieth centuries shipping trade. Now get this, her parents were kidnapped in an international fiasco while in the Congo over a decade ago. Due to a glitch with the ransom drop-off, they were executed. If you can call it that. I won't go into detail, but it was horrific."

"I can imagine."

"No, trust me, Chief, you can't. I saw photos. Their killers were making an insane statement."

"Oh drat. Were they brought to justice?"

"Really? Need you ask? The Democratic Republic of the Congo, Chief." Sometimes he thought his supervisor spent too much time behind a desk. "I remember reading it in local papers when it happened. Obviously, the released information, a publicly-sensitive prepared statement. A lot kept undercover. Thank the lord. It looks like Miss Brechenworth and her grandfather went to the DRC with the cash ransom. They returned with the money and two boxes of ashes."

"You weren't involved with any part of it, were you?"

"No. On another assignment, besides, kidnapping isn't my specialty."

"Good. She won't recognize you. Did you read the Reynolds file I sent?"

"Yep. Who would have thought it?" Lock frowned. This was not going to drop out of sight in a day. He hadn't even emptied out his exercise room of its equipment yet. He needed to get it done so he could set up the room for his parents to move in.

"What is she looking for and why?"

Lock noted the sternness in the chief's voice. "I don't know. I don't see an obvious connection," he admitted.

"Bunk. Find the darn link. What's your first step?"

"I'll do a little surveillance. In order to cut this short, I think I'll just talk to her."

"Use caution, Lock. With resources and knowledge of the law, especially D.C., she might be hiding some sharp talons."

"Got it. She's not a trial attorney, Chief. Relax. I promise I won't tick her off. I'm not a greenhorn at this. In fact, you might as well know, I'm scoring my time to retirement, Boss."

"I've been expecting it. You're well over the twenty, as it is."

"Yes I am. Over twenty-five, in fact."

CHAPTER 14

Late Thursday night into early Friday

Letsea tossed the covers off, sighed, and looked at the clock. At 2:11 a.m., sleep eluded her like a gentle breeze. One could feel it approach, next, it flitted away leaving her in a state of yearning. After steaming up the bathroom with a hot shower, she dried and redressed for bed then stared in the mirror. Her stomach tightened and she ran a hand through her hair.

"Paul Reynolds, what are you doing to me? It's December, for Pete's sake! I have a long list of Christmas things to get done. Preparation for two annual parties. A day of babysitting and Christmas shopping to finish. What do you expect of me?"

What do you expect of yourself?

Did she really hear something? It sounded like a rough, uneven whisper. A peek into the bedroom revealed zilch. Where did it come from? Verbal? Surely not. In her thoughts. "Reynolds, are you here?"

Naught.

As she crossed her favored antique hand-hooked area rug she turned on her heel toward the ivory French doors and inspected the softly lit hall. With the skeleton key, she latched herself in, sealing anyone else out. As a precaution, she palmed the aged brass and set it on the accent table. In the early years when she finally returned home from law school, lonely and frightened Gwendolene commonly locked the boogieman out and crawled in bed with her. Such a comfort when she was nearby.

She recalled how her grandparents aged uncommonly fast, due to fear, grief, and anger. Their anguish over how her parents suffered, too heavy a load to bear.

She didn't feel alone. As if it were the presence of—who? Paul Reynolds? Parents or grandparents? She sat, observing the shadows in her bedroom. The sheers over the large bay window allowed a luster from the outside lights. Only outlines of furniture and paintings were visible. Darkness prevailed. Was the gloom in her emotions or memories? Or...

"Paul Reynolds? Talk to me! Or are you going to make me drive back to Union Station?"

Would I really do that? she questioned herself. "Why are you in my thoughts?"

I was murdered, echoed in her memory. Memory? Or did he just say it again?

"The evidence is on the Wall of Honor at the FBI Headquarters. At least I know that much," she said aloud. "What else do you want?"

This is all you. You won't let go.

She saw no one and it sounded more like a faint, jagged whisper. She raised her shoulders. "I don't see how that can be. You're the one in my head."

Your head, not mine.

"Paul Reynolds?"

What?

"Prove to me it's really you so I know I'm not going crazy."

You're talking with yourself.

The uneven tone, ill-defined, enough to believe it to be errant thoughts or wind. Maybe the windows need to be sealed.

"Oh! Paul Reynolds, let me sleep, will you?"

By the by, I prefer Paul E. Reynolds.

What? Wait. "Paul E. Reynolds. What does E. stand for?" she whispered.

Edward.

"Oh!" Letsea jumped up. Did she read his middle name somewhere? Was it really Edward? Did pure imagination answer her own question, correctly? Unless he only existed in her head! "No. Paul! It really is you!" she shrieked.

Assume what you will.

Silence. After a long pause of breathing fast, she heard a knock on her bedroom double doors.

"Letsea, is everything all right?" asked Pauline Collins, her head housekeeper and cook.

She rushed to unlock the double doors and fumbled with the key. "Give me a minute, Pauline. I'm fine." She opened the door, relieved to see a friendly, familiar face. It confirmed it wasn't a dream. "Thanks for checking on me. I can't seem to sleep."

"I heard talking. I don't mean to disturb you. I thought you might be making one of your overseas calls. I'm still concerned. You need your sleep." Pauline held a small tray, nurturing and motherly.

A phone call may have been an easy cover for talking to herself in the middle of the night. "Sorry if I woke you."

"No, no. I brought you a cup of hot chocolate and toast. Just in case." Pauline, a staple around the house since Letsea's high school years. A natural caregiver and a major support to the whole family through, and after the ordeal with her parents.

"Thank you. Night-night, Pauline."

"Good night, miss."

She placed the snack on the round oak table. Was it Reynolds, or her imagination? If so, why?

"E?" Could easily be for Earl, Edmund, or Eugene.

"Paul E. Reynolds?" she whispered.

Her mind went quiet. Had sweet Pauline chased away the sleepless night or a lost spirit?

CHAPTER 15

Dark of the night Friday morning

Agent Lockhart left home hours before dawn. He wanted to learn the lay of the land in the quiet of the night. The estate, easy to locate. Signs of understated elegance posted the entrance to both Brechenworth Manor and The Queen Anne House. How had he lived his life in St. Charles and never driven down this outer-edge-of-town lane to see this estate?

The two stately old houses stood beyond the intricate double-lane green gates. The design on the barrier, a seascape. The decorative metal picket fencing defined the large yard while permitting a good perspective. He backed his black BMW between a couple of hedges. An acceptable shield to stay out of sight.

Trey studied both houses through binoculars. The prodigious blue three-story house with excessive gingerbread trim, a turret, and a wraparound porch. It looked fairy-tale-like, compared to the two-story folk Victorian he was raised in, yet, modest compared to its adjacent grandiose neighbor. Approximately forty yards of manicured lawn and a circle drive separated the two structures.

A green roof topped the imposing old-world-styled manor. Built with quarried natural stone, the three-story mansion had a four-story tower on the front east corner. Several chimneys gave him an idea of the considerable depth of the dwelling.

Newspaper articles, he spent the day before reviewing, did not prepare him for the prodigious size. Not the largest house he had ever seen, or been in. After all, his career involved discovery and revealing money fraud. Although white-collar crimes proved to be more violent than one should expect. Money launderers and embezzlers willingly murdered to protect what they perceived to be theirs. Interesting thing regarding criminals, they lived high on other people's money, impressing others. It was more than greed. They envied power and control, and had it. Until caught and put behind bars. Even there, they worked to maintain control of their endeavors.

Trey spent last evening combing over Miss Brechenworth's accounts. Through the estate, a noted, generous donor to several local charities. Donations were higher than she allowed for her personal account. Fortunately, there were no signs of fraud. What a relief. Pauline, a close friend of his mother's, lived-in, and worked for her.

Seeing the place, he instantly gained new respect for Pauline. His mother wanted to go inside this house for decades. Her friend so respected the family's privacy she'd never invite anyone over to her live-in apartment.

White Christmas lights outlined the architectural features of both houses. As private homes, never listed for sale, he found very little information available on the internet. Her social media presence simply nonexistent. On the laptop, he searched county personal and property taxes.

A prolonged high-pitched whistle escaped his lips. "Man," he spoke within the luxurious privacy of his sporty car. "That's got to be rough, no matter the size of your income." He remembered her official income being well below his. "Or lack of income," he amended.

According to county taxes, she owned over fifty vehicles. *What in the world?* He viewed only a summary. It did not list the make and models. *What does she have, a car museum?*

An upstairs light went out, a bedroom, he imagined. Did she just go to bed at four o'clock in the morning? He relaxed, but not for long. Headlights came around from behind the house and stopped under the car porch. A tall, young man got out and held the door open.

The original use of the car porch on the end, next to the tower, allowed riders easier access from a carriage. It had been updated and boasted a redesigned set of steps and a mechanical platform lift. Who needed a wheelchair?

Miss Brechenworth stepped outside. "Wow! Beautiful." Trey admired her as he refocused the field glasses. The lady dressed in a camel-color knit cable dress, matching shoes, and carried her woven camel-color overcoat. A glimmer of gold hung around her neck. The man took her coat and placed it in the back seat of her Lexus SUV, which also came camel-colored. Geez, he'd heard of matching shoes to an outfit before, but cars?

Her file said single. No mention of an ex, boyfriend or fiancé. The man could be a servant. "Yeah, I'll go with that one, an employee." Afterward, he considered why should it matter to him?

He sank low in his seat, grabbed his fedora, and placed it over his forehead. As the SUV pulled away from the house, the double green gates slid open like pocket doors. As soon as the Lexus cleared the iron barriers, they promptly closed. Adjusting his seat, he put his car into gear. His timing, impeccable, the adventure began early. Clearly, had he waited for a normal hour to drive over, he would have missed her.

Lock kept his distance and followed.

Twenty-seven and a half minutes later, she pulled up to the front doors of the Union Station. At four thirty in the morning? The hotel. By all means a tryst! The lovely lady had a secret lover.

CHAPTER 16

4:55 a.m., downtown St. Louis

With discretion, Special Agent Lockhart followed the prim and proper Miss Brechenworth through the front doors of Union Station. She stood to his immediate left, at the edge of the entrance. *What man in his right mind dare keep this glamour doll waiting?* He passed by and went up the long eastside staircase to the main floor. She did not. He wished she would make her way up and sit. Concerned she might leave, he wanted to position himself nearby. To stall, he walked around the quiet Grand Hall and kept going to the banister to look down at her.

Finally, he pulled three chairs and a small table into position, so he could comfortably see down the steps. As soon as the coffee shop opened, he hurried and bought a cup of coffee and went back to sit and observe the intriguing lady. He draped his overcoat on a chair, removed his hat, setting it on the table, and opened his laptop. With a cup in his hand, he didn't think it would be obvious he followed her.

A group of airline staff checked out, went down and departed through the front doors.

As soon as she was alone again, she faced the wall like she wanted to ignore the whole world, then spun to look around. As though playing hide-and-seek, but alone. Finally, she settled, faced the wall of the arch, and appeared to talk to herself. Gearing up confidence? Praying? Possibly. Other than Reynolds, what were her logistics? Where was her companion? He snapped a picture with his cell phone.

Except for a young man, in exercise attire, who crossed the lobby alongside the extensive bar, no one was around. Only she and he were in the humongous Grand Hall.

He hoped to hear Miss Brechenworth from his position, yet failed.

A waitress walked through, approached her, nodded, and went back to the coffee shop.

It dawned on him, whether she knew it or not, whatever she said in that spot could be heard at the other end of the Whispering Arch! Slow, to avoid her attention, leaving his overcoat and coffee, he put his hat on and tucked his laptop under his arm and went down the westside flight of stairs. If he was smooth enough, he could hear what she said.

To-go cup in hand, the waitress returned and inadvertently brought attention to him. "Sir, I'll be with you in a moment."

In an unforeseen change of plans, he headed their way as the fine lady opened her purse. Trey took his chance.

"Here, let me get that for you." He handed the waitress a ten-dollar bill and insisted she keep the change. In afterthought, he hoped it wasn't an expensive drink.

"Oh, snap!" Miss Brechenworth jerked her head and jumped back a step.

When the server expressed her gratitude, he met her with relief, apparently a ten *did* allow for a generous tip. Miss Brechenworth, on the other hand, conveyed utter fear. The last reaction he expected. A gasp, green eyes wide, her mouth open, and a hand clinched at her heart. She reminded him of Marilyn Monroe.

He held his hands up to show no harm intended. "Sorry, I didn't mean to startle you. I wanted to cover your drink."

She drew back. Her legs wobbled and she put a hand to the wall. Apparently, she needed support. "Maybe you should sit down," he suggested.

Frozen, she didn't move, simply stared. Her hands trembled.

"Please, before you fall." Trey offered his arm to help steady her. He refused to grab her. He told the chief he'd not tick her off. He failed to mention scaring her. The dismay in her eyes disheartened him. *Why did I take a case during vacation?*

"Where did you come from?" Her plump lips quivered.

"Are you all right?" Lockhart led her upstairs to his little niche of the grand lobby.

"I'm fine. Just fine."

So she said. He could tell she wasn't. "Have a seat." Pleased and surprised when she walked with him without resistance, though, he felt guilty for frightening her.

Despite the struggle, she managed to unhook the large single button on her wool coat. He helped her out of it, draped it next to his overcoat. She jerked forward, turned to look over her shoulder, and shuddered. He put his hand on her arm while she sat.

"Should I call for medical assistance?" he asked, genuinely concerned.

"If I flop out of my chair, sprawl on the floor, and flounder like a fish, please do call. Otherwise, I'll be fine. Thanks for asking." She closed her eyes, and a delicate upturn graced enticing her lips.

He lifted one corner of his mouth. So, Miss Brechenworth had a sense of humor.

The waitress followed and placed a to-go cup on the table. "Here's your tea." She paused. "Are you not feeling well? I can call for the manager."

Without opening her eyes, she said, "No thank you. I'm fine. I only need a minute."

The waitress furrowed her brow at him and put her hand on Miss Brechenworth's shoulder. "If you need anything, my name's Gina. Call out, I'll come."

He took charge of the situation. "Thank you, Gina. I'll sit with her for a bit." The girl looked at both of them before she left.

A few seconds later, Miss Brechenworth did a face-palm then rubbed her temples.

Lockhart leaned forward, forearms on his knees. "So, what happened back there?"

Clasping her hands on her lap, legs tucked together against the chair, she looked directly into his eyes. "I thought you were someone else." She glanced upward to his fedora. "Sorry. Thanks for the tea, by the way."

"I'm curious, who did you think me to be?" Who was she scared of? He sat back and interlaced his fingers. "My name's Trey Lockhart." He hoped she would introduce herself. *It's easier to converse with people when they know you know their name.*

She continued to look at him for a minute then spoke, "Trey? Hm. I'd think your friends might rather call you Lock."

His eyebrows raised. Did she know him? "Some do," he disclosed.

"Trey? So, are you the third in your family with your name?"

"Yes. I am Godrick William Lockhart the third."

"God-rick? Your parents set the level rather high in your playing field, didn't they?"

He laughed. "They are a gentle loving couple who want the best for their children."

"Good parents, then."

"The best," he agreed and looked at her expectantly. She shied from giving her name.

"I noticed it looked like you were testing the Whispering Arch. Just so you know, it doesn't work unless you have two people, one for each end."

"One would think that, wouldn't one?"

"I thought you were waiting to meet someone."

"Oh? I'm trying to figure something out in my head."

Palms to her face for a second time, he was relieved she stopped eyeing him. She pressed her fingertips to her eyelids before dropping her hands, and suddenly gripping the chair arms. Was she in pain? As quickly as she tensed, she eased, opened her eyes, and talked. Exactly what he needed of her.

"I'm looking for information on an ancestor."

Bingo. The opportunity I've been waiting for.

CHAPTER 17

Letsea, 6:40 a.m., Friday morning

Snap-snap-snap!

Letsea stared at the man in the black suit and thin black tie. Where did he come from? For a moment, she thought Agent Reynolds materialized.

It pleased her when the phantom uncle took advantage of the Whispering Arch to speak to her. The voice *of* Paul E. Reynolds. He said he was murdered, although there were those who tried to say he committed suicide, since they were incapable of publicly solving the mystery of his being killed.

In a whisper, she told her uncle, the Bureau declared it an unsolved murder. Nothing there to question, still Uncle Paul insisted eventually they announced it a suicide. Why?

She actually conversed with him! How on earth was it possible? Time to reconsider her lack of belief in psychics and everything she thought as nonsense.

Looking at the handsome, classically dressed man who kept an intent eye on her, she needed to change the subject, and reached for her drink and stopped. After all, her eyes were closed for a while. Her appearance may be fragile, but stupid she was not. Although courteous, he's a stranger and might have slipped something into the drink. Respectfully, since he paid for her tea, she picked up the cup. Then, to divert attention, asked, "Are you working?" She gestured toward his laptop.

"Yes, next to always." He removed his hat, placed it upside

down on the table, and moved his hand to the computer. "Are you?"

Slowly, she moved her head. "Not today. Do you always come to the lobby to do your work?"

Even as the words came out, she recalled the story of the night of Agent Reynolds' disappearance. It said he spent hours working at a table in the lobby of the plush Hotel Adams in Phoenix. She thought of the unengaged voice at the Whispering Arch. Maybe Paul E. Reynolds, even in spirit form, liked plush hotels.

Interrupting her thoughts, he answered, "Not always. I'm glad I'm here now though."

She set the cup down.

The man next to her seemed charming. *Indubitably, that's how con men get away with their schemes. They fine-tune their craft in places filled with strangers.*

"Care for something to eat? The restaurant will open soon." he said.

A glance at his left hand revealed no wedding band. *Dare he flirt? Well, Lockhart, the third, no sense in going there, I assure you. You won't be interested in my situation.*

Her mind wandered to the spirit of Reynolds and the sound of his voice. She looked Lockhart in his eyes. "May I ask you a personal question?"

"I thought we were already to that point. Please, ask away."

"Do you believe in psychics?"

The look on his face, unreadable.

"I suppose there might be a few who actually receive messages which can't be otherwise explained. I depend on instinct. However, I don't see myself ever paying money for someone to predict my future. Does that answer your question?"

"You nailed it. I agree, though sometimes it's hard to find answers."

"Maybe I can help you." He pulled a card from an inside coat pocket, extending it between two fingers. "I'm a detective. Is there something I can help you find?"

The card, a simple classic, black ink on heavy gloss white card stock. His name, followed by the title Detective, was centered. A phone number printed in one top corner. She touched the raised ink. Who used a printing press in this day and age of instant copiers, except those of excellence?

"Do you need to locate your relative?"

Locate? She knew exactly where he was. After all, she drove into the city to talk with him under the Whispering Arch. Reynolds' spirit tapped her on the shoulder blade again. *He's right here. Poking me*! She shifted. "I'm looking to fill in some gaps in my own research."

She pushed a deep sigh from her lungs. Despite being a stranger, he was a detective who listened attentively. Possibly he could help.

"It keeps me up at night." Once again, a touch grazed her shoulder. She glimpsed to see no one there. Mentally, she yelled, *Stop with the touching!*

"Who are you wanting to find information on?" Lockhart asked.

"His name is Paul—"

In that moment, a coin, seemingly from nowhere, rolled across the floor directly toward her.

CHAPTER 18

6:58 a.m., Friday morning

Trey followed the line of Miss Brechenworth's intent stare. Then he heard the light, sharp metallic rolling sound on hard floor. He watched a coin travel several feet. It came to a stop when it bumped into the toe of one of her pretty camel-colored pumps.

He looked around. Not a single soul nearby. Nobody walked through their area. He glanced up to the balcony. Perhaps someone tossed it as a joke. No, he didn't see anyone.

She leaned forward, stared at it, but did not reach for the coin. So, he did. "That's odd," he said, as he picked it up. He strained to look upward at the 65-foot arched ceiling. Subsequently, he squinted to get a closer look at the dime. "Sweet. This has been around awhile. 1929-S. It looks to be in mint condition."

"1929?"

Her voice, so hesitant. A mere whisper.

"Yes. Minted in San Francisco. A silver Mercury dime and not a soul to be seen around us. Do you think it fell from the ceiling?"

"I don't see how," she said as she looked up, "with all they've done up there over the years, including the light show."

She became preoccupied with looking upward.

"Maybe it came from one of the Christmas wreaths or garlands."

"Here." Trey stretched his arm toward her and noted her ashen face. "Your dime, not mine."

Hands clasped in her lap, jaw tight, she said, "You keep it."

The sight of flight in her eyes. He knew it. Masked fear. He tried to distract her. "You said you're looking for a man named Paul—"

She lunged forward. And her head jerked as she forced herself to sit straight again. She looked toward the main doors. Yep, there it was. The panic mode.

"Sorry. I need to go." Purse, tight under her arm, she jumped up and sprinted past the massive Christmas tree, then outside.

"What the heck was she all about?" Trey stuck his hat on, grabbed his laptop and both their coats. Whatever the reason, he snatched up the ten-dollar cup of tea, and followed her.

Outside, Lockhart saw her pull a car door closed. As he proceeded toward her, the cab pulled away.

He flinched, sorry to see her leave, then he put on his coat. What exactly was her problem? He walked back to his streetside parked car and took a sip of her unsweet tea. Freshly brewed and delicious. Certainly, the most expensive tea he ever tasted. He sighed, and considered what he witnessed inside. Letsea Brechenworth looked confused, and afraid. At least she didn't look ticked off at him. Even if she didn't know it yet, she did need him.

No doubt Miss Brechenworth would return for her car and coat. He would wait.

"Just drive, please," Letsea told the cab driver.

It was getting weird in the Grand Hall. She did not do weird, not normally anyway.

After the last poke on her shoulder blade, no—a flat-out shove! She needed to leave. The spirit of Reynolds wanted her full attention. With arms folded, she questioned why the trembling. Cold? Or fear of a ghost? She sighed. Her reactions to all that poking must have made her look daft.

Despite the fact, indeed a stranger, *but a detective, he* wanted to help. By the time dear old Uncle Paul asserted himself several times, she was ready to tell all, except for it being unknown territory. Paul *E.* Reynolds didn't want her to leave the arch, since he actually communicated with her there. He didn't want her to tell the detective either. Why not? Solving mysteries was Lockhart's livelihood, and he was friendly and cheerful. Nonetheless, one thing for sure, she had to get out of there!

After the cab pulled away, she turned to look out the rear window. Trey Lockhart stood on the curb, wearing his hallmark of a fedora, holding a computer, her cup of tea, and a puzzled look on his face. Two coats were draped over an arm, his black one, and her favorite handwoven llama hair one which matched her shoes. Left with no choice except to go back for the special wrap, a nervous twitch of a foot reminded her of the rolling dime.

A 1929 dime! The year of Agent Reynolds' murder!

Letsea rubbed the raised print on Lockhart's card, and watched buildings flutter by as they moved toward the Mississippi River.

She sensed someone sitting next to her and shifted. "Are you kidding me?"

The cabbie looked at her in the rearview mirror.

"Sorry. I hope you don't mind if I talk to myself."

"Doesn't everybody? If you're speaking to me, simply tap the back of my seat."

She tapped the seat. "Drive around for ten minutes, then take me back to the hotel."

She felt a presence again.

"How do you do that?" she asked in a muted tone.

You tell me. She heard the barely audible rough whisper, like in her room.

She looked up. A classic cab, mid-century modern, older model with a curved roof line. Could it create the whispering effect? No. Besides, at the arch, his words were articulate.

A pressure against her upper arm. No one appeared to be there, yet someone sat beside her. *What have I done?* With a tap on the front seat, she said, "You can turn back now."

Agent Lockhart sat and watched for Miss Brechenworth's return. He drank the tea and studied the coat on the seat next to him. Soft and warm, he rubbed the material. Then he looked at the collar for a label. He raised an eyebrow as he read. *Designed And Handwoven Exclusively For Letsea Brechenworth. Animal Safety Protected.*

"Huh. It must have cost a pretty penny." Or a pretty dime, he thought, and pulled the mysterious coin from his coat pocket to examine it. Maybe she attracted money out of the woodwork. Although he didn't see anyone around, he had to believe it was someone's crazy idea of a joke. It didn't make sense, otherwise.

Cabs drove by. Some stopped, some didn't. He was sorry she felt the need to run. It wasn't like she had done anything wrong. After all, she only searched the world wide web and made inquiring phone calls. The woman didn't even have a speeding ticket on record. Researching a murdered man of a hundred years beforehand wasn't a crime. Neither did they suspect her of one. Powers that be merely didn't want anyone to shine a light on the past. Skeletons remained in the closet for a reason. She had no idea what she tampered with. *So what was she afraid of?*

Surely, hers, nothing more than a genealogical search. *Dad enjoys those.* He was into discovery of and in many cases not repeating history.

His father, the one family member who knew his real profession. Everyone believed him to be an agent for the Internal Revenue Service, his original plan for a career. Instead, he accepted an assignment to the FBI. To avoid worrying his mother, he let the misconception remain. To quote his father, *"It is what it is."*

While Trey waited, he observed the magnificence of Union Station. An iconic building holding its place in history. "For the love of Pete." It's a similar version of the Brechenworth mansion. Same kind of stone, from what he could tell at night, except for her green roof. He pulled up a photo on his laptop. He looked at the lady's house and back at the station. Had Lemuel Brechenworth anything to do with trains? He read. No. His money was earned in a fleet of ships. Similar architecture, okay, the man had nothing to do with Union Station.

A cab stopped. Brechenworth stepped out.

He patted the dime, placed his hat, grabbed her coat, and hurried to meet her.

CHAPTER 19

Later, same Friday morning on the sidewalk in front of Union Station front doors

"Can we talk?"

Letsea turned from the valet attendant to find Detective Lockhart held her coat out, waiting for her to slip her arms into the sleeves. "You waited."

"Put this on before you freeze."

"Maybe I like cold air."

He slowly moved his head from side to side. "No, you don't. You're trembling. Here, put your coat on."

"Why didn't you leave it at the front desk? Or here?" She tapped the service stand.

"I'm not a dunderhead, Miss *Cinderella*. You ran off. Instead of a shoe, you left your coat behind, giving me an opportunity to see you again. I'm not passing it up. Besides, I do believe I can be of assistance to you."

She tilted her head. "How?"

"With your ancestor."

"Oh."

He continued, "You didn't tell me your name, but you have my card. If you didn't return, I hoped for a call. I knew you would want this back. Nice wool coat, by the way."

She twitched the corners of her mouth. "Llama hair."

His eyebrows arched. "Okay." He paused. "I didn't see *that* coming." He shared a friendly broad smile.

"Few do." *Mr. Lockhart, The Third!* Traditionally carrying on his family's name, of course. He had an easy to get to know attitude, though he could appear quite serious to a certain degree. She trusted the man's sincerity, good manners, and kind facial expressions. His blue eyes were appealing, as well.

She released a pent-up breath and slipped into her favorite coat. His amiability encouraged her response. She might be a fool, still, she offered him a hand. "Thank you. I'm Letsea Brechenworth. Nice to meet you Lockhart, *the Third*."

He chuckled.

After shaking her hand, he placed the dime in her palm. "Circa 1929 silver Mercury. As close to a mint state as I've ever seen, out of its protective cover, that is. The value of that could be a premium. You should have it checked."

"Where do you suppose it came from?" She wanted to hear his theory.

"Perhaps a painter with a sense of humor and a spec of putty." He warmly closed her fingers over the coin and held her hand between both of his. "It's my pleasure to meet you, Letsea Brechenworth."

She looked into his eyes and teased, "Do you still have my tea?" Neither did he have his laptop. So, she knew he had not been holding court on the pavement.

He hesitated. "I'm afraid I drank it. I didn't know how long you might be gone. I'll be glad to get you a fresh one."

Letsea pulled her hand free of his warmth and patted his arm. "No. I don't want you to go broke on tea." Since the man wore a nice Burberry trench coat and leather wingtips, she didn't think the drink should bankrupt him.

"Whatever you want," he said.

Being near the Whispering Arch might stir up Uncle Paul's energy. She needed more time to adapt. "Not important," she murmured.

"I'd like to hear more of the person you're researching. I'm sure I can help you."

"A family—um—connection back in the 1920s. It gets a little complicated. I shouldn't even be concerned with it. You see, I'm reading a series of books with an FBI agent and I somehow got this old family link stuck in my head. Not important, I'm sure."

"Oh really? Tell me more."

Pressure on her back thrust her forward and caught her off-balance. A glance behind revealed nothing there. No. Definitely something. Not a person. An it. Paul's spirit. An it. *It* should go away!

"Are you all right?" Trey narrowed his eyes.

His gentle concern reassured her confidence. She needed help from someone and it wasn't like the fictional FBI character would jump off the pages of those books and volunteer.

"It may take a comic-strip hero to get me there."

"Ms. Brechenworth, is tomorrow morning a good time to get together to learn more of this ancestor of yours?"

Her SUV pulled into the valet space in front of Union Station. They quickly came to an agreeable appointment. She gave him Paul Reynolds' basic information and her number and address. Lock, as she preferred to think of him, walked her to the driver's door, tipped, and dismissed the attendant. He held her door, made sure she didn't get her llama coattail caught when he pushed it closed.

Lock rushed back to his car, and through a steady stream of morning traffic, he followed her. A few short blocks away, she pulled into an underground garage.

By the time he found a parking slot, he glimpsed her stepping into the elevator. The floor designator indicated she went to the fourth. He took the stairway and luckily found her with an apartment door open. A quick walk-by revealed her attention on a sheet of paper.

Lock went to the main-floor front-desk lobby to learn the name on the apartment.

Attorney Seth Eadgard Purser. That sounded too familiar.

He walked a block to a deli he liked. Upon his return, with a sandwich and bottle of water, he stopped in front of the building. A moving van crew unloaded their packing supplies and hauled them inside. As soon as he got back in the parking garage, he checked for her car. She had not returned. Why did he give up vacation time?

To avert any surprises, he chose to put a tracking device on the SUV. Lock ran over and stuck one inside the tire well of her rear passenger side and hurried back to his car.

He placed a call to Seth Purser's law office.

"He's not here. May I take a message?"

"No thank you." He had a good idea where the man could be found. Four floors up. He called his boss.

"Chief, it's a genealogical search but, she may mean business. She has connections with Attorney Seth Purser. Do you remember Seth Eadgard Purser Law Firm in Philadelphia? They're his father and grandfather."

"Bunk!" The chief snapped, "It goes without saying I know the 'aim low and squeeze tight' Pursers!"

"Either way, here or there, Miss Brechenworth knows a powerhouse."

"Give me some good news, will you?"

"I'm meeting with her in the morning, at her house, to discuss Agent Reynolds."

Lock downright laughed when his boss cussed and disconnected the call.

He made arrangements to tap Brechenworth's credit card accounts. *Egads, a third Seth Purser, of all people.* He recalled the interoffice frustrations of a couple lawsuits they pressed against government agencies. Weren't two of them enough? While at it, he asked for a forward on what they had on the third Purser.

Two hours later, he considered she may be there for the duration. He decided to check the lobby again. Several movers hauled modern black furniture and boxes into the truck. "Who's moving?" he asked.

A worker shrugged. "Some rich guy."

He'd have to be, to live in this prime real estate.

Without hesitation, he returned to his car.

Eventually she stepped out of the elevator with two small children in tow. Where did *they* come from? The apartment? Did she and Purser share custody? "What the heck?" Nothing mentioned children. At the car, she removed their little coats and buckled them into car seats. No reason to have those if she didn't have kids, unless they were Purser's children.

He pursed his lips. Why on earth hadn't he looked inside her car? On account of his rush to be clear of the vehicle in case she should return right away.

He watched her interacting with the children. She smiled, chatted with ease and kindness. *Good parent, then.* He needed to recheck and confirm who the children were.

CHAPTER 20

Friday, late afternoon downtown St. Louis

"Aunt Letsea, where're we going now?" asked Chip.

"We'll see." She poked instant dial on her dash. "Doyle, I have the children. If you're home, I'll bring them over."

"What's Gwen up to now?"

"I have no idea, considering it's December, I didn't ask."

"True. Will you keep them? I'm going to be late at the office."

"That's fine. You'll find them with me. I do have an appointment at 10:30 in the morning. If Gwen will pick them up beforehand, I'd appreciate it."

"I'll do it. Tell them I love them for me, will you?"

"You just did. We're on speaker."

"Excellent. Hi, kids! What have you been up to today?"

"Mommy took us to Aunt Letsea in an apartment downtown."

"We saw the big arch and we had spaghetti."

"Whose apartment?" he asked.

"Seth's. He moved back to Philly," Letsea said.

"I'm not surprised. Saying goodbye, were you?"

"Goodbyes were Tuesday over lunch. No, I let the movers in to get his things. Gwen tracked me down."

"Daddy, can we have ice cream?" Lauren asked.

"Sweetpea, it's entirely up to your aunt." Doyle guffawed. "She *is* your niece, isn't she? Listen, I'll let you go. I have clients here. Love you all. Bye."

After cold, creamy praline desserts with fresh-baked shortbread, the kids were asleep in the children's room next to Letsea's.

Dressed in cozy pink flannel pajamas and house slippers, Letsea sat up reading. The further she read, the more she thought of her unusual day. No sleep the night before might be the logics behind her emotions. She considered her encounter with Agent Reynolds' voice. Unless she had gone as nutty as a fruitcake, and of course, 'tis the season for those, she actually conversed with his spirit. A *ghost*? No, she preferred spirit. She perceived s*pirit* as rational. A swift roll of her eyes confirmed her belief, nothing sensible in the whole phenomenon.

The difficult thing to grasp, after leaving the building, she still sensed his presence. Even in the cab. Moreover, she meant she *felt* him. He touched her shoulder, poked her in the back.

How is it even possible?

Letsea considered the Whispering Arch. Realization struck. The Union Station Grand Hall exhibited a sky-high arch. Perhaps, that could be the secret. Even the older model cab ceiling was coved.

Had she heard him in her room, or be it a flight of fancy?

Except for the long gentle curve of the bay window, all other architectural lines were straight. In consideration of a whispering arch effect, she wondered if there may be one in the manor. Grabbing her robe and cell phone she went for a walk.

Rex Kitty weaved between her legs as she, room by room, wandered the halls. A survey through the main floor revealed no arches, not even in the ballroom, which was the most extravagant room in the house. Columns accented the walls and met the lofty painting. No arches. It featured coffered accents, three-dimensional grooved wood panels, like the formal parlors on the main floor.

A walk through the basement kitchens, storage rooms, the swimming pool, and laundry room revealed no arches. She headed into Grandfather's basement billiard room and bar. Lots of lighted stained glass, yet not an arch in sight. From the bar, she took the hidden staircase down into the wine cellar and keepsake vault.

Arched doorways with brickwork divided the wine rack cellar.

She supposed her great-grandparents were in the mix of those individuals who avoided the prohibition laws. She whispered, "Paul?" No response.

The round tower came to mind, not particularly arched. The ceilings were finished flat, although Rex Kitty did not want to go inside the other night. Hmm.

On the way back to the main stairs she checked the entrance to the underground tunnel system which led to outbuildings and the old bunkers. Great-Great Grandfather worried for a war here on homeland. He'd seen way too much disgruntlement in other countries and had tunnels and underground rooms built for self-preservation. There were definitely arches in the tunnels. She whispered, "Paul? Can you hear me?"

Nothing. Maybe being underground affected the dynamics. The housekeeper's apartment in the basement being nearby, she didn't want her long-term, dependable employee to overhear her talking to a spirit. She hurried to the second floor and checked on the children before she continued her search.

Once again, Rex Kitty waited in the hall not going into the tower. She whispered, "Paul?" To no avail.

Taking the east end servants' stairs to the third floor, she studied more diverse sloped ceiling lines. They coordinated with the angle of the roof. She avoided Bob's room. As a trainee security guard, after Gwen married, she asked him to move into the main house. Before that, he roomed in one of the carriage house studio apartments, above the garage.

The third-floor tower room, identical to the second floor. Plus, a narrow decorative hand-built spiral staircase which led to the highest point on the estate. As a child, she was never permitted to climb the narrow steps to the watch room. After she took possession of the house, she ascended enough to peek into the top floor, but remembered little of it. For safety's sake, she patted her phone in the pocket of her robe, gripped the dark-oak handrails, and made her way up.

The topmost floor, like a lighthouse tower, a circumference of tall windows with curved seats. An addition of a small child's desk against the interior wall. The staircase continued upward a few more feet to an interior platform for a clearer view of the property. Straight above, a dome.

The dome, extraordinarily high and decorated with four carved beams, squared off the vaulted area with lovely wooden arches. The beautiful craftsmanship produced goose bumps. She had her own arch! Did it have the whispering effect? "Paul. Can you hear me?"

The pertinent question is, are you ready to listen?

CHAPTER 21

Saturday morning after midnight in the top floor of the tower

The curved window seat cushions were old and brittle. No curtains on the fourth level. Letsea's hands trembled as she fingered the sundried padding. She sought him out, yet still uncomfortable conversing with a dead man. But, if she could offer solace or insight, she was willing to try.

She whispered, "Paul?"

Here.

She rubbed a palm over an eye. "How do you see me helping you?"

I don't know beans about what you can do. I simply want it known I did not have any reason to kill myself. I could never have done that. His voice was distinct.

"I told you it's been written on the epitaph as an unsolved murder."

Death by mysterious circumstances, now. They ruined my good name in an attempt to cover up.

"Paul, I'm sure it wasn't in the official report. Not that I'm privileged to see it, and goodness knows I tried. Suicide, only a suggestion of possibility, decades afterward."

They've always known it to be murder.

"I can't change old perspectives."

There has to be a way to clarify murder.

"Why are you putting this on me?"

I'm not. This is all you.

Letsea stood, hands on her hips. Her voice lifted an octave. "That does it! I give up! This isn't about me! You were murdered." She covered her ears and reminded herself of the irony of her parents' violent demise. She let the tight muscles in her arms go limp. "Granted, in order to help, I need answers to questions."

Line them up, lady. Let's go.

"Hold on, I need paper and a pen." She turned and noticed an old journal and pencil on a child's writing desk. "Still here?"

Where else would I go?

"I'm sure I don't know. Okay. I'm asking based on what I read. First, did you really intend to go for a swim the night you went missing?"

The voice laughed, a hollow, severed sort of sound.

That's your first question?

"According to witnesses, you left the hotel to go swimming. Is it true?"

I said it, yes. There was an invitation, but one must use discretion. The temperature was blazing and it made for easy conversation.

"What do you mean?"

I never intended to go for a swim. Nothing like being ambushed into a so-called late night accidental drowning at a friend's house. The heat gave reason to say "I was thinking of swimming," friendly small talk. With incognito work, you have to be suspicious of everyone. Albeit, friendliness counts. Everyone needs friends, anywhere you can find them. You never know who will help you, give up your identity, or straightaway kill you.

Letsea swallowed. She guessed her parents learned that lesson the hard way. "A news article said the authorities thought someone blocked you in the road and took you for a ride. Did it happen like that?"

I did surveillance outside a dance hall. They found me parked on the side of the street.

"Who?"

The woman who came to the passenger window to flirt with me while I did surveillance.

"What woman?"

Flapper girl. A professional gal, I assumed. Dressed in fringe and tassels.

"What profession?"

Naïve thing, aren't you?

"Um." She paused. "Oh. What next?"

She seemed to take a cotton to me. I figured she might be a good source for information.

"Was she?"

For someone. To me, my detriment.

Her eyes widened. "A woman murdered you?"

She was bait. We talked. She flaunted, all giggles and smiles. My back against the door, to the open window. My blunder. With my attention elsewhere, I was suddenly bludgeoned on the back of the head.

"I thought you were shot?"

That came later.

"What were you hit with?"

Really? My eyes were in front of my head, facing red lips and an open cleavage. How should I know what he used? It hurt.

"Why did you tell others you were going swimming if you knew you'd be doing surveillance?"

Honestly? Holding stock on the swimming line, are you?

"The papers made a big deal of it."

Being the last thing witnesses heard me mention. Look, investigation is tricky and dangerous. It's not like I'd announce to the mafioso, Hey! Don't mind me, I'm just a spy.

She stopped writing and pressed the heel of her hand to her forehead. "Dramatic, aren't you?"

Dramatic as my life.

"Why did you go to a dance hall?"

I followed a tip. Supposedly, one of my suspects would be there, at a particular club that night around ten o'clock. I intended to see if I had a reliable source.

"Was it?"

I fell into the hands of someone's ploy.

"Did your friends know you were FBI?"

B.O.I. The Bureau of Investigation. The fewer who knew, the safer.

"What did people think you did for a living?"

I amused myself.

She heard a smirky tone to his voice. What an attitude, she

thought. "You mean, they thought you had money and time to do as you pleased."

A man has to blend in. They were the social class we needed to infiltrate. Several of my acquaintances were more than well-heeled. They were filthy-rich. It's how they flourished we needed to foil.

"You mean illegal drugs and alcohol?"

That's the way of it.

"Who in Phoenix knew you were BOI?"

Plenty did. Police, attorneys, judges, some in federal offices knew. Certain stoolies were aware.

"Stoolies?"

Informants, rats, tattlers, all were snitches for some sort of payoff. Actually, I preferred to get tips from folks without ever revealing I was a fed. The less said the better. Have you ever heard the phrase "tell no one"?

Her grandfather used to say "share with no one," along with "question everything." Plus, the whole legal field is based on privileged information. "Sure I have." She wrote fast to keep up. "Why might anyone want you dead?"

Are you kidding? To them, BOI stood for diversion of their wealth. Other investigators knew me. In fact, I wasn't scheduled to be there. They pulled me from my own assignment in Albuquerque. Sent me to Phoenix by reason of a family member of the agent assigned there became ill and he needed to leave.

"Albuquerque? I thought you were in El Paso. Why send you so far?"

What can I say? I'd worked Phoenix before. I knew people.

Apparently, they knew him too, she thought. A pressure throbbed at her temples. "If you drove to Phoenix, why did you rent a car?"

The BOI flew me in.

Hm. She tilted her head in thought. Flew? An image of an early biplane flashed in her thoughts. "Paul?"

What?

"I'm confused on every aspect of you."

It's a lot to take on.

"Did they have commercial flights in the 1920s?"

Nothing.

"Paul? Paul?"

Gone! Why did he leave? She set the worn pencil down, closed the old journal, grasped it with one hand, and rubbed her face with the other. She had even more questions than she started with. Her cell phone showed 3:53 a.m. She needed to try for sleep.

The light of sunrise awoke her. Letsea was still plagued by questions. What did Paul mean when he said he had been yanked out of his New Mexico work and sent to Arizona to replace someone? Who? Why? Did his death sound pre-arranged? What internal motive did someone have for needing him to disappear? Did he have information on another fed? Perhaps the agent he replaced thought *his own* life in danger. Is that why he didn't go in to work? Subsequently whoever took his place thus, fated to be doomed.

Early in the morning, she dressed in her running clothes, then grabbed her cell phone from the charger before she went out to clear her head.

First, across the hall to her office, to lock the journal in the safe. A peek-in on Chip and Lauren, then she hurried outside. She wanted to be alert and ready when Detective Lockhart arrived for their appointment.

CHAPTER 22

10:25 a.m. Saturday morning

Special Agent Lockhart hoped the interview closed the door on the roaring twenties file. Eager to get back to his vacation, even if it meant heavy lifting. He needed to get his parents settled in his house before his sisters and their families arrived home for Christmas.

After given permission to enter through the gates, he slowed his BMW to a stop on the decorative circle drive in front of the mansion's main steps.

He liked Miss Brechenworth. A sight to behold, except for appearing fatigued and tense. What did she fear? It was obvious in her expressions, and he doubted it started when he paid for her drink. Noticeable jitteriness, always looking over her shoulder. Hopefully his answers might help her decompress. With all she experienced with her parents' demise, solid validity to her apprehensions. Her anxiety was pretty steep, until he saw her with the kids. She became relaxed and chatted with ease.

He admired the house. The basement with large windows protruded a good ten feet above ground. A winterized bordered flower garden surrounded the house. At the base of the staircase, a mud chucker, to clean his shoes. He didn't need to, yet hey, as long as it wouldn't damage the shine. Afterward, he strutted up the long, straight steps to the front porch.

The scent of the Christmas wreath reminded him of his mom's apple cider. Fresh-cut evergreen lavishly trimmed with dried slices of oranges, apples, and cinnamon sticks. He noticed a boot scraper and a self-absorbing runner before the doormat. He wiped the soles of his shoes again, even though he knew they were spotless.

The same man who pulled her car around early yesterday morning opened the door, and watched him tending to his shoes. Gnawing curiosity kept him silent and his pulse sped. Seth Purser? Maybe. There were similarities, he was tall, thin, blond, and 30's.

As he stepped inside, his eyes were drawn to the foyer flooring, elegant gold veins of Calacatta marble. A bench and two wicker baskets were placed near the door, one empty and one with house slippers and disposable shoe covers. He grabbed a pair of coverings and slipped them on. As directed to a parlor to his immediate right, he heard the undertone of Christmas music, it gave the house a holiday atmosphere.

The man did not introduce himself as he took his coat and hat, hung them on old brass wall hooks, while he looked around the narrow formality. The furniture complemented the room. Ladylike and antique. Fragrant, fresh evergreen swags decorated the windows.

"Detective Lockhart, are you carrying a weapon?"

"No."

"I'm sure you won't mind if I verify it, sir."

He arched an eyebrow. "You want to *frisk* me?"

"If you would permit it, sir. To insure Miss Brechenworth's safety."

Agent Lockhart stretched his arms outward and remained quiet during the pat down. Relieved gut instinct told him to leave the gun at home. That, and being undercover, he made the choice. She wandered all over the city Friday. Alone. Where was her bodyguard then?

"We'll also need to make a copy of your license, sir."

"My license?"

"Your private detective license and your driver's license, if you don't mind."

Actually, he did. Considering her past and his true reason for being there, he decided to let it slide. No fight, no plight. Her house, her rules. He reached for his wallet and produced his ID and the P.I. card in his real name.

Left alone, Lockhart admired the furnishings. Hardwood floors polished to the hilt. A couple steps on a vintage wool rug reminded him of how his parents appreciated American history. *Who else has stood here?*

With his slightest prompt, he'd encouraged his parents to tell him of the Brechenworth estate. Armed with tidbits, he looked around. He smoothed fingertips over the rich grains of the English walnut table, with matching chairs, near the window. A fragrant arrangement with red and white carnations, it reminded him of the boutonniere he wore at his sister Faith's wedding.

He glanced back at the sofa and chairs. A twelve-foot tapestry decorated the north wall, and a couple paintings highlighted the others. However, the traditional fireplace of green tiles, with modern electric heat, particularly interested him. The parlor was not what he expected. A tall, lengthy room, although rather narrow.

His mother explained antechambers. Used when the owner preferred to go to the visitors rather than invite them into the inner sanctum of their home. After his chilly greeting, this, most likely was the sole room in the mansion he'd get to see. The Victorian farmhouse he grew up in did not have a waiting room.

"Mr. Lockhart." A woman, mid-forties, wearing a dark business suit and round tortoise-shell glasses, stood in the doorway. "Here are your ID cards." He slipped them in a pocket. "Miss Brechenworth will see you now. Please follow me."

They entered a well-appointed, extensive hallway with a sumptuous cushioned ruby-red carpet runner. He shook off the childish temptation to jump up and down.

A telephone rang and she stopped at a doorway. "Pardon me, I'll only be a moment." She went into a long narrow office to his left.

He used the opportunity for observation. A utilitarian servants' stairs, plainly made of chestnut, to his left. Ahead, to his right, at the front corner of the house, the main floor tower room door stood ajar. The blond man, with his back to him, faced a single security monitor. There were good views of the front and east yards. He stepped back when he heard his escort wrap up her call, ending his distraction.

"Sorry. This way, sir."

They walked east, where two tall, extra-wide, wooden exit doors with stained glass windows led to the car porch. They turned left, the last room at the back of the house.

"Ma'am, Detective Lockhart is here."

While standing in the hall, he glanced to the totally opposite end of the wide, long hall. Another pair of exquisite carved double doors on the other end.

It interested him how long and tall the rooms were. The house had depth. Her sitting room, well-lit by eastern and northern windows. He liked the evenness of the natural light. The windowpanes were no doubt original to the house. Visible waves in the glass revealed the age.

It appeared to be a breakfast room with table, chairs, and an antique tea cart. However, an old-style chaise lounge and a couple of armchairs, accompanied by vintage floor lamps, gave reason to believe the room simply intended for relaxation. A book lay on a side table. A comfortable place to read. He recalled she mentioned reading a novel about an FBI agent. His eyebrows involuntarily twitched. He wondered if she would be interested in getting to know a real-live agent.

Hey, Trey, don't go stupid on yourself. Business before pleasure.

Miss Brechenworth approached with a pleasant expression and held out her hand. Although she looked a bit tired, she was still stunning in her tan slacks and a long-sleeved green silk blouse. He shook her hand, but possibly by virtue of the antique setting, he fought an outdated urge to kiss the back of it. He cleared his throat.

"Please, Mr. Lockhart. Do have a seat. I thought perhaps the table at the window might work for your laptop." She sat across from him.

"This is fine, Miss Brechenworth. I've already started research on the name you provided. I printed these for you." He slid a small stack of copied newspaper articles toward her. "From the *Arizona Republican* and the *Phoenix Gazette* in August 1929. They describe the event as it unfolded."

"Thank you." She left the papers untouched. "Were you able to find any official FBI or police records in Phoenix?"

"Is that what you're looking for?"

He saw her body stiffen, stand, her stance firm and tall, hands-on hips then drew a deep breath. The manner of a trial attorney, he thought. Formidable enough to inspire both respect and fear, whichever the case may be.

"I want to know who killed Paul E. Reynolds. Why did the FBI choose to sweep known facts of his murder under the rug? Did the FBI know who killed him, and decided not to reveal the name? If so, why? And why did they try to ruin the man's good name by leaking a false story?"

Lock tightened his jaw, then he dropped his chin to chest. *Son of a monkey!* The little dazzler could well mean trouble. He absently tapped a fist on the table, released a deep sigh, and conceded. "This investigation may take a while, Miss Brechenworth. I promised my family I'd take vacation this month. Can we pick this up after the new year?"

She sighed. "I suppose. I'll look over these papers. Give Marcia your bill, I'll cover it."

He did not want to be dismissed. "There's no charge for those. Between Christmas events, I'll make some calls. I'll tell you what I've learned over the years. To expect the FBI to volunteer information is as likely as planting a two-by-four in the ground and expecting it to take root, branch out, and sprout leaves." Her eyes were on him without a hint of mirth. He shrugged.

"I got that impression myself. Mr. Lockhart, *'The merit of all things, lies in their difficulties,'* Alexandre Dumas, *The Three Musketeers*." Her chin jutted upward.

"Touché," he said.

Her chin lowered as she stared out the window. "I can't explain why, but I can't get Reynolds out of my head, and I desperately need sleep. Christmas is a busy season for me, too."

She turned, went to a 1940s overstuffed rose velvet chair, and slumped into it. She looked defeated. He noticed she wore house slippers. Tan to match, nonetheless, looked fluffy and warm. It made her appear ordinary and easy to approach.

"In your head, huh? I've been there, Miss Brechenworth."

She looked across to him. "Call me Letsea, please."

"Thank you. Frankly, some cases won't leave me alone. They follow me wherever I go." *And that's the blessed truth.* Her expression softened, as if relieved he appreciated her quandary.

He thought of a way to relate to her he understood what she meant. A practical application of a quote he'd carried in his memory for decades. If it helped, he'd owe thanks to his high school English-lit teacher, Mrs. Ormsby.

He did something he had never done while on the job. All pretense aside, he moved toward her, knelt eye-level. "Miss Brechenworth, *'Nothing makes time pass or shortens the way like a thought that absorbs in itself all the faculties of the one who is thinking. External existence is then like a sleep of which this thought is the dream. Under its influence, time has no more measure, space has no more distance.'* Alexandre Dumas, *The Three Musketeers*."

She leaned her head back to the cushioned headrest and burst into laughter. Her happiness made him chuckle. He moved back to the table. The secretary came to the door and looked in, then quietly left.

"Touché." She paused. "Care to stay for lunch Mr.— um, may I call you Lock?"

"You don't like the name Trey?"

"I won't say that. I have known several in my life. You are the first Lock. I like the sound of it. You did say some friends call you Lock, didn't you?"

He liked that, besides he wanted to put her at ease. "Fair is fair. Lock it is. I'd like very much to join you for lunch. Thank you."

She touched an intercom button on the phone beside her chair. "Marcia, will you please let Pauline know I have a guest joining me for lunch."

"Yes, ma'am."

He looked outside the window to consider what he heard. Pauline knew him, although not his real profession. How could he avoid seeing Pauline if she served the meal? A carriage house in the backyard caught his attention. He observed six garage doors in a long, wide, tall building appeared completely surrounded by decorative stone pavement. He recalled the absurd number of cars on her personal taxes. They couldn't all fit in the garage. Could it be an error? Unless she *did* match the color of her vehicle to her outfits.

"I'm glad you'll join me, Lock."

And there it was. To his benefit, they were officially on first-name basis. "Letsea, you have a lovely name. I've never heard it before. What's the origin?"

She moved back to the table and folded her arms. "Mother lived life rather avant-garde. The story goes, when she got pregnant, everyone kept asking what names she and Dad were considering if she gave birth to a girl." Letsea tapped her index finger to her cheek. "Mom said she used to tease them with, 'Let's see, what should we name a girl'? By the time I arrived, she'd said 'Let's see' so many times, she and Dad fell in love with it."

Lock chuckled. "What if you had been a boy?" He watched her face lose all humor.

"Truth be told, if they'd known they weren't ever going to have a son, they'd have named me Lemuel Brechenworth, the fifth. It's a family tradition I'm sure *you're* familiar with, Godrick Lockhart the third."

Such relief to see a mischievous glint in her eyes, until she bit her bottom lip. *Oh, cuss.* "So, Let's see, Letsea it is."

CHAPTER 23

Saturday morning continued

Letsea relaxed, believing her visitor to be helpful.

"What is your family connection with Agent Reynolds?" Letsea watched Lock take notes on an iPad as they sat at the table in the morning parlor.

"Reynolds' widow, married one of Mom's great uncles."

Lock scowled. "I see."

The detective was quite attentive as she continued to answer pertinent questions, most of which she recently learned the answers. The serious tone of his voice captivated her interest. Her mind wandered, undoubtedly where it shouldn't. He'd quoted Dumas. Ha. She felt a tingle up her back, all good until her ears grew hot. He was a handsome man in a rigorously thorough sort of way. She sighed and hoped her face wasn't red. The dark-blue suit, tie, and silver cuff links demonstrated Lock to be a smart dresser. His suit also complimented his blue eyes and dark hair. *Did he wear his hat today? Oh, snap. What was his last question?*

Chip and Lauren ran in and she enveloped them in a big hug. "What have my little darlings been up to?"

"Miss Pauline let us help make dessert in the pastry kitchen." They bounced with excitement.

"I see you got samples, hm?"

Their heads bobbed up and down.

Her niece looked at Lock, with her eyes wide. "Hello."

"Children, this is Mr. Lockhart."

"Lock, these are my—"

"Pardon me, ma'am," Bob interrupted from the doorway. "They got away from me. Your sister called, she should be here any minute and requested to speak with you privately."

The intercom buzzed and Marcia spoke, "Miss Brechenworth, your aunt is on line one."

She glanced at Chip and Lauren, while they amused Lock. Gwendolene made her grand entrance, wearing a wintery red leather short skirt, half boots, and a shapely cut leather jacket ensemble. Even her lipstick was the same dark-red color. Sis's pose exemplified that of a runway model. Large round sunglasses held back her long strawberry-blonde hair.

Gwen ignored the fact they weren't alone. A glimpse at Lock revealed his full attention on the children. He didn't even give her beautiful sister a single glance. If she were to keep score, he'd gain double points for that matter alone. "Hello, Gwendolene, I've been expecting you..." She glanced at the clock. "For a couple of hours, dear."

"Letsea, I need to talk with you. Can we go upstairs to your office?"

Bob stepped aside when Liza came to the door. "Pardon me, ma'am. I'm supposed to tell you lunch is served in the front parlor." She looked around. "Though, I only set the table for two."

"That's correct."

"Gwendolene, can you come back in the morning?"

"Not really." She half whispered, "You'll need your checkbook. And I'm hoping you'll keep the kids this afternoon while I take care of Christmas matters."

The children stopped chatting and stared at their mother, as though the key word to silence, Christmas. To top the day off, as if communicating with the spirit of a dead man wasn't enough of a distraction, her life brashly turned chaotic.

Letsea released a deep sigh. "Marcia, tell Aunt Mae I'll call her back as soon as I can."

"Yes, ma'am."

"Chip, take your sister, go with Mr. Bob. Find Miss Pauline and see if she has treats you can take home with you. And, dears, please put your shoes on now." She nodded to Bob.

"Gwendolene, upstairs."

"Liza, show Mr. Lockhart where he can wash up, then to the main parlor."

"Yes, ma'am. I'll be glad to take the children downstairs, too," Liza said.

"Very good. Thank you."

She turned to him. "Lock, I'll join you as soon as possible."

A glint of humor in his eyes, Lock said, "Smooth moves." He grinned on his way out.

And that's what I like about the man. The moments he's not so stern and serious. Another point earned. When did she start a point system on him? Oh yes, when he quoted Dumas.

External existence is then like a sleep of which this thought is the dream.

"Okay, Sis." They hugged. "What's up?"

"I need a check. It's important, Letsea."

"You haven't overdrawn your checking account again, have you?"

"No. Besides, Doyle took charge of the checkbook. Which is plenty fine with me."

"Is this something we should discuss with Doyle?"

"No. It's a surprise for him."

"How much are we talking?"

"Ninety-eight thousand *should* cover it."

Letsea lifted her eyebrows as her stomach muscles clenched. *What did she do?* "Gwen, I'm sure that amount alone is likely to surprise Doyle. Tell me."

"I can't. I want to surprise you too." Gwen's enthusiasm was childlike.

"Honey, it's safe to say, you already have. It's quite a chunk of change. When do you need it?"

"Now, please." Gwen held out a palm.

"Let's talk tomorrow. Right now, I have company."

Gwen pushed her bottom lip forward. "Will you cut me a check today, after your friend leaves?"

"How are you going to cash it, if you don't have access to a checking account?"

"Oh! I didn't even think of that."

"You call me after four o'clock and we'll figure it out, okay, honey? And, Sis, try to keep any future surprises low-key, will you?"

Gwen giggled, wrapped her arms around Letsea. "You're going to love this surprise."

CHAPTER 24

Saturday, lunch in the front parlor

He looked up from his seat at her shiny white baby grand piano, stood, and approached as Letsea joined him in the large open parlor.

"Sorry."

He didn't think she looked any worse for the wear after an unexpected conversation with the overconfident sister. "I hope everything's all right."

With a hint of a smile, she said, "Thanks, and I hope you didn't get bored."

"Not at all. You have a magnificent home. For years, my mother's been hoping you'd open it for a home tour."

"I'm not nearly so brave." She paused and tilted her head. "Where are you from?"

"Born and raised right here." He wished he'd been honest from the beginning. *A little late.*

"Then why were you at Union Station at five in the morning?"

"Wrapping up a case." He hoped she bought it. "Why were you there?"

"I've decided to think of it as sleepwalking. I guessed you were from out of area. I take it your mother lives around here."

"Both parents. At the other edge of town. Where the new roadwork is to begin."

She winced. "It'll be a mess while they work. I heard some people are being uprooted."

He nodded. "They've officially received their walking papers."

"Sorry. I hope they were fairly compensated. Some aren't."

Lock made a clicking sound when he opened his mouth and sighed. "Let's say I now know the meaning of highway robbery."

"Otherwise known as Eminent Domain. Did they have one of the older homes?"

"Victorian, more of a farmhouse really. Not anything like yours."

"This architecture is Romanesque Revival." She shrugged. "Doesn't matter to me one way or another. As long as I can keep the roofs from leaking. How long have your parents lived there?" She moved toward her chair. He reached it first and with both hands, he pulled it back, then tucked her closer to the table.

"All my life. It has fanciful scrolls, brackets, and embellishments. My kid sisters believed themselves to be fairy princesses." He joined her at the table where salads were pre-served.

"I felt the same. I grew up in the Queen Anne next door. My grandparents lived here, although I spent a great deal of time in this house."

"Why separate houses? Surely several families could live in a castle like this."

"The Queen Anne is the original house. My ancestors lived there during construction of this place. And there's nothing so grand about this, it's just a big house. One tower does not a castle make. My parents living next door was regarding independence."

"This is a lot like Union Station."

She placed one hand flat on the table and leaned forward. "I have no knowledge of any connection. It's the architecture of the times. The first Brechenworths spent a lot of time overseas, this is where they chose to settle."

The first Brechenworth? The entrée was served by the maid. "Thank you, Liza." Relieved he need not explain his presence to Pauline Collins.

A rush of voices flowed in from the hall.

"Bye-bye!"

"Bye."

"I'll call later," her sister said on their way out.

Letsea waved to them when they passed by in the hallway, then looked out the window. "There goes my pride, joy, and hope for the future."

Close up, he'd recognized Chip, Lauren, and their mother. He knew them from the community center and musical rehearsals. Puzzle pieces were fitting together. The Davis children were the two newest prodigies in the area. Through the large curved bay window, Lock easily observed the kids being packed into a red Audi A5 parked next to his car. It matched Mrs. Davis' disposition, bold and breathtaking, although the young woman was possibly more assertive than her ride. He chose not to tell Letsea he knew them, and considered if Gwendolene Davis mentioned to her sister that she'd seen him around. Perhaps luck remained in his favor.

"This meal is delicious." Naturally it was. He recognized one of his mother's specialties. She and Pauline regularly swapped recipes. He needed to change the topic away from family. "The fish, it's Perch, isn't it?"

"Yellow Perch. Pauline is an excellent chef. She sautés it in sweet butter and olive oil with a sliver of vanilla bean and a hint of lavender. It's one of my favorites."

His, too.

"Did Liza show you around at all?" she asked.

"Yes." The pretty young woman with black hair had a becoming accent he couldn't quite place. "She's very efficient and showed me your library. Quite impressive, I must say." He looked around the dual open parlors with pocket doors tucked away. He acknowledged the multiple crystal chandeliers at the remarkable high point. "I believe it possible to hold a conference in this size parlor." She smiled often. A pleasant reward she kept hidden yesterday. "I believe this is the largest hook rug I've ever seen." Her eyes brightened.

"It's original to the house. Most of the furnishings are. Hook rugs were my great-grandmother's hobby."

"She made this?"

"No. Shopped." She put fingers flat on the table and laughed. "Although, she made the one in my room. I love it, mistakes and all."

He'd like to see *that* for himself. "Nice." He cleared his throat. "Before we're finished, I still have questions regarding Reynolds."

CHAPTER 25

Saturday afternoon

"Lock, please tell me the areas of your work."

She had a way of changing the subject. He'd let it slide. The more she talked, the more he'd know her thought pattern and her personal characteristics.

After lunch, they went back to the cozy morning parlor. Positioned across from one another at the small table in front of the window, her gaze probed. He sensed her need to interrogate. "What do you want to know?"

"What do you normally investigate? I assume it isn't usually dead people. Cheating spouses? Scam artists? Insurance fraud? What exactly?"

"Financial matters mainly." He swallowed. Paper trails often led to more murders than she'd care to think of.

"Were you ever a police detective?"

"Let's say sometimes even our finest need extra help."

"I can't imagine why some people do the things they do." She rested her forehead to her palm.

"I know about your parents. I'm sorry you and your family went through that."

"It's in the past." Her voice, barely audible.

"So is Paul Reynolds."

She massaged her temples. "If only it were true. He prefers—ed Paul E. Reynolds."

What the heck did *that* mean? "For my own part, I wish the

whole world felt loved. Heal this craziness of hate and defiance. I'm all for finding a new career. Or retire."

"Paul E. Reynolds worked drug control," she said.

"Yes, I know."

"I read he lived in El Paso, worked in Albuquerque, killed in Phoenix. What was with so many locations?"

"With barely twenty years behind them, the FBI didn't have many field offices. Even today, their agents can be sent all over."

"BOI, at the time," she inserted. "He called it the Bureau of Investigations."

"Who did?"

"What?" She dropped her hand to her lap and looked startled.

"You said, '*he called it.*'"

"Did I? I've read so much lately I'm not sure who said what anymore."

"I understand."

"Lock, do you think most FBI agents tell their friends who they work for?"

"Sure, if they work in a forensics lab. If they work undercover, less likely. Why?"

"According to the newspaper articles, Paul E. Reynolds intended to go swimming at a friend's house. Would his friend know he was an agent?"

"I don't think they would go around announcing it. But I don't believe they worked undercover as such. Possibly a setup. Maybe shot on private property and hauled off in someone else's car to be dumped. The authorities didn't find blood in his. You know security cameras and DNA have changed everything in solving crimes these days."

"Yeah, right. Modern science didn't help much in the Congo a decade ago."

She may as well have struck him between the eyes. He didn't see it coming. "My apology."

"It's not like you could have done anything to help. Be that as it may, don't you think Reynolds might have been leery of accepting such an invitation?" she asked.

"If guilty, why would the man reveal Reynolds planned to come to his house at all? Unless, he did go and was murdered there. It may have been the man's way to divert authorities from his property, by stating he never showed."

Letsea sat back and stared. "I like the way you think. Maybe they did, but I never noticed any mention of authorities going over his property with a fine-tooth comb. Besides, it doesn't explain why someone hit him over the back of the head while doing surveillance, now does it? And who knew he'd even be there? Who else did his informant tell?"

"Do you mean the night of the murder? What surveillance?"

"At the dance hall."

How did she know?

Riveted by how *her* mind worked, he sat in silence as she squeezed her hands together. Where did she get information regarding Reynolds being hit? From behind, no less! The contusion on the back of his head was key evidence, never released to the public. What exactly had she been reading? Did she somehow manage to get into some of Reynolds' old, locked storage cabinets? He would have been notified immediately if she filed a motion or lawsuit for admittance to those files. *Son of a monkey!*

Who is her insider?

Chapter 26

First Sunday of December, daybreak, fourth floor of the tower

With the same old journal and new pen, Letsea sat on the circular, sun-worn cushion in the upper round room. "Paul, who shot you?"

I don't know who did the job or who paid him.

"What did he look like?"

With a crescent moon, I couldn't see enough of his face to know. If he'd focused his thoughts on me, I may have gotten into his head. He did a job. Over and done. No thought of me afterward. Except maybe to be paid.

"Oh! Earlier when you said 'my head, not yours', you were serious! People have to let you into their mind by thinking about you."

Never more so. His voice relaxed and so did she.

"Where did he kill you? In town or out at the canal? According to the newspapers, they suspected you were shot on a bridge and fell off of it."

He knocked me out in town. I awoke with the flapper in the seat holding a gun to my ribs, my wrists were bound. The stranger drove my rental toward Glendale. He forced me to walk to the bank of a canal. I figured either him or me. I mean, what did I have to lose? Two men with a mission. He held the iron and I wanted to live so I kicked and struggled. The rope on my wrists came loose. I hit him a couple times. The man shot me point-blank. He kicked me into the canal with his boot before I died.

Letsea's eyes welled with tears. "I'm so sorry it happened. You were just doing your job trying to stop dangerous drugs from ruining lives, right?"

Yeah, look where that got me.

She swiped at her face while still taking notes. "Did he shoot you with your own gun?"

Hah. What gun? I didn't carry a piece.

"Why not? You were a federal agent! Where did you keep it?"

BOI didn't issue guns to investigators except by special permits. I owned guns. I wish I'd chosen to carry one of them. My object that night was to simply observe.

Sadness turned to instant anger. "How are you supposed to protect yourself without a weapon?"

Therein lies the rub. Life is not only a puzzlement, but it is the dream as well.

Emotions hit hard, having wished her parents had carried a weapon. She pulled her feet up and leaned back against a window frame. Across the room, toward the front yard, she noticed a hint of daybreak reflected in the curved window. An odd reflection caught her attention. It looked like a tall man stretched out on the cushion on the opposite side of the room. She gasped, tried to swallow the sound, and held her breath. Could that be Paul's ghost? Very slowly she turned her head to see him. Nothing there. She released her pent-up breath and looked back at the curved glass.

An image appeared to be lounging with folded arms tucked behind his head. One foot flat down and knee raised, his other ankle balanced over his raised knee. The image wore a three-piece suit of pale linen. The shoes were white with brown wingtips.

Any thought of feeling relaxed flew straight out the window with its apparitional disclosure. Letsea glanced over her shoulder. The most physically visible, a hint of a cobweb. She paused. *What's happening?* Her writing stopped, since her hands trembled.

When she focused on the glass pane, the image became visible again until the light of the rising sun created a glare. Her eyes watered. It gave the effect of a starburst photo filter. Letsea drew slow deep breaths and rubbed shaky hands down her pantlegs and tried to carry on with questions. "Do you know what happened to your briefcase? They never found it."

I took it with me in the automobile. They must have taken it after he killed me. After the job, they didn't give me a second thought.

Her notes were scribbled since her eyes blurred. "What papers were you working on in the hotel lobby?"

Arrest and search warrants. There were many forms involved to get a judge to sign the orders. We had to prove probable cause. Plus, our superiors depended on the special investigators to know which judges were least likely to be paid under the table for tip-offs.

Time stilled. Tip-offs! "How were you going to make an arrest without a gun?"

The police arrest. It's their job. The investigator shows them who, when, and where.

As the sun rose, his image faded in the bright reflection. An urge to keep him talking pressed on.

"You *were* buried in Idaho, right?"

Morris Hill Cemetery, Boise.

"That's what I thought. I contacted them. They're going to email me a photo of your headstone."

I loved the service.

"You saw it?" She had flash images of her parents and grandparents' services.

I felt it through the hearts of loved ones. I will always love them. My wonderful family. I'm sorry they went through the ordeal, due to my career choice.

"My family, too." Letsea always hoped her parents could feel the love for them at their service. It was nice to know Paul was aware of his. It gave her hope wings of confidence.

The iridescent image faded. "Don't go. Tell me more."

Hey, little lady, please find a way to clear the insinuation that I killed myself. My parents taught me better.

"Wait. Tell me what it's like living in the 1920s."

You needed to be there to experience it. Great reasons to fear. At the same time, a new sense of freedom unveiled, therefore, more fear, for the loss of morality. Hold on to your loved ones. I've so missed holding Mills and my little man.

She sat up and looked at the empty space. "Mills?"

My wife, Mildred, Millie. I loved her so much. I can't explain the whole of my sorrow for what my sweetheart went through.

"You did love her."

I'd have given her the world had I been able. My beautiful Mills. My own Hot Tomato. I fell in love with her the first time we talked. She made the twenties roar, plus she gave me my boy. I wrote a letter to her the last night. I put it in my briefcase, but wish I'd mailed it.

"Paul, who do you think shot you? Or who wanted you dead?"

I reckon a lot of men wished me dead. By the by, the man who shot me wore a police uniform.

CHAPTER 27

Sunday morning continued

A thirty-minute hard morning run gave Letsea hope. She needed it to clear her mind of the masculine image in the fourth-floor tower room earlier. Never mind she accepted she'd conversed with a spirit. Was her imagination in overdrive? She never believed in apparitions. *So how did I hear and see one?*

The running trail was a flower garden labyrinth, a hundred and fifty feet behind the house.

With each footfall, surroundings declared their presence. A half mile away, cars sped down a highway. Dogs barked from the neighboring houses. A reminder of the stranger in the yard on Thanksgiving Day. *Why did he come here?* Her momentum slowed, eyes closed, to listen to nature's music. The sound of dried leaves danced across the yard in the breeze. They skidded over the asphalt footpaths and settled against the winterized rose bushes. Upward, birds called to each other as they gathered in the cluster of red cedar trees. A couple of red cardinals alighted on a bird feeder.

Aunt Mae and her gardener friends created a memorial for her parents and grandparents. Walking or running the labyrinth generally gave her a sense of peace. Although dormant for winter, she identified it as time alone with those she loved but no longer saw.

So why did she see Paul E. Reynolds? In a pane of glass, no less. Why couldn't she see him when she looked directly toward him? Unless he wasn't there at all. *If he wasn't, what did I see in the window?* She turned and jogged on the path to the house. Pauline's minivan, with engine running, was parked near the back basement door ramp. Letsea drew in a deep breath of cinnamon and headed into the kitchen where Pauline was slipping on her coat to leave for church. "Early start on your day off, I see," Letsea said.

"First Sunday of Advent. We're having refreshments after services. I want to be prepared." She flipped the cover back on a large fragrant basket of freshly baked cinnamon rolls.

"Mm. Maybe I should attend your church this morning."

Pauline tapped a glass dome stand on the countertop. "You're always welcome to join me. Meanwhile, I thought you might like a couple rolls."

"You know it. Mm." She reached for milk and a glass. "Thanks. Need help?"

"Not at all." She swung her purse over her shoulder and picked up the handled basket.

"Have fun today, miss."

"You too, Pauline."

After indulging in a warm homemade roll, she ran upstairs to prepare for church. Unlike Pauline's with two services, hers held only one. With time to spare, she checked her email.

Morris Hill cemetery forwarded a photograph of Agent Reynolds' headstone. Sure enough, it included the E. he preferred. After seeing military references on it, she called a veterans' admin office. Closed on Sunday. She flipped through her notes.

"Paul, those news clippings said you were in the R.O.T.C. while you were in college and from there, you went straight into the Army. After the war, you started at the Department of Revenue. That's where you worked with investigations on the Prohibition, isn't it?"

She looked around, half expecting Paul to answer, but he didn't. Not even the rough whisper used outside a whispering arch. She noticed the time and dashed downstairs. Bob had her SUV warmed, running, and waiting at the car porch.

When she returned home, she yearned to read Reynolds' official obituary. Her search revealed many Paul Reynolds in the past, just not her uncle's obit. Disappointed, she pushed all her notes of him aside. Time to get over Reynolds and focus on Christmas.

Her phone played Gwendolene's song. She answered immediately. "Hi, Sis, what's up?"

"Do you want to join us for dinner? You left so fast after the service, I missed you."

"Oh, sorry. I'm preoccupied, I guess."

"With what?"

"Um. Christmas cards. I need to finish writing notes in my cards so Marcia can mail them tomorrow. Gwen, remember Chip and Lauren are scheduled to sing a couple songs with the chamber orchestra at the volunteers' Christmas tea."

"Yes. They've been practicing. Thanks for asking them to participate. Even Doyle scheduled time to attend."

"I'm glad to hear it."

"I know you can't invite more guests than the ballroom will hold." Gwen hesitated.

"The count of volunteers has doubled this year. True, I cut the invitations to volunteers only, no plus-ones. Isn't it great to have so many people giving their time to the community? Doyle's always welcome. Honey, I need you to help me with this party. You're more socially involved than I am. The guests expect to see you greet them, with me. We'll put Doyle to work."

"I look forward to it, Lets. Oh, while Doyle's not within hearing, thanks for helping me with his gift. I'll go directly to the bank and dealership first thing in the morning."

"You're welcome."

"Dinner is at five-thirty, come, okay?"

"I'll be there. Love you, honey." Letsea was curious as to what kind of car her kid sister wanted to buy for her husband. Must be a nice one to need a hundred grand.

Christmas music played, and Rex Kitty curled on her desk while she wrote personal notes in her more intimate Christmas cards. Thank goodness Marcia already hand-addressed the card envelopes. The season was in full swing. RSVPs poured in for the tea party. The decorators were scheduled to arrive midweek.

Even being sidetracked by the interference of Uncle Paul, they were still on schedule with preparations for both the tea and the children's party for the local orphanage. Dare she not forget the Saturday of babysitting Gwendolene talked her into.

A dream private secretary, Marcia's organizational skills kept her tight to their schedule. She took a moment to feel gratitude for Marcia. She made a notation to shop for special Christmas cards for her, Pauline, Liza, and Bob. Their gifts were already wrapped and tucked away. Marcia included cards for the contracted services they hired to maintain the estate. "If not for dedicated employees, all the interference from a certain spirit could have thrown me off—my rocker. That's what you're doing to me. Paul, why don't you go back to where you were and let me figure out your situation when I have more time?"

Naught.

Interference? She pondered her use of the term. It led back to communications. Two or more waves of the same frequency either combine to strengthen or to cancel one another out. The greater wave... What was it called? She should look it up in Great-Great Grandfather's books. Is that how Reynolds' spirit managed to reach across time? Light, sound, or electromagnetic waves? Perhaps interference played a turn in how she so easily heard Reynolds speak inside a whispering arch.

One line from Paul kept repeating in her memory. *It's something you needed to be there to experience.*

Being there brought to mind the importance of opening statements and closing arguments in a courtroom trial. Both sides needed to convince the jury, and/or the judge, to see the situation from their perspective. You open with mentioning evidence they're about to see and hear. Then close with persuading them to recognize the same evidence as favorable to only their side.

Considering the evidence available from the 1929 Phoenix news sources, that's the opening. Those journalists seemed to have worked fast and furious to gather every possible bit of information available. The closing is simply a matter of relevant evidence.

"It's something you needed to be there to experience."

CHAPTER 28

Late Sunday afternoon at the Lockhart's old family residence

"Mom?" Lock called up from the kitchen.

"Godrick? I'm glad you're back. Did the furniture fit in your garage?" She surfaced at the upstairs landing.

"So far, but if you don't eliminate some of it, we'll need to rent a storage unit."

"Maybe we should. I don't like you needing to park your pretty little new car out in the cold this winter."

He thought of the six-car garage he saw behind Letsea's house. He believed his two-car garage plenty large, until he lined the walls of it with furniture. "Don't worry, Mom." He'd do enough of it for the both of them.

"I can't decide what to give up. We'll need all four of the bedroom sets once we find another house. The holidays won't be the same if we can't all stay under the same roof."

"You can sell mine. I can always sleep at my house and be back to yours for breakfast. You might rethink needing a large house. Mom, it's you and Dad, except for holidays. Downsizing might be the way to go."

"Oh, no you don't. You've missed too many Christmases as it is. I'm so glad you've finally settled down back here. Even so, the grandkids can sleep in your designated room. They're growing so fast. I can't believe how quickly kids go from cradle to college. I'm sure they'd like not having to sleep on the floor. Come on up.

You can help me wash down the back of the cabinets in the upstairs bathroom. They're all empty now. The labeled boxes are lined up, here in the hall."

As he headed up the stairs, his phone buzzed. A text from his credit card contact.

"Here." His mother tossed a damp cloth to him and motioned to the bucket of vinegar water.

He read his message. "Son of a monkey!" he exclaimed.

"I wish you'd stop saying that," his mother said. "Honestly, Merewood and I went through a few rounds, but you don't have to use your pet monkey for an excuse to cuss."

"Only a few? We all circled rounds with him. The little curtain-climbing, poop-hurling thief."

"I know he was a troublemaker, but a cute one. You gotta give him that much. Besides, you're the one who begged for a monkey."

She cleaned underneath the sink.

"Mom, I need to take care of something. Please don't crawl down there. I'll do it when I get back."

"I hate being such a bother to you, Godrick. But I really can use your help."

"Mom, it's not a bother. I volunteered. I'll be right back."

"Where's your father?"

"In the garage, sorting stuff."

He bounded downstairs and out the back door for privacy. "Chief, Brechenworth purchased a morning flight ticket to Phoenix."

"Follow her. See if she meets with anyone."

"I'm on vacation, remember?"

"I know you're good for it. I've always liked that you're totally dependable."

"Remember that when my annual review comes around. Gee, I feel a huge raise coming on, do you feel it too?"

"You're already maxed out, besides Christmas is a ways off."

"What?"

"You've got plenty of time for shopping and eating pumpkin pie."

Lock smelled the pungent odor of a vinegar-soaked rag draped over his shoulder. "Yeah, right. Find someone else. I'm on vacation." He hung up listening to his boss smirk. As if he had a choice.

He looked at the lone tree swing in the backyard and upward to his old treehouse. It didn't feel like forty years since he'd played up there. Or did it? He released a deep sigh. *Where did all the time go?* He figured he'd have seen children of his own playing in the yard. He didn't even have a prospect for a wife. The memory of Letsea laughing after he quoted Dumas to her made him smile.

CHAPTER 29

Sunday evening at a local soup kitchen

"Hey, Charlie, I saw a man at that lady's house yesterday."

"First time you've seen him there?"

"Yeah. It's been cold, so I've mostly been staying inside when I can. You been there lately?"

Charlie grabbed Otis's arm and pushed him against the wall. "Shh. Keep your voice low. Don't want someone else to beat us to our job. I went by earlier this week. There were Christmas lights strung up. Not good. Means she might be expectin' company."

"What do you think we should do?"

Charlie glanced behind them. "It means we're gonna have to be flexible and really prepared."

"To do what?"

"To be smart. Be strong. We want her money, right?"

"Yeah, but what'll it take to get it?"

"We have to kidnap her, Otis."

Eyes big as saucers, Otis stared and stuttered, "Ain't there an easier way to get her to hand over a bunch of money?"

"Like what, little buddy? Knock on her door, hold out an empty cup, and ask for a donation? Like, pardon us, ma'am, we're in need of twenty grand, will you help us?"

"Argh. Guess not."

"That's right. If we want it, we gotta take it." Charlie shook his head. "People don't give away big money unless they get a tax deduction. We gotta demand it from her."

"What if we get caught?"

"We won't. But if we did, jail is our retirement plan. So, we don't let nobody hook us. Come on, they're serving food now."

Otis planted his feet firmly. "Charlie, I don't want to go to prison."

"Why not? Worst can happen is we get room and board, clean clothes, haircuts, and healthcare is said to be great in there."

"Really? Who said? I think they make you work in the joint," said Otis.

"Hey, planning a kidnapping ain't exactly a life of leisure. We've got some heavy-duty calculatin' to do."

"Like what?"

"Whose car do we borrow? How we gonna take her, and where are we hidin' her? I have some ideas, but let's eat first, plot on a full stomach."

CHAPTER 30

Early Monday morning on a flight headed to Phoenix

Lock, cocooned near the back row in economy seating, knew Letsea was comfortably positioned beyond the curtain, behind the pilots. Odds were in his favor. Any need she might have should be covered in the luxury section. He would not be seen in-flight. However, the more he considered the situation, it could be advantageous should they *happen* to run into each other in Phoenix.

Lock closed his eyes to ignore the reclined seat suspended over his lap. Be that as it may, he found the loud snore more difficult to disregard. Why didn't he flat-out refuse to go on the trip? This wasn't an emergency. Truth be known, he wanted to help her. Maybe on the flight home, he'd claim a seat near the lovely Letsea.

The person behind him kicked the back of his seat for the umpteenth time. *Yeah. Merry Christmas to you, too, bub.*

Letsea stepped out of the elevator into the lobby of the Renaissance Hotel in Phoenix, Arizona. She noticed Detective Lockhart at the front desk with a newspaper in his hands. Absently, she poked the neck-height low bun and the cloche felt hat which matched her dress. Odd enough she was glad to see him there. She held an appreciation for investigators. Did she unknowingly coerce him to not wait until January to pick up her case? Plus, could

Uncle Paul's spirit come to her in the company of another? At Union Station, it seemed like his spirit wanted to push her away from the detective.

"Hey, I thought you were on vacation?" She smoothed her hand down the knee-length, topaz-shade, knit dress. She paused, tugged her petite cross-body purse, securing her room key.

Lock looked at her and arched an eyebrow. "Yet, here I am. What are *you* doing in Phoenix? I thought you were going to leave this to me."

"January is so far off. I thought if I came here, even for a day, it might help. I even tried to book the room Paul E. Reynolds last stayed in. They didn't just change the name from Hotel Adams to the Renaissance, they—"

"I know." He nodded. "A major fire and a purposeful implosion later, they built this entirely new expansive, all-luxury modern hotel."

"They have pictures of the Hotel Adams. I hope to get the feel of the 1920s," she said with elevated excitement for adventure not met in ages.

Lock rubbed his chin. "What are you planning to do right now?"

"They're pulling my rental car around. I want to check out the newspaper archives and museums. To see if there are any local stories still being touted."

"Mind if I tag along and see what we can come up with together?"

Relieved, she agreed. "Fine by me." Unlike with Aunt Mae's admonishment for her curiosity, with him, she sensed having a partner in her discovery. Even if she paid him for his time.

Being a gentleman, he held the rental car door open for her. She noted something comfortable about him. "Lock, I have a city map in my purse. How are you at navigation?"

"Can't say I've never been off-course, then again, I've never stayed lost. Where to first?"

"Start with the newspaper buildings, then the Police Museum. I also want to go toward Glendale and check out the canal where they found his body."

"Okay."

As he pulled out his phone, she pulled into a Wendy's drive-thru. He grinned.

"What's so funny?"

"I hadn't taken you for the fast-food type," he said.

"I haven't eaten since early this morning. Do you want something?"

"Definitely."

As she parked, Lock dug into the food bag, neatly folded down the wrapper and handed the burger to her, ready to eat. Her ice cream cup sat next to his coffee. She looked at the map while he searched websites on his cell phone.

"I'm sure the roadways are totally different in this century." He tapped the paper map in her hands.

"As diverse as the hotel?"

"Uh-huh."

"In Reynolds' day, the Phoenix population neared fifty thousand. What is it now." She remembered an old black-and-white photograph of the city streets.

"According to Google, over a million and a half. There's a hundred-year growth spurt for you." His attention went back to his phone.

"Lock, I don't mean to be rude, but I'd like a few minutes alone, to think. Please." She wanted to try to reach Uncle Paul.

"You want me to get out of the car?" He tilted his head.

She nodded.

"You won't drive off without me, will you?"

With her index finger, she crossed her heart.

"Okay." He got out, leaned against the passenger door, and finished his burger before walking around to find a trash bin. He paused at the front hood and looked at her.

She motioned for him to turn around. He walked away, whistling a Christmas tune. A clear musical sound. A relaxed feeling replaced her tension and she laughed.

"Paul, I'm in Phoenix. What do you want me to see? Hey, I'm not alone."

By whose choice?

Reynolds' barely audible rough whisper. More like her imagination than the clear voice from a whispering arch.

"There you are. What am I looking for?"

"Enough time?" Lock interrupted as he rapped on the hood.

She held up her index finger to stall him.

"Paul?"

Silence. What did he mean by *whose choice*? She motioned for Lock to get in the car.

"How did you do?" he asked.

She stared at him as a hollowness in her chest caused her to cringe. Did he hear her speaking to the ghost? "What do you mean?" She started eating her ice cream.

"Listening to your intuition, weren't you? Did you come up with anything?"

CHAPTER 31

Old downtown Phoenix

Lock quietly observed the Monday afternoon hustle-bustle of sidewalk passersby. He surmised some were Christmas shopping, while others returned to work after lunch. Without being obvious, he'd sneak glimpses of Letsea every chance he got. After all, she was easy on the eyes. Although, no denial she puzzled him. He didn't have firm answers for his chief as to why Agent Reynolds mattered to her. Family? He understood, yet why ninety years plus post factum?

For what possible reason were they parked in a refurbished section of what possibly had been the original part of downtown Phoenix?

Silent in the driver's seat, occasionally bowing, sometimes she looked up with a tilt of her head, as if listening or in deep thought. Did he do the same when he tuned into his own gut instincts. He suggestively intimated a search of websites, but everything concerning Miss Brechenworth captured his attention.

"How old do you think that building is?"

He looked at the corner office complex she pointed to. "Maybe sixty years, although it's likely been remodeled. What does that building have to do with anything?" He was relieved for the chance to ask without invading her solitude. So far, she hadn't ask him to get out of the car again.

"I'm not sure. I think there could have been a dance hall there." She rubbed the back of her head.

"What gives you that idea?"

She shrugged. "Just thinking." With a tilt of her head, she added, "Next to it might have been a diner. Maybe a barbershop and a jewelry repair shop farther on down the street."

He asked, "Been doing research?"

She shrugged then pointed to the right corner of the street. "A civic center there, wouldn't you think? One with both daytime and evening get-togethers and a beauty shop more along the center of the block."

"You've lost me," he admitted. "What about a dance hall?"

"I think there could have been a speakeasy through a secret door in the back of the dance hall. It may have led customers to a passageway taking them to a basement underneath a different business, like maybe a diner next door."

"What's your source?" He'd love to know.

She turned in her seat and looked him in the eyes. "I'm just thinking. You know, what if?"

Making it up, my...monkey's tail! She knew something. He needed to find out what and how.

"What else have you got?" S*eriously, what else?*

"I think Agent Reynolds might have been in his car, on surveillance, maybe right around here. On a hot August evening, he'd have the windows rolled down. He turned in his seat, leaned against the driver's door to talk to some flapper floozy, who leaned inside the passenger window flirting with him. At that time, he was struck on the back of the head through the driver's door open window. The killer and the floozy took him hostage in his own rental car and drove him out to the canal to finish him off, out of town. Away from others hearing."

"Is that a fact?"

Squinting, she lowered her eyebrows.

By Jupiter! He didn't mean to put her on the defensive. He shifted in his seat and swallowed. Thirsty and an empty coffee cup.

She leaned back and sighed. "It *could* have happened that way."

"I don't know anything to contradict your concept." He exhaled. "What makes you think he'd been hit on the back of the head?" He'd been curious since she mentioned it at her house on Saturday. *How does she know?* The question lingered in his mind.

She shrugged.

"Letsea, the first day we met at Union Station, you asked me if I believe in psychics. Are you one?" He didn't believe in psychics, as such, but he held gut instinct in high regard.

She shook her head vehemently. "I hope not. What do you say to us finding the canal where they found his body?"

"And forget the archives?" he asked. Recognizing her tendency to put too many irons in the fire.

"No. This shouldn't take long. It's like twelve miles from here."

"I'm game."

She drove like she knew the town. Not once asking for directions. "You're familiar with the area, are you?"

"I looked at the map earlier. Lock, do you always wear suits?"

His eyes widened. "No. Don't you like my suits?" He rubbed his chin and straightened his tie. Where was she going with this?

"They're quite nice. You aren't a mobster, are you?"

"Hardly." His pulse picked up and his muscles tightened. "Why would you think it of me?"

"If killed by a drug ring, most likely the mob did it, right? I read Capone may have owned a secret house here. What if the mob still wanted to stop any new outcomes from developing in the case?"

"With the history of organized crime, I can't imagine they'd be actively pursuing a coverup of a one-hundred-year-old murder of one man." *Yeah, who would do that?* His lips pressed together and he looked out the side window.

Another agent down. Lock watched the housing developments flutter by as Letsea drove. What if? He reminisced to an evening early in his career. The night he and his fiancée were walking back to his car after leaving a classy restaurant. They were gunned down by a passenger in a black sedan. He, the sole survivor.

Not wanting to revisit the memory, he needed to concentrate on Letsea.

It was fascinating to observe how answers materialize in a moment of quietude or shortly thereafter. His mother explained it to him as a child. "Be still and know."

He remained quiet, waiting for peace of mind to wash over and fade intense memories. Letsea, too, drove without speaking. Surely all those guesses she supposedly made up were due to her listening to the voice within.

Letsea slowed. The next exit might be her turnoff, except she didn't feel directions from Paul's spirit like she expected. So, she picked up speed to continue. The road crossed over a creek, or a canal? They passed an industrial area.

Weird how she clearly sensed Paul's communications downtown, even with Lock right next to her. Not so much out on the highway. She glanced at her passenger. He remained silent and stared out the window.

Oh, snap! Muscles in her jaw tightened. He went quiet on her. He probably got upset by her audacity. *Why didn't I think before asking 'Are you a mobster'?* The faux pas, however, was a done deal, no backsies.

"Turn here."

She gently released a pent-up breath. For a second, she thought she heard Paul. Lock spoke instead.

After the exit, she pulled over and stopped. "Did we cross a canal?"

"Yes. Though I understand there were several at the time. They've probably reconstructed the waterways since. According to the articles I read, they found his body in the middle of farmland."

"Yes, and we're not even close to the twelve-mile distance," she said.

"I'm not surprised. No interstate back then."

"Did you see the sign indicating Glendale? His so-called friend with the swimming pool. Quite a drive for a swim."

"So-called friend? The man expected Reynolds to arrive at his house for an evening swim. We've talked about this, but let's assume people don't swim at a stranger's house."

While parked, she turned in her seat to face him.

"Simply because someone makes a statement, it doesn't make it true. Maybe Agent Reynolds wanted people to believe they were his friends," she explained.

"It is possible he concealed his position while searching for clues."

Good, she thought, they were back on the same train of thought. "Lock, will you look up how long Glendale has been a town?"

"Sure… Founded in 1892, incorporated in 1910. Why?" he asked.

"Odd, don't you think? Paul mentioned to someone he planned to go swimming. He didn't say where, did he? His Glendale friend later said Paul never showed, yet Paul's body showed up in the same vicinity."

"I know. I think it's a big part of the authority's initial puzzlement." Lock gingerly leaned toward her. "Are you feeling okay? Your face looks a bit red."

Yeah, from embarrassment. "There's so much to give thought to," she whispered. "I'd like to drive back out here tomorrow. Meanwhile, you were right. We should have searched the archives first. We'd have a better idea of where we were headed if I'd stuck to the original plan. Sorry. Sometimes I get ahead of myself. At this point, you're probably wishing we'd taken separate vehicles."

"Let me be clear. That is not my thought at all. Since you mentioned it, do you want to go to the newspaper offices now?" he asked.

Her lips parted. "That or the library. Will you call and see which is the biggest bang for our use of time?"

"No problem."

Relieved to see him back in full spirit, contemplative daydreaming gone.

"Oh hey, earlier I found a list of speakeasies. We can check one out tonight if you want." Lock pointed to his smart phone.

"Oh. A real speakeasy? One depicting the 1920s, or just the name of a bar?"

"This one says, 'time sensitive to the Prohibition Era.'"

She looked to him. "Why didn't you mention it sooner?"

"You were in the zone. I didn't want to interrupt."

"Okay." She didn't argue. "First the archives and there's a police museum."

"Sounds good."

In my zone. Of course, she decided he'd probably help put her away in an institution if she told him her *zone* meant listening to a corpse of practically a hundred years.

A trip to the library covered archives for all area newspapers of the time. Three hours of working side by side with Letsea brought Lock a profound realization of the depth of her desired accomplishment.

Like a dog with a bone, searching records, making copies, and forwarding information to emails came off as second nature to her. With the efficient help of friendly librarians, time flew by. Her voice, the soft sweet fragrance of her hair, and the occasional gentle touch of her fingertips on his hand ignited all his senses. How long could he handle it?

After they hurried to the car, Lock searched his cell phone for their next stop. "You aren't going to like this. The Police Museum is closed for the day. We'll have to wait until tomorrow to get in. And it's too early for the speakeasy to be open."

"Oh. We could go back to the hotel, catch a nap and refresh."

Sounded enticing. "Or, brace yourself for this..." he joshed, "we *could* find a restaurant and eat dinner. I'm hungry and there is a little matter of the time-zone difference to consider. Frankly, I'm getting to the age where a nap is good too."

"I understand. What are you hungry for?"

He dropped his head back against the headrest and sighed. "Trust me. Whatever you want is fine by me." What he felt after a day with her resulted in a type of hunger he could not admit to.

"Oh my!"

Lock looked across the booth-table of the authentic Mexican restaurant. Enchanting Letsea, wide-eyed, stared at him. He drew in a breath. "Are the Chile Rellenos too spicy for you?"

"Not at all. It's fabulous. The blackened poblanos have a delicious smokey flavor. It's perfection. How are your fish tacos?"

"The best. Don't you like the margarita? You've barely touched it."

"I'd rather eat before I drink any. I'm really not much of a drinker."

"I see."

She smiled like a shy teenager. To learn more of Miss Brechenworth never ceased.

"I'd still like to go back to my room before we find the speakeasy."

Did she tell or ask? A fresh pinkish hue crept to her cheeks. To avoid staring, he looked at his watch. "Not a problem. They have late hours."

They fell silent and finished dinner. After the waitress removed the plates, she spoke up.

"You said January. Why are you even here?"

"Research. What else?" He watched as she dipped the tip of a little finger into her drink and smoothed it around the salty edge of the glass. Her brows were drawn, as though in deep thought. He certainly was. Could she be any more enticing?

For a moment, Letsea placed the fingertip on her tongue.

Yes! She can. I need help from her allurement.

"All I ask is for people to be honest with me." She paid the waitress for both meals, tipped, and left the drink virtually full.

Before he got up, he took a swig of her drink. Ah, mouthwatering.

CHAPTER 32

Monday night outside a Phoenix speakeasy

"Don't we need a password or a secret knock to get inside?"

"Letsea, the Prohibition period ended in 1933. I think they'll let us in." Amused by her enthusiasm.

"Doesn't feel authentic if you can walk right in without proving yourself."

The doorknob failed to turn. "What do you think? Should I bash the door down or beat on it?" Her stifled laugh tantalized his imagination. He drew in a breath, slow to release.

"Is there a secret doorbell? Or, try a knock." She tugged on his sleeve. "Make it interesting."

He tapped three times then whistled the chorus to the song "Knock Three Times."

She elbowed his arm. "That's my sister's ringtone!"

"Who's there?" came a rough, masculine reply from behind the door.

"Lock and Letsea."

The door opened. A man looked out and studied the empty stairwell behind them. "You alone?"

Lock said, "There's two of us." He liked the way Letsea rested her forehead to his shoulder. He wished he'd called his boss to remind him of his vacation and in no way did he consider *this* part of his job.

The door opened just enough for them to squeeze in sideways. Promptly the door closed behind them. Dead bolt flipped. *Are you kidding me?*

The doorman held out his palm. "One-hundred-fifty-dollar cover charge. Each."

Lock stepped aside to settle their entry fee. As the man faded into the dimness, Lock made an effort to read the tickets. Supposedly the entry fee came with a couple drinks. It should have included dinner or a Broadway show at such a price. Ultimately, for Letsea's experience, he hoped it met her expectations. Not much activity in the place. Simply a lazy, dark lounge. Not what he envisioned.

Dim lighting of red and yellow bulbs in sparsely placed wall sconces gave the long, narrow underground tavern an old dingy atmosphere. The walls of dark-red bricks made him feel as though in a tunnel. He waved smoke away from his eyes, hopefully it came from a fog machine. The only modern thing he noticed was a lighted exit sign.

He saw a half-dozen people, and heard music. The vibrant, golden sounds of jazz rang out. A saxophonist skillfully acquainted with his piece. The music was probably piped in on decent speakers. It saddened him to think Letsea might be disappointed. She really wanted the era to come alive.

On the way down to the bar, vintage cushioned chairs were paired off for couples. Lock glanced as Letsea gripped his arm, he liked the feel of it. He placed a palm over her fingers and guided her. When they stopped, he admired her with a redefined appreciation. "What do you think so far?"

She gave a slight nod but said nothing.

The bartender wore a black apron and long-sleeved black shirt. He looked invisible in the dimness. The bar, old-fashioned with a vintage coffee machine and brewed tea urn dispenser. Soft drinks were available in six-ounce glass bottles and a variety of fruit juices listed on a blackboard.

"Looks legit," he whispered.

"Innocent enough. I guess the alcohol is kept out of sight."

"How are you this evening?" The bartender looked beyond his shoulder and bobbed his head.

"Fine, thank you."

"Good evening," came a man's gravelly voice from behind. "I don't believe I've seen you here before."

As he turned, Lock placed his hand on Letsea's back. "First

time." He noticed the man wore a dark-blue, three-piece suit with bright white stripes, 1920s gangster style, with a thin white tie and a white Fedora.

"You'll need to know the house rules in order to stay." His dialect was that of a north-eastern city, his eyes dark and piercing.

Letsea inched close against him. He rubbed his thumb back and forth to reassure her all was fine.

"First rule, we don't extend credit, so don't even ask. No lettuce swapping. No tiger milk allowed. If you have any heaters, gats, rods, or roscoes, you leave them with the doorman. You got that?"

Lock covered his mouth to hide his grin. Who was this guy supposed to be? He didn't need to declare who he was. This was entertainment.

"In case of a raid, swallow fast. I'll have no discussion of politics, religion, or upcoming heists or crimes of any kind, understood?"

They both nodded. Letsea leaned into his shoulder. He thought she might bite him to avoid laughing aloud. She hid her mouth from the stranger. The little stinker. She wanted to know the feel of the Prohibition Era. Maybe they *were* in for an interesting evening.

"In here, we keep it civil, see? No fisticuffs will be tolerated. Grifters leave their work outside the door. Keep it clean. We bounce boozehounds." The stranger looked Letsea up and down then said to Lock, "You keep your flirting to your own squeeze." He gave Letsea a stern look. "That goes for you too, young lady." He tipped his hat and added, "By the by, you either drink it or leave it. No sauce walks out our door. Now do you understand the house rules?"

Lock said, "We got it." Wide-eyed Letsea, clinched his waist. He enjoyed her mood, but guided her hands away from his shoulder holster and checked the buttons on his coat.

Since he occasionally carried no "heat" when undercover, he wondered if this was one of those times he shouldn't have. But then, he never knew when he might need it. Still, relieved for the man's one-on-one instructions, it undoubtedly set the mood. The striped-suited stranger receded from view as mysteriously as he surfaced.

"Did you get all of that?" he asked.

"No. What's a rod? Like a steel pipe or something?" She let go of him.

He chuckled. "More like a pocket canon, I should think." He whispered, "You're cute, Letsea. Either way, I don't think we need to fret." He paused. "You aren't carrying a weapon, are you?"

She shook her head. "What's a grifter?" she whispered.

"A con artist," he said, putting his cheek near hers in order to whisper to her ear. "We're good there too, kiddo."

The bartender came around the counter of the bar. "You ready for the bees knees and giggle water?"

Lock agreed and followed directions as the bartender motioned for them to back up against the brickwork.

"Now, hold on to each other. Stand flat against the wall. Seriously. Don't Move. Not even a hair."

Lock reached for her hand. She squeezed his.

"Isn't this where they brought out the gats?" she whispered.

He said, "I'm hoping for something pleasant." He smiled.

The section where they stood began to move. It revolved as a door on a vertical axis. It turned into total darkness. The din of music and chatter increased, and they were still closeted inside the crazy-thick barrier between rooms.

"So, what did he mean by lettuce and tiger milk?" she asked, her words soft with a tug on his hand.

He got a kick out of her timidness. "I believe they don't want us to bring liquor inside or attempt to do any kind of business while we're here. Except to pay them cash. I'm not sure what lettuce is. I thought it currency. I may be wrong."

"A man who admits he may be wrong. Wow. What a concept. My father used to say, 'Princess, to save time, just assume your daddy's always right.'"

Lock laughed.

Like a single-door elevator, they were opened to a whole new scene.

To their left, on and around a small corner stage, a live band played swing jazz. Cymbals and drums ignited the horns and saxophone with a fiery energy. The center of the room was all dance floor. The crowd danced with a wild swinging spirit.

To their right, was an old-fashioned dark-wood bar backed by etched mirrors, and rows of bottles. Chalkboards decorated the walls. The rest of the perimeter was lined with continual wooden bench seating. Scattered along, there were chairs with small tables. Forty or so people danced or sat with drinks. The 1920s costumes captivated him. Flapper girls were lively dressed with lots of fringe, men in suits. Sweet.

Letsea stood close and he looked into her inquiring eyes. Oh, man, not only was she beautiful, looking at her made him feel young again.

After a big smile, she giggled. It made her appear a little tipsy and they hadn't even indulged in a drink yet. The inviting taste of margarita, hours earlier, with dinner didn't count. He cleared his throat, put a hand on her lower back, and cautiously led her across the room. He held a chair for her then sat on the bench. No waitstaff from what he could see. He leaned forward. "I believe we're meant to belly up to the bar." He stood. "What would you like?"

"Do you think they'll have Biltmore Reserve Chardonnay?"

He doubted they'd be so specific. He covered her head then ducked when a dancing pair of lady's legs swung close by. "I can't imagine why not. But if they don't?"

"Whatever. Not stiff, though, remember I'm driving."

He nodded then dodged his way to the busy bar, but kept glancing back. Not about to come so far only to lose track of her.

There were several large chalkboards listing specialty drinks at exorbitant prices. The free drink tickets did not include those. For her, house white wine. Jack Daniels, for him.

"Here. To quote the bartender, 'foot juice' for you and 'jag juice' for me."

She tilted her head. "What?"

He shrugged his shoulders and plopped a small box of mixed nuts on the table. She was probably going to have her first taste of cheap wine.

The band stopped. Applauded by a standing audience, they switched out with a smaller band.

She sipped her drink and wrinkled her nose. "Foot juice, hm?"

Rhythm changed to slow. A smooth pianist and accompanists. Fast-paced dancers rested and drank. New couples continued to arrive. A few began slow dancing. The energy enchanted his thoughts.

"Letsea, care to dance?"

CHAPTER 33

Dancing in the secret bar and dance room of speakeasy

L etsea felt his toned body as they slow danced. She considered if Lock jogged. Next, "Foxtrot." Slow, slow, quick, quick, close, turn, and repeat back. The man moved with experience. Although, out of practice, it reminded her how fun dancing could be with a partner who held his own.

"You're an excellent dancer." Lock looked into her eyes.

"Thank you, but my dance instructor didn't teach me anything like what we saw going on when we came in here. If it gets too fast, I'm down for the count."

"You took dance lessons? What did you study?"

"Ballet and ballroom."

"That explains your smoothness. It also means you can handle anything. Mrs. Bilyeu used to say, 'If you master ballroom dance, you're good to go.'"

She rushed to say, "You took lessons from Mrs. B's studio? Me, too. There weren't many boys in *my* classes though."

"There were never enough boys in dance class, period. That's how I got roped into it. I drove my kid sisters to class. Mrs. B. talked me into staying and taking lessons so girls would have an actual male partner."

"Apparently you didn't mind," she joked.

"Guess not."

The music switched to "Maple Leaf Rag." They kept up with the faster movements. "She said if I learned to dance proper, girls would flock to me. Powerful words to a sixteen-year-old boy."

"Did they flock?"

He chuckled. The tempo picked up again on "Bourbon Street." He took full charge and led her around the crowd with zest to his steps. "The only girl who ever matters is the one in your arms in the moment."

It felt nice to follow his lead. She missed the exhilaration of music and dance. Her limited recent dancing was a single closing slow dance at the annual tea parties for volunteers. Quite at ease, Lock led her around the room for several numbers. No wonder they called this to "cut a rug." A transformative energy. Someone started snapping pictures.

Her musings were interrupted by a flash of light. Her ex-boyfriend, Seth, popped into her thoughts. He refused to do the "Chicken Dance" at Aunt Mae's wedding reception last summer. For what reason did she talk herself into staying with him for three years? She knew why. Her dream for a family.

Putting hope in Seth was like throwing coins into a wishing well, only to discover it dry as dust.

To watch Lock, refreshing. When she heard the next song, "Black Bottom," she broke free. "I can't. It's too involved." She moved toward the table. *Great,* she thought, *I'm as boring as Seth.*

"Sure, you can." He followed. "Just kick your legs side to side and wave your arms upward. Dancing is not about following the rules, Lets, it's expressing how you feel."

"Those aren't the words of Mrs. B." He called her Lets, again. Hmm. *Why not?* She didn't want to turn into a fuddy-duddy. No sooner did they start when the music came to an abrupt stop.

The pianist hollered, "Switch." In swift movements, the small band cleared the stage, and the original ensemble returned. Brass, strings, drummer, and soloist all took their places.

"Folks, get ready! We're gonna take a little visit to Charleston, South Carolina. Everyone up!" announced the emcee. "If you need a couple minutes to practice, here's your chance."

People rushed to the floor. Cheers ensued as band members took their places with a brief non-harmonious sound of tuning. A few cleared off the floor to sit it out. She was with them.

"Hey come on. Where are you going?" Lock called out.

"Oh no!" She raised both arms into the air. "Nope, I can't do that one!" She headed back to their table, only to see it with new occupants and their drinks gone. Not that she cared for the drink after having left it alone. Or at all. She stopped, and Lock stepped up behind her, both hands on her waistline.

"What better way to experience a speakeasy? You shouldn't pass this up."

He spoke directly into her right ear, like he did earlier. She shivered, in a good way. *What is it with Lock?* She turned in his arms. "We traveled, long trips. I missed too many dance classes. I've never even tried the "Charleston". It's too complicated."

"Somehow, I doubt it."

She pulled on his arm as she made her way to the bench. Realization of the intimacy of her gesture caused her to let go.

An older woman, in full flapper attire with rows and rows of fringe, put her arm around her. "Come on, darlin', give it a try. I'll teach you." She pulled Letsea onto the dance floor.

Lock's eyes revealed a sparkle of humor. *You rascal,* she thought. He enjoyed her dilemma.

"First, darlin', your knees are either facing opposing directions or toward each other. Second, kick your legs behind you, swing forward. Third, when you bring your feet down, imagine you're squashing a cigarette butt—"

"I don't smoke."

"I didn't say 'smoke it,' darlin'. Consider it an imaginary nasty old lit butt on the floor. Squash it out, twist one foot on it, then the other." She explained the rhythm count, of when to start. The swing of her feet and legs. "Move forward with your right foot, back with your left. Switch. Feel it? Now twist your feet. Squash, squash. Feel your freedom, honey. Now swing your arms. Reach up, out, and down. You can shimmy, kick. Perfect, child! Now go have fun." The woman slipped a long rope of pearls, like Mardi Gras beads, around her neck and tucked something into the band of her hat. "Go get 'em, darlin'. Be free."

You have no idea how I'd love to feel free.

She looked at Lock, sitting on the bench watching, his head leaned back and shoulders shaking. New energy emerged, she marched over, pinched his sleeve. "Don't laugh thus, old man!" She pulled him to center floor. He didn't resist. A new wave of people rushed to the dance floor.

"Ladies and gentlemen, the 'Charleston'!"

She counted rhythm beats and started. Lock stood back, watched her for a few seconds before jumping in, clapping then moved into a soft-shoe routine without missing a beat. In swinging her arms, she back-slapped his elbow. "You know this dance!" she hollered. He moved in front of her, took her hands, and danced with her before letting go. She moved into lively steps. He watched and clapped again. His wide smile graced his face in a mischievous way. She enjoyed Lock.

When did she turn into an all-work-no-play, stick-in-the-mud? She was well aware of when it happened. It came with her responsibilities as an adult and heir in charge of the family estate. If her brother-in-law, Doyle, had agreed to her grandfather's will stipulations, Chip would be the rightful budding heir. She could have more freedom and not be stuck in such an awkward position.

Paul referred to Aunt Mildred as his very own "hot tomato." Did her aunt dance the "Charleston"? Undoubtedly, she did! It was living euphoria. She understood how 1920s dancing made the young generation feel a sense of freedom.

A warmth crept up into her heart. She looked at her partner. He held his arms toward her with a pleasant air and a grin. She wanted to melt into his look.

Don't go there! she warned herself. *He is not a date.*

Before she realized it, she found herself doing the hands to knees bit, white beads swaying the whole time. Lock knew how to dance. She roared with glee. She'd forgotten how good it felt to be unreserved. Perhaps because she was so far away from family and no one in Phoenix knew her.

As the song ended, everyone applauded then she noticed other couples were kissing, intently.

What was she thinking? She headed straight to the secret door.

"You want to go already?"

"I noticed the ladies' lounge out in the first room." She stepped into place and a younger flapper moved to set the secret passage in motion. Lock stood beside her.

They were closeted in darkness.

"I'm fairly certain some of the dancers are paid actors," she said.

"For a hundred and fifty bucks a pop, we're getting an audience participation show. Authentic enough for you?"

"Kind of fun, hm?" She pressed against the bricks then turned a cheek to the coolness. Her leg brushed against his. "Lock, are you married?"

"Never."

See? she reminded herself. *Not only is he not a date, the man is a confirmed bachelor. I should have known. Whatever I feel, get over it!*

The front room opened up and she aimed straight for the ladies' room. Among other things, she needed to splash water on her face and get her mind off Detective Lockhart.

CHAPTER 34

In the speakeasy's front entrance room

Lock looked around the crowded outer room. He leaned against the wall, waited in thought. Letsea showed moments where she acted like she doubted her abilities. Why? She was balletic. During the "Toddle", patrons created a large counterclockwise circle. She mingled and laughed at ease. So adorable. He grinned thinking of her little hops, skips, and slides.

"Lock!"

Startled, he tensed. "What happened?"

"You have to go into the men's room. Hurry! Check it out." She clapped her hands.

Her burst of excitement confused him. "Why?"

"You have to see it to believe it. Go in!"

He put his hands on her shoulders and backed her to the narrow wall between the men's and ladies' doorways. Letting her out of eyesight wasn't in the plan. "Stay right here." He looked her in the eyes and raised an eyebrow. "Stay put, hear me?"

"I'll wait. Go see."

He went into the men's room, took a moment, and went back out. "What?"

"What do you mean, 'what'? What do you think? Isn't it beautiful?"

"What's so special about it?"

"Didn't you notice a mural on the wall, mirrors, lights, the red velvet benches and chairs?"

"No." He studied her puzzled expression. "It must just be in the ladies' room. Ours is white."

"No. They wouldn't do that. Would they?" Her shoulders slumped. "That's not fair. The ladies' have a full-blown old-fashioned lounge. Decorative gold sinks with gold faucets. There's a long marble makeup vanity with mirrors. It's all red trimmed with gilt. A huge antique chandelier. One wall has a mural of *Baths of Caracalla* by Lawrence Alma-Tadema. You mean you don't have anything like that?"

He shook his head.

"*Tsk.* The men really miss out."

He tried and failed to hide a smile. "It sounds like they spent their budget on the ladies' behalf. Sorry to disappoint. No mural. No vanity or velvet seats. No red or gold."

Her brows pinched. "Chairs?"

"Letsea, there's only one chair in there and it's white porcelain with a hole in it. The sink matched the same color scheme. Silver faucet by the way. Too bad, I like gold faucets. For the men, it's just the nitty-gritty."

"Ooh," she groaned. "I'm sorry if I got your hopes up." She thrust her bottom lip forward.

He thought he *could* survive without all the comforts of an elegant washroom. However, her pouty expression he might succumb to. Her lips were an invitation. She'd refreshed her lipstick while in the ladies' lounge. Not ruby red. More like an apple. He closed his eyes briefly and sighed.

Naturally, she chose to wear red-delicious apple. Did she have any idea what she was doing to him? Yes. He suspected she did know. He imagined Seth Purser's stress level in code blue if he saw his girlfriend making this face to another man.

He remembered they weren't friends. She was a person of interest in a federal investigation. For what reason? Caring for the reputation of her deceased relative? *How did I even end up here? On my vacation, no less!* Lock fully realized his frustration with his job description. He liked this lady. Between his job and her boyfriend, he saw no hope left for him.

Seriously, he ought to retire instead of holding out for a higher pension.

Duty required him to forget the fun of dancing with her. He

spotted the exit sign and looped fingers around her upper arm. "Come on, Eve, time to leave."

They departed through a lighted tunnel leading to a long, winding ramp that took them ground level, far from the entrance.

"I'll reimburse you for the admittance fee," Letsea said.

"Whatever." He *could* expense it, but he enjoyed himself too much.

When they emerged ground level, he noticed a man step very close behind them and leaned even closer. Lock recognized him from working in the main dance room.

"Psst." The stranger whispered in a rough, edgy tone, "It looks like you two had a good time down there. I have something you may want."

Letsea spun away.

Lock reached for her, but she grabbed the right arm of the stranger dressed in a black suit, and his hat set flight into the darkness.

She twisted the man's arm behind his back. With a great deal of force, she shoved him against an iron handrail. In a direct and demanding voice, she yelled, "What *do* you want?" She pulled tighter on his arm.

The man groaned.

Lock touched her shoulder.

Without a backward glance, Letsea screamed, "9 1 1!"

The stranger whimpered, "No, not 9 1 1."

"Lets, let up on him. I think he's play acting a part from the speakeasy."

He slid his other hand down her arm, the one holding the man's wrist. Her pulse raced.

He hoped she felt his attempt to calm and ground the intensity of her response. Caught in the defensive mode, it took longer than he expected for her to come around. "Letsea, you can let go of him now. It's okay. I remember him from inside."

The man said, "Really, lady, he's right. I'm with the speakeasy. Holy cow! What are you a black belt or something?"

She was still in an adrenaline rush. Lock rubbed her arm. Her grip was remarkably tight.. He whispered, "It's okay. He's not a threat."

It appeared the moment of realization hit. She loosened her

hold.

"You aren't going to try to hurt us, are you?" Her voice strong and determined.

"No. I've got a picture of the two of you, dancing."

Finally, she let him loose.

He shook his arm and pulled a picture out of his coat pocket. They moved closer to a yard light and he shined a flashlight on it. "See? I sell them. It's only ten dollars."

"We'll take it." Lock handed the young man a twenty. "Keep the change." He slipped the picture into his right breast coat pocket and led her toward the sidewalk.

"Are you okay?" he asked. When she didn't answer, he wrapped an arm around her and pulled her to him. "It's okay. Truth be known, as close and mysterious as he was being, he got what he deserved for scaring people." Her head slumped against him. He knew the feeling of a charge of excitement and letdowns. After a moment, he heard her sigh.

"Do you feel better now?"

"I'm getting there."

So was he, she frightened him, too. Her swiftness and strength were unexpected. "I'm surprised you didn't land him on the ground. You have quite a defense technique."

She blew a heavy breath and said, "Years of self-defense classes will do it every time. I still need a minute." She stopped, bent over at her waist, put her hands on her knees, and intentionally blew out a couple of deep breaths.

"Take your time. Unless you're going to do the Charleston dance out here in the street." He fingered her dangling rope of beads.

"Oh, funny man, aren't you? By the way, I'm not even a white belt. You, Mr. Calm and Collected, don't tell me, you *are* a black belt."

"Fine. Let's say, I know a few moves. You know, for the occasions they're actually needed."

She tilted her head. "Haha. Where are we anyway? Where's the car? I need to sit."

"We exited through a different door." She walked slowly. He recalled walking her to a seat in the train station hall. Lucky him, she didn't flip him on the floor. Was it only four days ago? "Would you prefer I drive us back to the Renaissance?"

"You're not on my contract for insurance. Otherwise, I'd be grateful."

"I'm insured to drive any vehicle, as long as I have permission."

"Whose? Mine or the rental company's? Never mind, don't answer." She handed him the key.

CHAPTER 35

Hotel elevator, Tuesday at 1:15a.m.

"What floor?" As if he didn't know.

"Third."

He stalled for time. He needed to know what she planned to do with the Reynolds information.

"Letsea, have you read letters from Reynolds to his wife? Or a diary?"

Without answering, she reached into her purse. "There are several museums I want to visit. The history one, the police, and the Victorian museum. Melinda's Alley downstairs is supposed to have Hotel Adams history. I should go there as early as possible. I fly back after lunch." She turned her cell phone on.

He finally selected the third floor button.

"It's hard to remember having so much fun. Thanks for going with me."

"My pleasure." Indeed, it was. "Letsea, you deserve to be happy."

"Right. I think people attending speakeasies wanted to relax and be amused. Simply a place to gather and enjoy themselves. We didn't drink much and look at all our fun. Folks needed to give themselves permission to have a good time. A shame it was illegal."

"Speaking of—"

"My phone's been off. How did I go a whole day without using it?"

Lock waved his. "We've been using mine."

"Oh dear. My sister will throw a fit." She cringed and tucked her phone back in her bag. "Sorry. What were we saying?"

"The prohibition being unfair. It took over ten years before they finally repealed it."

They ignored the elevator door opening.

"Do you think people spent time in jail or prison, as a result of wanting to be entertained?"

"A lot did. For the first time in American history, our prisons were overcrowded."

The doors started to close, Lock stuck his arm out to keep it open, and she stepped out first.

"All from a few people thinking it a good idea to tell others how to live their lives." She shook her head.

"Not just a few." He softened his voice in the hallway. "Seventy percent of Americans were for the Prohibition Act, until it took effect. It got out of hand fast."

"How did they know they errored so quickly?"

He held out his hand for the key card and unlocked the door. "Simple. It showed in the numbers. Depending on the city, for every single legal bar forced to close, there were anywhere from six to twenty new *illegal* clubs to replace it."

She looked stunned. They entered her room. He glanced and noted a small tan backpack.

"That's hard to wrap my mind around. Being illegal, no taxes were paid."

"That and governments lost licensing fees and restrictions on when bar hours could be open."

"I understand a lot of police, even government officials were paid off to ignore their existence. And to warn clubs before a raid. So, bribery must have been a huge factor."

"Yes." He stood beside her room entrance door as she closed it. He decided to probe further. "I suppose it's possible Reynolds might have been bought off, too."

Her hands flew to her hips, clenched into fists. "Paul was sort of a low-key kind of guy, from what I've read. Friendly, honest, and discreet. The police liked him. Known for being good at his job."

He baited for another response. "Reynolds was well-liked by the wealthy. I wonder why."

"I'm disappointed in you." She broke eye contact. "The wealthy need be selective in their friends, especially due to all the scam artists out there. However..." She looked directly into his eyes. "The caliber of someone's character does *not* depend on their bank balance. Quality is utmost."

Ouch. She took it personally. Clearly, he slid down a notch in her opinion of him. "Sure. What do you know of your uncle?" he provoked.

"Paul E. Reynolds, plainly a military idealist. Highly respected by his supervisors. Did you know Hoover sent his best investigator here to Phoenix, to head up the investigation?"

"I may have read it somewhere," he admitted. *To do what exactly?* he questioned himself. *To lead the investigation or to control a cover-up?*

In defense, she said, "In an article I read, even his past Los Angeles supervisor of three years said he was unable to believe what happened to him. He verified Paul as a man of quality and diligence."

Lock hoped the Bureau had those same thoughts concerning him. With sadness in her eyes he felt culpable for planting insinuations on Reynolds. Obviously, she cared for the man. But, w*hy?*

"Stop looking at me like that," she snapped in a serious whisper.

His back straight to the wall, he forced his hands into his pockets. "How am I looking at you?"

"Like you feel sorry for me." She pouted.

"You are one curious lady." He watched her expression slowly change to intrigue. He needed to redirect the look in her eyes. "If I didn't know better, I'd think you personally knew the man."

"You're being silly." She stepped back and kicked her shoes off. "His murder made a huge story." Her pitch rose high. "You've seen it for yourself. The journalists were thorough."

"They sure were." He pressed his lips tight before he said, "You have an adventurous spirit."

"Not anymore. My parents were venturesome and liked thrills, but it did them in."

He wanted to stay clear of the *parent* topic. "You mentioned you've traveled."

"In my youth, my parents often took me with them on travels. Never a normal trip like to Disneyland, I assure you."

"Like where?"

"My first trip, to Edinburgh Castle, my second, Siberia."

"Cockle shells and monkey tails. In Russia?" He didn't believe either would be a suitable trek for the very young.

"The very one."

His head tilted. "How old were you?"

"Four."

"Tell me it was summertime."

She stepped close and placed a palm on his tie. "Do you have a problem with cold?"

He drew in a breath and looked into her eyes. "I can't imagine taking a small child to the coldest place on earth."

She tilted her head. "You mean the Vostok Station or Eastern Antarctica."

"Don't tell me you've been there, too?"

"Fine, I won't." She patted his chest and her eyes sparkled. "Pray tell, monkey tails?"

"My bad. How cold does it get in the northern hemisphere anyway?" He *should* leave before her friendliness went any further, but he liked her.

"The coldest I've ever experienced was negative fifty-seven degrees Fahrenheit. It can be negative ninety, but then, even Missouri can get pretty cold with wind chill."

He shivered at the thought. Freezing wasn't his favorite temperature.

Letsea edged up toe to toe. She smoothed her hands up his arms with a spirited look in her eyes. He saw a teasing Letsea and his heartbeat quickened. He liked the vision of her and wished he could participate.

"So, you're a warm weather kind of guy, hmm?" she whispered.

Bracing her balance by grasping his arms, she stretched to reach her face up to his. Her green eyes darkened then closed. He gauged the intimacy of her body pressing against him and his reaction. Her lips touched his. He stood still. The muscles in his throat constricted, he relieved them with a forceable gulp and hoped she didn't hear it.

His natural urges created a tug of war between his feelings and conscience. He wanted to show her how much he'd been thinking the same all evening. An impulse to capitulate his lies and seize the moment begged. No way he could give in, he had obligations to his job.

Mmm, her lips were everything he imagined them to be.

He stood perfectly still.

She pulled back enough to look at him. Her voice barely audible, she whispered, "Don't you *want* to kiss me?" She blushed.

He moaned and hoped it was silent.

She dropped down from her tippy toes and lowered her head briefly. When she looked up, her eyebrows furrowed.

"Are you holding back because I'm hiring you? I'm not your employer. Yours is contract labor. You didn't even bring a contract for me to sign." She leaned away and studied his eyes. "Or maybe you're just not interested?" She let her hands drop. "I'm sorry, I didn't even consider—"

Her phone played the same tune he whistled at the speakeasy door. "Knock Three Times."

"My sister. I have to answer this before she files a missing person report. Stay, will you?"

She took another step back and answered the cell.

"Hi, Sis."

"It's about time!" Gwendolene's voice snapped, easily heard within the couple feet of distance. "Why haven't you been answering your phone? I've been worried sick."

"Sorry. I turned it off on the plane and forgot to turn it back on, until a couple minutes ago."

Her sister's voice shrieked from the phone, "What plane? Where are you?"

"Um...Phoenix."

"Arizona? What are you doing there? When did you go? When will you be back?"

"I left St. Louis yesterday morning. I'll be home tonight. Honey. Don't worry."

"Letsea, you can't take off around the country all by yourself. The kids are performing at the historical theatre and you'll miss it."

Gwen spoke to someone on her end, "Are you hearing this? Letsea's in Phoenix! Why would she go cross-country all alone and not tell me?"

"Is she all right?" A calm man's voice seemed to placate her. "You might ask why she's there."

"First, honey, I'm not alone. I'm with a friend. Second, I'll be home in time to see the children sing." Letsea leaned forward, patted Lock's arm, then gave a gentle squeeze.

"What do you mean you aren't alone? Is Seth with you?"

"No. My friend's name is Lockhart."

"You mean Trey Lockhart from the house Saturday?"

"You know him?"

"Sure, I've seen him around."

The man spoke into the receiver. "Do you mean Godrick Lockhart? The Special Agent with the FBI?"

Busted! He clinched his jaw.

Letsea stiffened. Her chin raised and eyes widened. She stepped toward the door.

"I'll explain," Lock whispered. He hoped she would let him.

"Doyle, how do you know Godrick Lockhart?" she asked, then her lips tightened in a fine line.

Lock wondered the same thing. How did her brother-in-law know him?

"He was an expert witness in a case my law firm handled three years ago. Great guy by the way. How long have you two been seeing each other? You didn't mention—"

His wife must have snatched the phone back. "You two can gossip when she gets home. Letsea, what time does your flight arrive?"

Letsea's face paled. If anything, her expression turned cold and distant. As she withdrew, he nearly felt that negative ninety degrees Fahrenheit. He, however, knew regret. She opened the room door and jerked her head toward the hall. He slipped out. The moment the door closed behind him, he heard her speak to her sister and stayed to listen.

"On Saturday, he was right there and you didn't mention you knew him or say hi to him." She paused. "I didn't make introductions because of the chaotic conditions."

Lock sighed. Soon Letsea would know he knew Chip and Lauren and their mother from the community center. He'd rather have been the one to tell her. He didn't know Mrs. Davis was the wife of Doyle Davis, Attorney-at-Law. Why not? Oh, definitely time for a change. Her voice faded as she went deeper into her room.

He glanced at the closed door then walked to the stairwell to use some pent-up energy. Halfway to his own room, he exclaimed, "Son of a monkey!"

CHAPTER 36

Middle of the night Tuesday, in her room at the
Renaissance Hotel, Phoenix, Arizona

L etsea spoke into her cell phone search mode, "Agent
Godrick Lockhart, FBI." Soon enough, words popped up
instructing her to enter her security code. "Oh snap! Not
again."

Quickly, an attempt to back out of the site, to close the phone
down, was refused. It read "Checking for a security pass." One
didn't exist. The big blue circle set to spin until it read: Access
Denied. Again, she'd get locked out. Apparently, one could not
successfully search for FBI agents, dead or alive.

With the phone on its charger, she rolled over on the bed
wanting to deny her actions. More ashamed than angry. He didn't
come on to her. Oh no... The other way around. Holy cannoli! An
FBI agent no less! How ridiculous to make a fool of herself to a
fed. Had he not declared himself a confirmed bachelor, she may
not have been so brave.

Come to think of it, as of late, the FBI seemed foremost in her
thoughts. First, the conversation with the author, Gunner Hardyn
Chase, his books with the main FBI character. Second, Paul E.
Reynolds. *Now, Agent Lockhart.* Under different circumstances
maybe....

No. Surely, she shouldn't trust anything he told her.

With the cell in limbo, she got up, used the room phone, and
called both the front desk and the airline to move her departure up.

Ten minutes later, still dressed, she was back on the bed with feet high on stacked pillows and arms stretched out. The full extent of embarrassment overwhelmed her. She searched for a way to release misgivings concerning her unwanted advance on Lock. Where did the bravery come from? She closed her eyes in disbelief of her audacity. *Why did I have to kiss him?*

Recollections of the last week spent with her parents came to mind. It was spring break. Memories were both sweet and painful. At home to see them before their last trip, because they always offered her calmness. She was in need of tranquility in preparation for both the upcoming finals, and the bar exam. Her father, always at ease, told her, "It's a temporary fear, princess. Feel it, discard it, and move forward." Thinking of his sayings made her laugh and cry, at the same time. "Life is an adventure. Enjoy it." Well, she *had enjoyed* dancing with Lock.

She felt her mother's arms wrapped around her from their last private conversation. "Princess, imagine yourself enjoying your heart's desire. Surrender every opposing thought. When you know you can live your dream, surrender it as well, my love. Let God take care of the details. Your job is to be aware of and follow the harmony as it flows into your life."

Her parents weren't even hippies. Although, Mother's parents were in that category.

As a little girl, she watched as her parents danced alone in the grand ballroom. Arm in arm, Mommy and Daddy swinging and swaying in the arms of love itself. Was it so wrong to think somewhere she held a possibility of finding a kindred soul mate?

"Sweet Lord, what has gotten into me? I need your help." Tears trickled down the sides of her face. "Am I wanting a husband and children of my own so much that I'm totally out of control?" Shaking her head sanctioned more emotions to rush in. Finally, with time to draw in and release a few slow deep breaths, she found peace. Until thoughts drifted to recent events.

Lock totally acted *into her*. His hands on her hips, he whispered in her ear, more than once. His humor. They moved with compatibility. Oh boy, he knew dance. The "Charleston", hah! No past boyfriends would ever have danced it. They laughed together, even at each other. A connection. Shared a teasing bond. *Unless, he's that good of an actor.*

A deep sigh escaped.

For a time, in the speakeasy's hidden room, she knew affection, tenderness between two.

By the very nature of her enjoyment, a belief of him caring for her evolved. To Agent Lockhart, she was nothing but a task. He worked undercover! Much like Uncle Paul, good at what he did.

Her face scrunched, inflamed by his deception. He probably followed her to Phoenix. His reason to be there, to spy on her, and boy, did she ever fall for it! Her hands clenched.

Of course Lock fell silent after asked if he was in the mob. He did have an ulterior motive and didn't want to lose his cover.

The harder the attempt to not let tears well up, the more they did. "Augh!" After she dated Seth Purser for three years there were no tears at their breakup. Why now?

She squeezed her eyes tight. Seth wasn't her desired soul mate. At least he was respectful, polite to her family. Neither was he intimidated by wealth or notoriety. Mostly, he stayed around long enough for her to believe he would eventually come around to her grandfather's wishes. Her eyes popped open. Her first tendency was to legally quash that well-intended trust fund with a sense of avenge. However, Granddad, a lawyer, knew what he put into effect with his document. His intention, to secure the future of the Brechenworth name. He hadn't meant to repress her future.

Why was she so embarrassed?

Lock, a part of her life for four days, never even a date. *Get over it!*

Artwork on the hotel room wall became a welcome distraction, until her eyes closed again. Reflection on those other than earthly conversations with Uncle Paul nipped at her conscience. *It's not like I can say, hey! Don't mind me, I'm just a spy.* Neither could Lock.

Agent Lockhart must have followed her to Union Station Friday morning. A false belief they happened to run into one another. Having been in a deep whisper with Paul's spirit, the waitress interrupted them. Forthwith, Lockhart appeared like a figure from the past. Paul poked and pushed, tried to separate her from him. The ghostly spirit must have known Lockhart was FBI. Why hadn't he warned her when they talked in the upper tower room?

Did she snuggle up to and kiss a married man? A spy, dare lie, if he had a wife. Oh, how smooth. Surely, he's married. A man so attractive, gentlemanly, and humorous most likely wouldn't get to his age and not have fallen in love. Plus, he refused to return her kiss. Probably protecting the sanctity of his marriage. She pursed her lips. Unless there was something wrong with her? Did he detect her anxiety about getting too old to bear babies? The medical Privacy Act could never allow the FBI access to her doctor's records. Or would they?

A glance at the cell phone reminded her why they put Lock on her trail. All from looking for information on Reynolds. *Will there be a second agent on my case for trying to look up Agent Lockhart?*

After a final swipe of the tears, she sat up and slipped on her shoes.

What terrible deed did they think her guilty of? Okay, probably sticking her nose where it didn't belong, surely, not anything illegal. When a ghost asked for help, you didn't refuse.

CHAPTER 37

St. Louis Lambert International Airport

L ittle Miss Change-of-plans Brechenworth forfeited her Tuesday morning in Phoenix to catch a red-eye flight home. Lock followed Letsea through the airport.

Outside, Bob, the security guy, waited at a cream-colored Cadillac limousine. The kind with a black carriage roof, to make the luxury car appear as a convertible. Odd look for a limousine, yet elegant. Over a decade old, it still it looked sharp. Another of the fifty-some cars, no doubt. The chauffeur opened the rear door for her and took the overnight bag. *So, who's watching the property while he's away?* Apparently, Bob had more than one position at the Brechenworth estate.

What might it take to make this situation right with her?

His ride pulled up. He tossed his bag in the colleague's back seat. "Thanks, pal."

"Lock, what are you up to?" asked Special Agent Don Pfeiffer.

"Thought I was chasing a pretty little rainbow. Turned out, I dug a hole."

"Been there, done that, my friend. So long as the hole isn't your grave. Can I help?"

"Sure, get me home. I need to catch some shut-eye and come up with a new strategy."

"Seriously, what's wrong? You look dog-tired."

"I've been ousted by a relative of my assignment."

Don grimaced. "I hate when that happens, ole boy."

Lock leaned his head back and pulled his hat over his eyes. *Old boy*, more like, Don being a good ten years his junior. Maturity was a steady creeper.

"You're home, buddy."

"Already? I must have dozed through the morning rush. I'd invite you in, Don, bar none, things are a little complicated right now. My parents are living with me. They're settling in."

"What happened?"

"Eminent domain, that's what."

"So, your bachelor pad is closed. Guess no card games for a while, eh?"

"I'll be up to it soon, at your house," Lock said, reaching for the door handle.

"Barbie isn't though. We can always rent a cabin."

"Sure, as long as we aren't called into duty, and there's the conundrum. I'm supposed to be on vacation and look at me. Thanks for the ride."

The smell of breakfast greeted him at the door. "Smells good, Mom."

"What a short trip. I didn't expect you home so soon. Come eat."

He sat at the table with his dad while his mother brought hot omelets to them. Mom wrapped her free arm around his neck and kissed his forehead.

At this rate, he might get spoiled. "What about you, Mom?"

"I'm getting mine now."

"Trey, I tried to open the upstairs door, it's stuck."

"It's locked, Dad. It's my office. Due to privacy issues, I keep it secure."

"I see. We've misplaced a box of sundries. I thought it might have made its way upstairs."

"Nope. It's probably in the garage. I'll check later. Don't concern yourself with the upstairs, okay?"

"Got it, Son. No trespassing into your workspace."

"Speaking of your job, Trey," his mother said as she set her plate down and joined them. "Have you thought any more of retiring? Regardless of the fact you don't like to discuss it. Margaret Ormsby and I were talking a few days ago, and it came up you ought to take your pension now. You could do people's taxes. No traveling. You'd be home, maybe meet a nice young lady and settle down."

His mother sat very still with her hands clasped under her chin, a slight smile fixed on her face.

"I take it you'd like that."

Her expression grew bright. His dad chortled, "Boy, howdy. Me too, for that matter."

"You have a look in your eye. Mom, are you thinking of a particular young lady?" Who knows, it might help him keep his mind off Letsea.

"I am. In fact, you asked about her house last week." Mom crossed her arms on the table in front of her, leaned forward, and glanced at a stack of mail between them, then reached for a card on top of the pile.

He remained silent as his parents exchanged a *look*. His father gently shook his head. Mother scrunched her mouth into an odd shape. "What's going on?"

"Your father got an invitation to attend a Christmas tea party. It's for people who volunteer a lot of hours in the community. Ever since he retired, he's been volunteering at the senior center helping folks with their genealogy charts. The tea party is at the Brechenworth estate. Your father refuses to send in the RSVP because it's volunteers only. Not enough space for them to bring a guest. I want him to go so he can describe it to me."

"Mom, haven't you been volunteering too? Picking up trash at the parks, and who knows what else?"

"Only a couple months, not nearly enough hours clocked-in to qualify for the tea party."

He looked back and forth between the two. "What does this have to do with me?"

"Your mother wants to introduce you to Miss Brechenworth."

He swallowed. "We're in different social leagues, Mom. What might Brechenworth and I possibly have in common?" He visualized his early morning fiasco.

"Letsea's not like that, Trey. I've been asked to use her first name." His mother bit her lip to control her excitement. "I know you'd like each other."

"Mom, most rich people aren't exactly excited to associate with IRS agents." He sighed. After he retired, lies could be put to rest.

"Sure, if they cheat on their taxes. She'd never do that. Letsea has put this Christmas tea party on for the last five years. She's dedicated to showing volunteers how much their work is appreciated. Even *she* volunteers with one of the children's homes and helps with food banks and the community center when they need things. Did you know the Brechenworth estate paid for their solar panels to help with the cost of utilities?" She got up to put her plate in the sink.

As a matter of fact, he did know it, from reviewing her tax statements. "How do you know all this, Mom?"

"I worked in a tea room for twenty years. People talk." Her fingers squeezed his shoulder.

He tried to focus on conversation, yet his mind was completely on Letsea. He saw a message where she tried to look him up through the Bureau's website. Not that she could have gotten anywhere. Still, he questioned at the confusion in Letsea's eyes. Could it have been disappointment? Guess he'd find out soon enough. His only decision at this point was *when* to call on her.

"I never got to bed last night. I'm going to sleep for a while." And figure out a new plan of action. Some vacation.

Eight o'clock Wednesday morning Lock sat in his car in front of the Brechenworth estate.

Several delivery trucks and vans arrived and parked on the circle drive between the houses. The person in charge, a ponytailed young woman, met each driver and pointed in some direction.

Tables, chairs, and plastic tubs were hauled inside. A decorating company carried rolls of evergreen swags along with large red bows. They hung them on both the mansion and the Queen Anne.

He drove forward for a better view. A black sports car, similar to his, pulled out of a secluded area in front of the house. Experience compelled him to notice the license plate as it sped away. He parked in the vacated spot.

One team set up the painted life-sized Nativity. The decorators were utilizing a large double-door entry. Unlike the front porch with tall steps, the west wing doors were level to the ground with a wide, slight ramp of a sidewalk leading to the circle drive between houses. A team worked steadily to install a green canvas canopy over the entrance. Beside the door a sequence of exceptionally tall Palladian windows allowed a glimpse of interior. Saturday, Letsea mentioned several Christmas activities that needed her attention. Presumably, he witnessed preparation for the Christmas tea. A party so avidly attended, a restraint on invitations became necessary.

It was vital he speak to her. Observation didn't show any effort toward estate grounds safety. No Bob to be seen. Perhaps all his protective services consisted of watching the singular monitor in the tower security office. *Professionally, when opportunity knocks, you don't ignore it.*

He exited the car, punched the fob, heard the click, and walked through the open gate, past the activity and directly inside the west end double doors.

Tuscan marble columns embellished the walls all the way to the minimum thirty-foot-high fresco painting, a bright blue sky with clouds and birds. The grandiose peak of the ballroom explained the extra height in the other rooms.

Matching marble fireplaces graced each end of the inside wall. He noticed a half-circle platform stage on the north end. The size of the room, even with the diffused wintery light from the windows, gave him a sense of the freedom dancers would feel while gliding across the floor. That's why she took dance lessons, she grew up with a private ballroom.

Ponytail girl with a clipboard stood atop the entrance staircase which led into the home's main hallway. Busy collaborating with a man from the rental supply company, was Letsea. Dressed in a Cardinals sweatshirt, tight-fitting jeans, and the ponytail, she appeared younger than her age. He blew out a deep breath. *On your mark, get set...*

She pivoted and glared directly at him.

He drew in a deep breath and stepped forward. *Go.*

Letsea stood on the ballroom entrance staircase, monitoring

setup progress. She spied *Agent* Godrick Lockhart across the room. He came forward a couple of steps and stopped.

What is he doing in my house?

She, with incessant eye contact and a brisk stride across the luxurious room, stopped toe to toe with him. Though frustrated, she knew not to emphasize it among others, and suppressed her emotions to a whisper. "Follow me." She pointed. With a sharp turn and swift walk across the ballroom, up the stairs, and through the long hall, Letsea knew he'd follow.

"Miss Brechenworth, your Christmas tree has arrived. Where exactly would you like it placed this year?" asked her secretary.

"Not in the mood, Marcia," she said with a scowl and held her palm up. "You decide."

In the receiving parlor, she tossed the check-off list on the table, folded her arms, and turned. "What do you want, *Agent* Lockhart?"

"I didn't intend for you to find out like that. I wanted to tell you," Lock said.

"Missed that opportunity, didn't you, Agent?"

"Unfortunately, yes."

"Why are you here?"

"I still need to talk with you."

"What will it take to be rid of you?" She didn't deny the pang of disappointment. She so enjoyed his company. How dare he stand there looking at her with such restraint!

"An official interview. Provide answers so I can wrap this up."

"I've been answering your questions for several days, and look, here you are. What else could I possibly tell you that you don't already know? If you'll recall, *I started* the inquiries."

He lowered his chin. "Please, Letsea."

"Don't you realize that with subterfuge you've lost your first-name privileges?" She pinched the bridge of her nose and turned away. And there it was, a tweak of guilt. In the form of remorse. Revealing the reason for her interest would not happen. Her stealthy uncle Paul's spirit was still safe from the FBI.

Chatter resounded from the main parlor, where young people were setting up the twelve-foot tree and hanging fresh drapes of pine branches. She preferred privacy. "Meet me next door at the Queen Anne house at eleven-thirty."

"Fine. Thank you."

She pointed to the doorway, and he tipped his hat and left. An inclination to stomp a foot altered her thoughts to a memory of her father. *Feel the emotions, discard them, move forward.* "Yeah right," she muttered. "Easy-peasy, Daddy."

Letsea snatched up her check-off list and headed out to find Marcia. She paused in the main parlor and watched Agent Lockhart walk out of the gate. Already remorseful, she sighed. *Why did I just do that?*

CHAPTER 38

11:15 a.m. Wednesday, Agent Lockhart officially at the flamboyant Queen Anne

ock parked on the flagstone drive. Most of the decorators' vans were gone. Good thing too, he thought, dark clouds indicated a heavy downpour soon. Each step on the smooth walkway brought him closer to an awkward interview with one exasperated Miss Brechenworth. He kicked a stray pebble then for good luck, picked it up, slipped it in his pocket, and thought of the promise to his boss to not tick her off.

He admitted to himself, he was glad for the opportunity to see inside the upper-class Victorian home. Not as gigantic as the mansion but still a vast extravagant old house. The fully decorated wraparound porch had fragrant pine garlands. Decidedly, Miss Brechenworth, as his mother did, appreciated Christmas candles in all the windows. Undoubtedly preset to light up at dark. They were on, due to the brewing thunderstorm. Was she encouraging welcome, hope, or peace?

Sparse raindrops fell.

He pushed the vintage doorbell button, surprised to hear the musical refrain from "We Three Kings." Softly, he sang along. "O star of wonder, star of night..." It reminded him of the music rehearsal later, at church.

The door opened. Rather than inviting him inside, Letsea appeared indifferent. She released a deep sigh and said, "I see you made it."

"Yes. Thank you."

"I'm not happy with you, you understand." A squint of her eyes confirmed her words.

"I still have an investigation to complete. I can wrap the whole thing up today with an interview. Or the Bureau can assign another agent if you prefer. I wouldn't blame you."

"Darn straight you wouldn't." At the raise of her voice tempo, a flurry stirred around her feet. Before he got a good look, it disappeared.

She looked above his eyes, to his hat. Keenly aware she liked his fedora, he was proven right when her gaze softened a hint toward kindness.

Letsea stepped back and held the door wide open. "Well then, let's get this interrogation over with."

Not exactly welcoming words. One step inside and she stopped him.

"First, Agent Lockhart, I'd like to see your credentials." She had one hand still on the door, as if ready to slam it in his face in a heartbeat.

Okay, she hadn't softened. He flipped open the special ID wallet for her to see.

Letsea reached to take it. He pulled it away.

"Don't touch."

Her hand dropped to her side as she stepped closer to study the ID. "How do I know it's real?"

"Take my word for it."

She raised an eyebrow. "Since when can I trust you?"

"Take your brother-in-law's word for it."

"So, you really are with the Department of Justice. Might as well come in."

He came to a standstill at the elegance of the late nineteenth-century home. The floors, walls, doors, and staircase were all embellished by the use of different types of beautiful woods. Light shades of maple to the dark walnut. As if he'd stepped back in time.

If his mother should tour this house, she'd talk of it for years. The warmth of the home surrounded him even though its owner dispersed a chill.

A corner of his lips curved up as he hung his hat on a high hook of the large cherry wood Scarborough House hall tree. His overcoat next, and he peeked in the center mirror to be sure his hair wasn't askew. *Here goes nothing.* His dad would add, "Could be the start of something great."

"I made coffee. If you want some, it's in there." She pointed through the curved French doors to the round turret.

He stepped closer and leaned toward her.

"What? You aren't going to *frisk* me?" he said, hoping to lighten the mood.

"Why should I?"

Her cheeks reddened, enhancing her beauty. He'd seen her blush before, but not knowing how to answer her, he didn't.

She asked, "Do I need to?"

"No." Although he wouldn't mind if she did. Matter of fact, he'd enjoy it.

"Are you carrying a gun?"

"I am."

"Good, I'm sure you're safer with it," she said then blinked before she led him into the round room.

He admired the stately turret, even though furnished in other than Victorian furniture. Somewhere along the line, probably decades ago, someone updated the décor except for the federalist drop-front secretary with its tall glass-door bookcase. He also noticed a formal silver tray with a silver coffee set on an antique tea cart.

A classy meet-and-greet waiting room. He doubted she'd bother to invite him into the inner sanctum of the house this time. However, she cared for his safety, a positive start. "Thank you for receiving me."

"As if I had a choice," she muttered.

That quick, the mood changed. He reached for the coffeepot.

"Don't touch," she said.

Payback, he thought. He stopped, stepped away, and held his hands clear of the silver.

She motioned to a mid-century channel-back chair. "Sit."

Coffeepot in her hand, she looked at him. "Black, isn't it?"

"Yes." Oh, she'd serve him after all. *Nice.*

After handing him a cup in saucer, she put cream and sugar in her own, and settled across the room and held the cup in front of her. She used it like a shield. *Interesting.*

"Where do we start, Agent Lockhart?"

"Letsea, I hoped to have kept it simple from the beginning." He would not willingly forfeit the use of her first name.

"I know. This task is keeping you from your Christmas vacation. Honey, we lost all count of simple when you showed up in Phoenix," she said.

Honey? His lips spread to a more prolific smile. He needed something to help soften her mood. "True. I am glad I went though."

Aw, another blush on her cheeks and a light in her eyes. Were her thoughts of them dancing at the speakeasy? His were. Indeed, he'd never forget their night of dancing.

A shake of her head then her face paled.

He recalled how the night ended. *Drat!* He wished for a do-over from the beginning of the whole assignment.

"What do you want to know, Agent? I have nothing to hide."

She stared into his eyes as if waiting to see if he believed her. When she finally looked away, she glanced up and to her right.

Doggone! A flat-out lie? Avoidance yes, but lying? What was she hiding? He pulled out a tiny digital recorder and set it on the coffee table. "I need to record this."

"Whatever."

He pushed the red button. "This is Special Agent Godrick Lockhart, FBI, speaking with Letsea Brechenworth of Saint Charles, Missouri." He spoke the date and numbers into the device. "This interview is in reference to Special Agent Paul E. Reynolds of the Bureau of Investigations from 1920 until his death August 9, 1929."

Closely watching her reactions, he addressed her. "Letsea, a couple years after Reynolds' death, his widow married one of your great-great uncles, correct?"

She nodded.

"You'll need to speak your response."

She leaned toward the recorder. "To my knowledge, yes."

"I've heard you call him Uncle. He is not an uncle of yours. Correct?"

She cleared her throat and raised her eyebrows. "I use 'uncle' figuratively. The first husband of one of my great-great grandfather's brother's wife."

"You've mentioned to me, Reynolds was struck on the back of the head. Where did you learn this information?"

She straightened tall in her chair, glanced up—again to the right. "I don't remember. I must have read it somewhere."

Now she is lying. Where did she find it?

Body language was not a scientific law, since people were different by nature. They created their own distinct responses and habits. Hers were not consistent with previous conversations. Looking up and to the right often indicated one used their creative imagination to invent a reply.

She definitely wanted to avoid revealing something. What she was up to?

"Tell me why you believe he had a lump on his head. In Phoenix, you mentioned you imagined it. Why?"

She shrugged and shut down by squeezing her eyes shut as she gripped the chair arms.

"Come on, Letsea. A simple version of what you're thinking."

Her eyelids opened.

No mystery there, she glowered at him suspiciously, even tried to laser burn him with fervent direct-eye contact. He understood her frustration. Something she mentioned in private conversation became a point of contention. "What's wrong? Just say it?"

"Why is the FBI so interested in me?"

"For one thing, no information on a head bump was ever released."

CHAPTER 39

Noontime, Letsea interviewed in the Queen Anne house turret

"**A**gent Lockhart, you tracked me down before I ever mentioned a bump on Uncle Paul's head. I suppose your interest in it means it's true."

All of a sudden, Paul's spirit spoke loud and clear.

So, just tell the man what he wants to know.

Rex Kitty screeched.

Letsea's heart jumped into overdrive at having clearly heard Paul, with Lock in the room, no less! No rough undertone of a distant whisper. Clear as a bell. She looked at Lock. He couldn't have missed Reynolds' voice.

"Oh, snap!" Letsea cringed.

The frightened feline jumped, appeared to fly several yards from the top of the desk bookcase. He liked to perch and watch activities in the room. He landed in her lap then tried to climb over her shoulder.

Lock flinched. The cup clattered to the saucer. Letsea believed the cat got out of the bag, quite literally. She was positive Lock heard Uncle Paul's voice. No keeping the ghost a secret. She petted her cat and sat still to watch for a reaction from the one man she could physically see. First, Lock leaned forward to put the china on the table.

"Thanks for the coffee. No breakage." He stood and blurted, "Now, what in the world is that anyway?"

Tell him, Paul repeated.

She couldn't believe Paul wanted Lock to know of his phantomlike presence. "What?" she snapped, in dispute with Paul.

Rex Kitty's hair stood on end as he clamored. She worked at pulling her pet down to her lap as he fought. Her face tightened. What would Lock's further reaction be to having heard Uncle Paul's voice? She didn't know how to answer his question.

Lock closed in over her, his eyes wide. "What do you mean 'what'? What is that thing?"

She looked up to the flat ceiling. She never considered the Queen Anne might have a whispering arch. Having grown up there, she never noticed even an echo.

Paul's spirit adopted a combative tone.

Tell him about me. He wants to know. Go ahead. I'm not afraid of him.

Rex Kitty shrieked and pawed again. She held him tighter. "I don't believe you!" her sharp voice aimed at the unseen phantom scaring her cat. *Sure, no reason for Paul to fear an FBI agent.* She felt differently. She liked her life enough to not want to be institutionalized for hearing discombobulated spirits.

"What did I say that was so wrong?" Lock asked.

He looked confused then reclaimed calmness. It dawned on her he may not have heard Uncle Paul speak after all.

Several times, she blinked and tried to center her thoughts as though the hub of a three-ring circus with Lock, Kitty, and Paul all focused on her alone. First with hesitation, then she asked, "You mean my cat?"

"Is that what it is? Domestic or something else? It looks like some kind of mythological creature."

"He's a Cornish Rex." Why hadn't Lock heard Paul's spirit? Kitty obviously did.

"So, something else, then." Lock held out a hand toward Kitty. "I've never seen a cat with such a look before. Such long skinny legs, long tail, and good heavens, what big ears you have," he said to Kitty. "They look like ears of a rabbit. What did you do, have it shaved? He's so wrinkled."

Amused by people's reaction to the Cornish Rex for years, she said, "His name is Rex Kitty." At his name, the feline turned around, stood on her lap, showing his full height and face.

"Is it now?" Lock bent forward to scratch between the cat's

long ears. "And look at those big blue eyes. Almost humanlike."

Kitty turned playful, crooned his head and his supremely long ears against Lock's fingertips.

"Nice kitty. Are they always so tall and thin? And have such long ears?"

"You make him sound like the wolf in 'Little Red Riding Hood.' Generally tall. They have one layer of hair instead of three."

He interacted with her cat, and as she relaxed, her anger waned. His reaction was more like the playful Lock she knew in Phoenix. Not the agent with an interrogation still to do.

"How long have you had him?"

"A gift from a friend ten years ago."

"Oh. I guess Rex Kitty has withstood the test of time."

The cat started meowing and batting at the shiny cuff link on the sleeve of Lock's dress shirt. "Rex Kitty, be careful."

"He's fine. No sharp claws, from what I see."

"I keep them trimmed. I have to, with antiques everywhere."

"Do you think he'll let me hold him?"

She scooped him up and handed Kitty to Lock. Not Agent Lockhart, rather Lock. They had gotten off track and she was grateful for the reprieve.

"He's so light and incredibly soft. I can't believe how blue his eyes are and look at those round pupils. Not thin slits like I usually see." Lock sat back and stroked the cat.

"Meow, meow, meow."

Pleased, Lock appeared more comfortable. "The pupils aren't always so open. It's getting dark in here. I should turn on the lights." She reached to a floor lamp.

"Meow, meow."

"Talkative, isn't he?"

She snickered. "You have no idea."

"Miss Brechenworth?" Pauline called from the back of the house.

"I'm in the turret, Pauline."

"Oh. I don't mean to disturb you. It's after twelve. I brought lunch." In the doorway, she stopped and stared at Lock.

Letsea watched as he stared back at Pauline.

"Why, Trey, what are you doing here?"

"Um. Uh," he stammered.

"Don't you even think of harassing Miss Brechenworth with an audit. She's one of the most generous, honest people you'll ever meet."

He stared. "Not at all, Pauline." He stood, and set Rex Kitty on the floor.

"You two know each other?" Letsea asked.

"Oh, I've known him since his boyhood. I didn't know you two knew each other. Oh, Trey, your mother must be thrilled! I don't know why she hasn't told me."

"Uh. Pauline, Mom doesn't know we know each other. Please don't mention it before I get a chance to tell her."

Pauline patted her cheeks and scrunched her eyes, made the motion to lock her lips. "Tick-a-lock. I can't wait to hear her tell me. Sure, I won't say anything."

Letsea ping-ponged back and forth, watched and listened. "What am I supposed to know of this?" she asked and smirked.

Lock stepped up and gave Pauline a quick hug. "Thanks."

"I didn't know who you had here. Marcia said plus-one for lunch. So, I brought enough stew for two, fresh bread, dessert, and there's ice cream in the kitchen freezer. I'll leave you two alone." Pauline left through the back door, and Letsea heard the woman singing all the way. "On the first day of Christmas, my true love gave to me...."

Letsea raised her eyebrows. "An audit, Trey? Who are you, really?"

A hair-raising blast of thunder caused her to jump.

Ka-Boom!

Letsea felt the vibration shake the house. "Wow! Just how high *is* the authority of the FBI anyway?"

Paul piped in, *You, have no idea!*

CHAPTER 40

Lock carried the service tray, following Letsea into the kitchen. "Tell me how you got information on a head bump."

Letsea looked out the windows above the sink. All she hid was a disgruntled spirit. *Okay, ghost. Those aren't even supposed to exist, are they? Hah!* The image she saw in the tower window made it clear Paul *did* exist.

He placed the coffee tray on the countertop. "Now there's a downpour if ever I've seen one."

His elbow brushed her arm. She turned her head away and briefly closed her eyes to pause. Even after the night in her room in Phoenix, she wanted to feel friendliness toward him. "Sure is." She busied herself in the kitchen, warming the pot of stew and the coffee. She pulled out a clean cup and saucer for him and filled both their cups.

"There are plates in the cabinet, if you want to set the table." If kept busy, maybe he'd forget his question. "Remember the bowls."

She opened the plastic container of dessert. "I hope you like Gooey butter cake."

"Immensely. Well?" he asked. "You haven't answered my question yet."

It thundered.

She leaned toward the kitchen window. "What causes thunder, I wonder?"

"Lightning."

She didn't expect an answer. She knew what caused thunder.

She simply wanted to get him off her case. "I hope it doesn't fill the rain gauge. I don't want the ground to be soft."

"Stop avoiding the subject, Letsea. It's my guess you've read someone's diary."

Man, he aimed for the jugular.

Thunder cracked and rolled.

Tell him, Paul reinstated his earlier insistence.

"Hm!" She glanced at Lock's face to see if his expression changed when Paul spoke. It didn't. Apparently, he was incapable of hearing Paul. Why? She'd played with the Whispering Arch at Union Station all her life and never knew it to be selective.

Tell him!

Rex Kitty screeched and ran out of the kitchen.

"What a delayed reaction to the thunder," Lock said after the cat ran away. "Don't tell me Kitty can't hear with those rabbit ears."

Paul proved to be insistent. *Tell him and while you're at it, tell him my pocket watch belonged with family. Not stored away in a file. Tell him that!*

"I can't." *Oh, snap!* she was unable to handle this. The FBI agent looked at her as though she were crazy while a ghost filled with tension repined from the ethers.

"You can't what?" Lock asked. He tapped the recorder on the kitchen table. "This is still running."

Tell him!

She tilted her head toward the ceiling and released a deep sigh. She needed out of this. She spoke to both of them, "I can't." Mentally she begged Uncle Paul for relief.

"You can't what?" Lock asked again.

"I can't explain it."

"What are you *not* telling me?" Lock pressed.

"Call it woman's intuition, if you will."

Paul persisted, *Tell him!*

Lock insisted, "Tell me."

"Oh no!" *Not both of them! Simultaneously no less. Men! And ghosts!*

"Excuse me." Abruptly Letsea dashed to the servants' back stairs and raced to the second floor. Hands gripped the circular banister as she looked up to the domed ceiling at the center of the house. The round stairwell was open from the main floor all the way up past the third floor. She whispered, "Now talk to me."

Perhaps he will find it within himself to help you clear that awful rumor, said Paul.

"It doesn't make sense to tell him you're a ghost. I can't, please don't ask me again."

"Meow, meow, meow." Rex Kitty was being deliberately loud. He stood at the bottom of the foyer staircase, beckoning her. "Meow, meow, meow."

She walked downstairs, picked up Kitty, and sat on a lower step.

Lock came into the foyer from the kitchen. He sat beside her, propped his forearms on his knees, holding the recorder. "What else have you got?"

She sighed and reluctantly said, "It's my understanding Uncle Paul wanted the pocket watch to be returned to Aunt Mildred."

Thanks for telling him. Paul's voice sounded civil again.

After a sigh, she leaned back with her elbows on a step behind her. Perhaps if she listened with one ear to Paul, the other to Lock....

Lock angled himself to face her. "It's not like the watch was worth anything at that point. Presumably ruined, underwater for three days."

Letsea frowned. "It could have been repaired, if they got it to a jeweler in time."

"It's still evidence in an unsolved murder investigation. It revealed the time of death from when it stopped," Lock explained.

She listened to Paul's explanation in her ear and repeated parts of it. "Yes, I know. It stopped at 1:03. It was an 18-karat gold, precision clockworks, pocket watch. The BOI, FBI, whichever, should have returned it to Mildred. She wanted it back. It has—I mean, it had, a special meaning. Maybe she wanted it for their son."

"It was ruined. What good would it do anyone anyway?" Lock asked.

"Since when does sentiment need a reason to be of consequence?"

"I figured it was a wristwatch. So, this confirms you do have inside information. The time on his watch wasn't public either."

A barb stabbed her from his words. "What's that supposed to

mean? I read it in the Phoenix papers."

"The time released to the public said exactly 1:00, not 1:03. You obviously have or you've read a diary or a written source perhaps belonging to the family."

That, she thought, could be her out, but to what lengths would he go to get his hands on a diary that may or may not exist?

"Letsea, how did you know the time on the watch read 1:03? Certain information not made known to the public may have been mentioned to his widow."

She wanted a good cry, but was afraid, she'd nervously laugh instead. She wished for a family journal to explain everything. The whole story bound in a nice little book would be easier to believe than a persistent apparition.

She sat up, and Kitty moved over to Lock's lap. Letsea placed her face in her hands. "It's all so personal to me. I can't explain why." Knowing she muffled her voice, she stayed put and hoped he'd leave.

"Come back to the kitchen," he said. "The stew is hot. I've set the table. You need to eat. Then I have some information you should know about your beloved uncle. I think you deserve to know Agent Reynolds may not have been the stellar man you think him to be."

Chapter 41

uriosity as a driving force, Letsea wondered where Lock planned to take this. "What do you mean by 'Reynolds wasn't who I think he was'?"

Lock wagged a finger. "Eat first. We'll talk after lunch."

Did he think his information would make her lose her appetite? "Fine. At least tell me how you know Pauline." Best to avoid the ghostly eavesdropper anyway.

"She's my mother's best friend. You know, I'm surprised she hasn't retired by now."

"Me too. Most of the staff retired after my grandparents died. I'm glad she's still with me. I have great appreciation for Pauline."

He pushed the plate of fresh bread closer to her. "Apparently, she does for you too. Speaking of her, this stew is delicious."

"My great-grandmother's Irish stew recipe."

"Do you have an Irish bloodline?"

"She did. My great-grandfather met her in Dublin. Her grandparents owned a pub and eatery, ran by family."

He raised his eyebrows. "My mom's side does too. Is Brechenworth Irish?"

"My great-great grandfather didn't have family. He ran away from an orphanage-workhouse as a boy and never knew a real name or a birthdate."

"I've heard similar stories. My father is into genealogy, maybe he could help you learn more of the name."

"I already know. He made it up. He took parts of names of people who were kind to him and created his own. Then gave his son the same name, thereby starting our family heritage."

"That's what you meant by the 'first Brechenworth.' I wasn't sure. Where did he run to?"

"An East Coast harbor where he got a job on a ship. The captain mentored him. Ships became his home and he sailed the seas. He ended up married to the owner's daughter. Their son, my great-grandfather, took the family shipping trade to a higher level. My grandfather, however, suffered seasickness. Between a baby who couldn't be on the water and my great-great grandparents ready to retire and settle on firm ground, they sold the fleet. *Viola!* St. Charles is home."

"It's nice you know the history."

Even after her faux pas, he remained easy to talk with. Her attempt to persuade him into a kiss didn't seem to affect him though.

"I need to organize it. Family history packed away in oodles of trunks." She shrugged. "I've been busy trying to grow the estate funds to support its future. Maybe for a museum, so the name and its history will be remembered."

"How do you do it? You don't have a business, do you?"

"Managing this estate is my career. I focus on investments for growing the trust and my own future. We also have my maternal grandparents' properties in Vale."

"We? You and your sister?"

She nodded. "And Aunt Mae, Mom's sister. A property manager handles leasing and rentals for us."

"I see."

"Don't tell me you already knew."

"I looked at numbers, although I didn't know all the details."

All? What did her income have to do with Reynolds? Before she became agitated with him all over again, she changed the topic. "So, your father does genealogy charts?"

"Dad has a master's degree in American history. He worked the National and Missouri Parks. Retired a couple years ago, he's been volunteering at the senior center ever since. Helping folks to discover their family trees and roots."

"Does he spend a lot of time doing it?" she asked.

"He probably averages three days a week there."

"Is he coming to the Volunteers Christmas Tea? We're setting up for it now."

Lock tapped a finger on the table. "He didn't return the RSVP. He wants to wait until Mom can go with him. Hopefully next year. She's only been retired for a couple months and hasn't put in enough hours to attend."

Letsea lowered her face and released a deep sigh. "I should have foreseen this happening." When she looked up, he tilted his head.

"A few years ago, I threw a Christmas tea party as a tribute to community volunteers who put in a lot of their time. It's grown every year. In fact, this year there were so many volunteers I ran out of space to let everyone bring a plus-one. Which is exciting, on one hand. Not so much when someone doesn't want to attend alone. St. Charles is an ideal place to live, and everyone is so nice and helpful, but this may be the last volunteers' tea party. Or I need to reconfigure my whole plans for next year."

"How many seats will your ballroom hold?" he asked.

"One hundred and sixty with tables."

Lock glanced at the clock and drummed his fingers. "My mother managed a hotel conference center before she switched to a tea room. Maybe she can help with ideas."

He'd mentioned her before. "Your mother?"

"What do you want to know?"

"Her name might be nice."

"Alice Lockhart."

"Is she the Alice from the downtown Settlement Tea Room? She recently retired."

He bobbed his head.

"She's your mom? I know her! What a sweetheart, so uplifting and positive."

"Yes, my mom retired. She's been manager, cook, and her favorite position, waitress. Mom's a people person."

Letsea recalled Alice's kindness to her. Through her parents' ordeal, many close friends shied away. The most common excuse, *we don't know what to say*. Who would? Even the minister of their church struggled with visitations. All too known through media and gossip, she went to the Congo with her grandfather, to find a resolution to the kidnapping.

Instead of consoling, most friends avoided the family. Her

grandparents were crushed by the sudden lack of their companionship. Flowers galore, visitors near zilch. Some people cannot handle a tragic situation. Although the funerals were well attended, very few volunteered communication. Deputy at the time, Bill Ruell, his wife, and Alice, however, did chat with her afterward.

On her first time to the tea room after the funerals, Alice placed a long-stem white rose on her reserved table and offered sweet condolences. She remembered her recent visit with Alice at the community center.

Alice wanted to introduce her to her "paragon of a son." She put a hand to her warm cheek. Unhappily, she remembered Lock's insistence in the speakeasy's hidden door, he *never* intended to marry.

"Would your father come if your mother came with him?"

Lock chuckled. "I'm sure of it."

"Please tell them to call Marcia and RSVP for two. Today. Don't delay."

"Okay."

"I'll text them now." He pulled out his phone and started typing.

"Call her."

His eyebrows pinched. "It's easier in text."

"Why?"

"After I tell you what I know about Agent Reynolds, you might not want anything to do with me or my family."

Letsea looked at the cake on her fork, stabbed some ice cream, and swallowed. She pulled her phone out and called Marcia. "Add two for the tea, name's Lockhart. I'll fill you in later." She clicked off and put her phone away.

"Your parents are now officially registered. They are safe. You, I'm not so sure of."

As a diversion, she speared her fork into the frozen treat. "Speak your mind, Agent Lockhart. Let's get it over with."

He swallowed his last bite of cake and dabbed his lips with his napkin.

Letsea tapped the points of her fork on his empty dessert plate. "Stop stalling," she goaded. His hesitation made her nervous and no one deserved to be a witness of her anxiety.

"First, Letsea, if you do have access to a private journal or letters, please understand I'm not trying to take them away from you or any family member. Although, I increasingly believe there is something. And from what you've already mentioned, your information could help finally unravel a century-old cold case."

"Lock, it's all I want. To clear him of his alleged suicide. It makes no sense."

"It might. If you knew the bigger picture."

Lock appeared to analyze her. Watched her every move.

He cleared his throat. "According to the file I have, Agent Reynolds drank hard." He put his hand up. "I know, it's difficult to believe, especially as a federal agent during the Prohibition. I'm sorry to be the one to tell you, he most likely was an alcoholic."

No, no, no! thundered Uncle Paul's tumultuous response.

Letsea squeezed her eyes closed, her body tensed, hoping dishes wouldn't start flying.

Kitty jumped midair and shrieked. Lock reached out and caught Rex Kitty and attempted to cradle the squirming feline in his arms. "Good thing he hasn't any claws."

I was not *an alcoholic!* Paul's voice shook with emotion.

Lock stroked Rex Kitty's neck and spine. "He must have heard distant thunder. Are you a nervous kitty?" he asked the cat.

Letsea put her fork down. "Lock, you really didn't hear anything?"

Lock's face looked blank. "Well, it is still raining cats and dogs." He held the cat out to look at its face and smiled. "Unintended pun, Kitty."

All the while, she listened to Paul E. Reynolds rant on and deny the statement. It took all her resistance to not respond to the upset spirit.

"He was dying," Lock said. "The man was what they termed as a skirt-chaser. Letsea, Reynolds had gonorrhea."

Letsea closed her eyes, assumed that was the reason Aunt Mae didn't want to discuss Reynolds, the past scandal that embarrassed family. Paul went into a nonstop diatribe on J. Edgar Hoover's protectiveness of the Bureau and his failure to admit the investigation turned into a fiasco.

If he were alive, she'd tell him to take a few slow deep breaths. Were ghosts capable of breathing?

Paul stopped talking. After a long silence, he calmly said,

Unless, not solving my murder wasn't a slipup. Consider the possibility I was actually murdered by the feds. They couldn't solve it because it was a government frame-up. All real clues were distorted on the spot. Perhaps some of the reporters were planted, secret operatives.

Her jaw dropped open then she finally whispered to Paul, "Why?" Then looked at Lock.

Lock placed a hand on the table and slid it toward her. "I know it must be hard to hear."

She closed her eyes again and listened intently.

Paul continued. *The arrest warrants I worked on to process. A couple of them were for government employees.*

She cocked her head to the side and opened her eyes. "Lock, who do you think really killed JFK?"

Lock's eyes widened and he leaned far back. "Whoa. Where did that come from?" He pinched the bridge of his nose. "You know, not everyone can change topics as quickly as you."

"I thought Paul's death might have been part of a conspiracy. I'm so—"

"Don't apologize. I've noticed sometimes it's difficult to keep up with you. And yes, my job, my burden."

I have nothing to apologize for! She wished to ignore that she kissed him the other night. However, Lock avoided the possibility of conspiracy.

The ghostly presence hung nearby, but paused. Paul wanted her to relay messages from him to Lock.

Lock said, "Let's not talk about JFK. It's a lengthy conversation and I still need to wrap this up. I also need to be elsewhere at four o'clock."

"Fine by me. I have plenty still to do. Please, let's put an end to the drama and cover the facts," she hoped both Paul and Lock got her message.

"Letsea, just days before he died, Reynolds took out a life insurance policy on himself. Most likely, he took his own life. He was terminally ill. Why else kill himself? It explains the count of events."

Paul roared, *Lies! It's exactly what I need for you to dispel! All those lies!*

How does Lock not hear Paul?

"You see—"

"Stop." Letsea pushed her palms straight out in front of her. "Lock, wait. Give me a minute here." She needed Lock not to talk in order to hear Paul. "About the policy," she whispered. Lock opened his mouth and she waved a hand and shook her head.

Paul said, *I bought the insurance policy right after the St. Valentine's Day Massacre in Chicago. All of us operatives with any sense were trying to protect our families in case of our death. They lied, saying it was just before my death.*

Letsea told Lock, "Maybe because he realized how dangerous his job really was. He wanted to leave a sense of security for Mildred. Maybe you should recheck the date he purchased the policy. I think you'll find it was in late February of 1929. Right after the famous mob murders in Chicago." She closed her eyes to listen to Paul again. "Okay," she mumbled.

In a softened voice Paul said, *I loved Millie. I always worried for her safety. If I was ill, I had no knowledge of it. If my body was diseased, did the coroner put it on my death certificate? No. He did not. Did they list it on an autopsy report? No. Ask him, see if he knows. Tell Agent Lockhart to check it out. By the by, I was not a "skirt chaser." All a ruse, to give the impression I drank and went for the girls. Apparently good at my job, to a point. My assignment was to fit in with the party set. All part of being a federal agent.*

"Lock, listen to me! Paul E. Reynolds loved his family. He didn't take his own life. He was murdered." Once more, she looked up toward the ceiling, hoping Paul heard. "He wasn't sick. I saw a copy of the death certificate. Shot in the heart. There's no mention of any disease."

Lock watched her and spoke calmly, "The disease didn't cause his death, Letsea. It was a close-range gunshot wound. And was most likely self-inflicted."

NO! I was murdered!

Letsea looked Lock directly in his eyes. "Have you read a medical examiner's report? Is there even one to read? Probably not. You have been misinformed, Agent Lockhart. Reynolds was murdered."

"Yes, I have read it," Lock said.

Don't believe him, Paul warned.

"You'll never convince me, Agent. If one does exist, you best

THE DEAD FED SAID

have a forensic examination done of the paper. Learn the real date it was drawn up. Likely years, even decades, after his death. Who is going to question the newfound existence of false evidence planted afterward to appear real? It was created to cover their made-up story. Ultimately, the leader of the FBI refused to stand by and have the Bureau's reputation less than exceptional by not solving a murder of one of their own."

Lock spoke softly, "His own wife told the FBI he had gonorrhea."

That's not how it happened. They told her I was infected, then she uttered the words back in disbelief. They referenced her repeating it as "she told them." They do things like that. Watch what you say. Why do you think people always have the right to have their lawyer present? Authorities are allowed to lie to suspects and the public in order to trick them.

"You are talking conspiracies." Lock sounded ready to quash Paul's perspective. "That's ridiculous."

"Oh, really? A man does not shoot himself in the heart then throw himself over the rail of a small bridge, into a canal. Followed by driving his rental car back to town and parking it beside his hotel. The most unexpected act of all, even a dead special agent of the Department of Justice cannot professionally clean, wipe away all fingerprints and debris from his rental car. Can't you see a major cover-up? The whole issue proves it."

CHAPTER 42

"Letsea, there's a perfectly good explanation." Lock watched her lift an eyebrow and fall silent.

He continued, "Did you know a bus departed from the Hotel Adams every hour, every day? It drove directly to and from that very canal spot. The schedule advertised in the papers. It's simple enough. He picked his spot, drove back to the hotel, then took the bus out to the canal and stayed out there. He probably shot himself standing on the bridge's edge so he would fall in. Therefore, it would look like murder, and his wife able to collect the five-thousand-dollar insurance policy on him."

"Your narrative has so many holes in it." Her eyes narrowed. "If I hadn't seen your shield, I'd have to question if you really were FBI."

"Ouch." He leaned back, crossed his arms, and watched her.

"Why, pray tell, should any city bus travel twelve miles to a canal footbridge in the middle of farmland just to turn around and go back to town?" She tapped fingernails on the table. "And every hour no less? Without a newsworthy story, there's no logic for the trip."

Lock stared at her and silently agreed. *That's credible. Why should a bus do that?* He watched as she stepped over to the sink, emptied her coffee out, and poured a fresh cup.

"The only reason, Agent, to meet the demands for curious sightseers to see the location where the body of the dead fed was found floating, caught, and swirling in the water. When we have a chance to look at the copies of the newspapers before August 9th,

I'll bet a dollar to a donut there were no bus tours driving people out to the middle of nowhere. After the discovery of his body? Yes, that I'll concede to."

He inclined his head. "Sounds right." His version, lame, he knew. It didn't take a detective to see the discrepancies. It's what they gave him to dish out for this assignment.

She refreshed his coffee before sitting back at the table. "Anything I've ever read on a bus schedule they stop at places with public accommodations. A hotel, restaurant, bus station, or somewhere touristy or special events."

"Sounds right," he repeated.

"Come on, Agent Lockhart. Can't you see the man did not do this to himself? For Pete's sake! If a man took a bus to the middle of nowhere, got off but not back on, don't you think the bus driver and other passengers would remember him when the story of his disappearance then his death hit the front-page news?"

She crossed her arms and legs, under the table. He knew because she swung a foot and the toe hit into his shin. He'd let it go, wanting to keep the conversation moving.

She sighed. "Especially since it was such a big deal, it led to a state-wide search for his rental car. With G-men all over the place, no less. An active cover-up took place. If not, they needn't send you here to stop my research."

Lock pushed his cup forward and inched his chair backward, away from her walloping toe. He hoped she didn't realize what she was doing. Officially assaulting a federal officer. "Point taken. It's worth checking into."

"I suspect you've been given a summary of his case file. When you check, I believe you will find as his assignment, he needed to blend in with the party crowd. Which meant drinking, flattering women, and since he was working on drug enforcement, he probably demonstrated interest there too. I don't know by whom, yet he *was* murdered."

He cleared his throat. "I understand you believe that. Nothing I tell you will change your mind. What else can I say?"

"You said it. Nothing. Examine the facts, Agent. The file you see, is it large?"

"It's long, Letsea."

"Really? Is it big enough to fill several large filing cabinets?

Because if it's not, you aren't seeing all of it."

"How do you know how many filing drawers it fills?" he asked with a stern voice, hoping she'd back down. "Are you basing your facts on some conspiracy theory?"

"Interesting you should ask. Feds usually focus on closing doors on other people's questions, not opening them, don't they?"

He wrenched sideways and scooted his chair back farther. "Let's not go there, Letsea."

"Why? Are you afraid of opinions different from the government's word on how things happen? Do you believe as citizens we shouldn't question everything? Isn't that why you're here now? To prevent me from digging deeper into the Agent Reynolds case? Some countries are well known for shutting up criticism by not only arresting but killing those who voice an opinion opposing their government leaders. The last I heard, we still have free speech.

"Let's face it, Lock, with JFK, no matter how artful a sharpshooter one man might be, no one gunman, with a single shot, could have pulled off all those extraordinary angles from one direction. And JFK, too surrounded by Secret Service when it happened. As you look through this case file, ask yourself, in his extensive investigations, what might Agent Reynolds have known, about whom? And who didn't want it to go any further? Consider the possibility his murder had nothing to do with any drug dealings in Phoenix. It may have been a setup to remove suspicion from the true suspect's location, like El Paso or Albuquerque, or even Washington D.C."

He relaxed since she called him Lock again. "Letsea, will you consider what I told you today?" He swallowed his coffee. Huh. She and his dad thought alike.

"If you will consider the points I made to you." She asked, "Are we done? I have more to do for this party than you can imagine."

He watched her step over and glance up the servants' stairs. When she looked back to him, she had a faint smile.

What's up there? "You do realize you are an enigma, don't you?" he asked as he stood to leave and tucked the recorder in a pocket.

"Under the circumstances, I'll take that as a compliment. What will you tell your boss?"

"It's a family thing and you already know more than I do. Promise me you aren't planning to make trouble." Her all-too-brief pleasantness fell away from her eyes and she stared. He waited.

"I'm not a troublemaker. I sincerely want his name cleared from the accusation of suicide." She headed to the foyer and stopped at the hall tree. "Oh, yes. I want all the scuttlebutt to disappear."

Although he still didn't know how to explain her to Chief, he would try to think of a way to help her feel satisfied with Reynolds' case. "Your uncle was never accused of suicide. Rather, as a suggestion of a possibility. It's still listed as an unsolved murder."

"They changed it to 'mysterious circumstances.' It used to say 'unsolved murder.' If they weren't still pushing the suicide issue, you wouldn't have arrived here prepared to sell me on the idea of it."

Dagnabbit! He did his best to paste a smile on his face. Her points were valid. All he could do was stick to the approved file. Although something was odd concerning Letsea's fervent determination in regards to a man she never knew. She intrigued him.

In front of the hall tree, Letsea watched as he slipped his overcoat on. "It's still raining enough for this," she said and handed him an umbrella.

"I'd like to consider this investigation officially closed. I'll see what I can do to help you with whatever this is with your uncle."

"I appreciate it."

He reached down and petted Rex Kitty's neck.

She held the door open and as soon as he stepped out onto the porch, he turned and cocked his head to the side.

"Thanks for your time and especially for letting my parents attend your tea party together. I wish you all success with it. If there's anything I can do to help, call me. I'll gladly volunteer."

He held out his hand to shake hers.

"Volunteer? You mean as a friend might offer?" she asked.

"Sure, friends. That's all I ask."

His manner gave him laugh lines, like Frank Sinatra, relaxed.

"Considering you are Alice's son, we could give it a try." *Did I just give him another point in his favor?*

"Speaking of my parents, Letsea, I'd appreciate your not mentioning to them that I'm an FBI agent."

"You mean, they don't know?" Her body tensed.

"I never wanted Mom to worry about me."

"And you thought she wouldn't if you were...what? Out in the world doing audits for the IRS? Lock, she's your mother. If she can't see you, she's going to worry no matter what."

"You're probably right. Before long, I plan to retire. I'd rather she doesn't find out until after I do."

Aw, sweet.

"You poor misguided fool. Moms worry. It's their self-appointed lifelong job. Your secret's safe with me." She squeezed his elbow and breathed through a tingle of contentment. *By all means, let's be friends.* Even Uncle Paul mentioned the goodness of having friends.

Lock paused and appeared at ease. "Thank you, Letsea." Then he left.

"Hmm, Rex Kitty, we ended on a pleasant note. Didn't we?" She stepped out on the porch with her cat and watched Lock walk back to his car.

He didn't look back. No wave. He walked to his car and drove away. *Who leaves without looking behind them?* She sighed. *A good friend would've waved. Oh. It's all right, he's a new friend.* Then it dawned on her she didn't wave to him either.

After he departed through the front gates, she went inside and looked up at the fedora he left hanging on a hook. Lifting it, she held it then breathed in the aromatic fragrance of him. Fresh, clean, and masculine. She whispered to Kitty, "Mm. Like him, very fine indeed."

Looking in the mirror she placed it on her head and tilted it forward toward her left eye. After modeling it, she tucked her ponytail inside and started to leave. With a pause, she stood afoot of the main staircase and hollered up into the heart of the Queen Anne third floor dome. "Reynolds, we need to talk." After a pause, she added, "After the Christmas Tea is over." She reached down to pick up Rex Kitty, then she noticed Liza standing in the kitchen doorway.

With an inkling of nervousness, she said, "Don't mind me. I'm being silly."

"Silly is good, ma'am. I saw your visitor leave. I'll clean up and put everything in order."

Letsea thanked her, laughed, and shook her head.

Liza said, "I like the hat, although perhaps it could be a tad smaller."

Letsea glanced in the ornamental mirror next to the front door. "Really? I hadn't noticed." She grabbed an umbrella and headed back to the main house with Kitty draped over an arm.

The main reason a man might leave his hat behind, was for an excuse to return. What was her *new friend* thinking? Better yet, she asked herself, *why did I knowingly let him leave without it?*

CHAPTER 43

Late afternoon, second Saturday of December,
The Volunteers Christmas Tea Party

Letsea, with her sister and brother-in-law, greeted friends and met new attendees as they came in the west-side ballroom entrance.

Gratitude washed over her for the several city officials who volunteered to assist in any way. They fulfilled tasks such as valets, coat check, seating guests, and answering questions.

Inspired by the Phoenix speakeasy, Letsea rubbed her upper arms, considering the fixtures and accent furniture in storage. Next year, she wanted to have both the ballroom ladies' and gentlemen's rooms remodeled to a more stylish elegance of antiquity.

Gwendolene whispered, "Letsea, isn't that Alice from the Settlement Tea Room getting out of a car now?"

"Yes, it is, and her husband. Did you know they are Trey Lockhart's parents?"

"No idea of it. She's one lady you just have to admire. Sweet as a button."

Letsea greeted them. "I'm glad you both came. I hope you enjoy yourselves tonight."

"Thank you, I know we will." A council member helped with their overcoats.

Alice wore a midi-length tea dress of Christmas red satin beneath black lace. The black fitted bodice-vest with red ribbon tied in a delicate bow.

"Alice, such a beautiful dress. Is it vintage?"

"Thank you, no, but I do like the fortyish-retro look. Not that I'd personally know anything of the era, you understand." She tittered and said, "I would like to introduce my husband, Rick."

A handsome man, younger than she imagined he might look. He wore a black suit, red bow tie with a matching pocket square. The same red shade as Alice's dress. She held out her hand to him. Being quite the gentleman, instead of shaking it, he gracefully held it and inclined with a half bow.

"My pleasure to finally meet you, Miss Brechenworth."

While Gwen and Doyle spoke with Alice, Letsea used the moment to look for the resemblance between Lock and his father. Rick carried an air of enthusiasm. She witnessed such energy from their son while in Phoenix. No. She corrected her thoughts. Lock also displayed it when he quoted Dumas. She was glad for the amusing memory, since he appeared quite stern at times. Possibly job related.

"Have you two discovered the fountain of youth?" she continued, "You don't look as if you'd have a child Trey's age." Relieved she remembered to use Lock's family nickname. How old did she think he was anyway? Old enough to retire.

Rick laughed. "We were mighty young when our boy was born."

She tilted her head. Just how young were they?

Alice rejoined Rick.

Letsea motioned. "Come, I'll show you to your table." She led, and paused as they greeted friends while crossing the floor. "You'll find your place cards here." Pauline rose to hug Alice.

After all were seated, Letsea watched as the city administrator, from the stage, welcomed everyone and gave a brief agenda of what to expect.

Two musical ensembles were introduced. One, composed of a string trio with a harpist, celloist, and the violinist. They played first to set the mood with Christmas tunes, while guests arrived. Letsea noticed propped on stands were extra violins and a viola. They were well prepared and she appreciated the endeavor. The second, at rear center stage, a wind quartet of an oboe, flute, a couple clarinets. Surprised, a saxophone on a stand. Oh, they were in for a good time!

Her black grand piano was suitably positioned on stage. One of the council members volunteered as pianist. Earlier, in conversation with her, he shared his eagerness for her new after-party. His excitement, contagious.

Waitstaff busied themselves serving hot teas and hors d'oeuvres while guests were being seated. The meal began with soup followed by petite sandwiches and salads, everything gracefully served on dainty china. The staff kept service prompt and smooth. Letsea relaxed. All went as planned or smoother.

"Rick," Letsea said, "Trey tells me you are a historian."

"My boy knows me aptly. American history, in particular."

He was so polite. "I'd like to talk with you sometime. I'm afraid I have an overwhelming task ahead of me in organizing my family's history. I'm open to ideas."

"Discovery of who they are or something else?" he asked.

"Piecing together dozens of trunks of journals, shipping logs, paraphernalia of all kinds."

His eyebrows shot straight up. "All kinds?"

The way he repeated her words reminded her of when Uncle Paul described how Aunt Mildred repeated the FBI agent who gave her shocking news. *Oops. Wrong time to think of the ghostly-spirit.* She did not want him to make an appearance. "Shipping business records, maps as well as military, fashions, and personal belongings through the generations."

Alice laughed then covered her mouth. "Letsea, you've easily won his heart."

Rick added, "I'd like very much to see how I might help you."

Letsea enjoyed visiting with the Lockharts, but she also made time to mingle. Dutifully important to her to have one-on-one interaction with everyone present, including the servers. She wanted others to know she was a real person, not some fictitious, little rich girl all grown up, exaggerated by years of old rumors and fears.

The mayor addressed the guests, extended gratitude to the Brechenworth estate, her, Gwen, and Doyle.

She watched the music director and received her cue for the next phase of entertainment. A glance at Gwen, then they nodded and Letsea went to the stage.

"Thank you each and every one for sharing your time and

efforts with our beautiful community. To all of us at the Brechenworth estate, you are the heart of our historical and beloved town. You make a difference in St. Charles for all citizens, our visitors and therefore in the world. God bless you."

She sat on the piano bench, fluffed the skirt of her new gold French dress trimmed with Chantilly lace, a gift from Gwen. She played a medley, during which Chip and Lauren made their procession to the stage.

CHAPTER 44

Lock watched as his parents sneaked in and hung their coats, glad they were home safely. "Boy, howdy." He startled them. "It's after eleven. Am I going to have to put a curfew on you two?" They giggled like teenagers.

"You weren't waiting up for us, were you?"

"Sure, why not? Have you been drinking?" he teased.

His father clamped a hand over his son's shoulder. "Sure we have. Tea, coffee, water, and a copita of sherry."

What's a copita? His mother headed to the kitchen then aimed for their bedroom. Ten minutes later she was in the living room wearing her purple fuzzy robe and house slippers. She sat on the sofa and plopped her feet on the ottoman. His father sat beside her, scooped her onto his lap. She snuggled to him.

"Trey, close your eyes for a minute," his father said.

He pretended to, rather he watched them kiss. Feeling a tad embarrassed, he went to the refrigerator to see what Mom put away. "Is this for me? Did you bring me something to eat?"

"Trey, put the box back. Pauline packed leftovers. We'll share tomorrow but we get first dibs."

He closed the fridge, turned off the kitchen light, and sat across from them. "I feel like we're switching roles here. I take it you enjoyed yourselves."

"Oh my, yes. I can still smell the fragrance of the flowers. Chamber musicians took turns playing Christmas music while we ate." Mom barely drew a breath before she exclaimed, "Gwendolene Davis' children sang. You should have heard their voices. They remind me of you as a boy. They sound like young adults. The girl is three, and sang backup for her brother in 'Have Yourself a Merry Little Christmas' and they did a duet with Paul McCartney's 'Wonderful Christmastime.' They were amazing. You'd have loved it."

He heard them rehearse at the community center. He recalled they were Letsea's "pride and joy and hope for the future." The memory of their good time in Phoenix teased his senses.

"What did they serve to eat?" Lock asked, knowing she'd get to the topic sooner or later. He decided to be kind and get her started.

"Something for everyone. Smoked salmon, cucumber sandwiches, chicken salad, angel egg bites you'd love. So much, it's hard to remember it all. I'll probably have foods dancing in my dreams tonight. Oh, cheeses and fruits...the capri with fabulous fresh herbal flavors."

He knew better than to stop her commentary. Mom shared all she loved of the evening.

"Oh, Trey! The desserts were fabulous! Fresh sliced strawberries on a bed of fresh herbal cream cheese resting on tiny crumbly, buttery shortbread biscuits. A whole variety of petits fours." She kissed her fingertips and exclaimed, "Oh, the most divine mini raspberry-chocolate ganache cakes, layered with smooth raspberry filling, topped with fudge and fresh berries. We brought extras for the freezer. A day to remember for flavor, fragrance, music, and good company for sure."

"The tea party was over two hours long. As it wound down, Letsea invited anyone who wanted to dance to hang around for an all new after-party. They cleared the dance floor, pushed chairs to the walls. The musicians were fantastic."

His dad grinned, kissed Mom's cheek, and said, "Sweetheart, I'm so glad you agreed to marry me." He looked into her eyes.

"Okay, you two, what happened over there?" Lock figured if he didn't get them talking again, he'd have to go to his room and give them privacy. "So how many stayed to dance?"

"Over half the crowd. They played decades of music and closed the night with Jerry Lee Lewis's 'Great Balls of Fire.' Most joined in and sang the words. It was hilarious."

That explained all the kissy face they were doing.

Lock propped his feet up and pondered whether or not to ask in regards to the hostess. Finally, he decided not to be a coward. "I suppose Letsea's boyfriend, Purser, attended."

His father, with a light in his eyes, said, "Interesting you should ask. Not at all. She wasn't short of dance partners though."

He remembered holding her in a slow dance and her smile when she moved into fast steps.

Mom leaned into Dad's shoulder with a smile on her lips. After a long pause, his mother asked, "Why do you ask?"

"No reason." *Can't a guy be curious?* "Anything else?"

"When it was all over, Pauline took me downstairs to see the magnificent kitchens and her posh apartment. No wonder the gal doesn't want to retire. She's in a sweet situation, living the dream of a chef!" She sighed.

He looked at Dad. "You, too?"

"Letsea showed me the storage rooms housing family memoirs. She asked me for ideas in organizing her ancestry."

Dad smiled as big as ever. He was glad he suggested Letsea ask for his help.

"Son, I'm a happy camper."

Mom's expression changed. "Did you meet with the church music director again today? The congregants are going to be blown away the night of the candlelight service."

He shuddered. If she witnessed crime scenes the way he had over his career, she'd never use the phrase *blown away* again. "Yes, we rehearsed. So, did you learn anything new on the Brechenworths?"

His father said, "Nothing worth repeating. Just rumors and stuff."

"Like what?" He was an investigator and rumors often revealed facts.

"Well," Father started, "Old man Brechenworth, who got his fortune in shipping, didn't even have proper schooling. Since then, they've all been lawyers."

"I heard Letsea's father displayed tendencies more of a bread-spender than a breadwinner. A globetrotter. However, someone said he did earn good money in minerals. It explains why he and his wife were in the Congo. Checking out a mine for investments."

Lock had read it in the international kidnapping report.

"Even before the tragedy, Letsea's grandfather chose to leave the family fortune to her and skip her parents. Not even her little sister got a share. The trust listed Letsea next in charge at twenty-five years old. They say she's the sensible one."

"How is it even possible?" Lock asked. "It sounds unfair."

"Old traditions, really." His father said, "A privilege generally granted to the eldest son. The idea is to keep monetary strength in the family coffers."

"Coffers?" Lock smirked. "I haven't come across any chests of money in your move."

His father agreed, "I wish we had more to pass down. What little we leave behind will be divided equally among you and your sisters. I just wish there was some way we could prevent this great divide."

"I know," Lock mumbled. He knew what his dad meant. The old method still being used was psychological warfare. By dismantling people's faith, family, courage, and country. Attempts at separation happened through heated controversy, confusion, and violence. He closed his eyes. The enemy used various tactics to change how we see, feel and act. They aim to kill morale, incite fear and self-destruction.

Lock squeezed his eyes and reminded himself not to talk politics with his father after their lighthearted evening. His dad worried for the strength of the greatest nation being divided into so many conflicting agendas, so did he. But then, worry only served negativity.

He knew targeted tactics worked hard to take down *united we stand* with continued harassment by irritations of objection, guilt, blame, anger, and fear. His father, passionate on survival of the soul, to keep faith in God, not mortal matter. America strong was in a united oneness.

They prayed for all to recognize love and wholeness.

Lock considered what part the Prohibition Act and influx of drugs played in what was happening? Heavy duty, he surmised. Let alone leaders of certain countries with plans to nettle away freedoms and rights. Divide and conquer by infiltrating from within. Eliminate individuals' defense mechanisms, to make their take-over easier. He felt his jaw tighten.

For the first time, he considered of the roaring-twenties agent's own perspective. With what internal war did Special Agent

Reynolds really contend? Exactly what *was* in those many file cabinets that housed his file?

Aware of analyzing Letsea's protectiveness, he felt something for what the BOI agent dealt with on a professional level. Reynolds worked to stop illegal drug-smuggling from incapacitating our country's power. Was he also aware of multiple spies in major roles within the U.S. government? How did he view the importance and impact of his assignments? Was his murder one of those so-called *good natural deaths*?

Like so many, Letsea had attached her emotions. Not that *he* would do that. Sure. He opened his eyes and unclenched his jaw. But it explained her determination to stop a lie about the man.

If only we all remembered who we are as a whole. One Nation under God, indivisible, with liberty and justice for all.

"Godrick," his mother interrupted his contemplation. "Letsea is quite accomplished. On top of everything else, she played the piano. You'd be so good together."

"So." His father cleared his throat and continued after a long pause. "All estate money handed out goes through Letsea. I'm told she's a swing trader. She's extraordinary at it. Someone told me she's a billionaire."

"You're kidding?" he paused. That didn't seem likely. Nor did he see it in the financials he reviewed. Not that he scrutinized her retirement portfolio. Surely, a billionaire wouldn't stress about keeping the "roof from leaking." That financial list would be easy to check out.

"Bunch of rumors. No one really knows."

"You mean gossip, don't you?" Lock's jaw tightened again. "She throws a big shindig as an appreciation and some hang and gossip?" The desire to defend her struck him hard.

His father reiterated, "It's speculation, Son."

"Trey," said his mother, "we weren't going to mention it. You asked us, remember?"

"Sorry." He didn't realize the harshness of a reaction he'd feel. Apparently his mom noticed. He forced a relaxing breath.

Mom changed the subject. "A fine affair. Like a Renoir painting sprang to life. Groups of friends sitting around the tables chatting or Degas' dancers."

Lightening the mood, he asked, "You mean, some wore tutus?"

Surprised by the painted image he'd been given.

"Don't be silly. I meant in a poetic sense."

"It really was," agreed Father. "We've decided to get involved with the dance studio again, like we were when you were kids." His father patted Mom's thigh. "They have senior dance night and we have time now."

As Lock was going to let them have the living room to themselves, his mother said, "After the after-party, Letsea invited us to her family parlor where we sat comfortably and visited. She said it's still basically the original design."

He knew, he'd lunched there. "What did you discuss?" He reclined in his chair.

"Hook rugs."

He wasn't surprised.

Lock yawned. "I'm glad you had a good time." He stood to go to bed. "Good night."

"G'night, Son."

When he turned to the hall, he noticed they were kissing again. "Hey," he groaned, "you two need to get a room." As he went into his, he heard his father whisper and his mother giggled.

His parents set a good example of a happily-ever-after marriage.

He thought of Letsea. If he were able to get past the burrs under her saddle, she would be a lot of fun. What was the real source of, and how many irritations could she have? Oh yeah, still the matter of that attorney-at-law boyfriend. He sighed. "Good night," he called out as he closed his door.

CHAPTER 45

Monday morning Letsea supervised in the ballroom

Rental company workers loaded the last of the tables and chairs into the trucks. Letsea surveyed the room. Not bad, following a big party.

The cleaning service would come on Tuesday. She sat on the stairs and called Gwendolene to confirm next Saturday's event. The song "Wind Beneath My Wings" played in the main hall behind her. Gwen headed her way. She waved and turned off her phone and went to hug her sister.

"Why were you calling?" Gwen asked.

"Are we still on for next Saturday's Parents Day Out?"

"I hope so. The kids from Sunday school are excited."

"So, it's from ten in the morning until four in the afternoon?" Letsea asked.

"I'm hoping some can come earlier, say nine o'clock."

After a deep breath, Letsea agreed. *It's only an hour longer.*

Gwen smiled. "Good. I'm also hoping we can make pickup at seven instead of four, to give the parents much-needed time to themselves."

"Honey, I'm not sure."

"Here's the thing..." Gwen interrupted. "Word spread. I'm looking at more like ten kids."

Letsea's eyes opened wide and she stared. "Ten kids for ten hours?" She paused. Gwen's sweet expression made it obvious she was hopeful. "As long as you and Doyle both will be here."

"I plan to be. Doyle said it depends on his workload. Besides, you always have Marcia, Bob, and Pauline. I didn't want anyone to feel left out. Besides, we had fun last year, right?"

"Honey, it's Marcia's day off. Bob's already overloaded on duties. Pauline is planning to cook lunch for them. Afterward, she's gone for the day with her own family. I still have the children's home party coming up and Pauline will have plenty to do to be ready for it. Do you want to ask your housekeeper to come help babysit?"

Gwen winced. "No. I'm half scared of her as it is."

Letsea roared as if it was slapstick comedy. It felt good to laugh again.

"She's a tough old bird." Gwen promised, "We'll figure something out."

Later, Letsea worked diligently on filing legal forms to help her learn more details on her ghostly spirit. As she completed them, Marcia stepped into her office.

"The cleaning crew is gone. Everything looks good. Also, I spoke with the director at the children's home. They emailed this..." She handed Letsea a copy of the list. "Twenty-two kids. Their names, ages, and a general idea of what they like. A couple churches are doing the Christmas shopping, so that's covered. I'm sure they'll get nice gifts. We're down to the Christmas Eve party with dinner. Pauline wants to cook for them. A magician for entertainment. The DJ volunteered an hour of music for the dance. A photographer will be here for snapshots for the home's scrapbook."

"Sounds organized, as ever. By the way, I'm running errands this afternoon. In fact, I have several this week. I'll be in and out rather often."

Marcia said, "All right. Do you want Bob to drive? You won't have to find parking."

"No, I like getting out on my own." Besides, it crossed her mind to stop at Union Station on her way to an investment meeting.

Leaving the post office, she noticed Lock's car parked a couple spaces away. She waved but didn't get a response. The windows were darkened so she couldn't see in and hadn't noticed him in the building either. As he left her place last week, he didn't wave. Maybe he was not into the gesture. Besides she didn't have time to chat, she needed to drive into the city.

Union Station, a busy place, people roamed, although the Whispering Arch was vacant. Letsea went to the empty Whispering Arch and whispered, "Paul?"

No voice, no sounds. She leaned her forehead against the wall and mused if he simply left, gone from her life for good. Did she let him down? His problem, a conundrum she couldn't solve. She'd told him *after the tea party*.

"Hello there, babydoll. Aren't *you* gorgeous," came a clear, unfamiliar voice. She turned and saw a stranger ogling, looking directly in her eyes and puckering his lips. The man wore a white suit, black shirt. The buttons opened halfway down his front. A thick gold chain hung across his carpet of chest hair.

She said nothing. With the Whispering Arch, he probably heard her breathe.

"I see you're waiting for me."

She raised her chin and backed away from the wall toward the steps. She had no interest in an old man who tried to look like he'd stepped off a 1970s movie set. Upon glancing around, Letsea noticed the waitress, Gina, who brought her tea the day she met Lock. She secured her purse under her arm and scampered upward, for safety's sake.

Run, Letsea!

She made a beeline to Gina.

The first time Uncle Paul used her name, and he warned her away from the stranger who tried to pick her up. She shivered. It was nice to know Uncle Paul had a protective watch over her. Although, remaining in control, she was already on her way for refuge.

Gina met her near the top of the steps. "Stay clear of that guy in the disco outfit,"

Letsea looked back from a safe distance. The stranger stood alone, looking around the arch. She'd bet he somehow heard Uncle Paul's voice. Maybe she *should* have asked Bob, after all. She ordered a tea from Gina and walked with her.

"That piece of work is on the verge of nuisance. I'll tell you one thing, he's no John Travolta."

Letsea nervously smiled, took her tea, and thanked the waitress and silently thanked Uncle Paul. Oddly relieved he hadn't disappeared into the vapors of the universe, yet.

Gina walked outside with her to the valet and asked staff security to watch so she was shielded from the nutcase.

Safe. A glance at a clock reminded her it was time to head downtown to the monthly stock market meeting with friends.

CHAPTER 46

Early Saturday morning

Lock stood in the driveway with his hands on his hips. "Dad, it looks like this is the end of it. How are you doing?" His father walked over, stood beside him, and stared inside the empty garage.

"I guess for the circumstance we've been dealt, I'm as good as can be expected."

"If Mom would agree to an estate sale, I think you'd do well with it."

His father rubbed his chin. "She's not giving up her furniture or memories so easily. We'll see what happens after we find a house. It's not expensive goods, but they're antiques and it's ours."

Lock knew what he meant. After seeing furniture in both of Letsea's houses and comparing it to what he grew up with, it bore a striking difference. "That's that." Lock slapped his hands together then swiped at the dust on his jeans. "Dad, the only thing left here is sweeping out the garage. I'll come back and do that later. Let's get breakfast and coffee before we unload this last haul."

"Sounds good."

Mom had a fresh pot of coffee brewing when they walked inside his house, but she was crying. Lock was about to ask what was wrong, until he noticed his dad shake his head. *Dad's got this.* He pulled down three cups and filled them while his dad stepped up behind her and put his arms around Mom.

"Honey, we enjoyed fifty good years there. It's time we look for something new. Be glad we're not ready for a nursing facility."

"Better not be. After dancing last weekend, I want to do it more often."

"You know what else we should do?"

Dad turned her around and kissed her while Mom's arms encircled him. Lock poured their two cups of coffee back in the pot. He took his outside and began unloading the scrap boards and pipe from his dad's pickup. He stuffed it in any little gap he found in his garage. When he finished, he went inside.

Mom and Dad were having breakfast.

He hadn't realized how romantic his parents still were until they moved in with him. Were they always so lovey-dovey, or possibly emotions from the move triggered a fresh tenderness?

With the phone on the charger, he went in to get cleaned up, not in a hurry to sweep out the garage, yet relieved the old place was finally empty.

Showered, shaved with a pat of aftershave on his face, and dressed, he combed his hair. His early start to the day worked in his favor, except for not sweeping the garage earlier. It looked like some free time in his future so he'd start with breakfast.

He slipped his cell phone in the jeans' pocket, strapped on his back holster with the Glock, then reached for his wallet and IDs. The phone rang playing the "William Tell Overture." He remembered taking it off vibrate while loading the pickup. His boss was calling. For years, he considered them good friends, not so much this month though. He wanted to ignore it. Being on vacation, it should have been within his right to do so.

He sighed. "Hello."

"Lock, are you interested in a short quiz?"

"Not really, thanks for asking, Chief. Talk to you later."

"I'll be quick. Guess who filed a motion against The Department of Justice? She wants rights to review Agent Reynolds' case files."

He hissed. "Son of a—"

"Get on it." Click.

He closed his eyes and clenched his jaw.

CHAPTER 47

8:35 Saturday morning at the Brechenworth estate

Lock was surprised Bob not only let him through the gate without hesitation, he also let him in the mansion without frisking him. Clearly the security guard did not pick up on his level of anger.

"Miss Brechenworth is upstairs in her office. I'll call her to let her know you're here."

Ignoring the formal antechamber, Lock stepped into the main hall and watched Bob go through the doorway to his tower security office.

Through the empty hall, Lock headed up the main staircase he'd seen before.

The top of the stairs, on the second floor, flaunted an expansive hallway, in fact, an art gallery. Several doors lined the walls, but only one emitted light. He peeked inside.

The first contemporary room he witnessed in the old house, floor-to-ceiling white with modern furniture. He stepped through the doorway and noticed Letsea sat in front of a bank of ultra-wide curved computer monitors. She listened to the speakerphone intercom.

After making note of something on paper, she made eye contact. "Never mind, Bob. He's here with me now. Thank you."

Lock stepped into her office.

She looked from his face to the floor. Letsea's eyes widened, her hand pressed against her stomach.

"Don't walk on my white carpet wearing outside shoes. Take them off." She pointed to his feet.

"No."

She raised an eyebrow. "Off."

"They're clean, barely damp. Snow flurries."

A quiet stare from her caused a sense of restraint to wash over him. Her house, her rules, he didn't have to like it. Irritably he tugged his loafers off and held them dangling. It would be difficult to express his utter frustration in his socks.

"Um. What are you doing here?"

"You said you weren't going to cause trouble." He thought he sounded more like a child with hurt feelings. He cleared his throat.

"What?"

"You filed a motion against the DOJ."

"So?"

How can she not see it as problematic? "I'm trying to have a vacation and you keep messing with it."

"My wanting information on an agent who died a century ago has nothing to do with you. You interviewed me. Isn't your part done? My goal is not met, it's between me and the courts. Why do you think it's any of your business?"

She looked at her clock, and started closing down her computer system.

"It just is. Drop it, Letsea."

She stared at nothing in particular and murmured, "I wish it were possible."

It raised the hair on the back of Lock's neck. *What's the deal?* "Just stop," he ordered and gave her a testy gaze.

"Lock, it turned out, you aren't the private investigator I thought to hire. My interest in Reynolds has nothing to do with you. Not a single thing. Don't take it personally."

He knew she was right, so why did he feel otherwise? Because like it or not, she happened to be his assignment. Which happened as a result of procrastination on his retirement. All for wanting a better payout on his pension. He didn't want to work her case. His attraction to her hindered his professionalism, even with her eccentric, if not idiosyncratic nature. "What's your game plan?"

"Simple. Whatever it takes for the government to let me peruse the actual files."

"Letsea, even if you were granted permission, you'll never find every detail."

"Why not?"

She pushed her chair back and swung her knees out from under her desk. On her feet were house booties which looked like two plush toy white rabbits with long ears and little pink noses.

If he wasn't so frustrated, he'd laugh. The stubborn streak within him refused to change the topic. "Due to a fire, a lot of Reynolds case files were destroyed."

She lifted her chin. "In *whose* fireplace?"

Lock slowly blinked, breathed deep and slow. Truth be known, old gossip confirmed the burning of documents and photographs in *someone's* fireplace. Were those Reynolds files? Who knew? All before his time. He opened the door on the topic, so he had to gather the strength to face her, not wanting to arouse anger, also not wanting her to think of him as a jellyfish. *Geez-a-loo.* He shifted his head. *Time to retire.*

"Yeah, that's what I thought."

His jaw tightened. "Letsea, I need for you to stop your research."

"What's it to you anyway?"

"My supervisor is breathing down my neck. There's an issue with it being unsolved and the higher-ups don't want the repetition of embarrassment to resurface on their watch."

"So what? They throw *you* under the bus?"

Her intercom buzzed. "Miss Brechenworth, the kids are arriving."

"Thank you, Bob. Let them in from the car porch. Are Gwendolene and Doyle here?"

"I have yet to see them, ma'am."

"I'll be down."

She walked to Lock, bunny whiskers twitching with every step.

"Listen, our conversation is not over, but I have a prior commitment to tend to." She tilted her head. "Do you have plans for the day?"

A vision of him pushing a broom around the old garage came to mind. "I may be able to make a change. Why?"

"Do you like kids?" She smiled.

"Why? Do you want to get *married*?"

CHAPTER 48

Her mouth dropped open. Letsea stared and realized Lock was in a mood. Being flippant though? Okay then, one could give as good as they got. She closed her mouth, swallowed, and said, "Where are we going with this?"

He gave an awkward grin and tried to shrug off the comment.

"Go put your wet shoes on the floor in my bathroom. Through there." And motioned to her bedroom doors. *Act cheeky, will you?* A perseverance test for the secret agent awaited. He returned as she locked her office doors and slid the key in a jeans pocket.

"Downstairs, sport."

Bob let the tiny, noisy children trickle in.

Lock looked outside the thick door. Gwendolene met and directed the children inside from a line of cars. He went back to Letsea who handed out colorful socks for each child to put on whether they were wearing any or not. Little shoes lined along the wall.

"Having a birthday party?" he asked.

"Parents Day Out. Ten preschoolers from Sunday school. They're here for the day. And, you, sport, have volunteered to stay and play with them."

He teased, "Is that what you call it? Babysitting, more like."

Her eyes revealed a twinkle of mischief.

"First things first, shoes off, socks on, coats in closet. Yours too." She scrunched to the floor to slip socks on a little tike.

Focus went to the bunny feet. Whiskers twitched. *Oh, this ought to be fun.* Who could stay angry with a playful Letsea? Right as rain, he knew better, still, he personalized the assignment. He hung little coats, but kept his jacket on. "What next?"

"I made a list. It's flexible except mealtimes. We have games, puzzles, dancing, *which I know you're good at*, naptime, and a movie."

"I see. An annual event?"

"The second one. I'm not committed to a third, at this time. First is breakfast. Some may not have eaten and hungry kids become irritable."

He knew it to be fact. So did hungry adults. He'd skipped breakfast in a rush to get over here.

"Hi, Lets!" Gwen kicked off her tennis shoes and plowed through the crowd, carrying a couple of flat boxes. "I brought muffins. I'll set them on the table." Chip and Lauren joined their friends.

"On the sideboard, please. Pauline is cooking," said Letsea.

As ten preschoolers filed into the dining room, in walked another one with two older brothers. Lock didn't have to be a detective to see Letsea didn't expect any older children. Her face paled.

Integrity showed through, and she pulled up more chairs, then spoke in his ear, "I'm glad they're wearing socks. I don't have any their size. Thirteen kids, *phew*! I'm glad you volunteered."

"No babies, I take it?" he asked before any other surprises entered the house.

She cringed, gripped his arm, and leaned in to whisper. "I firmly insisted they all be potty trained."

"How were two of you going to handle all these kids?"

"Doyle will be here. He stopped by the office first."

Lock smirked. "I'm sure Doyle Davis found something pressing he needed to tend to."

Breakfast arrived in a dumbwaiter and the kiddos were excited to see it work. After eating, they moved to the ballroom, where incidentally, the lady of the house allowed no balls. However, they did play active games. During *Follow the Leader*, Letsea took a moment aside with him.

"By the way, Lock, you interviewed me, so this case is closed. You can stop *following* me all over town." She rejoined the children's line, where they were doing a bunny hop.

What?

He stepped up behind her. "What do you mean by me 'following' you?"

She spoke over her shoulder, "I saw you. Several times."

Next, they all swayed like trees in wind.

"When? Where?"

"You know, the post office, the card shop, hardware store, and a meeting in downtown St. Louis for starters." She went to congratulate the children for being so clever and start a new game.

During *Freeze Tag*, he caught up with her again. "What day do you think you saw me?"

"All week. Every time I ran an errand, there you were."

He didn't want to frighten her, but she needed to know. "I haven't followed you since Phoenix."

She stopped watching the children, looked him in the eye, and made a *Hmmm* sound deep in her throat. "Maybe you didn't notice me. We happened to be at the same places at the same time." She returned to the kiddos.

Right, as if he wouldn't notice her.

He went to the hardware store a couple times, not the other places she mentioned.

Later, back in the dining room for lunch, he asked privately, "What kind of car did I drive when you thought you saw me?"

"Lock, I've seen your car out front, remember? A little black sporty thing."

That's all she knew? No make or model? "Letsea, what meeting in St. Louis?"

"Friends. We discuss investments."

He asked, "How many friends attend?"

"Usually thirty. What does it matter?"

It matters! "How well do you know them?"

"We've been meeting for years. Come on, lunch."

While everyone, including her sister, were settled down to eat, he left to speak with Bob.

"Hello there." Lock entered Bob's round office.

"Bob."

Letsea interjected from the doorway. She'd followed him.

"Answer any questions Mr. Lockhart has. I'll be with the kids."

"Mr. Lockhart, what can I do for you?" He pushed his lunch tray out of the way.

"Miss Brechenworth mentioned someone with a 'sporty black car' has been following her this week. It wasn't me. How long do your security images stay intact?"

"It's on CDs. I wait six months before I reuse them." He pulled open a file drawer.

Bob was organized.

"I've dated and marked them with anything unusual."

"Good. Have you noticed any cars out front this week?"

"There are always cars parked out on the roadside. Gawkers, you know?"

"You mean to look at the houses?"

"Yep. Especially now, day and night, to see the Christmas decorations. Always has been, since I was a boy."

"You've been here since childhood?" Lock didn't expect that tidbit.

"Mr. Brechenworth hired me to keep his cars in order. Eventually I'd do anything they needed done. My dad worked security here for years. He taught me to take over when he retired."

"May I look at this week's surveillance?"

"Sure." Bob pulled up the recordings and showed Lock how to fast-forward, reverse, and pause. "They record by movement."

"Has Miss Brechenworth considered updating this security equipment?" Lock asked.

"She hasn't mentioned it. Really, this is all I know. I'm not exactly a computer whiz. Truthfully, I prefer working on the cars."

Cars? He took a chance. "I understand she has a lot of automobiles."

Bob cackled and slapped his leg. "Yeah. You can say that again. An awe-inspiring collection."

Probably not information a security guard should be sharing, Lock thought, as he scanned the visuals.

"Bob, what experience do you have with security?"

"I've been in training classes. Self-defense, Active-Shooter Encounters, and Street-Wise Safety. My next one is Street-Wise and Edged Weapons."

Locked sighed. "Good to hear. You're being proactive in learning techniques. Do you carry a gun?"

Bob unlocked and pulled out a drawer then pointed to it.

"Do you practice with it often?"

"Every month."

Lock nodded. More often than a lot of people, but how comfortable was he with it? Then noticed on the monitor, yesterday's CD, the same black sports car which drove away when he parked in its spot, ten days earlier. The screen view did not allow him to see the driver or license plate. Fortunately, he had the plate number in his notes.

"Bob, do you remember this car?"

"It's a repeat gawker. For a couple weeks or so. Similar to yours, sir."

"Make note of it if it comes back. Save this CD."

"No problem. One question, Mr. Lockhart. What's your interest in it?"

"Bob, that's just what you and I are going to figure out."

CHAPTER 49

An hour later...

"Bob, earlier you mentioned when you see anything unusual you make a note of it on the CDs. What do you consider 'unusual'?"

"You, taking liberty to walk through the open gates and into the house without an invitation the day they were setting up for the tea party."

"Saw that, did you? Why didn't you stop me?"

"I know she likes you." He shrugged.

Bob didn't beat around the bush, did he? "How so?"

"Miss Brechenworth invited you to stay for lunch on a whim the first day you were here. *That* is unusual. Besides, you made her laugh."

What a sobering thought. "Doesn't she laugh?"

"Not like *that*. Not since she was young. She does get tickled with the kids though."

As if on cue, the intercom buzzed.

"Lock, do you want to eat lunch?" Letsea asked.

"I could handle lunch, sure."

"Better come back to the dining room before I clear the table. Gwen is taking the kiddos to another room for a nap."

"Thanks. I'll be right in."

He reached to shake hands. "Thanks for your help, Bob. I admit, I'm concerned with the black car in particular."

"I'll be mindful of it. Do you think it might be dangerous?"

"Listen, that car parked out front for three hours yesterday alone. If it's the same one following her around town, we have a problem."

Lunch, a five-course meal on fine china. From the looks of the dirty dishes in the dumbwaiter, the kids were served on the same. *A brave lady.* Even his mother served on paper plates at times.

"Are they in the ballroom for naptime?" he asked.

"No. Gwendolene took them up to my grandparents' old bedroom. Two full beds, sofas, and chairs to sleep on."

"Like your room?" The largest bedroom he remembered seeing.

"Oh no, it's the entire size of the ballroom. Above it, in fact."

"You're kidding? Who needs a bedroom so large?"

"I suppose, those who lived most of their lives in little compact rooms on a ship, with lots of other people aboard."

Okay. That could make sense. "It's huge, then?"

"Like a penthouse." She closed the door to the conveyor and activated it. "You finish eating. I'm going to check on Gwen and the kids then run downstairs and load the dishwasher."

No wonder she stayed so fit. Walking this place was like a gym workout. He looked around the large dining room. The whole north wall, a glass-doored hutch for fancy dishes. He counted chairs. *Boy, howdy!* The table sat twenty-four people. The original Brechenworths must have enjoyed entertaining.

When finished, he walked his dishes down to the renowned kitchen. Commercial quality with a design of antiquity. Where was Letsea? The sound of water running sent him searching deeper into the multi-kitchen chambers.

"I thought I lost you," he said, entering yet another type of kitchen.

She rinsed dishes and loaded a dishwasher.

"Aren't you afraid of putting fine china in an automatic washer?"

"This one is especially made for delicate dishes."

"Boy, am I glad to hear it." He chuckled. "You worried me. Mom never let me put china in the dishwasher." He rinsed his own dishes, and she loaded them.

He leaned against the counter and looked at all the glass-door cabinetry. "What kind of room is this?"

"The butler's pantry."

"You've been hiding a butler?"

"He retired after all the grandparents passed. I try to keep expenses minimal and hire contract services as needed." She wiped out the dumbwaiter and slid the pocket door closed. "See? It goes from here to the dining room and up to the grandparents' room where the kids are. Convenient thing." With that, she turned her back to him, shoulders pulled forward as her head dropped.

"Letsea, be easy on yourself." He thought she might be crying and placed a hand on the back of her neck and shoulders.

"Did you figure out who's following me?" She turned around. Her eyebrows were pinched, and lips flat.

Okay, so no tears. He reminded himself of her defensive moves on the photographer in Phoenix. No way did he want to see her frightened. "We have a good lead."

Her face and shoulders relaxed. She sat on an old-fashioned step stool.

"Honestly, I thought you were following me around town. You know, doing your FBI thing. I felt a little affronted you didn't wave back."

"You waved at him?" he asked.

She nodded. "No response, but then you don't bother to wave, do you?"

"If I'd seen you, I would have. What do you mean 'I don't bother'?"

"The day you left from the Queen Anne. We agreed to be friends, yet you never looked back or waved goodbye. Who doesn't look back and acknowledge the person they're leaving?"

Lock stepped up, placed a finger under her chin, and paused. Their gazes met. "Someone who trusts and feels safe with the person they're leaving."

She sighed, "Hm. That hadn't crossed my mind." She placed her hand on his elbow. "Um. I need to check on the kids."

Did he read something behind her voice? Did she need to get away?

He stuck to her side as they climbed two flights of stairs.

Nothing dared stop him from seeing the gigantic bedroom. "Do you ever use the old cage elevator?"

"When we have something heavy or bulky to move. It's original to the house and came in handy when my grandparents were ill. Here we are."

"Boy, howdy!" He looked. "I can't say you didn't warn me."

"Shh." Gwen gestured with a finger in front of her lips. They interrupted her sister's reading.

Most of the kiddos were awake, quietly lying still. He nodded and took liberty to explore the elegant features of the room. The west windows were draped, covered in room-darkening shades. The north side opened onto a balcony. A large sitting area in the middle and a credenza at the dumbwaiter.

The modernized bathroom with two separate private compartments also contained zero entry shower, a walk-in tub, and a jacuzzi. "Now we're talking," he whispered.

The closet met the size of his living room and kitchen combined, complete with benches and chairs. The laundry room in the closet caught him off guard. When he came out, eyes wide, he stared at her. Letsea laughed.

The kids stirred. Gwen rolled her eyes and stood.

"It's okay, honey. I'm ready to take them back to the ballroom," she told her little sister.

"Fine. They're all yours."

Letsea wrapped her arms around Gwen. "*Ours*, dear. You aren't getting out of this so easily. Next, we're going to teach them the 'Chicken Dance' and the 'Hokey Pokey'."

Lock didn't even try to stifle his sense of humor. "Oh, their parents are going to be thrilled!"

"I know, right?" Letsea chuckled and ushered the kids out into the hall.

She definitely had a mischievous sense of humor. He watched as she ruffled the hair of one of the older boys.

"Did you sleep any?"

The boy said, "Naw, I brought a book to read."

"Good for you!"

After the dances, they set up several different carnival games. Cornhole and Ring Toss were favorites.

"What am I, a glutton for punishment?" Lock said and breathed hard, trying to keep up with the kids on the Hop Scotch. *The FBI could use Letsea as a physical trainer.*

He sat on the floor while the children took advantage of wearing socks to slide around the ballroom floor. When he looked up, Bob stood at the top of the staircase looking directly at him. "Excuse me, ladies." He walked briskly toward the staircase and followed.

"That car's back," Bob said.

Lock stood next to the Christmas tree to observe. Sure enough, parked in its usual spot was the black car.

His attention flashed to his feet then wiggled his toes. Ironically, he wasn't particularly interested in chasing down suspects barefooted. "Bob, did you see when it pulled in?"

"Yes, sir. I came straight to you."

"Good job. Will you grab my shoes? They're in Miss Brechenworth's bathroom."

"I cleaned them already. They're at the front door."

Lock slipped his shoes on and headed to his Beamer. His intention was simply to block the suspicious car in place and talk to the driver, yet he found the vehicle empty. The hood still warm.

Where did the driver go? He looked around the hedges and found nothing. Did he run off or get inside the estate grounds?

The Maryland tag was a different plate number than he remembered. Was that other car a gawker, like Bob claimed? With his cell phone, he photographed everything possible, including the VIN number on the dash. The heavier than average tinted glass was all too familiar. His pulse quickened. Occasional cars drove by.

He tapped the autodial on his phone. "Chief, did you put a tail on Brechenworth?"

"Just you. Does she have another?"

"Yeah. Professional." His muscles tensed. "Later."

With cupped hands beside his eyes, he peered through the darkened driver's side window, no keys, no papers, nothing. The doors locked. He rubbed his chin, stepped back, and lay on the ground to see beneath the car. Clear.

He slapped a GPS tracker in place.

Bob called, "How can I help?"

"The driver's gone. Did he get inside the gate? Pull up the security footage."

"Sir, the fence is tight, I doubt if he's on the grounds."

"Let me back in. I want to see the security coverage myself." He left his car in the road as a block and made a vigorous dash inside the gate, hastened up the steps, and through the door. Bob met him in the entry.

Lock headed to the tower office for surveillance images. "I'll call the sheriff, see what he knows."

Bob cleared his throat. "Shoes, sir."

He stopped. "What's the deal with no shoes!" he snapped as he tugged them off.

"Long live the memories of a disastrous stain, sir."

Lock paused, cell phone in hand and rolled his eyes. "Watch that car."

He made his call and requested code one and road-closed signs put in place.

CHAPTER 50

Letsea cringed, peering down through bare trees at the sight in front of the house. Thank goodness no flashing lights or sirens. A glance across her room reassured her the children were settled watching a movie.

With authorities in front of the house, memories of the Congo flooded her mind. In hindsight, miscommunication between governmental agencies played a major factor in not getting her parents freed from the kidnappers. The Embassy and FBI did everything possible to help, but inaction by the locals in charge in the Democratic Republic of the Congo created unnecessary delays, resulting in their deaths.

Murder. Murder exasperated by some crazy sense of revenge. She, with her granddad, security guards, and the cash ransom, still someone stalled the exchange. Why? Who possibly benefitted from causing the hindrance? It's not like anyone there kept the money.

Why should she be connected to murder victims? First, her parents, then, Agent Reynolds' ghost. *Now some suspicious car follows me!* Did it have to do with her parents or Paul's case? Of all people, why did Paul seek her out? Why were Lock's supervisors determined he dissuade her from researching the murdered BOI agent?

What did all of these situations have in common? The FBI? *Oh, Lord, please don't let this be some weird omen.*

Her arms crossed as her heartbeat pounded and roared in her ears. She wanted to make it stop, but recollections of the Congo horror still hurt. She grasped her stomach. *Please don't let anything happen to Gwen's family or Lock.*

"Letsea, what's wrong?"

To stop Gwendolene from looking out the window and becoming frightened, she forced herself back to the sitting area. "I'm tired, honey."

Gwen squinted and with a gruff undertone said, "It's those stupid dances. You always overdo things." Sis turned on her heel, flipped her hair, and barged out.

Me? Gwen was the exorbitant one.

She glared back at the window. Why should some unknown person follow her? Greed, no doubt. Ransom for her parents. Uncle Paul worked to stop influential drug lords of his day. *Who and why would anyone want me?* She often kept Chip and Lauren. What if her kiddos were in danger? Doyle needed to know. Gwen would be a worse basket case than her.

At home, in St. Charles, she knew most of the local law enforcement. Being personal friends with the sheriff and an FBI agent couldn't hurt matters. She clutched her hands and went back to the window. The overcast sky had darkened and night shadows made it difficult to see. The string of cars of onlookers was next to nonexistent. Why?

Lock moved his car back inside the gate, and he, Sheriff Bill, and a couple deputies stood on the road beside the mystery car and talked. *What's happening?* An urge to find out for herself was halted only by the need to stay with the children. Since her FBI friend didn't hesitate to take charge, she ought to relax and be glad she finessed him into staying.

A deep breath caught in her throat, remembering Paul's words. "You never know who will help you, give up your identity, or straight-away kill you."

Oh, Lock, be careful my friend.

CHAPTER 51

Lock opened one of the French doors. Letsea jumped up and met him in the hallway.

"What did you find out?"

She looked frightened. He pulled the door closed and walked her down the hall. "Everything's fine. We're figuring it out," he assured her. "What are the children doing?" He wanted to lighten her mood by changing the subject.

"A movie. What's with all the police cars?" She gripped his arms. "Who is it?"

"Precautions. I'll know more in a bit. When is dinner?" Heaven help him, he wasn't the slightest bit hungry. Still running on adrenaline as it was.

"Lock. Don't do this to me. Whose car is it?"

Her voice, suspiciously soft for someone with so much fear in their eyes. "Relax, will you?" He reached to place a hand on her back, but when she shook his arms, it landed on her hip. He let it rest there. "A name doesn't mean a whole lot at this point anyway. Can I help with dinner?"

"Gwen's taking care of it. It's a surprise."

He was sure of it.

"It might mean something to me, if I know the man. What were you all talking about for so long? What's wrong?"

He framed her face with his palms. "Nothing's wrong and we can talk after the kids are gone. Okay?" She stared. "Breathe. It'll wait. How long is the movie?"

"Another forty minutes." She pressed a hand to his chest. "Lock, I need to know what happened."

Through her anxiety, he recognized the defensive stance and daring look in her eyes. "Not a thing happened. You happen to have some overprotective men who care for you."

She raised an eyebrow. "Like who?"

Me. "Apparently every man that's ever met you. Including your brother-in-law and the uniformed." How, at this time, could he want to kiss her? In fact, he did.

"Promise to tell me what you know after the kids go home."

"Shush," he uttered with a finger to his lips then moved it to her's, and silently shook his head.

He wanted to kiss her with enough passion to make her forget her fears. He settled for seeing her face relax and breathing return to normal. Not being sure how much to tell her, by giving it time, he'd figure it out as the evening progressed. On a positive note, he managed to call Doyle Davis and get him in on the loop. They walked back to her room.

"Care to come in, sit with us, and rest?" She opened the door.

"Sounds like a plan." First, he went over to the windows. The black sports car was still in place. Eventually, the driver would return for it.

From the far side of the room, two things caught his attention. The hook rug near her bed must be the one she mentioned.

"Oh, isn't that special," he mumbled. His fedora hung on one of the bedposts. The hat he purposefully left at the Queen Anne house for an excuse to return. He liked knowing it held an honorable position on her bed and wished he could as well. His heartbeat picked up. Was it getting warm in there? *Sweet dreams, Letsea.*

Finally, he stepped around little children fixated on a large screen TV to join her on the sofa. In a somewhat reclined position, he crossed his ankles.

After a couple minutes, Letsea pulled her bunny-booted feet up beside her and leaned back. Her edginess must have drained her. He saw weariness in her eyes. But then, that was normal.

Letsea leaned to his shoulder. He pulled a little cushion from behind, plopped it on his lap, and encouraged her to lie down. She did. A sense of calm settled over him. Until—his cell phone vibrated. The ID read *Restricted*. "Lockhart."

"FYI, Agent, this is Rogers. The black car drove away."

"Did you see..." He stalled, fully aware Letsea listened.

"No, sir. No one approached it. No door opened. It just started and drove away."

Lock winced. So the driver never left the vehicle. They stowed away behind the seats where the side windows were totally blackened. *Oh crud.*

"Next step in place?" Lock asked softly and glanced at Letsea.

"Yes. We have an unmarked vehicle waiting as soon as they exit this road toward town."

"Tail only. See where it goes and if they meet anyone. What's your position?"

"I'm staying put. My eyes are open, Agent."

"Rogers, I appreciate it. Later."

Letsea looked up at him. "Is it that car?" she whispered.

"Later. Rest while you have a chance."

She sighed and closed her eyes.

His mind raced to think of who, with what agency or department, purposefully avoided making themselves known to local law enforcement. CIA? MBI? DEA? ATF? Interpol? Any alternative called for full alert. *What's going on out there?*

Lock watched little Lauren inch her way to the sofa and look at Letsea.

"What's up, kiddo?" he whispered.

"I don't like this part. It's scary."

Letsea reached her arm out, scooped her niece up, and they snuggled.

As the film moved toward a close, Doyle walked into the room, nodded to Lock, picked up Lauren, then sat in a chair, hugging her. He stretched his legs out with his daughter curled to his chest as she watched the happy ending.

The moment it was over, the kids jumped up to run to the bathrooms. Lauren wiggled loose from Daddy's arms and she and Chip led the way. Letsea sat up and tugged at her blouse.

"Hey, Sleeping Beauty, did you have a good day?" Doyle asked Letsea.

"Oh, look who finally arrived. Do we know if dinner's ready?" Letsea stretched.

"I brought pizza, Gwen put them in the warming ovens."

"I thought you were going to be here all day," Letsea said. "What happened? Did work at the office keep you detained?"

Doyle coughed. "Yeah, something like that. Gwen texted it was going smooth here."

"Sure, with help from Lock...hart."

When they all stood, Doyle shook his hand.

"I'm going to make sure the kids aren't wandering all over," Letsea said.

With the two men left alone, Doyle spoke up, "Hey, thanks, man. I appreciate the heads-up. Something's weird, the car's still there. I don't recognize it."

"You've been in the house for a while. It left. We're checking into it. Mind, keep your senses sharp and use caution. I haven't told Letsea *you* know."

"Good, she's as protective as a mother hen. So, you two are dating, right?"

"We're friends. Do you think dinner's ready?" *Is how I feel toward her so obvious?*

They moved to direct the children downstairs.

The pizza party was a big hit. Then parents arrived, and Letsea introduced him. They were all gleeful and grateful.

He liked the day's playful field of vision. Not everyone lived a life of a millionaire or one of catching racketeers. Some folks simply enjoyed a normal job and family life.

After all the families left, and the house was quiet, he spoke with Letsea in the receiving parlor. "There isn't any record against the owner of the car. You don't own the road, so there's no legal grounds that others can't park there."

"For hours at a time? He must have an agenda. We're the only ones down this far."

"I know. It's still a public road. I'll see the sheriff tomorrow at church and we'll meet Monday. It is a suspicious situation, but no crime has been committed, that we know of." After a deep breath, he asked, "Any chance you have any jealous exes?"

"None at all. What if this guy plans to kidnap Chip and Lauren?" Her shoulders tightened as she gripped his arm. "We can't let them be in danger."

"Don't think that way, Letsea." Although, he already had, and she could perceive every reason for it to happen. Concerned of the chance of a kidnapping, in the local field office the best source to bring in on this, none other than, Don Pfeiffer. One didn't thwart corrupt schemes by ignoring possibilities. *Anticipate the worst. Hope for the best.* Besides, he and the sheriff already put a protective strategy in order.

"I didn't have a chance to warn Doyle before they left. Gwendolene or the kids stayed by his side. I don't want my sister to get anxious."

"The sheriff and I already filled Doyle in on it."

"Good. I wish you'd fill me in." She followed him outside to his car. "So, you *do know* who it is."

"I told you to relax." He touched a fingertip to her nose. "Looks like you'll have to remove your bunny booties, since you wore them out here."

"I will."

"I'm sure of it. By the way, are you familiar with Summer *Chablis*?"

"A delicious vibrant, aromatic white wine." She rubbed her neck. "What does wine have to do with anything?"

"Just what I thought. Not a thing. I'll be in touch with you." He got in his car, started it, then rolled his window down. "Goodnight, Letsea." He made a point to wave. She giggled and gave an open-and-closed finger wave.

"Good night, Lock, and thanks for all your help."

"You're welcome." Suddenly he told her, "By the way, the owner of that car is listed as a woman."

"What woman?"

"I shouldn't release a name. It's probably a sightseer or a real estate agent interested in the houses. Don't stress. Now get back inside before I go. As a precaution, don't leave home without telling me first, okay?"

Watching her, he chuckled. She waved a last time and scampered up the front steps, bunny ears wiggling all the way. *Her children will be adorable.* Not for the first time, he considered where she and Purser were in their relationship. He'd yet to see the attorney. And why did Davis assume he was dating her? At over forty, if she planned to have her own children, she better get to it.

He didn't have anything against waving. Waving was a fine gesture. After clearing the gate, he also waved to Deputy Rogers on surveillance in the blacked out marked police car across the road. He pictured Letsea's sweet goodbye and smiled.

CHAPTER 52

On his drive home, Lock pulled over to read a new text. The sheriff informed him that the Maryland car reached Interstate 70 and floored it, like a projectile, toward St. Louis. The last he knew the Highway Patrol's eyes were on it. Lock glanced eastbound in the sky.

He looked for the information from the GPS tracker he stuck under it. "Crapola!" He zoomed in on the locator map. It was in a dumpster at the gas station off the road to the estate.

The driver retreated within the car the whole time. A contortionist, at that. She heard the device click into place and overheard their entire conversation on strategy. The fact she knew to remove the tracker said a lot of her experience. He made a fist and bumped it against his leg. "Why hide, Miss Summer Chablis? Unless you are up to no good."

Anxious to see what he would find on the Bureau's computer, he needed to run an extensive identity check. He headed straight to his house. Time to unlock secrets.

Mom and Dad were watching a Christmas movie and paused it while he hung his coat. Why the heck not? He stepped out of his shoes.

"Are you hungry, Trey?"

"Not really, thanks anyway."

"You texted you were at Letsea's house today. Did you have fun?"

As if he were twelve and getting home from a ballgame. "Yes, Mom. I stayed to help babysit a throng of their friends' kids." He headed up the narrow staircase to his office.

"All day? How many children?"

"Thirteen tikes. I've been on the run all day. I'm exhausted."

"I'll swan, Trey. I bet they felt safe being under the watchful eye of an FBI agent," his mother said.

With the office key in his hand, he stopped and looked down. "What did you say?"

"That's right. I am well aware you've been lying to me all these years, young man."

Lock stepped down a couple of steps and sat on the landing. "It happened unintentionally."

"Godrick William, how could you be so deceitful? An FBI agent, for crying out loud."

"Mom, I didn't want you to worry. How did you find out?"

His dad moved his head from side to side and gestured *not me*.

"Someone, who will remain nameless, mentioned it to me last week at the tea party. I figured they misspoke. It's happened before. I know because you just *now* admitted it and confirmed it to be true. It answers years of questions, for sure."

Caught by Mother's ingenuity.

"Mom, you can't tell anyone. No matter how dear a friend they may be. Not even Faith or Hope. My own sisters are not to know. I'm undercover. Top secret. Tell-no-one status. Mom, do you understand what I'm saying?" She'd spent years in a tea room. Gossip being entertainment. How could she keep this quiet? Another sign of the times to retire.

She puckered her lips, squinted, then closed one eye and stared.

"Mom?"

The blasted tea party. Letsea Brechenworth!

CHAPTER 53

After Lock left, Letsea used the underground passage to the Queen Anne house.

Automatic candles glowed in every window.

Letsea reminisced of good times while looking in her childhood bedroom. Wishful dreams and goals. Photographs of family, travels, and friends always offered good memories. *For a day of fun, it turned awfully scary.*

From whom did Lock think she needed protection?

Bob told her of the deputy across the road. It must be serious. She crossed the house to look out a front window. Why did Lock refuse to tell her the woman's name? Then, the possibility of knowing her scared her even more than if it were a stranger. Jealousy? Envy? Revenge? For what?

Good grief! Lock arrived angry, however it delighted her how quickly he changed his attitude and put the children first. He *would* make a good father. Too bad he didn't want to be one. To be honest with herself, he never said he didn't want children, only he never wanted to marry.

Everyone could use more friends though, right? If not for Uncle Paul, she wouldn't know Lock at all. And they grew up right here in the same town.

Thinking of the ghost, she strolled back to her room, turned on a lamp to chase lingering shadows. She stood in the doorway and called out to the center of the house. "Hey, Paul, the last time I was here, I told you we need to talk. Where are you?"

You've been preoccupied.

"You bet your sweet patootie I have. Talk now, Buster."

About?

Letsea crossed her arms. "Let's start here, did you really have affairs?"

I loved my foxy little Mills.

"Augh!" she groaned. "There has to be some measure of truth to their story!"

They work with deception.

"They're investigators, not magicians."

Not so different.

She held her head in her hands. If a ghost were to drive her crazy, she wanted time to get last-minute affairs in order. "How's that again?"

One lies to entertain, the other lies to obtain.

"To obtain what?"

Information.

"Did you cheat on Aunt Mildred?" Nothing like being duped by a lying ghost. "Tell me the truth."

Silence.

"I'll put you out of my mind, once and for all! You'll need a new go-between."

No one ever changed my love for my wife. I worked long hours away from home. It was important she and my boy were safe. Eyes wander. Doesn't mean I did. A man gets lonely.

"Who doesn't?" she snapped.

You too? Any man would want to be with you.

His first attempt at personal conversation. "I'm not looking for *any* man. I want a best-friend kind of husband, and why am I telling you this?" she vented.

You're telling yourself, not me.

"The point is, you cheated on Aunt Mildred."

I did not say that!

"Did Mildred want a divorce?"

Heaven's no.

"Regret sounds like an excuse someone might use to take his own life."

I was murdered! I was murdered! I was murdered!

It echoed. "Okay, I get it." She paused. "Tenacious, aren't you?"

What gave it away?

"First, you interrupt my conversation with Agent Lockhart while he was here. Don't ever do it again and stop scaring my cat!"

A hollow chuckle. *Fine.*

"How can you touch things?"

Like what?

"The dime you threw at me in Union Station?"

I carefully rolled it to you.

"Why?"

To let you know I was there.

"I already knew, you kept poking me. Where did you get the dime?"

Touching doesn't always work. Difficult to differentiate when it will or won't. The dime, tucked into the watch pocket of the suit Millie picked out for my burial. There's a little favor packet, mementos, in my coat pocket too. Sweet, thoughtful, Mills. It's wrapped in satin and tied with a bow. Her tears are on it. She did love me.

"No doubt, she married you after all." Her anger waned.

Forlornness, like a heavy shawl, pulled at her shoulders. She refused to sink to a low level of depression, but she needed an answer to a big question.

"Paul, help me understand what happened to the car you rented. Not only city, but a state-wide search couldn't locate it. Even before, and especially after, they found your body. A few days later, it turned up outside your hotel. Had it been there the whole time and they missed it?"

In plain sight most of the time. The grifter who cleaned it did it that night, right there in the rental garage across from the hotel. Later, he parked it on the street.

"It doesn't make sense. All officers had an eye out for your rental car."

No, they didn't. Cops searched for the license plate number, not the automobile. The same goon took the plate off, switched it for another, and left it on the streets. When they were ready for it to be found, they simply re-switched the plates. That night, the beat cop saw the plate and recognized it. Hidden in plain sight. In my day, most automobiles were black, green, or gray. Easy to overlook.

"Why would they choose to do that?"

It's the dough. The lookout was only a scared boy who wanted to be tough. When the payoff is big enough—man or teenager will do what he's got to do.

"Is the man who cleaned it and switched plates the same one who killed you?"

I'm not sure. I was more in the head of the boy and he didn't know much, except both excitement and fear. Plus, you can't have any idea of the perspective of being on this side of the veil.

"Tell me."

Expansive. My burden I bear, to have this false accusation struck from my record.

Car lights reflected on the walls as it pulled inside the gates. Letsea went to see out the windows of the second-floor turret. Pauline circled around to the garage.

"Paul, when I met Agent Lockhart that first morning, did you know he was FBI?"

Yes. He reviewed my case file, including some confidential information, with intention to discourage your interest.

"Which allowed you into his head, I get it. Do you happen to know why someone is following me?"

Silence.

"Where did you go?" She tapped a fist against the doorframe. "Sure, it's all about you, isn't it? Thanks for nothing, Paul *E.* Reynolds."

Letsea turned off her lamp and made her way back to the big house and met Pauline coming in from the garage. "Did you have fun with your grandkids today?"

"Oh my, yes. We went to the rides and attractions at Union Station. The grands had a blast on the rides and for my part, I have a new corn on my foot. How did you fare with the rest of Parents' Day Out?"

"A fun day."

"So, why the long face?" Pauline took her coat off then offered her full attention.

"Lock— Trey came. You know."

"He looked to be enjoying himself. That doesn't explain your expression. Do you want to talk about it?"

"Trey and Bob discovered someone is following me and watching the house."

"A small black car with dark windows?"

"You've seen it?"

Pauline nodded. "At first, I thought it was Trey's car since you know him."

"So did I. It's not. They called the sheriff, apparently no laws have been broken."

"There were two different black cars, in addition to Trey's. Did you know that?"

Letsea drew a deep breath. "No."

"It looked a little suspicious, so I wrote their license plate numbers down, one never knows." She dug in her purse and pulled out a notepad, tore out a sheet, and left it on the kitchen island. "The cars looked nearly identical. The Missouri plates back windows are all blackened. The Marland plates are dark tinted."

"How did you even notice two of them?" Letsea asked.

"You know there are so many more cars stopping to look this time of year. The other morning, while I pulled the parlor drapes open, I thought those two were repeats. For both of them to be here at the same time seemed odd. So, I went out to *supposedly* check the mailbox, four hours early, mind you, and I wrote down everything I could see. It's all in my notes." She patted the paper.

"Did you tell Bob?"

"I jotted him a note to come talk to me. As you know, we all get busy around here. I figured Bob to be in the car barn."

Letsea read Pauline's notes. "All black, two-door coupes. Trey's is BMW, the other with super dark windows is a Volvo, and the third one is a Toyota." Letsea looked up. "How can you tell them apart?"

"Simple, miss. I know my cars. Grills and wheels are the first giveaways. Are you planning to stay home for a while?"

"Um. Trey wants me to. I'll still go to church in the morning. I'll be vigilant to my surroundings."

"I see. You be careful out there."

"I will, although we still have the children's home party to do."

"Now, Miss Letsea, you know stores deliver. You don't have to run all those errands. Say, how'd you like a cup of hot chocolate to end the day?"

"I think I'd prefer sherry. You?"

"I'm up for sherry. Running around with my grands has me

worn to a frazzle. I don't know how you managed a long day of thirteen tikes."

"This is how... I'll get the sherry decanter and glasses." Letsea volunteered, "Let's meet in the pool room and soak in the Jacuzzi. You can tell me about your day with the grandkids."

"Sounds perfect. I'll meet you there."

They drank a couple of copitas of sherry and relaxed. Letsea asked, "Pauline, do you believe in ghosts?"

"No, ma'am. I do not. And every time I see one, I tell them I don't believe they're real and eventually they go away."

She pressed a hand to her mouth to stifle a giggle then sobered. "Are any of them Mom, Dad, or my grandparents?" She fell silent, and waited.

"Any of who? Didn't I clearly say they're not real?"

With relief, Letsea sighed. She and Pauline both burst into giggles before closing out the night and going to their rooms. Letsea took the sherry decanter with her.

CHAPTER 54

After midnight Sunday morning, Lockhart in his home office

The fact his mother learned of his position from *someone* at Letsea's party frustrated Lock to no end.

Mom clarified, "It's fearful enough to think you were IRS. I love you and it's my business if I worry. Get over it."

He'd like to give Letsea what for, for breaking her promise. Yet, there was plenty for her to contend with at this point with a surveillant on her tail. Why? How deep did it go?

Upstairs in his office, on his official computer, Lock did a search on the FBI database for the mysterious car owner, Summer Chablis. Although skeptical of her name, since once his assigned code name, alias, was Jack Chardonnay. His suspicions were confirmed when the search engine requested a second supervisor's consent to gain entry. *What the heck?* His own security clearance was foremost in the Bureau. *Why would I need backup consent to enter a general file search?* Or was it another arm of The Justice Department?

He called his boss for approval codes. Sunday or not, since when did Chief not answer his phone? He texted and emailed. Without upper management confirmation inserted in the allotted time span, the blasted system blocked him out. Was Internal Affairs involved? He may need to drive into the field office to solve this.

Why didn't Chief get right back with him? Did his personal interest in Letsea become so obvious he was kicked out of the loop? Unless Chablis wasn't as he suspected. *What's going on?*

Nothing for it, he needed to talk with Letsea. She could not go around telling people his profession. He always managed to keep his status behind closed doors with the local law enforcement and legal sector.

He'd stop by her place on his way to church. Allow enough time for a brief, and firm, conversation, then be on his way. Simple.

He received a text from the chief.

We'll talk Monday.

With his shoes left in the foyer, Bob led him to Letsea in the morning parlor.

"Why did you tell my mother..." He softened his voice. "I'm FBI?" Geez Louise, she was gorgeous, dressed in a tight cashmere ivory sweater and a tan plaid skirt with matching shoes.

"What makes you think I did?" Letsea put down a book and stood from the chaise lounge.

"Mom said she learned it here. You promised not to tell."

"Do you think I'm the *only* person who knows?" She stepped close, toe to toe.

Okay, it might be difficult to refute the question. Before an argument came to mind, he recalled Doyle Davis leaked it to her, over the phone, that night in Phoenix. "Did your brother-in-law attend the party?"

"Yes."

"I may have misplaced my frustration."

"Well, get over your annoyance. I need to leave for church soon."

"What? You said you'd let me know if you were to leave the house."

"I planned to text you before I left. I'm not skipping church the day after babysitting several of the congregants' children all day. Are you always so exasperated with people?"

Mainly, you! He went to a chair and dropped into it. "My expectation for this month has been anything but. Sorry."

"Don't be. We're past it, aren't we? You didn't get enough sleep. I know what that's like. What did you learn of my stalker?"

"I'm waiting for an update." He considered what he could and could not tell her. Truthfully, he knew very little and what he did know, so did the sheriff and deputies.

"It's a female owner." *From Maryland. Law enforcements are on the lookout to talk to her.* "Technically, she hasn't done anything illegal." *Except maybe speeding, and patrols didn't get it on radar.* "You may not be in danger. However, I'd feel better if you stayed to your house until we learn more."

"So, no real estate agent, hm? I knew you were bluffing. Besides, it's Christmastime. I have things to do and I still have another party coming up."

"Do you always have so many parties?"

"Sometimes. Don't you ever have parties?"

"Why would I?"

"What about fishing with the guys? Play cards or have a barbecue? Anything?"

"Yeah, I guess I do when there's time." He noticed the book she set aside when he entered and he leaned forward to look at it. "Is this the FBI novel you mentioned?"

"One of them. It's book six of the series."

"May I borrow one?"

"Sure, start with book one."

"Sounds good."

Letsea crossed her arms. "Lock, in view of Uncle Paul, are you ready to leave me alone?"

"I was ready on day two. Somehow, I think I'm in it for the long haul."

She pulled a book off a shelf and handed it to him. "I want it back. It's autographed."

He raised his right hand in the three-finger Boy Scout salute. "I promise."

With an impish upturn of her lips, she handed the book over. "Heads-up, scout, you won't want to stop reading."

"Perfect. Now, I'll drive you to church so I won't worry."

She walked across the hall and got a coat from the closet. "You worry about me?"

"Who wouldn't? I woke you from so-called 'sleepwalking' in

the Grand Hall of Union Station. On a whim, you fly to Phoenix to wander around. Now you want to leave the safety of home, knowing some undisclosed person is following."

She kept an eye on him while he took her coat from her hands and held it out for her to slip into.

"There may be two of them," she said.

He stepped in front of her to look into her eyes. While there, he buttoned her coat. He liked the closeness. "What do you mean, two?"

She reached for her purse and pulled out a small sheet of paper. "Pauline noticed two separate, but similar, cars parked out front. Here's her information."

He read the notations. "This confirms a major situation. First, those bushes in front need to go. Your current video images are poor. You need a new security system. I know a guy. I'll call and make arrangements. You need more cameras, live stream with instant review. This I'll say, Pauline knows both cooking and cars."

After church service, Lock opened his passenger door for her. Letsea liked his consistent politeness. "What did you think of the service?"

"You attend a nice traditional church."

His answer confused her. "Don't you like traditions?"

"It's fine. Mine is a little more...uh unconventional, I guess."

What was he not saying? "What do you do, worship snakes?"

He burst with laughter. "No. Not that radical. It's our music, it's newer. Service moves at a faster pace. Your hymns are old compared to our songs."

"I grew up there, so I guess it works for me." Although, after her parents' demise, she discerned being shunned. However, Gwendolene liked Sunday School, so she continued to attend along with Aunt Mae.

Her phone rang, and it played the music "*9 To 5*." "Excuse me." "Hello, Seth."

"Hi, baby. Gee, it's good to hear your voice."

Oddly, he sounded excited, though she rarely thought of him anymore. "What do you need?"

"I'll be in town Tuesday to sign some papers and pick up my car. I want to see you."

"Tuesday?"

"Thought I'd stay with you for a couple nights."

Surprised by his forwardness, all she could say was, "Oh?" It would be a first.

"We need to talk."

She clenched her jaw and closed her eyes. Talk? That didn't sound like a good idea, but she invested three years of her life with Seth. *What does he want?* She sighed. "I thought we already did."

Seth cleared his throat. "A new discussion, Letsea."

"What time Tuesday?"

"I don't know. I'll text you before I head your way."

Whatever. "If you get hungry, you should stop and pick something up." *Since, I'll not know when to expect you.*

"Baby, I'll let you know, when I know."

"All right. Until Tuesday." She put her phone away then rested her head back. In the quietness of the car, she sensed Lock's curiosity. How much did he hear? What might change his attitude toward considering marriage? Then memory hit, Trey. The third in his family. Even if the man changed his mind in taking a wife, still yet trapped in tradition with his name. The epitome of the reason, Grandmama emphasized running when you knew your date wasn't marriage material. *Don't let feelings get attached to a dead end.* She sighed again. She should have run from Seth years ago.

Lock said, "I heard you have plans for Tuesday. What about Sunday dinner, today?"

"No plans." She opened her eyes and looked at him.

"If you're willing, I'd like for you to have dinner with me and my folks."

She *should* eat. "Sounds good. Your mom is always so uplifting."

He cleared his throat. "Yeah, usually."

He stopped his car in front of a new house built with an old-world English style. Three different types of stonework and the front stoop highlighted the entrance through a two-and-a-half story tower. "What's this?"

"My house."

"You do like old things."

"There's nothing old here, except the style."

He got out and went around to open her door. "My parents aren't back."

"From?"

"Church."

"I'm sorry you missed your own service."

"Don't be, I'll survive."

She stepped inside. "Lock, this is lovely!"

The coatrack in the round foyer revealed a variety of hats and caps. He hung their coats, slipped out of his shoes even as she did hers. She tucked her pumps beside his black loafers.

Obviously, he liked blue. She knew by the sapphire accents. It complemented the off-white trim and light pewter-gray woodwork. *And his eyes.*

The living room and kitchen combined into a great room. A glass sliding door on the back wall beside the surrounding stonework of the fireplace revealed a patio. A narrow, floating staircase led up to a single door, bringing her attention to the cathedral ceiling enhanced by the height of the stone wall and wooden beams across the ceiling. A hall to her left had five closed doors. "Charming."

"Thanks. I aimed for comfort, though charming's good, I think." He went to the kitchen and lifted the lid off a roaster.

"That smells delicious." She stepped next to him and peeked in. "Where are your tongs?"

"In my hand." Teasing, he snapped them together in front of her face.

"Are you going to flip the roast over?"

"It's my plan."

"Great." She went up the staircase. The door was locked. "What's in here?"

He turned around. "Uh-uh. My office is private. No entry." He waved tongs in the air.

She stepped down and went into the hall to sneak a peek. Coat closet, laundry room, and a bathroom. She waited between the two opposite doors at the end of the hall.

Lock stepped up. "What? You want to see a bedroom?"

His blue eyes appeared darker, like thunder clouds. She nodded. He opened the door on the front end of the house.

"My parents' room."

Prominent visuals were the antique Rococo bedroom set. Stacks of boxes lined the walls.

"Lovely carvings. I bet your mother treasures this set."

"Dad's gift to her on their seventeenth anniversary."

"Makes sense. Traditionally, the furniture anniversary." She moved across the hall and stood in front of the other door and waited.

"That's my room. You don't want in there." Slowly, he moved his head back and forth.

"I figured. Yes, I do. you've been in *my* room. Open up." She tapped the door with a fingernail.

He pushed the door open.

"Nice." The same color scheme, a long wall closet, long queen bed, recliner with a reading lamp. Mounted on the wall opposite the bed, a huge flat screen TV. The backwall included a sliding door leading out to the patio. Simple and neat.

"No chest of drawers?" she asked.

"Don't need it. Shelves in the closet. Have you seen enough?"

"Hardly." She went to the door next to the TV.

"Hey, it's private," he said, but couldn't hide a grin.

"I figured so." She looked in his bathroom anyway. "Wahoo! Luxury, I guess. You do like blue, don't you?" She stepped in. All royal-blue fixtures with fancy gold faucets, a shower, and an oversized jacuzzi. When she looked up to the ceiling, she exclaimed, "Ooh! Look. A chandelier!" She looked out the bathroom door and found him next to the bed, reclined in his chair with his sock-covered feet in the air. He'd placed her book on the small stand next to him.

"It's a light fixture," he corrected her.

"Yeah, with hundreds of pencil-thin tubular crystals in varying lengths." She flipped the switch to it. "Wow! Look at that! Rainbows all over the place. It's a chandelier, Lock."

"Light fixture. It's rectangle. Not dripping in fancy tiers like an upside-down wedding cake." Yet, he grinned.

She stepped in front of him and tapped the bottom of his right foot teasingly and pulled on his big toe. "A crystal chandelier in your bathroom. I love it." She chortled and tapped his other foot. She pinched his other big toe then rubbed his foot. His voice, deep and raspy when he spoke,

"I wouldn't do that if I were you. It feels rather good."

"What?"

"The foot massage." He wiggled his toes. "A man could get used to this."

Surprised at her own brazenness to practically fondle his feet! *How can I feel so comfortable with someone I met such a short time ago?* Well, the man *did have* his playful moments.

"Should I be sorry?" she mumbled, rubbed his toes again.

"Please don't be."

"Trey, we're back!" announced his mother. "We got a call from Hope. There's a problem with the girls' hotel—"

His parents stopped talking in the doorway and stared.

She removed her hands from Lock's feet and stepped back.

"I'll swan, Letsea. I wondered who those pretty pumps in the entryway belonged to." Alice went silent again. Rick, his father, stood behind his mom and smiled.

Lock broke the tension when he said, "I invited Letsea for dinner. What about the girls?"

Alice, his mom, gleefully said, "That's wonderful!" Then answered, "Uh, oh, the hotel with their reservations is having some kind of a problem. They need to relocate to a different one. Hope said they're all booked up here. She thinks they may have to stay in St. Louis. We need to help them find a closer hotel. Um. I'll get dinner on the table."

That quick, she and Lock were alone. She heard a lilt in Alice's voice in the kitchen.

He lowered his feet and stood. "Dinnertime. I'll see how I can help."

"I'll help, too." She stepped in front of him to beat him into his bathroom, to wash her hands in his gleaming blue basin as he waited his turn. With a mischievous expression, he flicked the light on and off a couple times.

As she left, she jestingly said, "That is a *chandelier* in your bathroom, my friend."

After a delicious meal, Letsea savored her slice of triple-layered vanilla-bean cake with a warm peach sauce dribbled over it. She listened to the three playfully discuss the odds of sleeping arrangements to fit fourteen people inside Lock's house. It's one thing to get everyone in the great room in upright positions, but horizontal was an entirely different dynamic. They amused one another then ultimately agreed they needed to find rooms or be without sleep.

"I have an easy solution to your predicament," Letsea volunteered. "You can all stay in the Queen Anne house."

Alice gasped. "We could never impose. Although it's sweet of you, honey."

"There is no encumbrance on my part. No one lives there." Uncle Paul crossed her thoughts, though he wasn't alive. "There are plenty of beds, the dining table can be expanded to seat sixteen, and you can all be together under one roof." She wanted to help and hoped they would accept the offer.

Lock leaned forward. "That's very kind of you."

Rick said, "Indeed. We'd be fools not to accept your gracious hospitality."

Alice hugged her. "Thank you so much, dear."

Letsea patted Alice's back. "That's done, come over this evening and take a look. You can settle in tomorrow and be ready for your daughters' families when they arrive on Wednesday."

CHAPTER 55

Monday morning

"Mr. and Mrs. Lockhart, this is Bob, estate security, with details to cover with you," said Letsea.

Lock listened to Bob then raised an eyebrow. "We need to sign a legal form?"

Bob explained, "It's a guest registry. Straightforward really, it simply states you are Miss Brechenworth's houseguests until the third of January. It will give you all two weeks, and I can give you each temporary passcodes to get through the gate."

Lock read it in full. "I've not seen one of these before. Not a bad idea, just unexpected." A logical precaution to prevent squatters. "Sure, we'll sign." He'd not dispute her kindness of letting them stay on her property. Plus, easier to keep a close eye on her.

His mother made arrangements for Pauline and Letsea to join them for 7:00 p.m. dinner at the Queen Anne. Meanwhile, he went back to his house to retrieve wrapped presents while Mom planned meals and the grocery list. After the girls arrived, they needed to get a Christmas tree.

"Great!" Realization hit. After lunch, he still needed to do his own Christmas shopping.

When Lock returned to the estate, he noticed a black sports car parked on the shoulder in front of the house, and a sedan, farther down the road. Before he could block the sports car in, it fishtailed away. He pursued. It was the first car he saw, confirmed by Pauline. The one with a Missouri license plate, his search led him to a corporation instead of an individual. He called the sheriff and stayed on its tail until a delivery truck cut him off. His mark slipped out of sight.

Back at the estate, he recognized the dark-blue sedan still there. "That's just great." *Midnight Blue*, if his memory served, and of course it did. He parked devilish close and rolled down his window. "Chief. When did you get into the area?"

"Late last night. It's hard to find a room in this town."

No. Empty or not, he refused to invite them to stay at his house, especially after being locked out of the search mode. "So I've heard. Why in the name of all monkeys didn't you tell me you were coming?"

The chief shrugged. "Lack of sleep."

Chief's passenger cackled. Lock tilted his head to see a face.

"I still love Lock's kooky monkeys!" The passenger slapped his knee. Assistant Director Douglas, U.S. Department of Treasury.

"Didn't you get my text?" asked the chief. "Today's Monday. We have a meeting."

Lock looked at the overly entertained ride-a-long. "What brings you to Missouri, Douglas?"

"I have an issue with your case."

"With Reynolds?"

At that moment, the sheriff pulled to a stop. Lock re-angled his vehicle, and the sheriff walked between the cars. "'Everything all right here, Lockhart?"

"I'd like to have you take these two in for loitering, but my boss would object," Lock said then scoffed.

The sheriff bent over to look inside the sedan.

Lock introduced them, "Meet my boss, DOJ's Special Agent in Charge Paytah and Assistant Director Douglas. Gentlemen, this is the reigning authority of St. Charles County, Sheriff Ruell."

The sheriff took a couple steps back. "Gentlemen, is there something I need to know?"

Lock looked at his boss. "The black car that left from here, is it on your team?"

"Not that I know of." Chief looked at Douglas. "Yours?"

"Not sure."

Lock considered their words and softened his voice. "So you do understand I need your authorization to investigate Summer Chablis." His suspicions concerning Chablis rang bells in his mind. *Always trust your gut instinct.*

"Don't hold thought on her. Now this other car is another story."

Lock said to the sheriff, "You might keep an eye out for the Missouri plate I texted you. It was here, again, twenty minutes ago."

Agent Paytah asked, "Sheriff, what of interest can you share with us concerning Miss Brechenworth?"

"Sweet lady."

Lock recalled how easily she could snap at him. Even her harshness didn't dissuade his interest. Yes, Letsea could be sweet and funny, but determined.

The sheriff continued, "She's terribly dedicated, protective even, of her family. Devoted to community efforts. Awful ordeal with her parents being killed while traveling, years ago. Which is why you're all here, I should think. Hope it's good news for her." When no one responded, he tipped his hat and said, "Good day, gentlemen." He walked back to his patrol car.

"Hey, Bill. Hold up, will you?" Lock followed and leaned on his door. "I think we can officially cancel the BOLO on the Maryland plates. I suspect it's not a danger. If it is spotted in the area, I still want to know. Don't pull it over."

The sheriff raised a brow. "Trey, you're keeping your boss waiting on purpose."

"He deserves it. Arguable, I know, but I scheduled this month off."

"I understand, 'revenge is best served cold.' Will you be at the candlelight service?"

"I'll be there. Hey, Bill."

"Yeah?"

"Something's not right."

"Duly noted, Trey." Ruell pointed two fingers at his own eyes. "My eyes are open."

"Thanks." They shook hands, then Lock headed back to the

sedan. He silently stood there studying his SAC supervisor.

His boss finally asked, "What do you know?"

"Experience tells me something is wrong. I now suspect Summer Chablis is with Douglas, here. So, what brings Treasury to this case?"

Douglas leaned over Chief. "Seriously, there's reason to believe Brechenworth may be in trouble."

"What kind?" He asked, with brows pinched.

"What else do you know, Lock?" the chief questioned.

"Not enough. Her security guard is raw, yet stalwart. There's no real security on her sister's kids. The brother-in-law said he'd be watchful." Lock leaned over and looked at Douglas. "What brought your interest to this?"

"She's been known to write hefty checks, never paid to the order of cash before. She recently cashed one for a smooth hundred grand," Douglas explained.

Lock said, "It may sound suspicious. I'm sure she's good for it. No sign of drugs."

"Our main concern is blackmail," said Douglas.

The man finally got to the point. Lock cocked his head. "I don't think that's it. She'd have mentioned *blackmail* to me." At least, he hoped she trusted him enough to do so.

"Really?" Chief stated directly, "It's no secret, victims are told not to contact authorities."

"Who? And what is their hold on her?" Lock asked.

"She routinely calls the Embassy in the DRC, anti-kidnapping division," said Chief.

"It's not a big deal. She doesn't want her parents' case to be cold," Lock reminded them.

"This month, she actually received several calls from the Congo. Our international division checked. The Congo headquarters doesn't have any progress in leads on their case. Their division did not call her. Turns out, the calls were from a burner phone. Following those calls, she wrote the large check for cash. In addition, we've got this other angle on Agent Reynolds."

"She commonly pays with checks. Something's suspicious with needing that much cash." Douglas leaned back in his seat. "Surely she *knew* the bank would report it."

"Are you going to ask her?" Lock asked Douglas.

"Officially? No reason, yet. You well know the manipulations of cash gifts and tax evasion."

The chief spoke up, "At this point, we're more concerned for her welfare."

"You think there's a threat from someone in the Congo? Or perhaps, tempting her with an unofficial briefing on her parents' case?"

"Those are two theories."

"What's another?" Lock asked.

"Extortion. She might be planning to tempt *you* to get her the Reynolds' information she wants. A hundred thou could go a long way for a man who wants to retire soon."

Lock's jaw dropped open and he stared at his boss in disbelief. "Me? I'm not stupid! She filed a motion. The legal course." He swallowed. "Nor would I—"

"Easy, fella," said his boss. "We aren't accusing you of anything, but if she were to make you an offer...."

Lock leaned forward, braced his hands on his thighs, and through gritted teeth said, "This conversation is over! I am on vacation!" He got back in his car, and squeezed the steering wheel. After a few moments, he faced them both. "She wouldn't do that. You don't know who she is." He questioned why he thought he knew her enough to make that claim.

"Lock, we're longtime friends, but I'm still your supervisor. Don't push me. You were supposed to stop her from digging into a case file. That's all I asked you to do. And now she's filed a motion to gain full access. Exactly what I wanted you to prevent."

Lock said, "What can I say? She's pertinacious. A good quality if you ask me." He drew a deep breath and slowly released it. "Okay, send me the link and your notes on her call records. I'll ask her. And FYI, I am supposed to be on vacation!"

"Look at him, will you? He's fallen for the affluent beauty." Douglas laughed loudly and slapped Agent Paytah on his arm.

Chief asked, "You aren't getting too close, are you? You haven't slept with her, have you?"

"Of course not!" He briefly closed his eyes. But then, again, he'd be willing to. *Breathe.*

"Hey, if you're so close, do not ask her. Observe. Hint, even. See if you can get her to reveal her situation. Strict orders, do not disclose Treasury is cognizant of the cash."

"We're headed to the field office and staying at the Union Station hotel. Let us know what you learn, ASAP."

CHAPTER 56

Monday afternoon

"Lock, your room is on the second floor, middle room on the east side. I think you'll find it interesting," said his mom.

His father smirked and looked away.

"I think I'll go on up." He patted his dad on the shoulder and grabbed his suitcase and laptop. From the doorway, he noticed pastel greens, ivory, and antique furniture. *Awesome.* A Tiffany lamp on a large Victorian Rosewood accent table. *Letsea's old room.*

What did his mother want him to see? His attention was drawn to a photo board with snapshots. An antique Louis Vuitton trunk along a wall made his curiosity burn with temptation. He tested the latch. Unlocked. He turned his back to it. Did he want to see inside on a professional level or from his interest in her?

Old sporadic pictures of her with family, friends from teen through college years were pinned to the board. Dancing troupe. Letsea, cute in her youth. "Now, she's hot," he whispered.

He removed his shoes and stretched out on the bed with his arms behind his head. Why hadn't he already taken his shoes off? Then he remembered the Queen Anne gleamed with polished hardwood floors. Rugs were used sparingly, as though it were summertime.

It was time to reflect on the seriousness of Paytah and Douglas's concerns of Letsea being in trouble. They did not drive the distance on a whim. She must be in a bad situation. He moved to her desk with his computer and opened Chief's email file showing calls from the Congo. Sure enough, there they were, plain as day. He called her.

"Hi, Lock."

"Hi there, yourself. I want you to promise you won't leave the house without me. Okay?"

"I do have a couple errands to run. Can you be ready in ten minutes?"

What was so important? "I'll pull around to the east side to pick you up."

"Lock, I need to take one of my vehicles. I have to haul something. You can drive."

"I'll be right over."

He slipped his shoes on and took the moment to consider what Chief asked him. Did he feel too close? In the first weeks of training at the academy, they drilled into their heads not to get personally involved. *How easy it is to care. For her.* It was a matter of survival to keep a clear mind and not get tangled with emotions. Admittedly, his recent frustrations were preoccupations of her.

He walked through the kitchen. "Mom, I'm going with Letsea to run errands."

Mom's joyful mirth made his lips quirk upward then he kissed her cheek before he left. A dash toward the big garage found him face-to-face with Bob and the key.

"She's going to the post office and a party store to pick up some things she ordered for the orphanage's Christmas party."

"Okay, thanks."

Bob furrowed his brow.

"I'll stay with her. Don't worry," Lock said.

"Worry is all I do lately," Bob confessed. "What was all that out front, this morning?"

"Keep an eye on sporty black cars, especially the Missouri license plate one. Call me if you see it."

"You pulled up right after it stopped this morning. Boy, you were on it, but what happened with the blue car?"

"Forget about it. My contact. I better go."

"You can park your BMW in here. Nice car like yours shouldn't be left outside."

"Thanks, man. I appreciate that."

Bob directed him to a green van with the estate logo and handed him the key. Garage dual doors allowed him to drive straight out and circle around to the car porch. The garage was built to park twelve vehicles. Six could drive through. He handed Bob his car key, so he could pull it inside, then watched his delight. Bob did like cars.

Utilizing the opportunity while driving, Lock asked, "Letsea, have you ever had a stranger contact you to do something which only benefited them and not you?"

"Sure, solicitors. They come out of the woodwork."

Not what he meant, though it started the conversation. "Anyone way out of the normal realm of daily activities?"

Her voice dropped to a whisper. "Like who?"

"Maybe a foreign contact which surprised you and wanted you to do something unusual. Something wasn't right, but at the same time you felt trapped." How else could he allude to being blackmailed without saying the word?

"What did you hear?" she asked and stared at him.

"I think you might be in some weird dilemma and you aren't asking for help."

"Oh?"

"Tell me. You shouldn't bear troubles all alone."

"What exactly, Lock?"

He wished he knew for sure. Her answers made it clear. The boss may be right. He needed to get her to share it with him. He parked. "First stop, post office."

She jumped out and hurried inside. He followed, looking all around the streets for stalkers. They waited in line and finally walked out with a box heavier than anything she should have tried to carry on her own. He placed it in the rear of the van behind the passenger seats. They headed to the party store.

"Well?" he asked.

"Tell me what you're referring to and we'll go from there." She stared out the window to her right.

How does one explain an obvious person of mystery? He stammered then said, "Do you recall the limerick about a man going upstairs who met a man that wasn't there?"

Sharply she turned her stare at him.

She finally whispered, "Oh mercy. You know." Then bit her bottom lip.

"Sort of. I'd like to help, but you need to tell me what transpired to this point."

Oh snap, snap, snap! The Lockharts hadn't even spent a night in the Queen Anne and already Uncle Paul made himself known. How much did Lock hear? Why did she think Paul might spare the Lockharts? She knew why, because Lock was incapable of hearing him the day they were both there, with Paul in short temper. She closed her eyes.

At this point, Lock had a great deal of knowledge concerning Paul. He read a lot of the case and even toured Phoenix with her, trying to learn more. Yes, according to Paul's explanation of being *in someone's head*, Lock fit all the standard criteria needed to give Paul entry. *Wait. It didn't have to be so bad.* If Lock heard Paul, he'd know *she* wasn't crazy.

Her phone played "Knock Three Times." Oh good! She needed a distraction. "Excuse me."

"Hi, Gwen, what's up?"

"Oh, Letsea, I need your help. Doyle's whole family is coming in for Christmas and now I learn their hotel had to cancel their reservations. The area hotels are packed for Christmas. They can't all stay here. We only have one guest room. I need you to let us all stay with you. Please."

"Gwendolene, I made you the offer when you initially said they were coming. I'm glad to have all of you. How many are there?"

"Twenty."

Letsea said, "I'll need to have beds made up, we'll have to plan meals, too. Make a list. Relax, it'll be fine. We'll figure it out."

When she hung up, she looked at Lock. "I need to go by the housecleaner's office and beg, in person, for help over the holiday. And the caterers."

"What's going on?"

She tittered. "I'm going to have a full house for Christmas."

Lock glanced. "So, you do enjoy parties, huh?"

She patted her hand to his arm. "I do, I really do."

"What will it do to the children's home party for the orphans?"

"I'm not going to cancel it. I'll tweak the timing." In all her excitement, she squeezed his leg then looked at her hand. "Oh! Sorry."

"I'm not." His voice turned husky.

She folded her hands on her lap. *Why does he feel so familiar?*

"Letsea, it's good to see you so happy. I wish I could lend a hand to relieve your tension. Between your past and this current trouble, what can you share to help me figure this out?"

"It's how life is. Some days are easier than others. The pain of my parents' loss is always there, leering, like a permanent stain. It helps to stay busy so I don't concentrate on it so much. Time offers separation. The more positive things I experience, the less old tragedies are in my face, like it used to be."

"Busy? Like when you're having fun with the kids," he said.

"Exactly. Doing the kind of things my parents would be happy about. I can feel their joy more than my sorrow."

"Lets, do you ever hear from the people in the Congo?"

"I call them monthly. There are never any new developments."

"Have they ever called you?" he asked.

"Not since the first year."

"Never? Are you sure?"

The surprise in his voice made her glance at him. "Why? Do you think there's news they're not sharing?"

"I don't know, but they should be making an effort to communicate with you."

She patted his knee again and quickly removed her hand. "Turn right, here." She drew a deep breath, and released it, remembering her train of thought. "When I call them, it's always routine. They say, 'Nothing new. Sorry, we'll call if something comes up.' I ask questions and try to keep them engaged. I think they must have so many new cases, they're overwhelmed."

"Could be. Here. Is this your housecleaner's office?" He pulled to a stop and got out to open her door. "By the way, I contacted my friend with security services. You are on the top of his list in January."

She stopped before going inside. "I've put a lot of thought into that. I look forward to updating the whole system. There are outbuildings to be included with the cameras."

"Do they all have electricity?" he asked.

"Yes, and generators. My main concern, other than the houses and garage, is the car barn. It's huge and way out back. There's a large collection of cars. Bob tries to drive back there every day. Security cameras will be easier on him. Although, he *is* a car guy."

Lock guffawed. "Whether or not they will admit it, all guys are car guys. I'd like to see your collection for myself. My dad, too."

"Anytime."

"Do any of them run?"

"They all do and are licensed. Although, mostly they're used in parades. I do lease some to antique car museums. We call it, 'the car barn,' but inside, it looks more like a dealership showroom. It's been Bob's pet project, most of his life."

"Now I look forward to seeing them all the more." He opened the store's front door.

"Thank you." She patted his hand.

Avoid mention of Uncle Paul's initiation into the inner realm, unless Lock bluntly spoke of the spirit first.

Late Tuesday afternoon, it darkened earlier than normal with an overcast sky.

Bob called Letsea. "Mr. Purser's car is now entering the gate."

She decided to stay with her mom's suggestion to *part in good graces* and stepped outside the front door to greet Seth. "Hello, stranger."

Seth waited until the door to his sporty red car finished its dramatic close then bounded up the steps with enthusiasm she rarely saw in him.

"Hello, beautiful."

He grabbed her waistline and lifted her into the air. "Oh! Seth!" With her hands on his shoulders, she pushed. "Put me down." He let her slide down his front then hooked her in a bear hug and a very long kiss.

She pushed against his chest and twisted her neck to the side.

She had to break away from his embrace. "What's gotten into you?"

"Aw, baby, I've missed you something terrible."

He tried to kiss her again. She pushed away and slipped inside the door.

CHAPTER 57

Lock went outside when he noticed the Lamborghini Gallardo arrive at the gate. He watched from the neighboring front yard. None other than Seth Purser. His jaw tightened. *Shoot!* Just getting used to never seeing "the boyfriend" around and hoped he'd stay away, he sighed. *Here he is.* A slow string of headlights crept by on the road. Gawkers.

For all to see, Purser hugged and kissed Letsea before they went inside. The tall blond attorney appeared to be a fun-loving sort. Letsea's type. The lady did have a playful side to her. He thought of when she put her hand on his leg, and drew in a deep breath.

The lights came on in the front parlor, unable to see inside since the first floor stood too high. He observed the other windows. Her room, a soft glow as it did every evening. Bob's room, on the third floor, well lit, as was his tower office on the first floor. Bob came outside, and a chirp and click of the fancy car sounded through the quiet air. Its headlights flashed and the driver's door raised.

"Hey, Mr. Lockhart, did you get an eyeful of this speed demon? Do you want to go for a ride?"

Lock forced interest. Bob was excitable. "Where are you headed?"

"Not far enough, only as far as behind the house."

He moved in closer. "Thanks for the invite, think I'll pass. Have you driven one of these before?"

"My first time," Bob said. "Have you?"

"A few times, but they always belonged to someone else. Here's a word of advice, be gentle on the gas pedal. Depending on the model and how new it is, it can take you from zero to sixty in under three seconds."

"Wow! Guess I won't get wild in the yard then."

They both chuckled. "Well, be careful. Oh, you don't think she'll be going out again tonight, do you?"

"I highly doubt it. Ice on the way."

"Goodnight." He waved to Bob and headed back into the Queen Anne. He could probably get Bob to spill the beans regarding Purser if he asked. Her romantic life with any other man wasn't what he wanted to imagine.

He went to his room, Letsea's old, childhood room, and looked out the window toward the west end of the mansion. From his perspective, the big house looked totally dark except for the Christmas and yard lights. So close yet so far, the huge primary bedroom above the ballroom showed no sign of movement. What got into him lately? Letsea Brechenworth.

He grabbed the book she loaned him and settled down to read, but his thoughts drifted toward her. He got up and toured the old house, including the summer porch and private classroom.

"Here's goulash." Letsea set a bowl in front of Seth as they sat at an island in the kitchen.

"I'd planned to take you someplace nice for dinner."

"There's no reason. It's not like we're still dating." Rather ticked at his cocky assumption she cared.

Seth cleared his throat. "Yeah, well we should review that decision. Possibly update our status."

She scoffed. "I don't think so. You basically ignored me for three months then abandoned me. I'm ready to move on. You should too." She scooped a spoonful of the goulash and stared at it. "What was with your greeting on the porch?"

Seth kneeled to the floor beside her.

"What are you doing? Get up!" Surely, he wasn't carrying out what it looked like!

"A fiancé would kiss his bride-to-be like that," Seth said and reached into his pocket and pulled out a ring with a huge diamond.

"Letsea Nadene Brechenworth, will you be my wife?"

Her mind jumped to visualizing the memory of Lock playing with the children. Teaching a preschooler how to throw in *Cornhole*. She heard his gruff voice after she apologized for putting her hand on his knee. *Why not Lock? Why does he resist the idea of marriage?*

"Well, what do you say?"

"Seth—" Stunned speechless, she feared of never hearing those words. At least not in time to bear children. She seriously considered alternatives to carry on the Brechenworth name. Seth knew the trust fund deal too. He must have changed his mind. She blurted, "You live in Philadelphia."

"So, I'll gain flight hours. A lot of people have more than one house. I'll keep an apartment there and commute. This will be my home. Whenever you, with our children, want to visit, you can go out there."

"Visit? Ugh!" She clenched her jaw in anger.

He played on her emotions! *Children*, she pondered possibilities of the future. "But you didn't like the trust fund requirement I discussed with you." Even though there were simpler ways to honor her grandfather's ultimate wish, *it is what it is*.

"Baby, I'm sure I can find a loophole in the trust. Give me a copy of it to review. I'll find the aperture so we can both be happy."

She glared at him. Seth must think himself a magician! An astounding act if a pinhole of light did exist. Goodness knows those first couple of years she searched for an escape clause in the document. The older she got, the more she appreciated her name. "Granddad knew what he wanted and I understand why." And if Seth really loved her, it wouldn't matter. But, he wanted to revoke Granddad's wish in exchange for his own. *Egotistical jerk.* "Get off your knee. Go back to Pennsylvania."

He reached for her hand and she pulled it back. "Seth, you've been in my rearview mirror for weeks now. Until you called to come out for your car, you haven't contacted me once. You can't show up and put a ring on my finger and claim me as yours."

"Are you seeing someone else?" he asked.

She closed her eyes. *I wish!* The evening she laid on the sofa and rested her head on Lock's lap came to mind. The comfortable feel of Lock's hand resting on her hip. She'd felt a tug on her ponytail. *What's Lock's problem anyway?* Why hadn't he told her he's interested? *Unless he's not.*

"Letsea, hello. Where are you? Yes or no, are you dating someone else?" Seth baited.

In her heart, she thought, *how easy to be around Lock.* An image of them dancing came to mind. Had she fallen in love with him? But then, all that happened before she knew his job as FBI agent intended to stop her from researching Uncle Paul.

She doubted there was any chance with him. In the speakeasy, he said, "never."

However, it took time to develop a relationship. If she were to wait much longer, her biological clock would close down. She sighed, and opened her eyes. "No."

Seth stood and placed a hand on her elbow. "Here. Take it." He held it ready to slip on her finger. "Marry me, Letsea. You can have the wedding, the honeymoon, the family of your dreams. You can have all the children your heart desires. I'm sorry you felt neglected. It wasn't my intention. My heart has held you close for years now. Please be my wife."

"Eeh! Oh, no!" Pauline gasped and exclaimed from the doorway.

Startled, Letsea and Seth turned toward her. Pauline's eyes were wide and her mouth open even wider.

"I'm sorry! I didn't mean to interrupt. I was just going to get a bowl of goulash for supper. I'm so sorry."

Letsea was relieved for the break in tension. "It's all right, Miss Pauline. Soup's on the stove. Help yourself."

"Mrs. Collins," said Seth. "The Hungarian goulash is good."

Letsea noticed he said *good*, not delicious, and she cringed.

"I'm sure it is. Miss Brechenworth is an excellent cook."

"Oh?" Seth looked at her. "You made this? I didn't know you were a culinarian."

"By the way, this is American-style goulash," Letsea corrected his previous words.

As soon as they were alone, Seth asked, "What do you say, baby? Let's make it official." He pushed the ring on her left ring finger and it stopped at her knuckle.

If ever she recognized a sign, this was it. "No, Seth. You hold on to this beautiful gem. I'm not ready to formalize anything." She shook her head in slow motion.

"Don't say no, Letsea. I'm sorry I acted like a jerk. Between us, I feared ruining my career. Every decision needed to be precise. Me against a team of experienced, high-priced, arrogant attorneys. In an underhanded way, they assured me of a strategic plan to bury me. Good grief, there were times I thought I could hear the shovels crunch against dirt and rock to dig a hole for my body. I had to stay focused."

If she mattered to him, he would have shared his fears with her. She may have offered insight, or comforted him as needed. Instead, he deserted her. "Seth, you didn't communicate at all."

"Sorry. I was scared and desperate."

"And you didn't feel you could tell me?" Letsea sighed. "Most people take a vacation. You abruptly moved."

"My father encouraged me to join his firm. He knows how to handle the cunning."

"So, he can be shrewd?"

"Father is astute. At best, I feel safe under his protective shield and his legal team. I have a lot to learn and he knows the score. Obviously, there's much more to law than what's in the books."

It no longer mattered.

Letsea shivered, and noticed the pinging of ice against the high basement windows. "Your room is on the third floor, east end. Your bags will be in it."

"Sounds far away from you." He shoved his hands in his pockets.

"It is."

She put the pot of stew back in the refrigerator and handwashed the few dishes.

"Letsea, I'm sorry I hurt you, but I needed to break away from here. Don't take it personally. I want to be your husband. You are the woman I want to be the mother of my children. To have and hold." He kissed her cheek and slipped the ring into her palm, folded her fingers over it before he left her alone.

Eyes squeezed closed. *It* was *personal, to me,* she told herself.

Why does he think I'd marry him now? She thought of the children she wanted to have and Seth knew it! He used her heart's desire for a family to keep her from looking too closely at his downfalls. *How dare he!*

An image of Lock playing Simple Simon flashed in her mind. Swaying his body like a tree in the wind and laughing with the children. She couldn't picture Seth ever playing such games.

The moment Bob signaled for Lock, he totally moved into protective mode.

Seth moved away in fear.

She placed the ring on the island and finished with the dishes.

Later, she placed Seth's ring on her office desk, locked the door, and strolled to the manor's premier bedroom. Rex Kitty followed and stayed at her feet when she pushed back the drapes and blackout shade. The lights were on in her old room in the Queen Anne across the lawn. Lights came on and went off, one room at a time through the house. Captivated, she picked up her cat and watched.

Later in bed, she tossed and turned with memories of rubbing Lock's feet. After picturing him laughing, Letsea finally fell asleep.

"What is going on?" Lock's mother asked.

"Looking around. Getting some steps in. Honestly, Mom, I feel restless."

His father called up the staircase, "What are you two doing way up there?"

His mother answered, "Trey hasn't figured out he's in love with Letsea. He thinks it's restlessness."

His father joined them near the third floor. The three sat on the stairs. "It happened to me, Son. Only once I realized it, I didn't pussyfoot around. I knew your mother was the one for me. I proposed, although we were in high school, so we waited a couple of years, to grow up."

Mom leaned against Dad. "We knew we were meant to be together. Don't you feel that way with Letsea?"

"I haven't thought about it in those direct terms," Trey said. He assumed his libido was in overdrive and the internal id messed with him.

"Give it some thought, Trey." His mother tugged on the hem of his jeans, got up, and headed downstairs.

"Come on down, supper's ready," his father said, then caught up to his mom. He watched his dad put a hand on her waist and she stopped to kiss him.

After dinner, Lock picked up the thriller book and went into the casual family room where he found a recliner and reading lamp.

Am I in love? Maybe so. He revisited his history, to a time he knew love. Memories of how it felt to be excited, future bound, and craving his fiancée shook him to the reality of her violent death. For ages, he believed her death as a result of dating him. Relief flooded his senses to learn differently.

It could explain his resistance to acknowledge his true feelings for a woman he met such a short time beforehand. The major fact of her boyfriend was an issue. The man, no doubt over there with his hands all over her. Or more. He squirmed, opened the book, and found a business card tucked between the pages. A card, of the author, he flipped it over and noticed the man wrote his private cell phone number on it. Apparently, every man wanted Letsea's attention. Before he tucked the card between the back pages, he made note of the information, and forced himself to read. He had to stay sane and keep his mind off Letsea. After all, she was an assignment!

Hours later, he finished and closed the book. The house was quiet and dark, except for window candle lights. He looked at the clock. His parents were long ago retired for the night.

"Confound it," he uttered. No wonder these books held Letsea's attention. Gunner Hardyn Chase was an excellent writer. He already wanted to trade book one for book two.

Instead, he went to bed.

CHAPTER 58

The Lamborghini left early. Lock wasn't sure whether the hum of the garage door, the arrival of the housekeepers' vehicles, or the smell of Mom's baking woke him

The girls were arriving for Christmas, *still* for those little moments in between the bigger ones, he wanted to get his hands on book two of the Chase series.

Headed to the big house for the book exchange, he entered through the back entrance near the kitchens.

"Pauline, you're baking too?" The pastry kitchen countertops were filled with baked goods and Christmas candies. "You and Mom both." He eyed fudge in several flavors.

"Alice and I agreed to make different treats and breads then swap some out. Bigger variety for everyone. I understand Hope's family is already on the road. What time does Faith's plane come in?"

"Two thirty-five this afternoon. Hey, any of these ready to be tested?" He offered her a hopeful look, with his eyebrows raised, and reached toward a cookie.

Pauline motioned her okay. "Stop back later, I'll bundle tidbits for you. What's going on?"

"Letsea is letting me read a series of books she's into. I'm here to trade up." He waved the book in his hand. "Is she around?" She better not have left without informing him.

"I haven't heard anything from her."

He'd rather not think why she needed to sleep in.

"Marcia's in her office. She'll know where the books are,"

Pauline said.

"Great. I'll ask her."

"Trey, shoes off before you go upstairs."

"Indeed." He sat on the walnut steps and untied his trail boots to set aside before heading up the impressive yet practical staircase.

"Good morning," he said at the secretary's doorway. He showed her the book. "I'm here to trade for book two."

The secretary stepped up. "Miss Brechenworth mentioned you'd be looking for more. How did you like it?"

"Anxious for the next."

She pointed. "In the morning room." They walked toward the east end of the hall.

"Have you seen her this morning?"

"Not yet." She looked on the same shelf where book one came from. "I don't see book two here." She glanced at her watch. "I'll see if she's awake."

Marcia headed upstairs with him close behind. She tested Letsea's doorknob before a light tap. "Miss Brechenworth?"

He heard the sound of a skeleton key twisting in the lock and stepped back, out of Letsea's view. She opened the door. "Sorry, I didn't sleep well."

He rolled his eyes.

"Is there anything I can do for you?" Marcia asked.

"Have someone bring me coffee, please," Letsea muttered.

"I'll do it. We're looking for book two of the Chase series. It's not in the morning room."

"I forgot. It's somewhere in my office. I bet he's clamoring to get his hands on it." After a yawn, she said, "I told him he'd not want to stop reading until he's done. Oh, Marcia, tell Lockhart he's welcome to drive the passenger van to the airport to pick up his family. It'll save them from driving two cars and being cramped."

Marcia looked over her shoulder at him. "I'll be sure he knows."

He mouthed "thanks" and saw Letsea hand Marcia a key and closed her door.

Marcia crossed the hall, unlocked the office, and went in.

Lock followed. His socked feet sank deep in the high-pile carpet. He wiggled his toes. While the assistant searched for the book, he admired the plush white wool rug under her desk, then looked up to the ultimate computer system. He noticed the sparkle of a ring with a gigantic diamond next to the keyboard. *Oh, come on! I don't have a chance, do I? I'm not in her league.*

"Found it!"

He heard a pleased reaction near the updated electric fireplace between the large windows. Contrary, sorrow hit him with anger at himself. *Blasted assignment.* Why did he have to go and fall in love? That's when he knew. He *was* in love.

"Here. I'll swap books with you." Marcia looked at him and furrowed her brows.

"Thank you," he said and hurried downstairs, put his shoes on, and aimed straight out the back door. Book two better be even greater than the first one. He desperately needed a worthwhile distraction.

"Hey, Chief, did you find out anything new on the calls from the Congo?" Lock sat at Letsea's little desk in her old room and studied the call list on his laptop.

"Just what you have on the link I sent, and that particular burner phone has not been used since she cashed the check in question."

"I asked her about communication with the Congo. She said their authorities never call her. I'll scrutinize the call list and zero in on her activity timeline. I have an idea, but I still need more information."

"Good luck. Don't be surprised if she's hiding a threat. At this stage, if you need to, call her on it. Dang it, get her to tell you what's going on. Don Pfeiffer is your contact here. He'll take over as soon as she admits there's a situation of blackmail. Got it?"

"Got it, sir. Did Agent Douglas interview her bank?"

"Yes. The teller who cashed the check is on vacation and they couldn't reach her. He's retrieving the surveillance coverage and a photocopy of the check."

Lock thought that if the clerk used her smarts, she wouldn't answer her phone when work called on her vacation. He definitely learned his lesson. But then, by job description, he was always on duty.

"Brechenworth didn't show signs of stress or fabrication when I asked her, sir."

"Maybe she's good at lying."

"I don't think so, Chief. I believe she's being honest." At least, concerning her parents' ordeal.

"You can see for yourself the calls exist. Keep me updated. I'm heading home." *Click.*

He looked across at book two on the bed. "Right now, I'd like to blow something to smithereens like you do, fictitious FBI agent."

Instead, he scrutinized the call list.

Letsea headed to the kitchen and stopped to see Marcia. "Did he get the book?"

"Yes, ma'am. Grabbed and ran with it."

Letsea said, "I knew he'd like the characters and storyline. Uh, what time did Seth leave?"

"Gone before I got here. The housekeepers are here making up all the beds. Liza's on it. She's having them lemon-oil polish all-natural wood in the house, while so many are here. The caterers called to confirm meals. Pauline took care of it and is busy baking and singing Christmas carols."

"Perfect." *Right?* There was no reason for anyone to venture to the fourth floor of the tower. Although, someday she should have new window-seat cushions made.

Lock pulled through the gates and looped around behind the big house. Faith giggled and he felt her drum the back of his seat.

"Trey, how on earth did Mom and Dad manage to get this place for us?"

"Mom knows the owner from the tea room, and we are in the Queen Anne, not the mansion."

"I remember her, you know. From dance classes. She's a lot younger than me, but oh man, graceful from the start. 'Our little swan,' Mrs. B. used to call her. Letsea's dad was a hoot!'"

"You knew him?" Lock asked. He stopped the van in the circle drive between the two houses so they would first experience the main grand entrance instead of the kitchen.

Faith swatted his shoulder. "Not personally, but her parents often attended practice and watched from the sidelines. I could tell they were filled with pride and he had humorous expressions. After class, he'd scoop her up and congratulate her on an excellent job. We were in separate classes, but I always thought it cool they were there so often. They traveled a lot, so sometimes they'd all be gone for weeks at a time."

"In separate classes, how did you even see her?" he asked.

"You'd drop us off early, before her class closed. Lordy, when I heard they were murdered, I prayed and cried for her, even though she was an adult when it happened. So sad. As a kid, she was so cute and always happy. She must have been devastated." Faith opened her door and let the kids out. "Do you think we might see her while we're here?"

He walked to the rear of the van. "There's a chance, but she does have a houseful of her own guests arriving tomorrow, so I don't know."

Carlton, Faith's husband, loaded down with luggage, asked Trey to get the last few bags.

"I can't imagine what all you thought you needed to bring." He usually carried one carry-on and his laptop when he traveled.

"It's the girls' stuff," Carlton said. "And Christmas gifts."

"Yes. It's Christmas," Lock agreed. He went the simpler route. Cash and cards, except for a couple of gifts. He sighed. One thing for sure, he wasn't giving anyone a five-carat diamond.

Faith's fourteen-year-old son, Bo, sidled up next to him. Unbelievable how fast the boy grew. "Here, Bo, grab a couple of suitcases."

"Hey, Uncle Trey, who got murdered? Does that mean this old house is haunted?"

CHAPTER 59

Wednesday afternoon

L ock met her in the main hall. "Letsea, I need to talk to you. It's important."

She motioned for him to come upstairs. In her office, they sat in the pair of modern white chairs near the balcony doors. "What is it?" She thought he looked tense with his jaw tight. She pressed to the back of the chair to brace herself.

"Do you remember what you did on the first Monday of this month? Talk to anyone? Go anywhere?"

"Same as the first Monday of every month. I got up early to call the Congo's anti-kidnapping office. They're seven hours ahead of us and I like to talk with them before their lunch break. Later, I searched stock news updates for possible investment opportunities. I also talk with my sister and aunt, usually more than once a day. I went to bed early."

"What happened the next day, Tuesday?" he asked.

"Oh. I met Seth for lunch and I went to the zoo." She watched him open and close his mouth without saying a word. She explained, "The young children's choir performed at the zoo."

Lock raised a brow. "So, you weren't home at noon?"

"No. Seth and I were at Union Station. Purser is his last name. *Should* I need an *alibi*," she said in jest, hoping to change his direction. He managed to narrow down the time of Agent Reynolds' first declaration to her in the Whispering Arch. *How sharp of a detective is he anyway?* She clenched into cushioned arms of the chair. "What are you getting at, Lock?"

"Hang in here with me, Letsea. Were you home by, say 2:30 p.m., Tuesday?"

"I think so. I always like to check my investments before the closing bell. Easier done on my home computer than a phone." She remembered the day, in her car, reading articles on Reynolds. Marcia called and startled her. *Oh, mercy! Does the DOJ keep tabs of every online search to their dot-gov website?* "Why is that time important to you?"

"In a minute. Tell me the rest of the week. Did you stay home every day, all day?"

She leaned forward. "Tell me why this is important, or I'll not answer any more questions."

"Work with me, I don't want to lead you into answers. It's important. I need to talk with your assistant, too. She takes a lot of your calls, right?"

"A leading question might be helpful." She sighed, got up, and pressed the intercom button on the landline phone. "Marcia, will you come to my office, please?"

"Yes, ma'am. My pleasure. I'm stuck on a line with one of those scam artists. Persistent devil that he is."

"Why don't you hang up?" she asked.

"He keeps calling back."

Lock jumped from his chair and said, "Don't hang up. Ask him to hold."

"I'd be glad to leave him on hold, indefinitely, for all I care. He's a nuisance."

Lock typed on his phone. "Tell him you'll put the call through, but it'll take a moment. Stall."

He put his hand on her waist and guided her to sit. "Letsea, do as I tell you. Leave the phone on speaker. I need to hear what he's saying. Stay calm. Keep him talking. Don't say anything in the affirmative, never say 'yes'."

"Calm? What do you think he wants?" she insisted.

"We're about to find out. Answer it."

"Hello." He pulled up a second chair to sit knee to knee with her, and they locked eyes.

"Is this Miss Brechenworth?"

She leaned in toward the phone. "What do you need?"

"You having nice day?"

"Not particularly."

"Sorry for that. It important you received my call, ma'am. I am Mark, with your security protection plan." His accent and broken English made understanding him difficult. "According to our record, your computer has serious intrusion. Someone trying to hack your system. I can help you and stop intruder from taking over your private files."

Lock rolled his eyes, motioned with a fast-paced finger across his throat, a signal for her to cut the call. He looked at his phone and resumed typing.

"Oh, really?" She told the caller, "I'll tell you what, give me your home phone number and I'll have my security guard call you back so we can get this figured out."

"I cannot my home number," he said in broken English.

"You called me at mine and I'm on both the state and federal No Call Lists."

Click.

A flicker of a grin passed his lips. "Good girl. Except you should never converse with them. Seriously, many of these callers record voice conversations so they can duplicate yours easier. Anything you say they'll edit your words to falsify sentences for scams. They want you to say the word yes." He glanced at his phone. "Hey! On a positive note, it looks like we have his GPS coordinates. Good job." He typed for a few more moments.

"Who did you think called?" she asked.

"Let's look at a calendar. We need to review your steps this month."

Letsea squinted her eyes. "Tell me what you're looking for." She reached for her daily planner book, put it on her lap, and pressed against it.

"It'll help to build a timeline of your activities from the first of the month." He touched the speaker intercom button. "Marcia, I'll stop by your office on my way out. Save the steps."

"Thank you, sir."

Her muscles tightened. "Why? What did I do?" She held her breath.

Lock took hold of her hand, maintained eye-to-eye contact. "Breathe. The Bureau wants to protect you. Between stalkers and a couple of other details, you may be in danger. So do as I say, don't leave your house."

"I thought you were all over my uncle's history." She watched for his reaction.

"Priorities switched when we learned you were being followed."

She speculated if they trained FBI agents to not show emotion. She drew in a defensive breath. "What do you want from me?"

"Answers."

After crossing her arms, she said, "Seems like we've been through this before."

"It doesn't make this any less important."

"Fine. What do you want to know?"

"Starting on the first Tuesday of this month, have you talked to anyone you don't know?"

"Naturally, I have. I went to Phoenix, held a community tea party, been shopping—"

His right hand went up flat. "Stop. One day at a time, start with the first Tuesday."

He patted an arm and she dropped both hands to her lap.

"Letsea, breathe. I'm for you, not against you."

"When, exactly?" she asked and opened her daily planner. She swallowed a gasp, slammed it closed, and tossed it aside on her desk.

"What happened before or after your date with Mr. Purser?"

After a deep sigh, she shrugged. "I don't remember."

"We can order a list of calls from the phone company for your current cell phone."

"You think it's important enough?"

She noticed his eyes widened as he caressed the back of her hand, from her wrist to her fingers. Such gentleness intended to help her relax. Instead, warmness fervently moved in.

"Okay. You can do it."

"While you were at lunch, did anyone else approach you?"

Yeah, the voice of a dead FBI agent. "Let me think." Not willing to expose her ghost or possibly her own insanity. "Oh, a Cardinals player started to approach, but Seth pulled me away. I'd liked to have met him."

"After that?" he asked.

"I went to the zoo, came home. Do you think it's a hacker or scammer?"

"Could be, however, we think it might be more personal than either of those."

She squeezed his fingertips and studied his eyes. "Who?"

"Has anyone asked you for money lately?"

"Sure, charities and my sister."

"Does anything unusual come to mind?"

"Not really. I wish you'd tell me what you're thinking."

"We'll know more of your timeline after we get a look at your current cell phone records."

"Lock, why don't you want my house phone records?"

He patted her hand, stood, and stepped back. "We already have those."

"Did you obtain a warrant?"

"The Bureau didn't need to. You and your grandfather signed a release over a decade ago. You must remember they promised to monitor calls and emails. It's based on international safety concerns between you and Africa. We have records for your landline and the cell phone number you used at the time. Now you mostly use the old one for online searches. We need to view your current call record on the cell number you gave me. Do you agree?"

"If it'll help put all this behind us. Sure."

He gave a pleasant half smile. "All we need is for you to sign here with your finger." He held his phone steady while she signed it. "I'll run an errand and be right back." Lock left.

She opened the daily planner to the Tuesday in question, and re-read the unforgettable words she had written in red ink to make note of when she had heard them. *I was murdered!*

Solely alone to consider Lock's words about her phone records.

How closely has the FBI been monitoring my calls through the years?

CHAPTER 60

Brechenworth mansion early Wednesday evening

At home in his office, Lock searched information from Letsea's current cell number records. He focused on cell tower locations, and alignment to incoming calls from the Congo. He printed what he needed and returned to the estate.

Having noticed Purser's fancy car at the car porch, he knew of the boyfriend's presence. Quietly, he entered through the back door, removed his hat and shoes, then headed up the wooden staircase to the main floor. His steps slowed when he heard Purser's fast clip and rather haughty voice in the front main parlor.

"Don't be ridiculous. We have three years of our lives wrapped up with each other. You cannot seriously think of severing a solid relationship now."

Letsea asserted with a firm voice, "We've already covered this, Seth. The answer is no."

"Don't you still want children? You're losing time. Have you seen your doctor lately? What did she say?"

Lock heard a long pause and cringed. He once thought the same thing, but hearing it voiced was incredibly rude.

"How dare you. It doesn't concern you! It's over. I'll go get your ring."

In stocking feet, Lock aimed upward for the hall and veered into the library. Though hidden, he easily heard their discussion. He felt the tension of her anger, yet she did not leave the front parlor as he expected.

"Letsea Nadene, we are *not* finished. I don't know what has gotten into you. It is essential you come to your senses. I need your commitment to our future family."

Silence.

Whoa! Lock rolled his shoulders. *Purser is bold and pushy.* He considered his possibilities with her, with this dimwit out of the way. Probably less, should she catch him eavesdropping on such a private conversation. He waited through her silence and easily imagined her defiant, piercing, angry green eyes cutting ties with Purser.

"Keep it, Letsea. Wear it. I mean to leave here trusting we are engaged."

"Can't happen, Seth. I'd never marry without love."

"Aw, baby," his voice softened. "I love you. You know that."

"That's the first time you've ever said it. Besides, while you avoided me these past several months, I realized I do not love you. You did say, 'Philadelphia *is your* home.' Seth, you will never live here."

"If I'd known I'd lose so much in the process, I would have passed on my last case. Even with the grand settlement, baby, it's not worth losing you over."

Lock drew in a deep breath. He wished to see their faces.

"You never *had* me. I am the one Granddad put his trust in. It's part of who I am. I reject any legal challenge of it. Two years ago, you obviously resisted the terms of my trust fund, as is. You still do. I should have listened to my intuition. You'll never change."

Lock rested the back of his head against the hardwood wall. *Atta girl, Lets, kick him to the curb.* Huh. The Seth Eadgard Purser Law Firm of Philadelphia, Pennsylvania, he thought of them as shysters of the courtroom. After all, who else is undaunted by the DOJ? Oh yeah, Letsea. He took a deep breath, closed his eyes, and sighed. Puzzle pieces were finally starting to fit into place!

"First, I'd like to shower and change. We can discuss this over dinner. Where do you want to eat? The roads are clear so I won't take no for an answer tonight," Purser said.

"You're going to have to. I have a previous dinner engagement with friends. Your bag is packed and in Bob's office. I'll go get your ring now."

Lock heard the rapid pitapat of hard leather-soled shoes as she scurried upstairs. *Why is she wearing outside shoes in the house?* He recalled her balletic feet in a pair of classic pumps. Realization struck, she must be power-dressed to maintain her confidence and control of the situation. Smart girl. *Bare feet or slippers show comfort, possibly compliance, they lessen her show of strength and ultimately the effect.* Willing to bet, not casually dressed to send off the arrogant ex-suitor. He thought of her wearing the bunny booties. *Good heavens,* he thought, *she's both beautiful and funny.*

Purser yelled up the staircase, "Who *is* Bob?" Then paced at the foot of the stairs.

Lock rolled his eyes. *What a dunderhead. How can he not know Bob?* The security guard with a crush on his boss and an even bigger crush on her collection of cars.

As he heard her coming back down, Purser growled, "Don't be unreasonable, Letsea."

"Let go of my arm!" Letsea's voice firm. Lock braced his hand on the doorframe, ready to pounce.

"Ouch!" Purser yelped.

"Seth, don't ever touch me that way again," she ordered in an eerily calm manner.

"I'm sorry, but hear me out," Purser insisted in a low, slow, controlled voice.

Lock clinched his jaw. He didn't want Letsea to know he listened in, although he refused to let Purser hurt her. Of course, she knew self-defense. He was proud of her. He listened, shifted backward to stay hidden from view as she and Ex-Boyfriend walked down the hall toward the security office.

"Here's your ring. Your bag is in here. Now you need to leave."

He peeked. They both moved out of sight into the security office.

"Ow!" Purser squealed.

"I told you no," she said in a hardened tone.

Lock remembered the photographer in Phoenix. He had an idea of Purser's current position.

Oh yeah, she's got this, he thought, then stole his way down the stairs to put his shoes on. He listened, but their conversation was low, no further hollering. He exited the back door and circled toward the Lamborghini Gallardo

Purser stepped out on the car porch, while Letsea remained

inside. "Take care of yourself. I'll see to me." She shut the castle-like thick door in a sweeping, firm thud, emphasizing her rejection.

Well done, Letsea! Purser stood looking dumbfounded, alone on the side porch. Finally, he stepped down to the ground, circled his Lamborghini, and hit the key fob. As the parting lawyer encroached on the driver's side, he looked over his shoulder, startled.

"Who in hades *are* you? How did you get inside the gate? Oh. You must be Bob. I hope you're not expecting a tip," he said scornfully.

"I have my own passcode. Special Agent, Godrick Lockhart, Federal Bureau of Investigation. No tip obligatory. Seth Purser the Third, we need to talk."

Letsea, in the round security room, pushed the gate button open. Why hadn't Seth pulled out? She turned for a better view, looking out the large curved window toward the car porch. Lock stood near one of the stone pillars talking to Seth. In jeans, a worn brown leather bomber jacket, and a rugged leather fedora, Lock still outclassed Seth in a business suit. She sighed questioned if they were talking about her.

She hoped her new security cameras came with audio.

Lock appeared to be in control. Seth, totally in defensive mode. His arms moved, talking wildly with his hands. It reminded her of a monkey! If he acted so willy-nilly in a courtroom, he'd prove to be ridiculed. *Where did the big defense attorney disappear to?*

Knees quivering, Letsea swayed then braced herself and took some calming breaths. Finally, she left the men to finish their alpha contest. No doubt, cool, calm, and collected would win. Besides being older, Lock had more experience. She headed to her room to calm down and change clothes.

Her phone played "God Save The Queen." She reached for her cell with a trembling hand. Not wanting her aunt to hear the tension in her voice, after the second ring she took another deep breath and answered. "Hello, Aunt Mae, how are you?"

"I haven't talked to you all day. Did your guests get settled into the Queen Anne?"

"Well, the Lockharts are all here now. I'm having dinner with them tonight, and I look forward to meeting the rest of the family. How are you and Uncle Robert?"

"Same. Letsea, honey, I talked with your sister a bit ago. Did you know she's planning to bring their suitcases over tonight? She wants the kids' clothes to be there, steamed and ready for the candlelight service ahead of time."

"Yes, she also wants me to give her and Doyle my room to stay in."

"Lock the door, take the key. Stop giving her everything she wants," said Aunt Mae.

"Auntie, I told her no. She pouted, but she'll figure it out."

"If you aren't careful, she'll move you to an old third-floor servants' room."

"I had those remodeled. They're really very nice."

"You've done a lot for the old place, honey. Oh, they say a storm is brewing up north. Fortunately, it'll be a few days until we see it. Candlelight service will be a beautiful night."

"I know, I'm so excited."

"Honey, I'll let you go. I wanted to check in with you."

"Thanks, I love you, Aunt Mae. Sorry I didn't call earlier."

"I know you're busy. I love you too, honey. Bye-bye."

As she hung up, she walked to the window in her room and watched Seth's car drive away and the gate close. Bob must be back in his office. His survey of the car barn was longer than usual. She was certain it was his way of giving her privacy while she dismissed her visitor. She brushed her hands together. "Good riddance, Seth."

She looked along the road out front. A couple of cars were parked waiting for the Christmas lights to turn on. At least no sporty black cars were about. With onlookers, she and Pauline would cross in the tunnel instead of on the lawn. No need to encourage the grapevine with the appearance of an empty house.

Her room suddenly brightened inside and out. Automatically the window candlesticks lit, as well as the outdoor draped string lights around both houses and the fence line. A picture-perfect Christmas for all to see. Right?

In her walk-in closet, she smoothed her hands down the tight wool dress and decided to change into something more relaxed for dinner with the Lockharts. Maybe she'd go with the Christmasy Bohemian-chic look. What if she were to wear one of her own fedoras? Or, Lock's?

She glanced to her dressing room mirror. "Just what *is* picture-perfect anyway?"

Her frustration resurfaced. "Three years I spent on that jerk!" she screamed. After taking off her shoes, she threw one and then the other across the room. "I should have kept his stupid crackerjack ring! I could have donated it to a charity auction."

CHAPTER 61

Wednesday evening at the Queen Anne

Letsea rested her chin to her palm. Glances up and down the expanded table revealed pure joy. Not surprised Alice had a loving family. The comical aspect caught her off guard. Long after dessert, they all sat around the table sharing memories, children included.

Lock leaned toward her and whispered, "You okay?"

She saw both concern and crow's feet humor lines. "My jaw is sore from laughing. You have an awesome family."

He said, "They keep me on my toes."

"Apparently, so did your monkey. Whatever made you want one?"

"He was cute, but boy, did he turn hyper when he didn't get his way."

His sister Faith piped in, "Nothing like having an uncontrollable primate rule the household." She rolled her blue eyes.

Faith, a natural comedienne, shared hilarious stories of childhood. She clearly enjoyed picking on her brother. The funniest quips were about school activities and Trey's pet monkey, Merewood. He must have been a handful.

Alice suggested, "Tomorrow we can form a caravan to go to Trey's house and dig for the boxes of photo albums and Christmas ornaments. What else?"

Hope stood. "We should go by the old house to look around one last time."

"As if we won't be popping back over there all week," Faith piped in. "Let's go out to eat then hunt for our Christmas tree."

"Letsea, you should come with us," invited Hope. "We have a ball! You won't regret it."

"I'd love to. My sister's family starts to arrive in the morning. I'll have a houseful." She thumbed toward the big house. "Sorry. I'm sure I'll be missing great fun."

Rick, Lock's dad, clapped. "There's a family room toward the back of the house and an awe-inspiring Victorian parlor. To which do we retire?"

The ladies voted for the parlor. It opened to the main entryway. As soon as Letsea stood to move out of the dining room, Faith rushed up beside her.

"I simply adore your Boho skirt." She twirled in her own. "Where did you find it?"

"Thanks. My sister, Gwendolene, does my fashion shopping."

"She has a great eye for style," said Faith. "Didn't she model?"

"Still does, every chance she gets." Letsea was proud of Gwen's talents in the fashion world. Plus, she received marvelous discounts.

Pauline said, "Look. All three of you girls are wearing flower child dresses."

Free spirit, her mother called it. She loved memories of her mom.

"Ladies, let's dance." Hope pointed at the piano. "Trey, play something for us to dance to. With Carlton, if we had a violin, we'd have a duet."

"The music room on the third floor has a couple," said Letsea.

Bo, the youngest grandson, jumped up. "I know where it is." He ran up the stairs.

"You play?" she asked Trey.

"I used to. Guess we'll see if I still have it." Carefully, he moved through the crowd and sat at the black baby grand and pecked on the keys.

Nico, Hope's husband, said, "Fortunately my wife didn't volunteer me!"

Trey, and his father, guffawed. Then he made a great effort to warm up the eighty-eight. When she moved in closer, he said,

"Nico has talents, music isn't one of them."

Bo handed Carlton a violin and scrunched his face when his dad tweaked the strings to tune them.

The unity of Lockhart family ties reminded her of the fun she enjoyed growing up.

"What are we playing?" Trey asked.

Hope blurted, "Tchaikovsky's Sleeping Beauty!"

Carlton complained, "Why can't it be something easy, like 'Twinkle, Twinkle Little Star'?"

Alice chimed in, "Now, Boys, it only takes a few minutes to get the hang of it again."

"Grandpa and Grandma, come sit on the sofa. We kids can sit on the floor," said Katie. "I'll take pictures."

"Come on, Letsea, Hope, let's warm up too," encouraged Faith.

Glad they did, she needed to stretch, especially after a full meal.

By the time everyone gathered to watch, the guys were ready. She, Faith, and Hope were centered in the main entry hall near the staircase. During the introduction, with eyes closed to experience the rush of music, energy pulsated in her body. Lock and Carlton played with the fervor of a tiny orchestra. Their passion, notable exhilaration.

On cue, they danced. Twirling and gliding in long flowing skirts and loose blouses. Like being born again, fresh, surrounded by new caring, fun-loving friends. Such a pleasure to be with the Lockharts, she blinked away tears of solaces. The ebb and flow of the musical rendition finally stopped. After their finale, the three closed with a circled hug.

Nico, in his Greek accent said, "Aw, *The Three Graces* stand before us!"

Faith murmured, "Luckily with clothes on."

The comical aspect of the evening brought the calm of tranquility and offered her rare peace.

In a few short seconds, applause and praises sung out in the old house. When Letsea looked over her shoulder to get a glimpse of Lock, the only thing she saw was Gwendolene standing in the foyer, staring with her mouth open.

Her heart stopped.

"When did you learn to dance like that?" Gwendolene asked as they walked back to the big house through the tunnel.

"Before you were born, you little snippet."

"Those window sheers merely highlight. No privacy from the cars."

"Who cares?" She didn't. What a revelation. A night of pure fun! Letsea looped an arm around her little sister's elbow and asked, "What do you need?"

"Your help. I don't know who I should assign to which bedrooms."

"Honey, why don't you let them decide? Great-Grandmama's rule number two, 'Guests rejoice, when you quiet your voice, and offer choice.'"

"Dare I ask for rule number one?" Gwen quizzed in a dull tone.

"'It's easier to please, when guests feel at ease.'"

"Doyle's family already have reservations toward me." Gwen slumped against her big sister, took a deep breath, then stomped a foot. "I want everything to be perfect!"

Letsea framed her hands around Gwen's face. "Whose world is ever perfect? Half of the country is wanting to restore the good of who we are, and the other half condemns the imperfections and wants to move forward by pushing every aspect of our lives into government control. A large percentage of which, don't even realize the underlying communistic objectives of what they're promoting. Where's the perfection there?"

"Granddad used to worry."

"Yes, he did. Remember FDR once said, 'There is nothing to fear, but fear itself'? Granddad called that a 'Heads up'. Yes, he worried about tyrants creating fearful events. As though scaring us to forget the strength of who we really are, both as individuals and as a nation. Gwen, life can be beautiful, yet as we well know, it isn't ideal all the time. Everyone lives life from the perspective of their own personal experiences. Granddad wanted us to be brave."

"Brave? I just want to make sure my in-laws think good of me."

"It's none of your business what they think of you."

Gwen stepped back, hands on hips, and snapped, "What?"

"You can't force others to like you. Nor would you want others to control *your* thoughts." Letsea explained, "Life will be easier all around by letting them know the genuine person you are in your heart."

Gwen looked confused. Letsea rested her forehead to her sister's. "Blessed be, we still have the right to think whatever we want. So do your in-laws."

"Doyle is often telling me how to think." Gwen's bottom lip revealed a pout.

"Doyle is a man with opinions, but he's fair and he listens. I'm sure he thinks he's always right, until he changes his mind. Of course, I don't know, I suppose, in a loving marriage there is truth to the words, 'The two shall become one,' in more ways than physical. Perhaps the more you openly communicate, the more alike you will become. Do you remember how Mommy and Daddy often finished each other's sentences?"

"No."

"Well, they did. So did our grandparents. With so much in common, they lived on the same wavelength. Often, they knew what the other thought before they voiced it."

Letsea realized she longed for familiarity in a relationship. She reflected on the playfulness of Lock. It gave her hope. Be it his job, or not, his protectiveness reassured her. What he might think of her, shouldn't matter. Not that she wanted to share her ghost with him. *Oh, snap!* She *did* care what he thought of her.

"Letsea?"

"Sorry, Gwen, my mind wandered elsewhere. Do you realize you're always trying to show the Davises how perfect you are? It's a not-so-subtle way of saying you think you are better than they are. Is that what you want?"

Gwen stomped a foot. "Absolutely not, but I don't want them to think I'm a bimbo, either."

Letsea strained to keep the frivolity of Gwen's words to herself. "Honey, everyone who knows you, knows better."

"I do want their stay to be perfect. If it reflects well on me, so be it."

"Gwendolene, you don't have to prove yourself to anyone. Relax. They're going to enjoy their time here because they're all together. Remember, you are not the pinnacle of their visit. You are a part of the whole family. This is Chip and Lauren's musical debut to Doyle's family. Relax. Meals are already planned, with choices available. Daddy used to say, 'Life is a buffet, by golly, get a big plate and enjoy it!'"

"I wish I remembered them more," Gwen whispered.

She kissed her sister's cheek. "Your extended family will get to know you and love you even more as you loosen up. Let them relax and enjoy each other's company." Letsea was still invigorated by the Lockharts' thrill of togetherness.

"Don't try to kid me, Lets. Your tea party is no buffet."

Letsea playfully swatted Gwendolene on her bottom and they both chortled on their way to find Doyle and the kids.

Doyle stood and greeted them when they entered the front parlor. "They're asleep." He motioned to the kids on one of the sofas. "Mom, Dad, and all the grandparents' arrive on the same plane at 9:37 a.m. Uncle Robert volunteered to drive the limousine to the airport. I'll drive the van and greet them. Robert will bring them here. I'll wait to pick up my sisters' families. The last plane comes in at 2:22 p.m." Doyle asked, "Did you figure out your sleeping arrangements?"

"Yes," Gwen said, "We're going to let them pick their own rooms."

Doyle's eyes widened. "Really?" He glanced at Letsea, kissed Gwen on the lips. "Darling, they'll love that."

Letsea's phone played the theme song she assigned to Lock, "Mission Impossible." She stepped away. "Hello, Lock."

"If it's not too late to talk, I have a timeline. I know we'll both be busy tomorrow and I don't want to put this off."

"Come on over. Access the tunnel beneath the kitchen stairs. It comes out in the basement. You'll find me in the library."

"I'll be right there."

She watched Doyle and Gwen gather up sleepy kiddos into their arms to head home.

The tunnel was wider than he anticipated. He looked at the walls. Notably, white ceramic subway tiles weren't as intimidating as the Paris Catacombs. He shivered, remembering the sight of bones and skulls. For what reason did the Brechenworths create underground passages?

Recalling Letsea during the evening, her quick wit spoke volumes of her disposition. Disappointment pinched at his senses when she left the house after introducing her sister to the family. Hopefully, they would be alone.

Lock pointed to his timeline chart. "Here's what I have. This red line shows incoming calls on your landline. Congo calls are circled. This green line reveals the location of your current use cell phone. The blue line is your old cell, which you carry and never answer. Monday morning, you called the Congo on your house phone. Later that day, someone from the same area code called twice, from a burner phone."

Lock watched her closely for any reaction. With pinched brow, she studied the chart.

He explained, "Their calls were short, two minutes or less each. Tuesday, noon, another came in." He pointed. "See. You were downtown at that time, however, at 2:23 p.m. this call came in, the line opened for fourteen minutes. It indicates a conversation took place. By cell tower records, you were home and online using your cell. Do you remember being on landline with anyone at that time?"

"I've contemplated it after our conversation yesterday. I used my cell phone and searched for information on the dead fed." She cleared her throat. "Sorry. Agent Reynolds. Marcia called and said this guy needed to talk to me. About a stockholders meeting. I don't recall details. Marcia may have told him to call back after closing bell." She shrugged. "I don't think he did, nor do I see how stocks have anything to do with my parents' ordeal. I hope this helps."

"It does. All of it is reflected here in the timeline. If they're using stocks as a ruse to confirm your current whereabouts, it could be quite relevant. Do any of the companies you hold stocks in actually have business in the Congo? Minerals, maybe?"

"I suppose cobalt is a possibility. I'll check on it," she said.

"Thanks. Look, on Thursday. See, they called again." He tapped. "You appear to have been home then. And the last call made from the same number was on Saturday. I know you were here, upstairs with your sister while I waited."

"I don't remember. Marcia can probably tell you. The woman keeps impeccable records and has a memory to match. Did you talk with her already?"

Lock raised a brow. "Briefly, I didn't have this chart yet. What time does she arrive?"

"I expect by eight in the morning, she leaves at noon and is off until after Christmas."

"Fine, I'll be over early. Thanks, Letsea."

"Lock, I appreciate your looking out for me, even if your efforts are misguided. I haven't talked with anyone from there who's called me. If I didn't like you so much, your questions would scare me out of my wits."

She likes me? He paused. "Can I ask you a personal question?"

She shrugged.

"What did you see in Purser?"

She looked to the floor. "I refuse to answer on the grounds that I may appear the fool."

He caught his breath. She pretty much answered his question. He exhaled. "Okay. By the way, my sisters begged me to convince you to join us tomorrow. If not for the whole day, do come with us to pick out a Christmas tree. It's always a fun time." *Yay, for kid sisters!* He longed to spend more time with her.

"If I have time I'd like to. The kids have rehearsal for candlelight service, and I may need to take them."

He lifted his chin, fully aware of the children's rehearsal. Apparently, Letsea still didn't know the whole extent of the services. "I understand. Our church is having one of those too." A crowded pew would give opportunity to slip his arm around her shoulders.

He gathered his chart. She looked even more tired.

"I enjoyed seeing you laugh tonight, even if a good part of it was at my expense. My sisters won't let me live down some of their most entertaining memories."

Letsea clasped her hands. "You have a great family. Treasure every minute with them."

Recognizing his blessed family, the utmost thing he held dear to his heart. She was the first lady in ages he considered bringing into the fold. "See if you can squeeze in tree-hunting time." His natural instinct wanted to kiss her goodnight. At this point, he didn't dare. He looked forward to finding a time when he could. "Good night, Letsea." Her green-eyed gaze tugged at his core.

"By the way, Lock, you do still have it."

"Still have what?" He raised a brow. Whatever *it* was, she must like it.

"Your musical talent, what else?"

His heart thudded loud. "I'm glad to know I have something you like." He wanted to show her what else he could still do. With an internal groan, he said, "'Night."

"Night-night." She waved by wiggling fingers.

On his way back, he realized the calls from the Congo may be much to do about nothing. What if they weren't? Agent Douglas and Chief believed she paid a bribe. That, being the key to this whole issue. He needed approval from Chief to talk with her on the matter of the hundred-thousand. If he didn't get it quick, he would not go lightly. It was imperative he claim that piece to the puzzle. Most likely, nothing but a stupid befuddlement, an anonymous end-of-the-year donation. If so, it must be an issue she felt passionate over.

Except for the blasted stalkers. No denying their existence. As soon as he officially made it back on the clock, a trip to Philadelphia was in order. Time to explore his theory on Purser's involvement. No black sports cars have hung around since the time of Purser's arrival to the estate, nor tonight, after his rejection and departure. He believed in a definite connection.

His main concern, who at the estate had been talking to someone in the Democratic Republic of the Congo?

CHAPTER 62

12:05 a.m. Thursday

Preoccupied with thoughts of Lock's timeline and all it revealed of her private schedule, Letsea went around turning off lights. The security office light shone into the hall and it caught her attention. "Bob, I didn't expect you to still be up."

"I'm outlining a work schedule. Mr. Davis asked for extra security this week. I spoke with Marcia and we decided there needed to be extra help all around. Liza volunteered to work straight through, she'll need help though."

"Marcia and I did discuss it. How's it going?"

"Good. Deputies Rogers, Farmer, and Allen are in for rotation. Two of the caterers' servers will do whatever household tasks may need done."

"Sounds like you have it figured out. If the deputies drive marked cars, will you make sure they park behind the house? In fact, I'd rather not have any cars park on the circle drives. Leave those for drop-offs and pickups."

"Actually, I have it on good authority, a patrol car in a prominent visual spot is good crime prevention."

"Okay." She considered his point. "Use the front, eastside."

"I can work with that, ma'am."

"Thanks for all your good work, Bob. Good night."

"Yes. Good night, Miss Brechenworth."

Later, as she climbed into bed, Letsea contemplated what she would give to feel the Lockharts' kind of love again. To create a forever family with humor, support, and an unconditional love like her parents provided.

Look at Gwen. As her guardian from an early age, she pampered her little sister. Eyelids squeezed, she prayed, "Dear Lord, should I ever have children, I want to teach them to recognize their life's calling, their natural talents. May they perceive Your perpetual grace and soar in Your loving embrace. And, not be control-freaks. Bless and protect my family and friends. Please guide me to make good choices and forgive me for not always putting my full trust in You, as I should. Amen."

The time had come to stop giving Gwen whatever she asked for. Were her sister's shortcomings her fault? *I need to set things right.*

Startled awake by a bright light passing over the walls of her room, Letsea grabbed her robe and dashed into the hall. It reflected through the hall's glass French doors, and it came from behind the house. At five o'clock in the morning, she crossed to a north side bedroom to see out the back windows.

Bob, on an ATV heading down the lane to the car barn. To retrieve the limo, no doubt. He'd been fussing over it, getting it waxed and ready. She watched until the headlights faded behind the grove of red cedar trees.

Realizing a good opportunity to touch base with Uncle Paul, she hurried up the servants' stairs, making her way to the tower's spiral steps in the fourth level.

"Paul?"

Here.

"I have company arriving today. Please don't try to talk to, or scare them."

They won't hear me.

"I want you to know, I filed a motion to review your case file. I'm sure it'll take a while. I won't forget you. I'll do what I can."

I trust you.

She sighed. Somehow, ghostly trust meant a lot. "Is there anything else I need to know?"

I was murdered.

"Stop repeating it, I'll always remember."

I'm waiting for closure.

"I get it." So was she.

My gratitude for taking this on.

"I hope my efforts help."

I'm not sure what good it'll do to read the files. Remember, many critical top-secret details were destroyed.

"I'll remember to read between the lines."

I wish to tell you the ultimate solution, I just don't know what it is.

"Paul, I've thought about the odds of your having an affair. If you did, I don't approve."

I wouldn't either.

"An affair is not the same as committing murder. It's also no reason to avoid solving one. A good man, doing his job. A superior job, too, from what I've read, ethical and efficient. People noted you were a delight."

Humor is a desired state of mind, but I took my responsibilities seriously.

"Paul, no matter your personal choices, I'm willing to go to Washington D.C. and plead a case to read what I can of your file. I'll do it. By virtue of the fact, you deserve peace."

Thank you. So do you.

"You are welcome, my friend."

Goodbye.

Although she suspected a long road ahead, the carefree evening with the Lockharts did help relax her view on circumstances she was dealt.

In her room, she picked up book ten of the Chase thriller series and read until sunrise. She recalled Marcia said Lockhart retrieved book five already. She pondered if he slept as little as she.

After a chilly morning run and breakfast, Letsea went to her room to get ready and decided to call Aunt Mae before she got busy and forgot.

"Good morning, Auntie. Will you join us for dinner tonight?"

"I think it's best they have time to visit first. Won't they be thrilled to see Chip and Lauren?"

She sensed her aunt's lighter mood. "I understand Uncle Robert's going to drive the limo."

"Oh my, yes. He just left for your place wearing a black suit. Bob promised to let him wear a chauffeur's cap." Auntie laughed. "You never know what will tickle a man's fancy. Men. Bless their hearts."

They shared good humor. When Lauren ran into her room, Letsea wrapped up her phone call. Chip and Gwen followed.

"They're on their way to the airport," Gwen said and walked into the bathroom to refresh her lipstick.

Letsea stood in the doorway. "Everything's going to be great. If you feel overwhelmed, take some slow, deep breaths. Reach out for Doyle's help."

Gwen tilted her head.

She moved next to her sister and fingered her strawberry-blonde hair. "You must have slept well. You are absolutely glowing this morning."

Her sister gave a shy look. "Lets, something you said last night really hit home with me." Gwendolene hugged her. "I love you."

"I know. I love you, too. But sometimes I feel like I've spoiled you." There. She said it.

Gwen agreed, "Yes, you have. Doyle gets a little miffed with me when he knows I'll turn to you for something I want." They squeezed hands. "I'm so glad you brought him home from school and introduced us."

"As it turned out, *you two* are perfect for one another. I'm glad you're happy."

"I love him so much. It's hard to put into words." Gwen placed her hand over her heart. "It's in here."

Letsea noticed the glistening in her sister's eyes. "Your heart shows it, honey. This week, try hard to remember his family is your family, too. There is no competition, whatsoever."

"I will."

"There's something else. The Lockharts invited me to join them today as they run errands. I'm going with them. You can do what is needed here without me. You're a grown woman, nearly twenty-five, wife, and a mother of two. You can handle this."

First, Gwen pulled in her bottom lip, and finally said, "That I'm so much younger than Doyle is part of why his sisters don't care for me."

"Then it's time you show them you are an adult. Be the hostess, let them know you care for your whole family. Remember, let them relax. Ask them how you can help and if they need anything."

"You really like Trey, don't you? What happened to Seth?"

"Trey and I are friends. I'm not sure if there's anything more to it. Seth is gone."

"He was just here."

"Exclusively to retrieve his car. I don't expect to ever hear from him again." Not to be unkind, but she was done with him.

Nico announced, "Look who's here!"

Lock's sisters openly showed their excitement. He kept a cap on his.

The men headed out to get vehicles.

Carlton sidled up. "I see Mom has her eye on having Letsea for a daughter-in-law."

Nico squeezed a hand to his shoulder. "About time, I say. She fits our family."

Yeah, Letsea's wonderful. Good luck, Mom.

After finding the family photos and Christmas ornaments, they caravanned to the empty family house.

At their old home, they walked through every room, reminisced, and shed a few tears. Lock found Letsea on the back porch watching his nephews climb into the old tree house.

"Did you build it?" Letsea asked.

"With Dad's help, yeah. Somehow, I always thought I'd see my own kids exploring my past haunts. I imagine come spring, those trees will be cleared away, as the house will be."

Letsea stared at him.

"What?" he asked.

Her lips curved upward. "Nothing."

What's she thinking?

Dad announced, "It's after one o'clock. I'm hungry. Let's head to the buffet."

No one argued with his logic. At the restaurant, they were pushing tables together when Letsea's phone rang and she walked away to talk.

Most of them were at the buffet when Letsea returned, face pale and brows furrowed.

"What's wrong?"

"I need to leave. I can call for a ride."

"No. I'll drive you wherever you need to go."

He looked at her downturned facial features. "What happened?"

"That was Uncle Robert. My aunt is missing."

CHAPTER 63

Thursday afternoon, driving across St. Charles, Missouri

"What do you know so far?" Lock questioned.

"When Uncle Robert got home, Aunt Mae wasn't there. Her purse and car are. He's panicked. He checked the house. Called the neighbors. She's gone. He called me. I called Auntie, it went to voice mail. I checked with Bob and she isn't at the estate either."

Lock pulled into the driveway of an old classic red-brick Italianate. An older man sat on the small porch. By the time he turned off the engine, the frantic man stood at the car door.

"Letsea, where's Mae? There's no note. We always leave notes."

"Uncle Robert, this is Godrick Lockhart. Lock, this is Robert Evans. Uncle, Lock's going to help us find her." She got out and rushed around to give him a hug.

"Are you Rick's boy?"

"He's my dad, yes." As a friend of Dad's, hopefully early suspicion of the spouse as first suspect could be dismissed. "Mr. Evans, tell me what you know."

"See for yourself. I can't think straight. What if she's fallen somewhere, and is hurt, and I can't find her? She's not answering her phone, either."

"Does she have a GPS app on her phone?"

"Yes, but I don't trust it. It's on battery saver and shows she's home."

"Does she ever go for walks around the block?" Lock asked.

"In the cold? No."

Letsea made for the front door, the uncle followed.

"Wait." Lock caught up to her and rested his hands on her arms. He spoke softly, not wanting to further upset either of them. "First, we only peek inside, don't touch a single thing." He knew anything may be evidence.

She turned in his arms. "It shouldn't matter. My fingerprints are all over this house. I'm here every week."

"Okay. Today, don't touch. It may be important. Wait here. Don't even touch the door or threshold."

He looked back. "Mr. Evans, have you moved anything since you returned home?"

"I don't remember. I checked from the basement to the attic."

"Okay. Will you wait out here while Letsea takes a look?"

The man sat on the front steps. Lock scanned the doorway. "Okay, Letsea. Only one step inside to look."

He lowered his hands to her wrists. "Do you see anything out of place?" She nodded. "What?"

"Here. The foyer rug is gone."

"Don't move." He turned to the gentleman outside. "Do you know where the rug from the entrance might be? Cleaners, maybe?"

"I didn't even notice it missing."

"Mr. Evans, I know it's cold out. You can sit in my car if you want."

"I'll wait here."

"Okay, Letsea. Let's move forward a couple steps." Parlors flanked both sides of the entryway, and Letsea leaned to observe both rooms. She strained against his grip to focus on the dining room then stopped.

"What do you see?"

"Her purse is on the table. She's kind of germophobic and doesn't believe a purse should ever be placed on a table where you eat."

What he worried about, even more, was the suspicious appearance of smeared blood on the doorframe leading into the kitchen. *That's settled!* "Let's go out the way we came in." He turned her around. "You can sit in my car and stay warm while I talk with your uncle."

"Shouldn't we finish?"

"I think it's best to wait for Sheriff Ruell or the police to get here before we go any further."

Letsea watched Lock text and talk on his phone while he paced. He glanced at her several times then sat on the porch and spoke with Uncle Robert. In barely a breath of time, Sheriff Bill Ruell parked behind Lock's car. He stopped at the driver's window.

"Letsea, sweetie, hang in there. Maybe it's time for a Silver Alert. Do you think?"

"She'd be furious for the embarrassment if we find her having tea with a neighbor. Trey Lockhart might have an idea of what to do. Thanks for coming, Bill."

He patted the inside of the door. "You look cold. Do you want this window up?"

"No. I want to hear."

"Sure. We'll do everything we can."

She watched Bill shake hands with Uncle Robert and Lock. Most recently, he helped outside her house with the mysterious black car. By all appearances, Bill was happily married with several children. A memory flashed of the night he took her to a school dance. They were such different people back then, young and naïve.

From the time she and Granddad left for South Africa, as both a friend and deputy, Bill checked on the family every day.

She thought of Gwen, gasped, and dug out her phone to call the house. Bob answered.

"We don't want to scare Gwen, but Aunt Mae is missing. The sheriff is here looking. Please tell Doyle and—"

Bob interrupted, "I'm aware, ma'am. Lockhart called a few minutes ago. Mr. Davis isn't back from the airport. I'll fill him in when he arrives. Mrs. Davis and the others don't know. To be safe, they're sending Deputy Rogers here early. I'm told to tell you to ask Lockhart if you have any questions. They know you had a stalker, so they're on top of it."

"Thanks, Bob." She hung up and looked at Lock, Special Agent of the FBI. No suit and tie. He wore jeans, trail boots and that brown bomber jacket of his, and of course that leather fedora.

A couple of marked police cars and an unmarked one parked in front, on the street. A crime scene van arrived next. *Well, this can't be good.* She clutched her arms and braced herself, as both uniformed and plain-clothed officers rushed to the house. She shook, wishing it from cold air but knew better. She screamed, "Lock!" His eyes met hers and he headed her way.

"They're here to look for clues." He sat in the driver's seat.

She watched as Uncle Robert walked with a police officer to a marked vehicle and sat in the back seat. "What's going on? Where are they taking Uncle Robert?"

He rolled up the window. "They want to keep him warm, while he tries to remember a sequence of events. It's nothing personal, Letsea."

"It is to me! This is my aunt!"

"Give me your hand." He held out a palm.

She placed her left hand in his right and he folded his fingers over hers. He closed his eyes and prayed out loud.

Her trembling eased a bit and when he said, "Amen," so did she.

"Is prayer a standard technique for the FBI? Because, I like it."

"I doubt if you'll find it in the training manuals, but you might be surprised how many agents apply it."

She squeezed his hand. "Do you think someone kidnapped her? It's staggering to think this is happening again. And right here at home. You knew something was up, didn't you? It's about those black cars. I can't believe you led a prayer for me." Although, that he did, relayed comfort.

"I'm a federal agent twenty-four seven, three-sixty-five, but in this moment, I am also your friend. I pray. Get used to it."

Relieved, she rested her head back. "All right, then." A movement in her peripheral vision caused her to turn. The police car with Uncle Robert drove away. "What's going on?"

"Standard procedure."

He squeezed her hand and held on long enough to offer reassurance. Plus, he took it to God, the highest level possible. Even higher than the Justice Department.

Sheriff Ruell strode back to Lock's car. "Trey, why don't you go ahead and call Don Pfeiffer to come over."

"I already did, he's on his way. I also called my boss and Letsea's security man at the estate."

"Good, good." Sheriff bent to talk to her. "Letsea, we have some questions for you, then we'd like for you to do a walk-through with us. Tell us any little thing you see out of place. Her house is like a museum, everything looks perfect."

"I'll do it now." She started to open the car door, but Lock still gripped her hand.

"Wait a minute," Lock said.

"Trey, if you want to walk with her, we're good with that. You do seem to have a calming effect on her. One of the CSI personnel and Detective Travis will take her through."

Bill asked Letsea, "When is the last time you saw or talked with your aunt?"

"This morning. On the phone. Right after eight o'clock."

"Do you recall her mood?"

"Happy. Doyle's family arrives today and Robert helped by picking up his parents from the airport in the limo. When I called, Uncle Robert just left here for my house."

"You're saying you talked with her after Mr. Evans left."

"Yes."

"What did she say that made you think she was 'happy'?"

"We laughed."

"Really? Well, good. You say, Mr. Evans drove the Brechenworth limo?"

"Doyle has two groups to pick up at the airport. The first group are older and it's easier for them to get in and out of a car than the passenger van."

"Flight arrival time?"

"9:37 a.m."

"Sweetie, what time did Mr. Evans return to the estate?" Bill asked.

"I don't know. I've been with the Lockharts. But, Billy"—she couldn't stop the whine in her voice— "if you suspect Robert of wrongdoing, you're mistaken. He loves her."

CHAPTER 64

L ock cut in. "Obviously, you two know each other. Am I missing something here?"

Bill's eyes widened. "Letsea and I have known each other all our lives. We even dated in high school. Why? Do you have a problem with it, Trey?"

Yes, he did. Lock sighed and pushed back against his car seat. "Not if your wife doesn't, *sweetie*." He'd rather not feel territorial but tightened his jaw and wished he could be so familiar with Letsea.

Bill asked her, "The last I recall, Mae was a widow. When did she remarry?"

"Well, *Sheriff*." Letsea glanced at Lock and lifted her chin. "They married last August."

"When did they meet?" he asked.

She blinked. "They were high school sweethearts. Then separate colleges took them in different directions."

"How long did they date before they married?"

She shrugged. "A few weeks."

Whoa, that did not sound good. Lock didn't like what he heard. Only weeks? It crossed his mind, he'd only known Letsea a few days, and he already visualized what it might be like to be married to her. So maybe he shouldn't judge.

"It's not a money thing, Bill. There's a prenuptial agreement between them."

"How do you know?" Lock asked.

"I drew it up and witnessed them sign it. So did a notary and a judge."

With a studious look in his eye, Bill said, "Do you know who her beneficiaries are?"

She squeezed his hand and Lock felt her tremble, he caressed her hand with his thumb.

"Gwen and I are, along with some charities. Bill, I don't like where this is headed."

"Let's hope it doesn't come to that," Bill said. He patted the door and stepped back. "I see Don's here."

Lock turned to her. "Hang in here, okay?"

"I'm scared out of my mind. Who's Don?"

He rubbed his thumb across her hand again. "I know, listen, I need for you to wait in the car. He's a friend. I'll be back for you." Lock went to greet his buddy.

"Thanks for coming." They shook hands and headed to the house to talk with the CSI team. They filled Don in on what little they knew, including the Congo calls and stalkers. It turned out, Supervisors Paytah and Douglas already had a preliminary discussion with him during their quick visit. While Don suited up, Lock walked back to get Letsea.

"Try not to jump to conclusions." He put his hand on her back as they walked up the slight grade to the house.

Lyle, a CSI team member introduced to them, spoke softly, and stayed close to Letsea's side. He helped her slip blue disposable booties over her boots. Not that she was inexperienced with those things. Next, he helped with rubber gloves. Lock followed and noticed everyone on official business wore a body camera. He did not.

Again, she stood in the foyer and looked around.

"The rug from here is missing."

"Can you describe it?" Detective Travis asked and took notes.

"It's an antique hook rug, six-by-seven feet, greenish with a large bouquet of flowers."

It *would* be a hook rug. Lock cringed. They are lighter weight and pliable. Perfect for rolling a body into, plus the ideal size. Why didn't Mr. Evans notice it missing? Letsea did.

"Anything else?" Detective Travis watched her closely.

"Not here, but in the dining room." They all moved forward several feet. "It looks in disarray. She never puts her purse on the table, plus it's open, with her keys and wallet out."

"What else is in disorder?" Travis inquired.

"She's tidy to a fault. See those papers, she never leaves anything out of place."

"Where are they normally kept?"

Without touching, she leaned over them. "Those are bill statements. They should be in her little office space waiting for me to stop by and pay them. Um, except Uncle Robert's planning to take over doing it soon. I'm going to show him my system. I haven't yet."

"How long have you been doing this for her?"

"Years. Since her first husband died."

"What did he die of?"

"Pneumonia."

"I see."

"What do you see?" She snapped as shoulders straightened.

Lock watched her blush as anger crept across her cheeks.

"Uncle went through surgery, while recovering in a nursing facility, he caught pneumonia and died!"

Lock knew her capable of spitting fire when prompted. Hoping to calm her, he rubbed her shoulders. "Easy. They mean well." He rested his chin against the back of her head.

Letsea drew in a deep breath. While releasing it, she appeared to notice the smear on the doorframe to the kitchen and stepped toward it. He feared her reaction to the clue of violence.

It appeared thick red, like a busted blood clot with a swiped fingerprint through it.

"We took pictures and a swab for DNA testing," said Lyle.

"I highly doubt you'll get a blood type." She sniffed it. "It's a special raspberry curd with a touch of dark chocolate."

"How are you so sure?" Travis asked.

Lock recalled the treat box Mom brought home and put into the refrigerator.

"Auntie loves those raspberry ganache cakes. She recently took several home after a party. She freezes them then treats herself to one every few days until they're gone."

Lock said to the crime scene inspector, "Seriously delicious. I got to have part of one."

He felt her shiver. "Do you need to step outside?"

"No. May I look in her little office?" Letsea looked at Travis. "It's right here behind the door under the staircase."

CSI, Lyle, carefully opened the door and she stepped in and looked around. She pointed.

"I need to open that drawer."

Lyle opened it.

"The checkbook is gone!"

"Wouldn't it have been in her purse?"

"No. She has a desk-size, three-ring binder checkbook. She carries a credit card and cash. It's a disaster waiting to happen to carry your checkbook, it might get into the wrong hands."

Lock thought, they also might get into the wrong hands tucked away in a desk drawer.

Letsea moved back to the center of the dining room and looked at the walls.

"What do you see or not see?" Lock asked.

"Whoever was here is not an art critic," she said.

Detective Travis coaxed, "Because?"

"Because that"— she pointed to framed art on the east wall— "is an original, signed piece by Pablo Picasso. It's prominently displayed in this very spot so the sun will never reach it."

Travis whistled. "What could that be worth?"

Letsea shrugged. "Shortly after Picasso's death, its insurance appraisal came in at $20,000. Who knows now."

"What's with all the weird triangles?" someone asked.

"Modern art. Who knows?" answered another.

Letsea looked at him, shaken, still dry-eyed. "Actually, it's a portrait of my aunt Mae, in her youth."

Lock caught a glimpse of her keen wit, amongst a very serious situation, then overheard a conversation.

"Sheriff, you should see the paper we found in the backyard, near the driveway," a deputy called out, through the kitchen door.

Crime scene staff and the other detective headed out the door. Don Pfeiffer came down from upstairs and also headed outside.

"The morgues and the local hospitals are clear. The station is still checking the greater area."

Letsea sighed and closed her eyes.

"You're doing very well with this," Lock whispered. Obviously not everyone knew family was here.

She turned and leaned against his chest. "What do you think happened to her?"

"They're gathering facts, don't jump to conclusions." Like his tendency to do.

"Miss Brechenworth," said the still-unnamed detective. "Does this look familiar?" With tweezers, he held out a single sheet of paper with fold creases.

When she reached for it, Lock caught her hand. "Don't touch."

"I know." Letsea looked over her shoulder, and quipped, "Touching is a real issue with you, isn't it?"

He nodded, and held his tongue. *It isn't the time for a tease or snide remark.*

"It's an old bank statement," she said. "It should have been shredded last January."

"Why do you say January?" asked Detective Travis.

"She shreds seven-year-old statements every first Monday of the new year, unless New Year's Day falls on Monday. Then she shreds on Tuesday."

"You make it sound like clockwork," Lock said.

"It is. She's very precise."

"Good to know. That generally works in our favor," said Travis.

Lock noticed something on the statement. "I see a heat mark at the top. And those circles impressed through the folds look the size of a snuff tin."

The crime scene staffer held open an evidence bag while the detective holding the paper with tweezers slid it inside.

"I believe you're right, Agent. No burn marks, but the waviness in that corner does indicate it's been near intense heat. Good call, sir."

His *good calls* through the years made for his job security and pay level.

Letsea squared her shoulders and stomped a foot. "Oh, snap! Auntie burned her papers again! She promised to shred them."

Lock looked at her face and raised an eyebrow.

"Aunt Mae hates the time it takes to shred paper."

"So, almost a year ago, this paper should have been destroyed?"

"That's right."

Lock suggested, "It could have made it into a fire then lifted out with rising heat and a gentle breeze, it floated away. Did she burn papers in a fireplace or burning barrel?"

Letsea turned in his arms. "In the backyard. I told her, she's not supposed to burn, but she doesn't see it that way. Says, 'Fire, purifies.' I insist on a shredder, however, the ones she buys are slow and they jam, plus, it's a hassle to empty the basket. Aunt Mae thinks you can dump a whole stack of papers and burn them all at once and be done with it."

A young deputy asked, "Can't you?"

A resounding response of, "No!" came from investigators.

Lock held the bagged bank statement. "By the looks of the worn folds, I'd say someone carried this around in a pocket for that long." He opened the bag and sniffed. "It smells more of mint tobacco than smoke." The detective re-zipped and logged it in.

"There's a burn barrel in the backyard, sirs," informed a deputy.

Don Pfeiffer, Lock's friend, a local kidnapping specialist with the FBI, stood outside the kitchen door. "We now have several officers doing a knock and talk in the neighborhood for witnesses and security camera catches."

They informed Don of the missing checkbook.

"Is her photo I.D. card here?" he asked.

"No, sir," replied a white-suited investigator. "Her wallet is, but no driver's license. I understand she carried a credit card. I don't see one in the wallet or purse. No cash either."

Finally in the kitchen, Lock noticed a full cup of tea. Also, an empty dessert plate and a plastic container were on the countertop. A small fork lay on the floor. Letsea stiffened and drew a deep breath. Through the open back door, he looked at Don's frown. "Letsea, how much cash does she normally carry with her?"

"I bring her two-hundred and fifty dollars every week from her bank. Last week, I brought her a thousand, since I knew I'd be distracted and it is the holidays. It's good to be prepared."

Son of a monkey!

Detective Travis said, "Miss Brechenworth, if you have authority to put a stop on her bank accounts, you can save us time from getting a court order to do so."

Lock contemplated. Missing cash, photo I.D., checkbook, credit card, and a soft rug, along with a defenseless, affluent, elderly woman. "Oh, bloody hill!"

CHAPTER 65

Lock and Don Pfieffer stood in the backyard near the cold, rusty burn barrel, half full of ashes. Gloved CSI were sifting through it.

Don said, "I admit, this looks like a kidnapping. I already have the recorder set up for incoming ransom calls. My team will be here promptly and we're still trying to locate her cell phone. Lock, what are you thinking?"

"We know what day the old statement most likely got dumped here." He touched the toe of his boot to the barrel. "The question is, which direction did it float and how far did it travel? We do know who can give us an idea of the weather on that day, don't we?"

Don said, "Fortunately we have friends at the National Weather Service. It'll speed things up."

"Yes, it will," Lock agreed.

"I'll give them a call," Don said. "Looks like you have your hands full. By chance, is Miss Brechenworth the 'pretty little rainbow' you were chasing, earlier this month?"

Lock glanced at his friend then stared up to the bare canopy of elm tree branches. "Yep," he mumbled.

"Oh, man! She's gorgeous."

"Yep."

Don clamped a hand to Lock's shoulder. "Well, friend, good luck with that. I'll let you know what I hear with the weather conditions."

Lock went back to his car where Letsea spoke on her cell with the bank, putting a hold on her aunt's accounts. He watched Don scrutinize the marked-off area of the yard where they found the old bank statement.

He waited until she put her phone down. "What can you tell me of this meeting you went to in St. Louis? The one where the black car followed you."

"I told you before, it's a group of friends. We get together once a month to discuss investments."

"Remind me. A stock market meeting?"

"General stuff. Who's doing what, when, where, and how. Latest quarterly reports. Who's producing game changers. We're watching for any new strategies. That's it in a nutshell."

"Thirty members, didn't you say? What do you know about them?"

"We mainly discuss the market, so, not much."

"Can you get me a list of who they are?" he asked.

"Lock, if you think these people have anything to do with Aunt Mae, I can't imagine it. They don't even know my aunt. Besides, we educate each other on earning money the legal way."

"Their names?" he repeated.

"We have an email newsletter. I can give you the name of the guy who sends it out."

She got back on her phone, searched, and texted. Meanwhile, he watched several deputies depart. The CSI team packed up, stripped off their protective coveralls, and left. Bill, the sheriff, ducked under the do-not-cross yellow tape and headed their way. He rolled his window down.

"Lock, Don's here with his team and Detective Travis is staying. Otherwise, we've got all we can find. The place is immaculate, any indication of a"—Bill paused and looked across at Letsea—"mishap, is far and few. What there is, we've collected and documented."

"Sweetie, you were a lot of help in there. We'll figure this out. Try not to worry."

"Phew!" She exhaled with exaggeration.

Lock added, "I guess that says it all."

Bill said, "I'll pull my car out so you can leave."

"Billy!" Letsea rushed to say, "What's with Uncle Robert?"

"They took him to the hospital to get checked out. He's

hyperventilating. We wanted to make sure he's not having a heart attack."

"He didn't do anything wrong," she insisted.

"I believe you." Bill tapped the roof of the BMW then walked back to move his car.

Letsea looked at Lock. "I want to go to the hospital and see my uncle. I texted you the contact info for the guy who does our newsletter. I still think you're barking up the wrong tree."

Lock rolled the window up, shifted his car into reverse, and said, "Somewhere is the right tree and we'll bark until we find it."

She clicked her seat belt into place and whispered, "Thank you."

Lock decided to dig in with questions while he drove. "Is there a possibility your stock market friends might know where and how you live?"

"The man who originally invited me to attend the group, knows me. He's been to the Queen Anne, years ago."

"You dated him?" As he saw it, he needed to know.

"A couple times. Way back when."

"Who broke it off? You or him?"

"There wasn't anything to break off. We hung out a couple of times, that's all."

He paused, but asked anyway. "Why just a couple of times?"

She leaned toward him and blurted, "I didn't like the way he kissed." She stared at him.

"Ah. So, the kiss is a make-it or break-it deed with you, huh?" He drove out of the old neighborhood toward the hospital.

"It can be. One thing I've recently learned is if a guy refuses to return your kiss, there's a reason for it. Have you ever heard the saying, 'Always kiss me goodnight'?"

"Not really."

"Hm, *that* explains a lot," she said pointedly.

Her kiss, in Phoenix, clung painfully in his memory. Oh, what he'd give for a do-over.

"Letsea, can you think of anyone who might be angry, jealous, or revengeful for your not continuing to date them?"

"Not really. I've learned to not carry dead weight. Being the first girl born on my father's side of the family, my grandparents were strict. Insisted guys be worthy and they pressed the point.

There's only one reason to date. In college, my parents once flew two-thousand miles to meet my friends. To give approval of my dating choice."

Lock whistled. "Sounds domineering."

"I was raised with the adage, 'The secret of a happy marriage is finding the right person.' As soon as you're aware they aren't your forever mate, get the heck out of there."

In light humor, he teased, "It's not a Dumas quote, is it?"

"Nope. It's a little Julia Child and a lot of Grandmama."

"So, to confirm, no jealous ex-lovers?"

"Hah!" She shifted in her seat. "Don't you live by an adage?"

"I do." At a traffic light, Lock said, "'In life, what is sacred? What is made by spirit? What is worth living for? What is worth dying for?'" He paused to watch her reaction.

The corners of her mouth curved upward.

"I'm afraid I butchered Lord Byron. Hint. They all have the same answer."

"Love," they said in unison.

Silently, she stared out the window.

He cleared his throat. A gut feeling on the bank statement angst him. It must have something to do with Mrs. Evans' disappearance. He didn't sense a common connection to the Congo, possibly a stalker. Especially if they knew Letsea and Mrs. Evans were related.

After he parked in the hospital parking lot, he looked at her. "I'm proud of you for all the things you noticed at her house."

"What kind of friends do you think I have anyway?" Letsea's face reddened.

He wanted to be sure they were true friends and not after her money. "I'm thinking of all angles here," he answered.

"Concerning my aunt or the stalkers?"

"Both, actually. Our goal is to keep you and your family safe. Therefore, I expand the perimeter of things going on with you so I can see a bigger picture."

Without another word, she opened the door and ran toward the E.R. entrance.

Settled in a room, Evans slept. Letsea sat beside him.

A nurse adjusted tubes and bags of liquid dangling nearby.

Lock's phone vibrated. "I'll be down the hall."

"Hi, Don," he answered.

"Hey, we've got a viable lead. The man across the street recently returned home. As he left this afternoon, he saw an old Chevy, white panel van, back up into the Evan's driveway. He even gave us a partial plate number. Two men walked behind the house."

"Now, there's news worth hearing," Lock said.

"There's a BOLO on the van now. The neighbor is at the police station giving an accurate description of the two men to an artist. I thought you'd want to know."

"Thanks. Do you happen to know the age range of the men?"

"'Most likely over 50. They looked worn and tired,' is all I got. I'm waiting for the sketch."

Lock went back to Evan's hospital room. She rested her head on crossed arms on the bedside.

"Letsea, honey, let me drive you home." *Honey? Jiminy Cricket! It felt good and easy to say. S*he looked like she didn't even heard him. "Letsea?"

She raised her head. "They expect he'll sleep through the night. I really do need to check on Gwendolene and say hi to Doyle's family. If I don't, she'll know something's wrong."

"Why tip-toe around Gwendolene?" he asked.

"After our parents' ordeal, we lost all of our grandparents, in quick succession. Gwen was a child. After years of counseling, she still gets very emotional. I don't want this to trigger her grief all over again. I'm a bit protective of her."

"I can see your concern," he said.

"There's that. Also, she bewails like you've never heard before."

"Come. I'll drive you home."

CHAPTER 66

Queen Anne house at 8:15 p.m.

L ock found his family listening to Christmas music and decorating the tree. It stood beside the fanciful staircase, which made it easier to decorate.

He said his greetings, hung an ornament, then slipped into the kitchen to find something to eat. Chili with all the toppings. As he sat, eating and contemplating the events of the afternoon, his dad walked in.

"Anything you can talk about, Son?"

Since her neighbors already knew, why not? "Letsea's aunt, Mae Evans, is missing."

"Oh, no! She and Robert are fixtures at the senior center," Dad said. "How is he doing?"

"He's in the hospital. They're being cautious of his heart."

"If there's anything I can do to help, I will."

"Do you happen to recognize these two men?" Lock showed his father an illustration on his phone.

"Sure. That's Charlie and Otis."

Lock's eyes widened. "You know them?"

"They live on the streets. Always willing to give tourists an opportunity to feel good for their kind deeds, by encouraging people to donate to their cause."

"What cause?"

"It's usually a pint in a plain brown bag, Skoal, or smokes."

Snuff fits.

"Where do they hang out?"

"They walk the streets and parks. When it's cold enough, they'll go to a warming shelter. Trey, I don't see it. They're friendly, not thugs."

Lock knew, by being nice, way too often criminals got away with murder.

"It's thirty-eight degrees out. Not near cold enough for shelters to open." Dad called out, "Alice, honey, come look at this picture."

"Mom, do these two men look familiar?"

"Look at that." She looked to Dad. "Isn't that Charlie and Otis, from the streets?"

"I thought so."

"Trey, what are you doing with a drawing of them?" she asked.

Dad answered, "Mae Evans is missing."

His mother stood there with her mouth open.

"They have reason to believe Charlie and Otis have something to do with it. Do you happen to know where they normally sleep? Last names, anything?" his dad asked.

Mom shrugged. "I've seen them in the alley behind the tea room plenty of times. There's no place to shelter there. I don't think those two are capable of doing anything so bad. They're polite. Mae, missing? There must be another explanation."

Mom sat, picked up a fresh baked Santa Claus cookie, and bit its hat off. "Mae's a tea room regular, plus, I see her and Robert at the senior center. You know, I have noticed Charlie and Otis walking along the river bank before."

"Mom, what were you doing down by the river?"

"Picking up litter. Double duty. It beautifies the area after others thoughtlessly drop trash. I also get more steps in. It's good exercise."

He thought of the old bank statement. "What kind of trash do you generally find?"

"Bottles, fast-food wrappers, and cigarette butts." She wrinkled her face. "You'd be surprised at the amount of mail with names and addresses blowing around out there. I don't think those are intentional though."

"Thanks. If you think of anything else, call me." Lock left in a hurry and called both Don and the sheriff to tell them his latest news. He drove from Riverside Drive to North Main to survey activity.

Dark out with the partial moon behind passing clouds, he strained to see people between city lights. A group of young people walked on the Katy Trail.

His car's speakerphone beeped. Don called back. "Hey, records indicate last January, the first Monday, we did have wind currents from the west-southwest blow through here. Between eight and eleven-thirty in the morning. And yes, a breeze strong enough to blow paper toward the east-northeast parks and the river. I'm headed your way. Lock, hold on, the sheriff is calling. I'll tell him your whereabouts."

While on hold, Lock continued to drive and looked at everyone in vehicles, on the streets and paths.

"I'm here," Don said.

"Any ransom calls yet?" Lock asked.

"No. Their friends calling to talk. Seriously, Lock, with her I.D. card and a desktop checkbook missing, I think they planned to make her write a check. If they're older and homeless, I doubt if they're electronically savvy. Besides, where would they take her? She has to still be in the van. They aren't going to do away with her, or leave the area until they extract the money they want."

"I agree." Don added, "All area enforcements are checking white vans. We've posted a message to be notified of any reported stolen ones. Although, the description includes a lot of gray primer stripes where the paint is peeling off."

"Don, we can't let it go until tomorrow. If we don't find her—" Lock paused.

"Spill it," Don said.

"Homeless aren't going to miss a chance to eat tomorrow. Surely, they'll go to a soup kitchen, unless they found money to eat elsewhere."

"Like the cash missing from Evans' purse?" Don said.

"Yes. If they consider her cash a lot, they could have filled the gas tank and be far away by now." His phone beeped. "My dad is calling. I'll talk to you in a bit." He accepted the call.

"Trey, your mother remembered something. Just a bit north on the Missouri, there's an empty lot. It's closed off, but it's common for her to pick up a lot of blown household trash along that particular fence line. There's a tiny, cinder block utility building just inside the gate. Last month, she noticed and reported the lock had been jimmied. There were things in it that looked like a homeless person might collect."

"Mom shouldn't be out there by herself. What if someone were in there?"

"I know. She and I will talk it over."

Lock took directions, called Don, and drove toward the site.

Relieved, he watched the moon peek out to reveal a white van with peeled paint, parked next to the tiny shed. He confirmed the find with Don then easily slipped through the opened gate. He listened to voices in the van long enough to identify the situation and rushed back to his car at the end of the dirt drive.

Within two minutes, Don and the sheriff arrived blacked out, no siren, no lights, no headlights. Speaking softly, Bill informed them, "More squad cars coming."

Lock said, "They're in the van with the motor running. She's alive."

"How do you know?" asked Don.

"I heard her. Mrs. Evans is well on her way of castigating the devil out of them."

Three patrol cars, also in blacked out code, pulled to a stop. One deputy stood with cars on the road. Lock, Don, and Bill with four officers quietly approached the little building and van.

Guns drawn, the deputies charged and ready, they spread out to cover all doors of the van and the one to the building. In synchronized motion, they flung all doors open. "Freeze! Hands where we can see them!"

"Well! It's about time!" squawked Mae Evans.

A man, bent over in his limited attempt to stand, dropped to his knees, groaned, and placed his hands on his head. His left eye was acutely swollen. An officer handcuffed him and led him to a patrol car.

The bewhiskered shorter man breathed with a high-pitched whistle wheeze. He frantically looked back and forth, finally he appeared to cooperate. He slowly climbed out the van's rear end and balanced on the ground, where he forthwith slammed a door into Lock and slipped away, leaving his coat at Lock's feet. The man attempted to scurry with a severe limp. Lock and two deputies took after him.

"Stop!" Lock ordered in a commanding voice, and charged his gun. The cocking ringtone seriously confirmed his intention of being obeyed.

The frightened man stopped and promptly collapsed to the ground. Lock stood over him, a deputy's flashlight disclosed bloody scratches on his face, and his eyes were red and puffy. The man wheezed and struggled to catch his breath.

"Holy smokes." Lock returned his gun to the holster.

Sheriff Ruell stepped up and said, "Frisk and read him his rights."

One of the male officers cuffed the offender. Lock said, "Have a medic check them both out." He walked back to the van where Don stayed with the still-ranting Mrs. Evans.

"You won't believe what those deplorable, wretched creatures did!" Every word, hollered at the top of her lungs. One of the female officers stayed right at her side.

"They knocked on my back door! Bullied their way inside! They grabbed me! Idiots! I kicked, then poked them in their eyes! Fools! They shoved me down and rolled me in a rug! I'm so angry I could spit nails!"

Both kidnappers handcuffed, deputies placed them in separate patrol cars. The sheriff told his officers, "Carefully gather evidence piled on the utility building floor, and call for a tow truck."

No humans inside, but a calico cat trembled in the cold. Lock rolled his eyes and scooped up the cat from the deputy who held it out, obviously not a cat man. Did this cat belong to Mrs. Evans?

Lock sat on the back end of the van and listened to Letsea's aunt's diatribe. Don stood with him. In fact, he thought she delivered what sounded to be a fairly accurate rendition of the event as it must have happened. Her statement, recorded multiple times on body cams. After a lengthy period of time, she calmed and sat next to him. Her legs dangled over the bumper.

"Who are you?" she snapped then squinted.

He pulled out his shield, as did Don, and they showed her. "FBI."

"I'll swan. I thought the FBI always wore suits." She eyed his khaki pant legs.

"Not all the time," Lock said. Although Don wore a suit.

"Well, I'll be." She paused. "Do you have a phone? My

husband is probably worried sick."

"Speaking of phones, we've been searching for your cell. Do you know where it is?" Don asked.

"One of those bumbling idiots stuck it in the garbage disposal! They should know better. No peelings, no eggshells, no pits! It's a long list and now I guess we need to add no cell phones to it! Idiots!"

"You should go to the hospital to be checked out," Don said.

"Oh, phooey! Just let my husband know I'm on my way home."

Lock thought Mae Evans a woman of spunk. Maybe Letsea got hers from her mother's side of the family. "Did they tie you up at all?" he asked. How else could they have taken her?

"They tried to duct tape my hands down. I'd sneak my teeny-tiny sewing scissors out of my pocket. As soon as they thought my arms secure, I'd snip myself loose. The tall guy feared I was a witch. So, I let them have it with the wrath of God on their heels."

"I'm glad you seem unharmed. We're still going to take you to the hospital. You can see your husband there, okay?" Don said.

She tilted her head, squinted, and firmly pressed her lips together. She fixed a quiet stare which looked like she might be equipped with otherworldly powers.

Don took a step back.

"It's not a choice, Mrs. Evans," Lock said. "You have to be medically checked. You and your clothing may contain evidence. And the police need an official report. Did they tell you why they took you?"

"Oh, the creatures made me write them a check! Fools!"

"Did you?" Lock asked and glanced at Don.

"The exclusive cooperative way to justify them not taping my hands behind my back." Mrs. Evans, pointed over her shoulder. "It's in there somewhere."

Don climbed into the van from the side door. "Here it is." He waved it, shined his flashlight on it. "Pay to the order of cash, twenty-thousand. Is this *your* signature?"

"I wrote it for the amount they insisted on, but I signed it Mortimer Snerd."

Don tilted his head. "Who's that?"

Lock grinned and said, "I'd say you're a clever lady."

She released a well-earned sigh. "You know it. Mama didn't

raise any dummies."

"What else did these guys do?"

"I'm still livid they ate my chocolate raspberry ganache cakes! There were just two left and they ate both! They're a secret recipe, made by some undisclosed baker. I can only get them at Christmastime." She sat there shaking her head then snapped. "You have no idea how I look forward to those petit ganache cakes."

Lock said, "I do understand your frustration to miss out on that particular dessert. I did get a bite and I still keep thinking I want more."

"Where did you find one?" Mrs. Evans asked and fell quiet.

Lock thought, his cover already blown, what did it matter? He needed to put his retirement into action and stop stalling. "My mother shared one with me, after Letsea's tea party."

"Who is your mother?" her voice still sounded sharp, yet not raised.

"Alice Lockhart."

"Oh my, she's the sweetest lady. Always be kind to Alice."

"I do my best. I love my mom."

Mrs. Evans patted his arm. "Good boy."

Lock liked the idea of being called "boy." A stir of youthfulness.

Don said, "It looks like your anger served you well, Mrs. Evans. But who is Mortimer Snerd?"

She looked at Lock and said, "Kids. They've missed out on so much, haven't they?"

He snickered, even though the insinuation meant he appeared older than his age. *There went short-lived youthfulness.* "Don, Mortimer Snerd was a real dummy from the early years of television."

"You, of all people would know that tidbit." Don dismissed him with a roll of his eyes and waved over the other female officer to pull a patrol car closer for Mrs. Evans. They needed to transfer her to the hospital.

"Absolutely not!" she barked. "I will not be seen in a police car! I'd rather walk back. Of all the embarrassing things!" She grasped Lock's arm. "FBI don't always drive marked cars. Do you?"

Kindly, he said, "No, ma'am, I don't."

She looked at the officer. "I'll ride with him. I know his mama."

"I'll get my car." He stood, still cuddling the cat.

"You will do no such thing. I'll walk with you."

Lock offered his arm.

"So, tell me, FBI agent, have you met my niece, Letsea?" She stopped, totally changed topics, and pointed inside the van. "Someone, get my checkbook and my hook rug. I can't lose it! My sister gave it to me."

"It's evidence. I understand important memories. I promise to see you'll get it back."

As they passed the patrol cars, she shook a finger at the perpetrators. "For shame. Shame on you! Your mother's heart is breaking!" She let go of him and walked the remaining distance on her own standing.

The calico still cradled in the crook of his arm. At the car, he asked, "Is this your cat?"

"Heavens, no. Cats tend to shed. I thought it odd you'd bring your pet to work."

"Anyone want to run this cat to a vet for a checkup?" he called out.

One of the female cops volunteered.

He pulled his phone out to call Letsea.

It went to voice mail! Now what? Why would she not answer her phone?

CHAPTER 67

3:12 a.m. Friday, Christmas Eve morning,
Brechenworth mansion

Letsea heard a tap in the hall and opened the office door. "Lock. Over here. Quiet, guests sleeping. What did you find out?"

"Knowing others were asleep is why I didn't call your house phone. You aren't answering your cell. I came inside through the hidden tunnel. I hope that's okay."

Comforted by the fact he trusted entering her home to be acceptable. "You're fine. Sorry. Cell's charging in my bedroom. Unable to sleep, I decided to work. Did you find Aunt Mae?"

"Yes. She's fine and sitting with her husband."

Letsea closed her eyes and sighed. "Thank God. And you, too, I'm sure."

"It's a team effort."

"What happened? Is she hurt? The truth."

"Her pride, yes. She *was* kidnapped. Quite honestly, she's a pillar to be reckoned with. Holding her own until law enforcement arrived."

Letsea rested her head on his shoulder. "She, Gwendolene, and I took a series of self-defense classes together."

"I believe it."

"Where did you find her?"

He led her to the sofa, put an arm around her shoulders, and explained what happened.

Although, she suspected he didn't tell all. When he explained Auntie's fury at losing her last two chocolate ganache cakes, she disclosed, "They're Auntie's favorite, but laborious to make." She sighed. "She's furious I won't tell her where to order them. She can be tenacious. What can I say? I'm protecting my secret source from being overwhelmed."

"I'd like to learn that recipe for myself," he said.

"When would you ever have time to bake?"

"I've decided it's time to make time to do all sorts of things."

She peered at him.

"It's time to retire."

"So young? Can you afford to?" Would he even answer a question so personal?

"As long as I keep my expenses below my pension. I've been preparing for it. Do you want to go see your aunt now?"

"After she has time to decompress. You don't know how hardnosed Auntie can be. Robert has a soothing way with her. Did he wake up?"

"Long enough to squeeze her hand and wink."

"Letsea, I know today's been stressful." Lock turned toward her and said, "I'd like for you to join me tonight, for our Christmas Eve Candlelight Service. It might help you relax."

"Chip and Lauren are singing in the one at our church. I can't miss their performance. What time does yours start?"

"There are two services. Seven and eleven o'clock. Seventy-five minutes each."

"Ours is at nine o'clock," she said.

"I can guarantee you we can make all three services."

"Do you *need* to go to both of your services?"

"I promised my mom. It's part of her gift," he said "Are you still giving the party for the orphanage?"

"It's all planned. The children, with their group families, will be in the ballroom. A magician, dinner entertainment, a D.J. for dancing. Liza, the servers and security will be here. They don't need me. I'll have early dinner with family here in the main dining hall. A brief exchange of gifts, then off to candlelight service."

"I'm confused. I thought you wanted to attend the children's party."

"It's their celebration. I'm supplying space, servers, and a gift for the group. Pauline is cooking the dinner. Liza's perfectly dependable for overseeing things. When Pauline retires, I expect she'll apply for main housekeeping supervisor. She has a degree in hotel management and hospitality."

"Liza has a slight accent," he said.

"Her prominent language is English, although she's fluent in several languages."

"Like what?"

"French, Spanish, and Swahili. I don't remember all the others. Originally, she planned to be an international interpreter."

He scooted to the edge of his seat. "Where is she from?"

"I'm not sure, but her parents live in Kenya. She's worked here since college."

"South Africa? Are you kidding? As in bordering the Democratic Republic of the Congo?" He stared.

"I've never thought of it that way."

"Wait a minute." Presently, a whole new door opened. He pulled out his phone and stood. "Excuse me." He walked toward the fireplace then looked back. "What is Liza's last name?"

"Martin."

Lock texted his boss. "Call me. ASAP." His phone buzzed.

"Chief, I have a possible lead on the Congo kidnapping of the Brechenworths."

Letsea stood, hands on hips. "Liza's not the type to have anything to do with it."

Lock reminded, "Just doing my duty."

His boss asked, "What are you doing with Brechenworth in the middle of the night?"

"Talking," his voice stern.

"Letsea, where can I go to be alone?"

She left the office.

"Chief, will you have Supervisory Agent Douglas and his team contact the international division and do a check on Liza Martin? Tell them to focus on her family and especially her past connections."

"Talk to me, Lock. What do you have?"

"Liza Martin has worked for the Brechenworths for years. Her parents live in Kenya. Boss, the Congo calls may simply be her family keeping in touch. The skeptical part of me considers, if Liza worked here before the incident, possibly she told someone in Kenya or the Congo the Brechenworths would be traveling there."

"Feasible, Lock."

"Therefore, kidnappers could have pre-planned their attack knowing of the family's wealth. If so, Liza may have been in on the kidnapping from the beginning."

"We'll get this information to the proper team. Thanks, Lock, and good job on the recovery of her aunt. Pfeiffer wants you to transfer to his team. Just so you know, I said no." He hung up.

Lock found Letsea sitting on the side of her bed, covers rumpled and she looked adrift. He sat beside her. "How long has Liza been with you?" She collapsed against him and he put his arms around her for support.

"Don't do this to me. I depend on Liza. She helped take care of my grandparents after my parents were killed. Lock, she wouldn't have anything to do with hurting Mom and Dad. She's good and kind."

He'd heard that before. In fact, his parents thought much the same of the men who took Mrs. Evans.

"You mentioned, 'since college.' Tell me about her."

"She worked here part-time while in school. After graduation, she came on full-time. I feel blessed to have her. Please, don't tell me I've been wrong in my discernment."

"I'm sure she's fine. However, as a precaution, she needs to be checked out. Does she live here or elsewhere?"

"She has one of the studio apartments above the garage, but she's not always there."

"Is she married? Have children? What's her status?" he asked.

"Engaged once, they broke up." She tapped his chest with a fist. Her eyes closed.

"Hey, you're exhausted. You need to get some sleep."

"What a concept," she murmured. "Thank you for rescuing my aunt."

He helped her roll into bed, and straightened her blankets over her. "Sleep tight," he whispered. He touched a finger to her cheek then turned off her lamp.

On his way to the door, he stopped, looked back. In the soft glow from outside lights, he noticed his fedora still hung on the bedpost. "Good night, love," he whispered. He could easily get used to this.

CHAPTER 68

Letsea loved a house full of cheer and chatter. She enjoyed visiting during the early dinner with much to be grateful for, starting with Auntie's safe return. Although, she didn't speak of her ordeal, Auntie was unusually quiet.

Immediately after dinner, Gwendolene stood, tapped crystal stemware, and made an announcement. "Everyone, I have a very special surprise. Grab your coats. Come outside."

Gwen pulled her aside. "Letsea, thanks for making this possible. I'm so excited."

She rested her forehead to Gwen's. "You're welcome, Dear."

Doyle worked his way through the crowd to Gwen's side. "What are you up to?"

"It's my surprise, for you! Merry Christmas, darling."

In front of the house, they gathered along the front steps. On the circle drive, Letsea saw a white Cadillac Escalade, glimmering from all the yard lights.

"Wow! Way cool!"

"Look!"

She felt a rush of energy through the early night air. Her sister absolutely knew how to present a gift with flair.

Chip, Lauren, with cousins, scampered down the steps. Their squeals warmed Letsea's heart.

"Darling, come look inside." Gwen opened the driver's door.

Letsea detected sharp judgement when Doyle glanced at her. *Oops, guilty of indulging Gwen's wishes, again.* Who cared? Gwen positively glowed and that thrilled her.

Sis opened a back seat door. Doyle looked inside, and his expression lit up with a huge ear-to-ear smile. Gwen hugged him and they whispered. Doyle gave his wife a very long, romantic kiss. He stood with his arms around her. Then called Chip and Lauren over and picked them both up in a hug.

Letsea drew in a deep breath. Happy for her sister, but she wanted a life like it of her own.

Doyle raised his voice above the crowd's chatter. "Everyone! We need a larger vehicle to hold all the child seats. We're going to have another baby!" he proudly announced.

Doyle's whole family crowded closer. Letsea heard echoes of cheers and excitement. She was glad for them. *Really, I'm happy.*

A tightness spread across her chest as her heart beat faster. Tears welled in her eyes. At the point she struggled to breathe, she slipped back inside the house.

Although happy for Gwen and Doyle, and happy to welcome the new baby, grief struck at an alarming impact. Not for their joy, but for what she deemed as selfish for what she desired and did not have. Why couldn't she have the family she so wanted? She thought of Lock and recalled he visioned his children playing in his old tree house. Lock wanted children, too. Tears filled her eyes. She met him merely three weeks ago, and she loved him. *Is it even possible?*

In the main floor lavatory, she let the tears fall. Committed to not letting Gwen see her cry, she splashed her face with cold water. Then snagged her car keys off the hook in Bob's office, and ran to the garage, where she jumped in her car to fall apart without being overheard.

Letsea struggled to breathe in gulps as tears fell. After she emptied the tissue box, she searched for napkins. She was determined to get her act together before time to leave for the candlelight service, yet unwelcomed tears flowed nonstop.

CHAPTER 69

Lock heard the excitement outside and stepped out on the wraparound porch to find Doyle's family in front of the big house. He noticed Christmas onlookers stopped instead of doing a drive-by look-see and cringed. Even the Evans' were there cheering along, but he didn't see Letsea. He waved.

Doyle yelled, "We're going to have a baby!"

"Congratulations!" Lock hollered and waved again. *Lucky you.* He strolled toward the kitchen door, where he glimpsed Letsea run from the mansion to the garage.

He waited, yet she didn't come out. Something happened. *What's wrong?* He went to check on her.

The moment he opened the side door, he heard her distress. If it's what he thought, he could relate. He tapped on her driver's door window.

She jumped and screamed. "What are you doing out here?" she snapped, while swatting tissues from her lap.

"Checking on you. Roll your window down."

She blew her nose instead.

He tried to give a pathetic, sad expression and tapped on the glass again. "Come on."

She gave a poor lopsided attempt at good cheer then let the window down. "You should go away."

"Why? I have sisters, I know what crying looks like. What's wrong?" He chose not to mention he'd shed a few of his own over the years.

"Leave me alone, I don't want to talk about it."

Her face was red and soaked, her eyes swollen. "Okay. Be that way. Leave me in a state of worry." He watched her pout and he couldn't resist further comment. "You have nothing on my sister Hope's tantrums." He intentionally smiled big. "Hope is the reason Faith has such a good sense of humor."

Letsea offered a faint chortle.

"There's my girl."

Letsea blew her nose again then leaned back and breathed in gulps.

He plucked up his nerve. "I understand you're going to be an aunt again."

Tears streamed anew. In a strong measure, he identified the source of her agony.

"I'm happy for that," she whimpered.

"Sure you are. I can see it all over your face." He peeked inside her car to make his point. "And your car seats and the floor."

"Lock, have you ever regretted anything?"

"Sure I have." He regretted not returning her kiss that night in Phoenix. "I take it you have too."

She nodded. "I regret not figuring out a way to have children of my own."

"Huh. Imagine that." He tilted his head. "I know a way. Do you want me to tell you about it?"

She cracked a grin and chuckled, albeit he saw one sad, crooked endeavor.

"I'm serious."

So was he, but maybe she wasn't ready for that side of him. "Tell me." He squatted to meet her gaze. "Talk to me."

"I've always wanted a family, but I have strict regulations to live by. According to my grandfather's trust, I am responsible for securing the next generation. If I don't adhere to his wishes, I forfeit the estate. I tried to talk Gwen and Doyle into compliance, nonetheless he wouldn't give in. There's more involved than these houses."

"It must be a very strict directive."

She squeezed her eyes closed then looked directly at him. "I can only pass the estate on in the name of Brechenworth. Otherwise, I have to turn the estate into a charity or divide it for other charities."

Lock whistled. "Sounds like you need to find the right husband.

How did you put it yesterday? Your forever-mate. Get married and have a bunch of kids."

She gulped in a deep breath. Tears cascaded from her chin to her coat.

He waited.

"It's not so easy," she finally said. "I should have adopted, or gone the scientific medical route. I might have gotten away with it. It's my fault, I stalled. I wanted the whole dream. I still do."

He stood and stretched his back and sneaked a glance at his watch. "Gotten away with what?" And this being the big question he'd been wondering for days. "What *is* your dream?"

"A husband who loves me for me, regardless of trust conditions, and children of our own. I want a happy family!" She whined and plopped her forehead to the steering wheel.

"Letsea Brechenworth, is that all you want? What if you were to marry me? We could fill your house with children. It's been said they're cheaper by the dozen." He had dreams, too. She heaved a couple times, caught her breath, and looked up at him.

"You aren't funny, Lock. I'm sharing a sacred secret and you're making fun of me because I can't find love."

"Can I come around and sit inside with you?"

"It's unlocked."

He brushed wads of tissues to the floor. "I'm not teasing. Are you? Who doesn't love you? Everybody loves you." Lock reached over and grabbed her face, forcing her to look at him. "Open your eyes, woman, I'm in love with you." *Since, the first morning at Union Station. You took my heart then left in a yellow cab.* "Letsea, are you afraid of me?"

"Why do you ask?"

"You're hiding something."

"Maybe, a little," she murmured.

"A little, my foot. At times, you tremble and display a mature defense mechanism to calm yourself. Not that you're doing it now. Why would you ever be frightened of me?"

"I believed you. It infuriated me when you lied."

"Yeah, you made that clear. Here's the thing. I'm not the only one here who has lied. In fact, I do want to help you. Every day, I hope to see and talk with you. My days begin and end with thoughts of you. If that isn't love, I don't know what is."

Her face drooped. "You don't understand."

"Then explain it." He folded his arms.

She raised her shoulders high, before dropping them with a deep loud sigh. "I need for the man I love to love me *enough* to accept the name Brechenworth as his own last name. Instead of my taking his as mine or keeping my own. Granddad believed it's the only logical way the name Brechenworth has a chance to survive. At least for another generation.

"To my knowledge, I am the last Brechenworth. My grandfather wanted to honor his grandfather's good name. I'm expected to give birth to baby Brechenworth. By doing that, I'd fully inherit all parts of the estate."

"That's it? You mean you'd consider marrying me if I agreed to take your surname in our marriage?" He glanced at his watch and cringed. "Letsea, I need to go get dressed. Will you please stay here? I'll be back in fifteen minutes. We are not finished talking, but I have to change."

He placed a kiss on her forehead. "I want to give you a real kiss. This isn't the time. I know you put a great deal of stock in first kisses. Since I'm in a hurry, and you're crying your eyes out, it'll have to wait. I want it to be perfect." He tapped her nose. "I'll be right back, love."

He opened the door, stepped out, and looked back at her. "By the way, you're beautiful as you are. I'll bring you a cold damp cloth to cool your face."

Stepping around to her open car window, he leaned in and kissed her cheek. "Don't go anywhere."

The moment he stepped outside, he pumped his fist in the air and raced to the Queen Anne. Without a doubt, being late to the service would not be the ideal way to pop the question of marriage. If Letsea still waited in the garage, he knew he had a chance.

His family, dressed, ready and waiting.

Carlton asked, "What's with your crazy expression, Trey?"

He hurried past them going up two steps at a time. "You all can go ahead. I'm taking Letsea." He heard his sister's cheer. It furthered a tingle of excitement. *Never would I have expected our conversation to lead where it did.* He finally knew Letsea's deep secret. He could handle it, in exchange for a wife like Letsea.

His mother knocked on his door. "Do you need help with your

tie?"

"No, although help with the cummerbund sounds good."

While his mom fastened the hooks, he tied his bow tie. After he slid the black formal coat on, he heard his dad's voice. "You'd think you were going to a wedding."

He hoped so. The sooner the better. He loved Letsea Brechenworth!

"You make the name Lockhart proud, Son," his dad added.

He tensed. He didn't have time to think of the prearrangement in her trust fund, but if she were willing, how might one avoid the trust terms? Impossible.

He recalled her words to Purser. *I reject any legal challenge of it.*

Conditions were set in stone.

CHAPTER 70

Letsea in her car

He loves me? Then again, trust fund conditions hadn't set in. "Nevertheless, he said he loves me," she whispered. No need to feel any more attached than she already did, unless he's the real deal. A quiver of doubt stabbed, and history haunted her thoughts.

Men. As soon as realization hit that they'd need to forfeit their hereditary surname, they left, or wanted to contest it. To think, all her ancestry mothers traded in their names.

Maybe she did need a candlelight service. But three services in a row? Letsea looked in the visor mirror. *Egads!*

She dashed to the house to scrub her face. In the kitchen, Pauline and servers scurried, so she went to a basement lavatory.

Sounds of the children's party from the ballroom renewed her heart.

Once, she considered turning the estate into a supportive children's home. Since her ancestor ran away from a nineteenth-century cruel one, it may well be a healing measure. As such, she wouldn't have to ask a man she loved to butt heads with his soul.

She dried her face and thought of Lock's parents. Rick and Alice were such good people. How unfair to ask Lock to forsake their name. She knew Granddad's intention for putting it in his trust, to honor his grandfather. Is it worth dishonoring such a loveable couple? *If* he was serious. *Open your eyes, woman. I love you.* She bit on her bottom lip.

She heard the Davises in the front parlor with an early gift exchange. The elevator moved and she speculated the grandparents went to take a nap before service. The house buzzed with excitement, why shouldn't she? *No matter what may come, he loves me.*

Conversations and sounds articulated in the walls of the basement. She never noticed it before. Usually, when she went to the basement, no one was upstairs. Except maybe Bob and Agent Reynolds' spirit. To her knowledge, Paul kept his word. No one mentioned having heard a ghost in the house.

She needed to figure out a way to help Paul find serenity.

No wonder Pauline always knew what transpired in the house. She heard her talking to Paul the first night his rough voice came to her room. She brought toast and hot chocolate to help her sleep. Had Pauline heard her talking to Uncle Paul in the tower?

Sweet Pauline must know a wealth of secrets and emotions through her years there.

Lock considered the rules by which Letsea lived. She needed the man she loved to love her *enough* to accept her as is. That included her name, very likely the reason for being single at forty-one years. *One doesn't sidestep anything so important.*

When he entered the garage, she stood dumping an armful of tissues into the trash can.

Relieved, he said, "I'm glad you're still here."

"You're my ride. Where else would I be?"

"You look great, Letsea. How do you do it?" Lock tossed something behind the seat.

She stretched to see it. A damp cloth in a plastic bag. "I already washed my face. I didn't want to go upstairs and be seen, so I don't have makeup, my purse, or cell phone."

"You don't need them. You're beautiful as you are and you can use my phone, if need be." He started the engine and pulled out of the garage.

"Lock, I'm not sure what to think of our conversation a little while ago."

"Don't think. First, let's get through all these services." He pulled into a full church parking lot and looked for a spot to park.

She knew what *don't think* meant. Restrictions in the trust hit him. Lock loved his parents. He would not give up his name. Or the legacy of possibly bringing the number four Godrick Lockhart into his family. Friendship. That's all he originally asked for.

Why can't I accept he loves me and if I need to surrender the estate, so be it. I'd rather have love and a family than property, right?

He opened her door, and when she stepped out and looked where they were, she said, "This is your church? It's Pauline's church, too."

Inside, Alice sat near the front with a *reserved* sign. Lock let her in to sit next to his mom. He slid in close beside her at the pew's end. The sanctuary was crowded, unlike her church with its sparsely filled pews. Letsea glanced at Lock and fidgeted with the vigil candle an usher handed her.

"You look nice," she said. "I didn't realize it to be so formal."

His gaze was receptive. Multiple friends stopped to shake hands and greet his family. He introduced her, but she already knew most of them.

"Are you feeling better?" Lock whispered.

"Just tired."

"What will it take for you to get a good night's sleep?"

She shrugged. "What will it take for the FBI to rectify a wrong on Agent Reynolds?"

"Have you always struggled with insomnia?"

"A couple weeks, I suppose."

"Three weeks, *I* know of." He raised an eyebrow. "Peace be to you."

Peace eluded her since *I was murdered* resounded from the Whispering Arch.

Overhead lights blinked then dimmed. Congregants hushed. The minister welcomed all and opened with prayer and a hymn. He proceeded to sit in a front pew. A weathered manger with a glowing light from within sat center stage.

The narrator's voice came over the speakers. A single star-bright light shone from the ceiling toward the manger. It reminded Letsea of the sunrise when she saw an image of Uncle Paul reflected in the curved glass. What an unusual year.

Distanced from Seth. Aunt Mae got married. Gwendolene pregnant. A spirited revelation at the Whispering Arch. She squeezed her eyes, but random thoughts didn't stop. A ghost! Stalkers! Aunt Mae kidnapped! She leaned forward. Police everywhere. Lock! Agent Paul E. Reynolds' expectations of her! Trip to Phoenix. Lock and her dancing in the speakeasy. She caught her breath. *Lock loves me.* FBI. All those newspaper articles on the Dead Fed. She sat back. The 1929 reporters, doggedly followed a city full of government agents, as if they actually tried to solve the murder themselves. How crucial Agent Reynolds' murder, at the time. The cover-up of it *still mattered*! Why? And what could she possibly do? *Lock loves me. Dare I believe it? Yes! Lock loves me. Lock loves me!*

He wrapped an arm around her.

She wanted to bury her face against his chest and say, *I love you, too*. Instead, Letsea glanced up to the high arched ceiling.

Oh, snap! An arch! Promptly, she attempted to dismiss her onslaught of musings. No way did she want Uncle Paul's voice to materialize in her head. She put her face to her palms and drew slow deep breaths. As Lock's hand rubbed her back, she refocused on the narrator.

Lock released her and stepped to the aisle. She sat up, what was he doing?

A trio of musicians played from the stage wings. Lock, a baritone, harmonized with two other men, from their own varied seats. They sang "We Three Kings." *Lock can sing!* Of course Alice wanted him here. She heard the voice of a professional singer. *Why choose the FBI?*

Right or wrong, Lock became her safe haven. As she listened, she relaxed.

When he sat, she placed a hand on his. "Beautiful," she mouthed. When his fingers interlaced with hers, a tingle moved across her neck. She saw him tilt his head and watch her.

The service interposed segments of reading Nativity scripture and songs correlated to the scene. Lock sung from the aisle again.

Alice held her hand as he did.

At one point, Lock moved to the front. Alone, center stage, a cappella, his voice, deep and rich, resonated to the beams and the arched ceiling. "O Holy Night."

Letsea closed her eyes to feel his voice, and recalled his words. *Open your eyes, woman. I love you.* She looked at him. Lock didn't need a huge S on his chest, the tuxedo framed him as her handsome hero. He'd been watching out for her safety all along. When he stretched out his right arm to emphasize words in the song, his hand pointed to her, or his mom? She swallowed back a murmur, and again he looked directly at her.

She trembled and gripped the edge of the pew. A moment later, Alice's hand held hers. She glanced at her friend and remembered Lock's words. *I promised my mom.*

Lock, the good son. A good man. Might he be hers?

When Lock returned, he put his arm around her and in the process, touched Alice's shoulder.

When her friend, who owned the party store, sang, "A Baby Changes Everything," Letsea brushed tears from her cheeks. Lock handed over his freshly pressed handkerchief, and pulled her closer to him. At least she didn't sob out loud. Although, another woman did.

Nearing the end, the choir, from the rear of the sanctuary, sang. An experience to behold, even more so, being unable to see their many faces. Every note clear.

The dim lights faded off. The starburst softened until it, too, disappeared. Attention drifted to a single alter candle shining from within the manger scene in front. The choir sang, a message of light, love, and the blessing of oneness, then went silent.

Candlelighters lit their tapers from the representation of the Christ light. They shared the flame with those in the outer-aisle seats. Each person shared their light with their neighbor one at a time.

When Lock held his candle to hers, a warmth ignited in her heart. After she held her flame for Alice to light from, Lock pressed his lips to her temple and squeezed her shoulder. Goose bumps tingled on her arms.

In a domino effect, the sanctuary glowed bright by the sharing of light. The choir sang a short medley of songs including "This

Little Light of Mine."

Lauren and Chip slowly walked up the center aisle, singing, "Somewhere Out There." Excited, she squeezed his hand. "I didn't know the kids would be here." The look in his eyes revealed he knew. Awareness clicked. That is how he guaranteed they'd not be late to any of the three services.

The minister stood at the front and silently demonstrated time had come for all to extinguish the flames. As they did, the bright beam of starlight shone down on the manger and a spotlight on her two babes in the light. Chip in his own astonishing baritone which belied his years. Lauren in angelic soprano finished their song. The ceiling lights slowly went from dim to bright.

The narrator said the name of each participant. At the reading of their name, each stood in place, and next, they all played and sang, "We Wish You A Merry Christmas!" The choir chimed in by singing a closing prayer.

Letsea meditated. She finally knew what she was led to do, to find desired peace. Following the ceremony, she needed to call Marcia.

After congratulating performers and the children on a beautiful presentation, Letsea found her sister. "They were breathtaking. Why didn't you tell me the children were singing here?"

"Trey hoped to surprise you," Gwen said.

"He certainly managed it." Letsea hugged her sister. "Congratulations, honey."

Doyle and Lock walked up behind her. "We need to head out."

She looked to Lock and said, "You said you'd loan me your phone." She held out her palm.

He placed it there. "If it buzzes, don't answer."

"Fine. Kind of like your 'don't touch' rule, hm? I'll meet you back at your car."

She headed outside. Lock followed at a distance. She called Marcia. "Merry Christmas. I'm terribly sorry to bother you tonight, however I need your help. I need a roundtrip red-eye ticket to Boise. A florist there who will deliver on Christmas morning. A hotel reservation with early check-in privileges, and a rental car. I want to leave here ASAP tonight, after two o'clock in the morning...."

Next up, the program at her own church. The same as she remembered every year. The one instrument being the organ. Hymns, choir, front and center. Aunt Mae among the faces. "Thank you, God." A long description of lit-candle etiquette proceeded the same annual sermon in the midst of service. The splendor of the night were the soloists. Chip and Lauren sang, "O Holy Night" and "Mary's Boy Child."

On their way out, after service, Letsea introduced Lock to her friends.

All the family members were in the Lockhart's church for the last service. Letsea promised herself not to break into tears again. Any more, and she'd be dehydrated. Yet there they were, dripping off her chin. Rick passed his handkerchief to her. She couldn't remember the last time she felt so moved by a service, glad to experience it twice.

Afterward, Lock caught up to her. "We're going to drive around and look at Christmas lights."

"Have fun, I need to get home. I'll go with Gwen in Doyle's new ride."

"The Escalade I saw earlier? Is it new?" Lock asked.

"Yes. Gwen's way of surprising Doyle with her baby news. Complete with three child seats installed."

He whistled. "You mean she went out and bought a new Cadillac? Boy, you all sure live a different lifestyle than I'm used to. Wait. No communication between them? Over a huge purchase?"

"It's not like it's out of their household budget."

He paused. "You bought it."

"Gwen bought it."

"You paid for it."

Letsea shrugged. "What if I did?"

Her sister and the kids were her heirs. Whether she got to keep and pass along the estate and the original funds or not, she worked hard to build her own financial portfolio. Why should they wait until she died? *I'd rather witness their happiness.* As her sister, it wasn't fair for Gwen to be left out of the wills. Surely, not intentional. In addition, Letsea managed the 25 percent Gwen did inherit from their mother's parents. Doyle wanted to be the sole provider of his family. He may have frowned on Gwen relying on Letsea for extras, even so, he welcomed Letsea's help with their retirement funds.

"You wrote a check for one-hundred-thousand dollars, paid to cash. For the SUV," Lock said.

She noticed, not a single question in his statement. "There's no reason not to. If it's what she wanted, so be it. And how do you know the activity in my bank accounts? Are you *still* investigating me?"

He sighed.

After midnight, Christmas morning, Lock called his boss. "Brechenworth wrote the check to cover the cost of a vehicle for her brother-in-law. Christmas gift. No blackmail, no bribe. No extortion."

"That's it?" Chief asked.

"Pure and simple. And so go the lives of the wealthy. Merry Christmas, Chief."

"Thanks, Lock. Merry Christmas."

Lock looked at the list of recent calls on his phone. Letsea borrowed his phone to call who? He typed a brief text and sent it to the number she called. His phone rang immediately.

"Letsea?" He heard a woman's voice.

"No, this is Lockhart. Who is this?"

"Miss Brechenworth's personal secretary, Marcia."

He learned an eye-opener! His heart dropped to his stomach. He needed to act fast! Marcia volunteered to help. "I'm relieved Miss Brechenworth won't be traveling alone."

"Son of a monkey, Letsea!"

CHAPTER 71

"You found me," Letsea said as Lock settled in the seat beside her on the plane.

"Yeah. You should have invited me."

"I've taken enough of your time away from visiting family as it is. You don't need to come. I'll be home before nightfall."

"Ditto. What are you thinking anyway?"

She placed a hand on his arm. "Actually, I'm thinking how elegant the services were." She closed her eyes. "I can still hear the richness of your voice." The seductiveness, but she withheld that part. He sang Christmas songs to her. She hugged herself.

"You have some amazing hearing. I stopped singing three hours ago."

She playfully batted his arm. "I should have known you'd follow me. Lock, there's something I need to do for my own peace of mind."

"I'm glad to hear it." He raised an eyebrow. "So, what's in Boise?"

"Paul E. Reynolds' grave."

He remained silent. It didn't stop him from gazing at her. "Lock, what are *you* thinking?"

"I worry. We have yet to figure out the unknown stalker. And you want to fly across country, alone, again. Please, talk to me."

She wished she could. The fact he came made her giddy. "I'm glad you're here. Maybe I'll get the kiss you promised."

Lock squinted. "I have a good mind to make you wait."

She pretended to pout. As he leaned close and his lips touched hers, a voice came over the intercom. Time to fasten their seat belts. He pulled back to his seat.

She wanted that kiss. "Ugh."

He looked at her. "I'm not going to start anything I can't finish." She watched him make a point of buckling in.

By the time they were settled, she thought there might be a chance for her kiss. Except the plane already prepared to land in Chicago for their connecting flight.

Lock carried her little overnight backpack. She wore her purse beneath her long winter coat. His hand on her at all times. At their terminal, they waited for permission to board the second plane. He kept looking at her. At her lips, in particular. His blue eyes turned deep, rich.

"Just do it," she whispered.

He pressed a hand against her back, and it caused her to stand taller, the other behind her head pulled her closer and she whispered, "Finally."

When his lips met hers, her arms wrapped around his waist, beneath his coat, hands spread on his back. The need strong, in the moment it was all she could ask for. At first, she reveled in the tender touch, then pressed letting Lock know she welcomed him to deepen the kiss. He moved against her. Lost in the persistent caress, she gasped for breath and he paused and rested his cheek to hers.

"Do I need to stop?" he whispered.

"Oh, please don't." Her fingers strengthened on his back. His lips firm and determined and she wanted him all the more. Nothing in the universe mattered in that moment of time. The two together, tasting, feeling, embracing each other was everything. No man ever made her feel so desired as Lock. He parted those delicious lips from hers and rested them to her temple. When he pulled away, she saw confidence in his upturned lips and sapphire eyes.

"Just try to tell me *that* didn't pass your kiss test."

What test? She quivered, not releasing the feel of him. His eyes were stormy and she raised on her toes for more. As their lips met, she heard the announcement to board their flight. Good heavens! She'd forgotten where they were!

A spontaneous applause broke out from onlookers.

"Let's go, love." Lock walked with an arm around her waist

through the passenger boarding bridge.

After they were seated, Letsea faced him, a quivery giddiness dancing in her veins, and pulled her bottom lip in.

"What are you looking at?" he asked. "Do I have lipstick on my face?"

"Better not. I'm not wearing any."

"Hush." His lips touched, caressed hers again.

"Nice. I expect when we're alone, you'll knock my socks off." She hoped.

Lock looked at her feet. "I've got my work cut out for me, since you're wearing knee-high boots.

She must have blushed but didn't care. Lock loved her and she loved him.

After the plane settled airborne, Lock asked a steward for a couple of blankets.

"Are you cold?" she asked.

He shook his head and looked straight ahead. "Not in the slightest."

Letsea giggled. She wasn't alone in feeling something marvelous.

Chapter 72

Boise, Idaho

"First," Letsea said, "I need to stop by the hotel to pick something up."

Lock set the coordinates and drove. "It's darker than I expected. What do you say we eat breakfast first?"

She typed on her phone. "Okay, the hotel has breakfast. We can check in, eat, and by the time we're ready, we can get inside the cemetery."

"You think this will bring you peace?" he asked.

"I depend on it."

At the hotel, they were told, "The florist already dropped off the flowers."

"Perfect."

Lock looked at her and did not say a word.

She touched his elbow. "I know it may seem silly to you, but it means something to me."

She mattered to him. He placed a hand over hers and asked the clerk, "Where's the restaurant?"

"Room service, sir."

"Indeed." He removed his overcoat and they went ahead and placed an order.

A desk clerk brought out a large bouquet of white roses. "Congratulations, sir."

"Thank you." Lock figured the clerk must think it's their wedding day or something. Letsea, all wrapped up in her long down coat, he, still in a black-tie monkey suit.

Letsea signed the registration and he said, "Those are beautiful. Do you want me to carry them for you?"

Letsea teased, "Might as well, they go nice with your tux."

"Hey, you didn't allow time for me to change, thank you very much."

"I don't mind. I like your cummerbund."

He looked down then back at her. "Some of the other musicians preferred vests."

"I'm glad cummerbunds won out. Vests don't distinguish it as formal attire, nothing more than a nice suit. Gwen said certain fashion designers want to abandon the cummerbund, so they can bring it back in a few years, to keep the fashion wheel rolling."

She acted mischievous on purpose. "Will you please stop saying cummerbund?"

She laughed. He loved to see her relaxed.

When they reached the room, Lock fumbled with the key, between flowers, his coat, and her overnight bag.

"Here." She snatched it from his hand and waved the door open. "I noticed you didn't get your own room."

"I'm not letting you out of my sight." He watched her drape her coat on a bed.

"Good, two beds. I hope we'll have time to nap before our return flight."

"Got it." Different visions danced in his head, but he settled for being with her. Roses placed on the desk, coats hung, shoes off, and thanks to hotel amenities, he went to brush his teeth. Letsea stretched out on the first bed. He bent over and kissed her before he sat at the table, rubbed his hands over his face, and yawned. "Your insomnia is costing me sleep. At least, that and *those books* of yours I'm reading."

"They are exciting, aren't they?" She pulled one out of her travel bag and waved it at him. "Which book are you on now?"

"Number eight." He stretched, undid the bow tie, and let it dangle. "Look at you, everything you need. I didn't have time to pack a thing."

She looked at him and her jaw tightened. "Lock, what you said, last night in the car—"

"Come here." He rolled his chair away from the table. "I meant it." He wrapped his arms around her and rested his head against her body. "I don't know how you managed to do it. In less than a month, I find myself totally enamored."

She held him, fingered his hair. "Me, too." He exhaled, glad to hear her say it.

He wished to kiss her again, but there was a knock on the door. "Oh, that's great. Now what?"

"Room service."

"Breakfast."

"I'm hungry for more than food. In due time," he smirked, aware it was too soon to advance to his intimate visions. Beforehand, he needed to know Chief removed him from her case.

"The Field of Honor section." Letsea pointed.

Still dark out, Lock angled the car as close to the cemetery lot as possible to utilize the headlights. When she hurried out of the car, he said, "Zip your coat. It's below freezing here," and opened his door.

She complied, then leaned in. "Lock, will you wait here, please? I want to do this alone."

He wasn't expecting that response, but maybe he should have. "Okay if I walk around? I need to stretch my legs." She pulled the hood of her down coat over her head and reached into the back seat for the bundle of flowers. "Knock yourself out. No, don't! I mean, fine, walk. Be safe."

"How many flowers are there?" he asked.

"Thirty. One for each year he lived on earth."

"I thought he was twenty-eight years old."

"Twenty-nine, plus I included a rose for the eleven months and six days of his last year. I'm sure they meant something to him."

With the headlights shining, he watched as she located Reynolds' headstone, bent, and brushed her gloved hand across it. She placed the bundle of long-stemmed roses in front of the marker then traced a finger along engravings of Reynolds' final identification. He saw her place something tiny on top of the monument.

When she shot a couple pictures with her cell phone, he assumed she had finished. He was wrong. She bowed.

Lock wondered what she possibly read to draw her fifteen-hundred miles away, on Christmas morning, with two houses filled with guests. To what? Lay flowers in memory of a man she never knew. When she looked up, he expected her to return to the warmth of the car.

She did not. He watched as Letsea stood in the cold and whispered. He didn't know if she were praying or wishing to communicate to him. Should he encourage her to come back? Not if the love he felt for her was real. She traveled a far distance to do what she needed to do.

With a defiant stance, hands on hips, she walked around the grave. Lock caught a glimpse of her glistening face. She talked. He lowered his window to listen, still not understanding the soft farewell.

Lock realized, whatever she thought of Agent Reynolds, he probably crushed her heart when he told her the things about the man which were less than flattering. He should have known she sensed a personal connection to Reynolds from the fact she researched his death. He noticed a fine mist falling on the windshield. It created starbursts of watery beads.

Fog moved into the beams of the light. He considered her health then heard a faint mumble. He refused to distract her by turning on the windshield wipers.

Having left the car running, he stepped out and walked around, wanting to hear her words. Inaudible, he looked at other headstones. He shined his flashlight and read inscriptions. Morris Hill Cemetery was filled with notable history. Upon his return, he noticed the incredible.

Letsea appeared to talk to a distinct pillar of fog. She paused, and spoke again. He glanced around, it was a lone column of fog, narrow and tall, above Reynolds' grave. The woman he hoped to marry was in the middle of a conversation with the odd cloud! Did she relate a familiarity between Reynolds and her parents by reason they were all murdered? He needed to understand what this man in history meant to her.

It was going on ten o'clock in the morning, with moving clouds in a dark sky. Obviously, a storm was brewing. Lock got inside the warmth of the car. Not hearing her words anyway, he raised the window and the heater. He caught his breath when he saw her engulfed by a concealing cloud of mist. The background, darkened by evergreen trees, made it difficult to see her through the thickness. What he noticed, due to the car light beams, Letsea became encircled by streaks of visible wind current.

Lock blinked. He witnessed the unbelievable. The mist on the glass accumulated and reflected dozens of iridescent orbs. He let the windshield wiper make a single swipe to clear his view. When she backed up, free of the obscure invisibility, she held out a hand, and something appeared out of nowhere in her palm. She folded her fingers over it. Small orbs of light floated in the distance. A deer stood statue still and stared at her.

Gazing into the fog, Letsea moved her head from side to side and her hood slipped down. She slipped her hands in her pockets then stood as still as the doe.

Lock recalled her laughter the first day in her house when he quoted Dumas to her.

Nothing makes time pass or shortens the way like a thought that absorbs in itself all the faculties of the one who is thinking. External existence is then like a sleep of which this thought is the dream. Under its influence, time has no more measure, space has no more distance.

He wanted a life with this woman, who lost so much. Tragedy haunted her past. This beautiful generous soul wanted a husband and family to love and cherish.

He breathed in deep. For whatever explanation, she, still single, as though waiting for him to find her. Lock loved Letsea and wanted to be the man in her life, husband, the father of her children. What he didn't want to do was hurt his father by disowning his name.

The fog lifted above, as a canopy, snowflakes twirled. Letsea stood fixated in front of Agent Reynolds' gravestone. The headlights shone a circle around her. The snow gave an appearance of a figurine in a shaken snow globe. Mistiness of fog drifted, and made it look ethereal. "Letsea, come to me," he whispered with grit. He prayed this graveyard visit not to be her swan song.

Lock stepped out of the car and stood by the door, willing her to return, still not voicing a word to interrupt. The fog faded away and she turned to him. It relieved his heart. She held out a hand for him to come.

Lock approached and pulled her into a hug. "Doing better?"

"I believe I am." She pulled away and gestured to the headstone. "Lock, this is the final resting place of Agent Paul E. Reynolds, Special Agent of The Department of Justice, B.O.I. and World War I veteran."

He looked at the object resting on the stone. The 1929 Mercury dime that rolled to her, across the floor in the Grand Hall of Union Station.

It crossed his mind, whoever came to remove the flowers shall find the dime. He'd not ask why, yet hoped someday, she would tell him.

"I'm ready now, Lock."

He walked her to the car, saw her seated, and leaned in to kiss her. "Love, I don't know what the significance of what I saw here, but I'll never forget it. I'll be right back."

He stepped toward the gravesite staying clear of the headstone and the dime. "Agent Reynolds, I don't know what hold you have on my future wife. Take note, I thank you for being the catalyst who brought me to Letsea."

Due to the pending storm, they opted to wait at the airport for their return flight, cuddled together in a lounge.

"It looks like you found your peace this morning," he whispered.

Letsea wrapped her arms around his neck. "I found peace last night at the services. This morning, I released an obligation. From here forward, I trust I'll know when, where, and what is mine to do."

Bob dropped off Lock and Letsea at the car porch, of the Brechenworth mansion. Gwendolene met them inside the hall door. "I'm glad you're home." The ladies hugged. "Some people from The Justice Department came here this morning, on Christmas morning and took Liza. What's going on?"

Letsea glanced at him then spoke to her sister. "Don't worry, honey. Go back to your family. I'll check into it."

Letsea looked at Lock. "What have you been up to? I told you Liza is good."

"I'm sure you're right. I had to tell my boss of the connection."

"Because twenty-four seven, three hundred and sixty-five, you are foremost an FBI agent. You have no empathy for the support I received from Liza during the most horrific time of my life. Young and graduating college, Liza chose to stay with my family. She helped Pauline take care of us."

"I understand, still, I cannot ignore a lead. I'm sure they're only questioning her."

Letsea looked away. "Good night, Lock."

He watched her pick up her cat and go upstairs.

CHAPTER 73

Early morning, day after Christmas, in the Queen Anne house

Lock awoke thinking of the story, *The Count of Monte Cristo* written by Alexandre Dumas and recalled his words. *All human wisdom is summed up in two words, wait and hope.* Oh, that's just great! Hadn't he waited long enough to find her?

He considered how long Letsea waited for love. Symbolically imprisoned by her grandfather's wishes. She didn't appear to have any revenge. Maybe a cry for justice on her parents' behalf. She hoped for real love. She's not asking for the love of her life to make an identity change like Dante did. At most, a name change.

He took a hot shower while mentally reviewing the mysterious scenes in the Idaho cemetery. Even more important, their kisses, to and from, along the trip. He wanted Letsea in his arms, his life, his bed. Nothing could nix his newly acquired dream. Dressed, he headed downstairs.

Lock's father poured a cup of coffee and sat with him in the kitchen. "Morning, Son. Did you have a good trip?"

"Different, but good."

"From what we saw, it looked mighty fine to us."

"Dad, what are you talking about?"

"After you went to bed early last night, we turned on the TV. Someone filmed you and Letsea kissing in an airport. The national news picked it up as an 'I'll Be Home for Christmas' story. I barely managed to stop your sisters from waking you."

Lock's eyes widened. "So obvious that it was us?"

His dad laughed. "Oh, yeah. Your sisters are already planning your wedding."

"The girls are jumping the gun on this, aren't they?"

"Are they, Son?"

He recalled Letsea's obvious disappointment with him turning Liza in to the feds. Not sure what to say to make a difference. Especially since he didn't intend to give up his name for hers. History and ancestry were Dad's joy. Being his one and only son, how callous to hurt his father by giving up his name?

Was it fair to ask it of a man? Probably not, yet she didn't make the rules, she just followed them.

One thing for sure, it never made sense to leave a risk unchecked. He needed to go into St. Louis. Finally, the time had come to speak to the company manager who owned the second black spy car.

"Dad, I'm going back to my house to change clothes. I'll be running errands in St. Louis."

"Be careful, the streets will be packed with bargain shoppers and teenagers."

"I will." He patted his father's shoulder and started to leave through the basement door which led to the underground tunnel, and he stopped. "Dad, what do you think these tunnels were originally used for?"

"My first thought, the Prohibition. Of course, these houses were built before it was passed,   an uprising for it stirred a long time coming. They owned shipping fleets. There's no telling what imported merchandise may have been stored here. Traditionally, worldwide, plenty of the wealthy and powerful secured secret passages to protect their families in case of invasion. And boy howdy, the world still has power-trip takeovers! Then again, it might be nothing more than a safe way to get between buildings in winter. Letsea is letting me read her family's journals. I'll let you know if I find out."

At home, he worked out with the weights, showered, and dressed in a Brooks Brothers dark-gray power suit and patent leather dress shoes. He went upstairs to his home office. Lock opened his email to find a dozen friends, including Chief, sent him a link to a newsworthy story. He and Letsea in a hot embrace at the Chicago O'Hare Airport.

Chief's email was to-the-point sharp.

Agent Lockhart, what are you thinking?
Is this Brechenworth in your arms?

He adjusted his tie then opened the link. "Oh yeah, that's her," he spoke aloud and relished in the memory of their passion. He looked beside the computer screen at the photograph he bought from the man outside the speakeasy. He and Letsea dancing and laughing. That night rated high on his favorite memories list. He thought how much fun his life would be once he managed the hurdles yet to jump.

Lock called Don Pfeiffer. "Remember I told you of the two black sports cars with stalkers on Brechenworth?"

"I do. Do you want help?"

"Absolutely. I'm going downtown to talk with the owner of the company."

"I'm in, if it'll wait until this afternoon."

"This afternoon works. Thanks, pal."

Lock hoped to get it over with in the morning, though he'd not pass on the opportunity to have Don's support. He looked at the clock and decided to use the time to transcribe the interview, at the Queen Anne house, to text. First, he watched the video of them kissing again. He chuckled and held on to hope. All he needed to do was simply *wait*. Right?

He set up the digital recorder to play the interview and the speech-to-text recognition app to transcribe it to his computer. He listened to his introduction telling date and purpose of the interview. It transferred fine to the computer, so he leaned back and listened to their voices, periodically glancing at the monitor to be sure it still typed.

The tone of Letsea's voice clearly revealed her frustrated as all get out when he arrived. He gave her credit for her resolve in proving her point on his lie. He wished he had told her he was FBI from the beginning.

By listening to the interview, he remembered her specific reactions of long pauses. Also, distractions, such as the thunderstorm. Recalling his own disappointment when she showed her first signs of deception. Why and what did she hold back?

When he asked why she thought Reynolds was bludgeoned on the back of the head, she closed down and fell silent.

So, just tell the man
what he wants to know.

The cat scared them with a screech and leap.

As he casually watched the screen, he realized words appeared which he did not hear on the recorder.

"Oh, snap!"

"What in the world is that anyway?"

Tell him.

Where did it come from? He scooted close to the desk to better focus.

Again, Lock heard nothing, just silence, yet the speech-to-text typed.

Tell him.

Rigid in his seat, not sure what was going on, he grabbed the recorder to turn it off. Gut instinct prickled on the back of his neck and he set it down and let it continue to play.

Had the program updated to some kind of AI system he wasn't aware of? Or possibly some digital interference? Or a frequency problem? His office both was soundproof, and high security bulletproof. It wouldn't be neighbor's transmission of radio waves.

Why did the computer type words he could not hear? He watched the interview continue to type on the screen. He zeroed in on her voice modulation, especially when her energy level rose and dropped around the pauses of silence. He heard his words, her words, cat sounds, so where did those other words come from as dictation printed on the monitor?

Tell him about me. He wants to know.

Go ahead. I'm not afraid of him.

Lock pushed his chair away and stood. "What is happening?" *Who is not afraid of whom?*

The computer typed their conversations about her cat and with Pauline when she came to the doorway and the crash of thunder.

Ka-Boom!

"Just how high of authority does the FBI have anyway?"

You have no idea!

Lock gripped the desk. It crossed his mind someone was playing a joke on him. He knew it wasn't possible. He listened to them talk about weather, food, and Rex Kitty.

"Stop avoiding the subject, Letsea.

It's my guess you've read someone's diary."
Tell him.
"Huh?"
Tell him and while you're at it, tell him
my pocket watch belonged with family.
Not stored away in a file. Tell him that!
"I can't."
"You can't what?"
"I can't explain it."
"What are you *not* telling me?"
"Call it woman's intuition, if you will."
Tell him! "Tell me."
"Excuse me."
Letsea abruptly dashed up the back stairs.

A long period of silence while Letsea and her cat were gone from the kitchen. Occasionally, the text typed the rumble of thunder.

He recalled finding her sitting on the foyer steps with the cat.
"It's my understanding Uncle Paul wanted the
pocket watch to be returned to Aunt Mildred."
The computer also heard and typed,
Thanks for telling him.
Again, Lock heard nothing.
They discussed the watch.
Voice recognition typed.
It was an 18-karat gold, precision
clockworks, pocket watch.
Before he actually heard Letsea say it. Then typed it again, as she did.

He sat back, at full attention, listened, and watched additional text on the monitor.
"Confirming you do have inside information...
...You obviously have a diary...."
"It's all so personal to me. I can't explain why."
"Come back to the kitchen..."
"...I have some information you should
know about your beloved uncle..."
Lock cringed knowing what else he said to her, and her reaction. They spent a bit of time talking about family, eventually

leading back to the topic of Reynolds.

"First, Letsea, if you do have access
to a private journal or letters...
... Your information could help finally
unravel a century-old cold case."
"Lock, that's all I want.
To clear him of the alleged suicide...."
"According to the file I have,
Agent Reynolds was a hard drinker...
...Most likely an alcoholic."
No!!

Rex Kitty screeched!

Who said no? Lock tapped his fist to the desktop.
I was not an alcoholic!
"Lock, you really didn't hear anything?"

He tried to soothe the frightened cat.

"He was dying."
"The man was what they termed
as a skirt-chaser..."

He and Letsea were silent, even so, the computer continued to type sharp opinions on J. Edgar Hoover's protectiveness of the Bureau and his failure to admit the investigation had been a fiasco.

Unless, not solving my murder
wasn't a slipup.
...because it was a frame-up.
all real clues were distorted
on the spot.

Letsea whispered.

"Why?"

Lock answered her.

"I know it must be hard to hear that."

The computer heard and typed.

The arrest warrants I was processing.
A couple... ... Were for
government employees.

Lock's right heel tapped in a nervous gesture. He swallowed and hung in there, glued to the monitor. Words in front of his eyes with no comprehension of how they came into conversation between him and Letsea. But for possibly one explanation.

Letsea not only heard it, she also responded to Reynolds' voice! The words on the screen, *My* watch. *I* was actually murdered by the feds. *I* was processing arrest warrants.

"Lock, who do you think
really killed JFK?"

It continued. He refused to look away, not sure those silenced typed words would still be there when the program finished. He didn't know how the realm of paranormal worked. He thought of Letsea standing at Reynolds' grave site, praying. No, talking to his spirit. As he watched, Lock prayed for understanding and patience. He grabbed his phone and started videorecording activity on the monitor.

As soon as the interview completed, he immediately reviewed the whole typed account. After he saved it several times and printed it, he created a new file and went back to isolate the reactions from the unheard voice.

Good lord, Letsea is *psychic!*
Lies! That's exactly what
I need for you to dispel!
I bought the insurance policy
right after the Saint Valentine's
Day Massacre in Chicago. ...
They lied, saying it was just
before my death.
Tell Special Agent Lockhart
to check it out. By the by,
I was not a 'skirt chaser'.
it was a ruse, to give the
impression I drank
and went for the girls.
apparently, I was good at my job,
to a point. My assignment—
To fit in with the party set.
... All part of being a
federal agent.

It sounded right. No telling how many times through his career he shammed criminals, to catch them in the act. Lock trembled at the thought of those pretenses being used against him.

No! I was murdered! Don't believe him.

Watch what you say. Why do you think
people always have the right to have
their lawyer present?
authorities are allowed to lie...

Lock sighed. No wonder Letsea kept saying she "could not explain." She was some kind of a mystic and so was her cat!

He glanced at the time, locked the recorder and the printed copy away in the safe.

He realized Letsea would not tell him her secret. She feared he'd not believe her or think her crazy. The sad truth is, if he hadn't read those words for himself, he might have thought just that.

A promise to Gwen to join her and Doyle's family for brunch is what forced Letsea to wake up. The first full night of sleep, in weeks.

During brunch, family filled her in on who got what for Christmas and praised the children. At peace with Lauren cuddled on her lap and Chip beside her.

"Letsea," Gwen said, "Your gifts are still under the tree."

"You don't need to open them now on our account," said Doyle's mother. "We do want to thank you for sharing your lovely home with us."

"It's my pleasure, and thank you. You are always welcome here. With the new grandbaby coming, I expect to see you back soon." She rocked Lauren.

Conversation led to memories. When movement caught Letsea's eye, she noticed Liza standing in the hallway. "Pardon me."

She led Liza to the morning room. "Are you all right?"

"Yes, ma'am. I don't know what to say."

"What happened?"

"Government agents came and took me for an interview. Mainly they wanted to know who my friends were in my college years. And my correspondence with my parents. Especially, when I started to work here. I think they suspect I had something to do with—"

Letsea watched Liza's eyes widen and tears fell.

"I didn't do anything intentionally wrong." Liza cried. "They asked what kind of things I told my parents about your family. Miss Brechenworth, my parents are good people. They'd never hurt a soul. Their life's mission is to help those in need. I'm sorry." She continued to cry.

Letsea wrapped her arms around Liza to soothe her fears.

"Should I pack my things and leave?"

"Of course not."

Lock stood in the executive office. The visitor chair seats were lower than the manager's desk chair. Intended to intimidate, he refused to put himself and Don in such a position.

"We can't help you, agents. Our clientele is privileged information."

Don spoke, "You can help us now in private, possibly prevent another drastic situation from occurring. Or you can be made to do so in open court." Don plopped a subpoena on the desk. "The family we are referring to has already suffered three kidnappings and a double murder. One, years ago, the latest, suspiciously, only last week. During your employee's watch. Should your stalking private investigator be connected to this or another crime, in any way, your company will be charged as an accessory before the fact."

"Just a minute." The CEO left the room.

"Don, when did you get it?" Lock whispered and eyed the paperwork.

"The day you gave me information on the black cars. In search for Evans. You were right, Summer Chablis is with the department. International Affairs."

Lock smirked. "You could have told me over the phone."

With a grin, Don said, "Yeah, well I like to see your expressions."

When the CEO finally returned, he held a single sheet of paper.

"Here is the name of our client and the information they asked for."

"What of the job report your client received?"

"Our P.I. thought it more to do with a relationship issue. It's a simple list of comings and goings. That's all I have to offer you at this time."

Lock read the paper he held. It's all he needed.

Seth Eadgard Purser Law Firm,
Philadelphia, Pennsylvania.

CHAPTER 74

Lock stopped to check in with Bob. "How's everything going here?"

"Quiet. The Davises are gone. I set an appointment with the security company you recommended. If you can be here, I'd appreciate it. You'll have a better idea of what camera system is needed than I ever would."

"I'll plan on it. Text me the time. Bob, what can you tell me of Seth Purser?"

"Drives a fine car, but not much personality to him."

"What do you mean?"

"I've never seen him happy, and look who the man dated." Bob scoffed.

"Never?"

"No. He's always seriously preoccupied."

Lock tilted his head. The image of Purser lifting Letsea into the air, the night on her porch, crossed his mind. He couldn't imagine her with anyone somber. On the contrary, he didn't want to picture her with anyone other than him.

"By the way, your family, Miss Brechenworth, and Miss Pauline all went to the Settlement Tea Room for a late lunch. I tried to talk her out of going with them."

"She'll be fine." Lock swallowed. Chances of a threat to Letsea were slimming by the hour. Plus, Nico and Carlton were very protective. Besides, he knew her big secret, a ghost. "I'll be driving out early. I have a flight to catch at four in the morning." He longed for retirement, when he'd sleep regular hours.

"Do you want a lift to the airport? I don't mind."

"Sure, if you want, thanks, Bob." They shook hands.

Before leaving the main house, Lock stopped in the front parlor and noticed Letsea had not opened all her gifts. He slipped an envelope under the tree.

The clouds covered the moon like a veil. By the time Letsea got in the house it was late. They were caught in a long and slow line of cars who waited to see her lights and decorations. Hope and Faith were hilarious, imitating others' surprised expressions when they noticed the gates open for them to drive in. She paused. Like her parents, the Lockharts were fun to be around.

She placed her shoes in the basket inside the door and stepped into the front parlor to draw the drapes mostly closed, letting the lighted tree peep through. Beneath the tree were several gifts. Picking up a couple, she settled on the nearest sofa.

From Gwen and Doyle, she received a specially designed, animal safety protected, handwoven, green mohair sweater. She slipped it on and knew the warmth of Gwen's affection.

Chip and Lauren gave her hand drawings and a new pair of house booties. She chuckled while putting them on. This year, they looked like sheep. Last year, they were bunny booties. She went back to the tree for more and noticed the card envelope. From Lock, she held the most romantic card she ever received.

To the woman I love. It included a short yet ever-so-amorous poem. It was signed. *Letsea, I love you and look forward to many happy years together. Love, Lock.* Inside he taped a key.

She clutched the card to her heart, leaned back, and daydreamed. In the garage, on Christmas Eve, he seemed open-minded to the idea of taking her name. She was happy.

Philadelphia, Pennsylvania

"I did not hire a P.I. to follow Letsea," Young Seth Purser

insisted. "Why would I? I broke up with her to move back to Philly. You're wrong, Agent Lockhart."

Lock, dumbfounded at the gall of the man to deny his involvement. He stepped close enough to stretch out his arm and slap a hand on the humongous Mahogony desk Seth Purser sat behind. He leaned toward the young man's face. "We have documentation proving someone from this law firm has put Letsea Brechenworth in harm's way. If not you, who?"

"Honestly, I have no incentive to do it," Purser said.

So, Lock tried a different tactic. "Before something drastic happens to her, we need your help to figure out what's going on."

"What are you talking about, sir?"

"Miss Brechenworth's aunt, Mae Evans, was kidnapped, last week. Suspicions are high someone intends to do harm to Miss Brechenworth, unless we can thwart the attempt. If you are not the one who placed the hire, surely, you want to help keep her safe."

"What can I do?"

Lock squinted, leaned on both arms, and asked in a hard voice, "Who else here has an interest in her? I need to speak to that person to eliminate them from our kidnapper suspect list."

Purser abruptly stood. It forced his luxury office chair to roll back a few feet. "Have a seat. I may be a while." He left.

Again, the visitors' chairs were shorter. He disapproved of the old-school way of manipulation. He walked around behind the desk and looked out the plate-glass window at the cityscape. The Senior Seth Purser, came in, stood still, and stared at him. Lock knew this little power game and he wasn't falling for it either. *First to speak loses.*

Seth Purser, Junior entered, stopped, glanced at his father, before fastening his gaze on Lock.

Lastly, Seth Purser, the Third, finally returned, and Lock focused attention on Letsea's old friend. Three silent Seth Pursers against one.

He quietly waited. *Dang, they are good.*

Lock wanted an opportunity to put them in their place. Still annoyed at their attempt to make the FBI look like a circus a few years ago. *Respectfully, my only purpose today is to solve Letsea's situation.*

Previously Lock decided to wait out their game all day, if need be, *or* he could get the ball rolling. He'd rather be home in time for dinner. He broke their icy resolve. "Gentlemen, which one of you put out a *hit* on Letsea Brechenworth?"

"What the—" the old man exclaimed as he kept a fairly blank face. The man, approximately ten years older than Lock, barked in a gravelly voice, "Who did what?" His facial expressions remained undisturbed.

"Father! What have you done?" The youngest Seth suddenly jerked sideways.

Lock hoped they wouldn't turn violent. He kept a sharp eye on their movements. The boy aimed an evil eye to his father. "I told you to forget her. She's innocent!"

"Shut up, Trey!" the father said in a venomous tone.

Whoa! That's why Letsea prefers calling me Lock, instead of Trey.

The eldest one's eyes slightly widened before he quickly closed down again.

Lock relaxed, although interesting to observe a somewhat-controlled nonverbal yelling match. Bit by bit, he knew his answer and realized the weak link in the Purser chain, Seth, the Third. Trey Purser first jumped at the chance to accuse his father of underhanded maneuvers. The two older men glanced at each other with a united front. They mentally forced the youngest one down and brought him under their constraint of muteness.

"Gentlemen, why?" Lock pushed for an answer.

They remained quiet, including Letsea's old boyfriend.

Standing behind the huge desk, Lock took charge and put both hands on it and leaned, looking at each Seth Purser, one at a time. "Gentlemen, our goal is to protect Brechenworth from harm in all conceivable ways."

The grandfather crossed his arms. An engorged vein grew on his forehead. Lock motioned to the two shortened leather visitors' chairs. "You're welcomed to have a seat."

"She's not in harm's way by us," declared the father.

"We haven't anything to do with her," stated the grandfather.

Lock looked at the young man who still said nothing. After a minute he raised an eyebrow.

The boy caved. "Is she all right? My family thought it crazy to have not married her." He glanced at his father. "When I told them the stipulations in her family trust, they told me to get a copy of it. After all, there are always covert provisions to find a way out of a contract."

Lock knew the stipulation young Seth referred to. "What did it matter?"

"To break the trust limitation. To free her from the burdens."

"To free her, or you?" Lock stared him down.

Both older men cleared their throats. Then Trey Purser blurted, "You can't understand. I am the third in my family with the same name. No prudent man should give up a family legacy. In order to marry her, the husband has to forfeit who he is and take her name. I may have been persuaded to let her keep her own name, but it wouldn't have been enough."

"So why put a spy on her trail?"

"It wasn't me." He looked at his father.

The two older men stood like statues with a look of stoic resignation. They restrained from conceding to anything. Lock slid a subpoena across the desk, pulled out his handkerchief, and wiped his fingerprints off the polished wood while they examined the formal summons.

Eventually, he left with a verbal agreement, promising they had no interest in Miss Brechenworth. They never placed her in any harm, nor would they. Not joining their family, firmly, her loss, not theirs.

Purser, the Third, accompanied him to the main floor. Lock understood the boy's way of saving face.

Alone in the executive elevator, the young man asked, "Is Letsea all right?"

"She's under protection. The FBI does not take kindly to kidnapping, you understand."

"Letsea is the classiest woman I've ever known. She's kind, thoughtful, and patient beyond belief. But that freaking trust is a ball-breaker, if you know what I mean."

Lock knew. Although after his visit with the Purser clan, he saw it in a whole new light. *Maybe I'm not a* prudent *man. I've often been told I'm an out-of-the-box thinker.*

CHAPTER 75

Lock's family, nestled in the den, played cards, told stories, and laughed a lot. He tapped his father's shoulder. "Dad, I'd like to talk with you." They moved to the kitchen toward rum cake and coffee. "Since you do a lot of ancestry charts, have you ever heard of a man taking his wife's last name in marriage?"

"Sure. Men who have no connection with their fathers and those of means. In several countries, when a couple marries, everyone keeps their birth name. The wife is not even allowed to take her husband's name. Why? Are you now considering marriage?"

"I'm curious, Dad."

"Is that Letsea's dilemma? Is she supposed to marry a man who will take Brechenworth as his own surname?"

Lock barely moved his head up and down.

"Well, it can be tricky, especially here. There are only a few states which will allow a man to take his wife's surname and Missouri is not one of them."

"Then how is it even possible?"

"Petition the court for a change of name. I think they usually allow it, if you do it clearly before the wedding is announced. Otherwise, it might be a costly court battle, if they'll do it at all. I guess a couple could get married in one of the states which do permit it. You know, it's more common than you may think for people to change their names." His father guffawed. "From what I saw on the news, you two are hitting it off pretty well."

Lock rubbed his neck. "Dad, I love you."

Rick patted Trey's hand. "I know you do, Son. Still, you should marry the one you love. Don't forfeit a life of happiness for a technicality."

"Dad, genealogy is so important to you."

"Because it's filled with peoples' stories. If you were to change your first, middle, or last name, or even all three, it doesn't change who you are. No matter what legal name change a person does, they can always be traced back to their birth name."

"Take the original Lemuel Brechenworth, for example. I've been reading his diaries. Now there's a man with determination for better living. His life started in an orphanage, the birthdate by approximation and without a legal name. A nickname, period. Lemuel found knowledgeable people worthy of respect and worked to earn theirs. He fell in love and married a shipowner's daughter and credits his success to his wife. Powerful reading. I can see why his son and grandson want to honor him."

"Dad, someday, I still hope to honor you."

"You already do. The best son a father could ask for. Besides, switching a name doesn't change the bloodline or your DNA for that matter. Family history remains the same.

"Speaking of, Trey, you'll never guess what I came across on Letsea's mother's side of the family. An ancestral great aunt who was once married to an FBI agent. Get this, the man was murdered, on the job. They never even solved his murder. Can you believe that? Son, you best be careful out there."

"Where's that journal?" A shiver ran up his spine.

"It's more of a family ancestry booklet. It's in the turret. I'll get it."

Lock followed his father to the tall antique secretary desk bookcase. The same one Rex Kitty hid on and jumped down from his first day in the Queen Anne. Lock looked at the booklet. Not a diary like he expected.

After talking with his father, Lock remembered how Letsea described the original ancestors during his first day at the estate. He got it. She loved her family, as he loved his.

The musical doorbell rang and played, "Do You Hear What I Hear?"

Lock stepped up and opened the door, not surprised to see Letsea. "Come in, please."

Rick greeted her then retreated to join the family in the den.

"Care for rum cake, coffee, or perhaps ice cream?" Her penchant for ice cream had not escaped his notice.

Letsea's eyes widened as she saw what he held. "Where did you find that? I've been looking for it for weeks."

"Dad found it in the turret bookcase. He said you have an interesting family." They walked to the back and he pulled out a kitchen chair for her and set the booklet on the table. He scooped vanilla ice cream onto a plate, then put a slice of rum cake beside it, and poured her a cup of coffee. "How are you doing?"

"It's too quiet over there." She bobbed her head toward the big house. A burst of laughter drifted into the kitchen. "Not so much here."

She looked directly at him. "Lock, I received a call today from the Congo."

"Another burner phone call?" He rubbed his forehead. *I'll be—*

"Um. No. The American Embassy and the office of anti-kidnapping. This is the first time they've contacted *me* in over a decade. Although, I did my research on my precious metal stocks. I do own shares of a company which manufactures electronics with cobalt. They have a strong presence in the DRC. At best, I can think of one single reason why they called from a burner phone. A group may have wanted enough votes to take over the company board of directors at the annual meeting."

"Reasonable idea." He brought her back to topic. "What did Congo police say?"

"After all these years, they finally have a lead on my parents' case." She set her fork down and sighed. "I'm sorry I acted the way I did on Christmas night. It turns out, it may have something to do with Liza's family." She rushed to say, "Not them personally, you understand. Liza's parents moved to Kenya to start a mission. They built it to house classrooms, a soup kitchen, food pantry, and short-term shelter."

Lock reached over and caressed her hand.

"When they received letters from their children, they were excited to share their news. The police think someone staying at the shelter may have overheard correspondence being read aloud and adopted a plan for robbery or a kidnap. Liza, excited for part of the family she worked for to be traveling their way, wrote to her parents with the planned trip. Her parents are now looking for her old letters to match up shelter registries to learn who may have overheard the schedule."

"I'm told it's a long shot, still the closest they've been so far. Most likely they were not experienced kidnappers, rather people with haphazard plans. It would explain the bumbling mess with the ransom. The murders were likely more out of fear than revenge."

Lock thought of the homeless men who kidnapped her aunt. One pleaded guilty and acted like he looked forward to being back in the clink to his "three hots and a cot". The other, not so much.

Lock stood to hug her.

"Come over here." With his hands on her waist, he encouraged her to sit on his knee. Letsea hugged his neck.

"It's weird," she said. "It's not solved, yet it's a feasible explanation of how it may have unfolded. Nothing will ever bring them home, even so, I don't feel like I'm in limbo quite like I did. You recognized the connection with Liza, even though she didn't do anything wrong. Neither did her parents. It's fair to share our excitement with friends."

She leaned back and looked him in the eye. "Thank you, Lock. How did you know?"

"I didn't. Granted, it's safe to say, I don't believe in coincidences either."

She placed her fingers on his cheeks. "Lock, thank you for the beautiful card. I love it. We may be rushing things, since we've only known each other such a short time." She paused. Their eyes met. "I love you, too."

Warmness swept over him. "Letsea, you mean everything to me." He tilted his head and kissed her.

"What's the key fit?"

"I've already given you my heart. To show my commitment to you, I figured the innermost and symbolic gift I could offer is a key to my home."

After a small gasp, she leaned forward, then kissed him. "It's more romantic than anything you might have done. Will this let me inside the secret upstairs room?"

He touched the tip of her nose. "Sorry, love. That's still FBI territory."

"I get it. I keep my office locked, too. How long until you retire?"

With her in his future, a no-brainer. "ASAP."

She looked down, leaned her head against his. "Does this mean you will actually consider marrying me under the terms of the trust?"

Relieved he spoke with Dad, his heart fluttered. "Dearest, 'A rose by any other name, is still a rose,' inspired by Shakespeare. I love you. I want you. My dear, I need you." He pulled her closer. He'd never get enough of her. "We should always be willing to discuss any topic freely. Even our ghosts and skeletons in the closet. FBI cases are restricted though."

"Do you mean that?" she whispered.

"Absolutely. No more secrets, okay?"

Letsea brushed her lips to his. Playfully, he caught her bottom lip before deepening the endearment and consequently his desire. He shifted and caught his breath.

"You're a great kisser." She giggled, rested her forehead against his, again.

He whispered, "Did you happen to see the newsclip of us kissing in the airport?"

She leaned back. "Naturally I saw it! Faith played it multiple times yesterday when we all went out to eat. She can be relentless in making a point."

Lock laughed out loud. "And so goes Faith. It's her way." His entire family rushed into the kitchen.

"Well, look at you two, how cozy!" Faith declared.

Lock chuckled and looked at Letsea, who bowed her head. She looked serious and bit her bottom lip. He raised an eyebrow. *What happened here?*

She leaned in and whispered, "We need to talk." Then stood and offered her hand.

He accepted the gesture and waved to his family. They walked over to the main house.

CHAPTER 76

In the privacy of her home, Lock asked, "What's wrong?"

"Maybe nothing. What you said due to honesty started me thinking. There's something I need to tell you before we go any further."

On one hand, relieved, she'd finally tell him of her ability to hear Agent Reynolds' ghost. On the other, nervous of the doubt he heard in her voice.

"Let's go upstairs."

They held hands. *It's a good start,* he thought until she led him to her office and not her bedroom. She let go to unlock the door.

"Have a seat." She turned on her computer.

"What's going on?" Would she show him a preview of the trust agreement, before they were officially engaged?

Carrying a single sheet of paper, she said, "Let's sit over here." At the white wooden conference table, she sat across from him.

A no-touching distance. *This can't be good.*

Rex Kitty jumped on the table and watched them.

"Lock, I have a secret I need to share with you. Before I do, I need you to sign this." She slid the paper across to him.

"A nondisclosure agreement? Is this necessary? We're talking about being married, aren't we?"

She released a sigh. "That's the point. We aren't married. We haven't agreed to any vows. After I tell you this, you may change your mind concerning a future with me. I need legal reassurance it won't go any further than here."

Satisfied she was ready to talk, he forced a blank expression.

Did she really think he'd not marry her as a result of her ability to hear a ghost? Yes, the interview transcript shocked him. Furthermore, he already accepted it as some uncanny phenomenon. After all, it wasn't his job to solve *all* the unexplained mysteries of the world. He read through the document. "Okay. I'll sign. Fire away."

She held out a pen. Rex Kitty batted at it.

He signed and handed it back to her, folded his fingers together, and rested his arms on the table. Casually he said, "Okay, beautiful, hit me with your best shot."

"I am Gwen's birth mother."

His heart sank to his stomach. "Wait. What?" *What? Did I hear that correctly?*

"Legitimately, she is my sister because my parents legally adopted her as their own. However, I am her birth mother."

"I certainly didn't expect that. I saw a picture of you holding her, as an infant. You couldn't have been more than—"

"I was too young. Most of my life, I grew up homeschooled, tutored, and sheltered. For high school, I wanted to see what public schools were like. I was naïve. This guy I met, so very friendly." Her eyes welled with tears. "I didn't know how stupid I'd been."

Letsea picked up her cat and petted between its long ears. Consequently, avoiding eye contact with him.

"Afterward, I didn't even realize what caused my body to change. My mother figured it out. She, Daddy and I went on a long trip to Iceland. When we returned home, my parents introduced my little sister to everyone. There was gossip, but then there always is."

He pitied the young Letsea. The woman he knew seemed to have a handle on it. He whispered, "Does Gwendolene know?"

"Yes, I explained it to her when she got her driver's license. We keep it as sisters. It works for us."

"Does she know who her birth father is?"

"She's happy with the one she knew as Daddy. She's never asked."

"Does he know he has a daughter? Is it someone I know?" He pictured Sheriff Ruell, calling her sweetie.

"Don't let your imagination run away here, Lock. He was young, too. He and his parents all signed away their rights so the adoption would go through smoothly. We both still had higher education ahead of us. It's not like he could afford child support anyway. He left for college and his parents moved. End of story."

She looked to the ceiling and released a sigh. "Well, except on Thanksgiving Day, I think his father stopped by here. The man didn't say his name and told a story of looking for his lost dog. I think I recognized him, but it's been over twenty-five years, so I'm not sure. He might have been Gwen's natural paternal grandfather. Doyle was there and the man didn't ask anything about family."

"Okay. So, do you still want more children?" he asked.

"Yes. I want children. She's my sister, remember that."

He smiled and reached across and poked her hand. "Secretly, you're a granny."

"I know." She smirked in a shy way. "My love for the kids is immeasurable. Nevertheless, to them, I will always be Aunt Letsea."

"Okay. I'm good with it. As long as you know I'd love to experience fatherhood."

Letsea stretched her hands across the table and clasped his. "I thought you should know now."

"I appreciate the information. And here I was all prepared for you to tell me about the ghost of Special Agent Paul E. Reynolds."

Letsea gasped. "How did you know? Boise cemetery, maybe?" She squeezed his hands. "You don't think I'm crazy, do you?"

"When it first registered something's not normal, it crossed my mind, *I might be going bonkers*. Finally, I realized you could hear him. A lot of things started to make sense at that point." He rubbed his thumbs on the back of her hands. "I guess there's more to life and the universe than I previously realized."

"I'm glad we can talk openly on the subject of Uncle Paul. Though I still need to find a way to help break the lie. He wants a correction made on the alleged suicide. At this stage I don't know how many people would even know about him." She went to the safe and removed a book. "Here's the journal you've been itching to see. But it's not from the past. These are my notes from talking with him just this month. Me interviewing Agent Reynolds."

He flipped through the pages. His eyebrows shot upward. "The man who shot him wore a police uniform?"

"Yes, and get this, Uncle Paul's hands were tied with a rope. Not handcuffs," she said.

"Huh. Letsea, we might explore the possibilities of you contacting the author Gunner Hardyn Chase. He might want to write a book about a real FBI agent, historically murdered with documentation. Not that I can reveal FBI secrets. But there's a lot here."

"Lock, I think that's what started this whole thing with Uncle Paul coming to me in the first place. When I bought all those books from Chase, I mentioned my murdered FBI ancestor. He showed interest and gave me his business card with his cell phone number. It's somewhere around here."

"I have it. When I came across the card tucked in one of the books, I typed his information into my phone contact list."

"Why?"

"A private number. I'm FBI. I never let significant information slide. It may be evidence."

"Good thing to remember." She tapped the table. "I have a gift for you. I'll be right back." She left the office, and of course, he followed.

In her bedroom, she reached for his fedora which still hung on a bedpost. He stepped beside her and she placed it on his head. "I knew it. It's perfect for you," she teased and tilted it toward his left eye.

"I like to think of it right here." He moved it over to her head.

He kissed her, broke their embrace, and closed the drapes. She giggled and he scooped her up and started to drop her on the bed.

"On the sofa," she whispered.

"Okay, but the bed has more potential."

She cupped his face with her palms. "There *is* one more little, itty-bitty thing I should mention. Since, I got pregnant as a teenager, the trust clearly states I remain chaste until I'm married. I promised Grandad."

"You're kidding." He stood straight and stared.

She saw surprise in his eyes and understood, after all, he knew she'd had boyfriends.

He whispered, "You're celibate?"

She nodded.

"So, we're talking a very short engagement, right?" He playfully dropped her on the sofa and knelt before her.

"Yes, please. Extremely short." She knew she blushed. "Plus, before we're married. I need to have some extra insulation work done in the house."

"What does that have to do with planning our wedding date?"

"Maybe nothing. Or everything, in privacy."

"You look mischievous. What are you up to?"

"*I* have a mischievous look?" she teased with a shrug and whispered, "You know, insulate our *privacy*."

His eyes widened. "Oh!" He nodded. "Right."

Lock laughed in a painful sort of way. For a moment, he thought she changed the subject again. He sat beside her and pulled her close. Ah. He just realized why Bob thought Seth Purser always looked *seriously preoccupied*. She dated him for three years. *Patient beyond belief.* Purser also called her "innocent."

Lock tugged Letsea onto his lap. "Do you have any idea how special you are to me?"

"For now, show me with kisses. I adore your kisses."

So, he did.

EPILOGUE

July, two and a half years later

Letsea stood under the Union Station's Whispering Arch and heard a clear voice.

"Dearest, you are the love of my life."

Holding back her merriment while facing the wall of the arch, she whispered, "I'm glad to know it. Because we are going to have another baby. Lemuel is going to be a big brother."

"Awe, love. You don't say?" Lock reveled in her tease. She heard his chuckle.

Living the dream, she particularly loved the humor which accompanied every aspect of her charming life. "Darling, you mean you already suspected it?" She bit her bottom lip to stop a burst of hilarity.

He added, "Dearest, I *am* retired FBI. Of course I recognized the symptoms."

She listened for another witty remark, but instead, she felt his hands on her hips. He nuzzled her neck from behind and caressed her extensive baby bump. She quivered with delight.

"Silly woman," he whispered in her ear. "Don't think you can pull one over on me, dear. I'm no greenhorn at detective work."

She laughed aloud then turned and wrapped her arms around his neck. He chuckled and stepped backward to make room for seven months of growing baby number two, between them.

"What shall we name her?" he asked.

With her index finger, she tapped her chin. "Maybe we could...

Or maybe we—"

"Uh-uh-uh, Letsea, don't go there. I know what you're doing. We are not naming our daughter MaeBea."

Her turn for a hearty laugh. "I was thinking of, Alicerose Lockhart Brechenworth."

"After our mothers. I like it. Are you sure you want Lockhart for a girl's middle name?"

She kissed him. "I fell in love with Lockhart. It's a beautiful name. I think of a gold heart-shaped locket."

She felt him touch the one dangling around her neck. A gift from Lock which held miniature pictures. Them dancing at their wedding and the first family portrait with baby Lemuel.

"How did I rate being so blessed?" He kissed her.

"Mr. and Mrs. Brechenworth." Gina, the thoughtful waitress they came to know and appreciate, stepped down. "A man asked me to give this to you." She pulled a large long-stemmed white rose from behind and handed it to Letsea.

"From who?" Lock looked around.

"He's already gone. He said to tell you thank you." Gina waved and left.

Letsea looked at Lock. "Is it possible it's from Uncle Paul?"

"More likely, a complete stranger admiring your beauty." He scanned the area.

"What are you looking for?"

"I'm not sure, maybe a surge of old coins rolling our way."

Letsea laughed. "Honestly at this point, there's not much left to surprise me. I bet our favorite author planned it. What time is it?"

"We came early. Gunner isn't due for another fifteen minutes." Lock's phone buzzed. "It's Doyle."

Letsea watched.

"Hey, what's up?"

"You don't say."

"Okay." He chuckled.

"Sure, I'll talk to your wife." He raised an eyebrow.

"Hello, Gwen."

"Is that right? Wow, and you want *me* to be the one to tell her? You two are a couple of cowards, you know it."

Eyes widened as he covered the microphone.

"Dearest, prepare to be surprised." He smiled.

"Oh? Okay, bye-bye, Gwen."

Lock couldn't keep a straight face. "First, Doyle has a favor to ask of you."

"One for which he thought he needed an arbitrator, I see." She crossed her arms. What was her brother-in-law up to?

"He said a couple members of the Chamber of Commerce asked to use one of the Aston Martins in the Christmas parade this year."

She grinned. "I suppose Doyle's willing to drive it for them."

"If he does, it sounds like he'd be dressed as an elf." Lock tilted his head upward and roared with a hearty laugh.

"The kids would love it," she said. "What did Gwen want?"

"Brace yourself. It's a heads-up. Aunt Mae is going to insist you order twice as many raspberry ganache cakes for the volunteers' tea party this year. She thinks there should be plenty of extras for everyone. She'll help pay."

"Double?" she blurted. Eyes widened as she shook her head. "No way."

Thoughts swirled and she leaned against Lock's arm.

"Apparently so." He led her up the staircase to a chair. "Honey, simply tell them it's your private recipe and *you* are the one doing the work to make the cakes every year. It's too much for you, or us, to handle. Better yet, share the recipe. We were exhausted from making two hundred of them last year. I don't know how you've done it without Pauline's help."

"Originally, I thought of it as my anonymous gift to the volunteers. Besides, seven months ago, we weren't *too exhausted*, if you'll recall." She teased and rubbed her baby belly.

"We should ask Mom, Dad, Pauline, even Mae and Robert to help bake them."

She changed the subject. "Oh look, here's Gunner coming now."

Their friend approached. "I knew I'd find you two near the Whispering Arch."

Lock and Gunner shook hands and did a one-arm man hug.

"Where's your family?" Letsea asked.

"The ladies planned a full day of shopping and the boys and grandkids are thrilled to have the hotel room so close to all the rides and entertainment. You've got me to yourselves all day. Where's your boy? I thought you took him everywhere."

"He's at home with Mom and Dad." Letsea stood.

Lock said, "We're fortunate. My parents live with us, they volunteered to keep Lemuel today. Did you check out the Whispering Arch?"

"I visited down here at four thirty this morning." Author Gunner Hardyn Chase looked at Letsea. "Like you described your first day here to talk with Agent Reynolds."

"We'll show you the house and the tower room where I had several conversations with Uncle Paul."

"I'm excited. Do you think the spirit of Agent Reynolds will talk to me?"

"All the detailed research you've done, no doubt, he's already in your head somewhere. So maybe."

Gunner handed her a folder. "By the way, here's an early draft layout for the book cover design. I want your opinion."

Letsea looked at the color layout. Eyes teared. Special Agent Paul E. Reynolds, B.O.I. was the spark that changed her life from worry to finding true love. She hoped Gunner's story helped his cause. After they were in the van, she handed it to Lock.

"Is it close enough for you, dear?"

"Yes." She read the bold red title, *The Dead Fed Said*. I love it. Hey, let's go for ice cream and celebrate. Oh, by the way, Gunner, thanks for the lovely rose."

"What rose?"

ON WRITING, NOTES OF SINCERE APPRECIATION

To Critique Me Friday, this dedicated and talented team has helped me reach the point of publication of this novel. I would not be here without your support. I thank you all: J.C. Fields; Lori Copeland; Sharon Kizziah-Holmes; Michael Lee; Shirley King McCann, and in memory of Heather Burch. I genuinely appreciate your sharing your wisdom, and insights. You enhance my writing experience. I joyfully look forward to Fridays.

To the editorial team at Decadent Publishing, I appreciate your good work and perspectives on this story. Thank you, Kate Richards, Addison Williams, and Nanette Sipe.

I thank you, Jaycee DeLorenzo for the cover design, patience, and your creativity.

I am incredibly grateful to Patsy Bennitt and Tina Vyborni for proofreading.

Sharon Kizziah-Holmes of Paperback Press, my gratitude is beyond words for your help from beginning to end. Your professional formatting and services made this possible. Your lightheartedness and insistence, to be applied as necessary, is appreciated.

To members of writing groups in which I participate. Ozark Romance Authors, Springfield Writer's Guild, and Sleuths' Ink, what fun and educational meetings we have. Thank you!

To those who have always believed in me, you are part of who I am. In beloved memory of my parents, Manford and Ida Bookout, who always believed I could tell, and write my stories. They so envisioned me as an author from an early age, they gave me a typewriter for my seventh birthday. I love you!

To my amazing sister, Linda Kerwood, and brother, David Bookout, who read to me, and helped their baby sister, learn to read and write. Then as our parents did, encouraged me ever since to "go for it", whatever I decided "it" was. I adore you both!

To Debbie Ralston Groseclose. My supportive, and encouraging friend, filled with zeal from the first day we met- over five decades ago. I love you, and appreciate your presence in my life.

Thank you to Sherry Cantrell, Sylvia Richardson, and Julia White, such precious friends. I appreciate all your support and encouragement to keep writing. To Neosho Daily News and the Branson Beacon for asking to publish my poetry, way back when. To Barbara Quin who, decades ago, asked me to contribute a story to her anthology, "Spirit Dancer". You opened a new shiny gate for me to walk through.

To Sue Baggett Day, Minister; and Rev. J. Douglas Bottorff; Rev. Trish Hall; Rev. Jacklyn Mace, who kindly suggested the performance of a children's play I wrote replace a Sunday morning Christmas sermon; and Rev. Pat Powers, all who in their own way, lovingly moved me forward into new territories of self-expression.

To Cait London, thank you for your encouragement and advice, including: "Sounds like you should check out Sleuths' Ink." Hah! I love a good, well-meaning suspense or mystery.

In treasured memories of, Russ and June Bowe; Nancy Daily; Jean Stark Hebenstreit, CSB; Ruthann Herring; Joe Le Vanti; Ogden D. and Alexandra Scoville; and Harry Sparks who emboldened me with enough confidence to take the next step. They all set forth mighty-fine examples.

To Lois Curran; Kathleen Garnsey; Sharon Kizziah-Holmes; Tierney James; Susan Keene, and Shirley King McCann. All who continually help strengthen my learning curve, challenge, apprise, support, and are an everyday delight. And in honor of Shirley's ever important question: "Where's lunch?" You know, for the meeting after the meeting. What fun. I give to you all deep and lasting gratitude, sealed with love.

To my husband, family, in-laws, nieces, nephews, cousins, aunts and uncles, who have ever asked, "So, when will I be able to read one of your books?" It is with love I thank you for your interest and enthusiasm. Here's your chance. Enjoy. To these wonderful, encouraging friends and family, who have stuck by my side through my adventures. I love you all.

Thank you, Librarians! The most dedicated, helpful assistants in the world of writing.

Thank you, *Arizona Republican* and the *Phoenix Gazette* of August 1929 for adventurous news reporting that lives through time. And to, *Phoenix Magazine* for remembering and breathing energy into history. To the World Wide Web for a vast degree of answers. My gratitude for the classics of Alexandre Dumas.

To the memory of Paul E. Reynolds, who lived a life of honor and dedication to our country.

To Randy Bunn, who graciously compiled the family history booklet that brought Paul E. Reynolds to my attention. Such an inspiring treasure of remembrance of generational family. Thank you so much!

Thank you Rick Bookout, Bill Terkeurst and Alec Wade; staff at the historical Union Station -Hilton, Renaissance Hotel, and Morris Hill Cemetery, for help with specific research details to help keep me in alignment.

My further appreciation goes to the staff of Nixa Arby's, Marco's, Godfather's and Wendy's. All friendly and helpful places for the times I need a break from the office and I can go to read what I just wrote.

To my readers, I hope you enjoy this story as much as I enjoyed writing it. If so, I have over a dozen more stories, of course, they are in need of edits. What a joy that would be! Leaps through time and space; romance; challenges on several levels; overcoming limitations, poor decisions and fears. Realizing when fears have purpose; and bringing strengths to light so they may flourish. Recognizing determination, faith and so much more.

You all are awesome! I am blessed by you, Conetta

About the Author

Conetta not only loves to write, but she's also an avid reader. She has stories published in numerous anthologies and "The Dead Fed Said" is her debut novel.

A member of Critique Me Friday; Ozarks Romance Authors; Springfield Writer's Guild; and Sleuths' Ink.

Happily-ever-after married for over forty years. Husband, Thom and she live in the beautiful Ozarks. She enjoys a good cup of tea, art and antiques, fun with friends, is faith based and looks for the good in life.

Enjoy!

www.ingramcontent.com/pod-product-compliance
Lightning Source LLC
Chambersburg PA
CBHW021435240626
47153CB00001B/157